ANNA JACOBS

Calico Road

HODDER

A CIP catalogue record for this title is available from the
British Library.

ISBN 978 0 340 82142 8

Typeset in Plantin Light by
Phoenix Typesetting, Auldgirth, Dumfriesshire

Printed and bound in the UK by
CPI Group (UK) Ltd, Croydon, CR0 4YY

Hodder Headline's policy is to use papers that are natural, renewable
and recyclable products and made from wood grown in sustainable
forests. The logging and manufacturing processes are expected to
conform to the environmental regulations of the country of origin.

Hodder and Stoughton Ltd
A division of Hodder Headline
338 Euston Road
London NW1 3BH

This book is dedicated to the people of Lancashire, whose history and culture have inspired me all of my life.

PART I

1827

I

September

Meg Staley hurried down Weavers Lane looking for her younger brother Shad, who was no doubt getting into mischief again. Her mother had gone wild when he hadn't come home on time and since her older brother Jack was still at his reading class, Meg had offered to go and find Shad. Anything was better than staying home when her mother was in a temper.

She tried to avoid the drunken men clustered round the doorway of the Black Swan, but one of them caught her by the arm.

'Let go of me!' she snapped, tugging away from him.

He laughed and his grip tightened. 'Give us a kiss an' I will.'

She kicked out at him, struggling to get away, but he didn't seem to feel her blows and his grip didn't slacken. With a sinking heart she realised he was so blind with booze that he didn't know what he was doing. 'Will no one help me?' she yelled.

Another man lurched forward, also well gone in drink, and she winced, terrified he would grab her too. Then she recognised him. Well, she knew most people by sight in Northby, it was such a small town, and Ben Pearson had once lived in their street. Now he lived near the bottom end of Weavers Lane, the less respectable end.

To her relief he took his companion's arm and said, 'You're frightening the lass, Ted. Let her go.'

The drunken man blinked at him, then his grip on her slackened and he muttered, 'Sorry.'

'Thanks.' Meg turned away but to her dismay Ben followed.

'You shouldn't be out on your own at this hour,' he said, still in that slurred voice.

'I'm looking for my little brother.'

'I'll help you.'

'I don't want your help. Go back and lap up some more booze with your friends. You're all sots!'

'You're sharp-tongued tonight.'

'I'm tired. An' I don't like tosspots.'

He stayed with her, frowning now. 'Is that what I am?'

'Everyone knows you spend all you earn on drink. An' I've seen you myself many a time staggering down the street.'

He laid one hand on her arm. 'Eh, I don't like to think of that, you being so scornful about me.' After a pause during which he studied her face, he added softly, 'I'd give up the drink for a lass like you.'

'Don't be silly! Why should you do that for me?' She didn't pull away because somehow she didn't feel frightened when this man held her. In fact, she felt sorry for him. He'd been married once, then a couple of years ago his wife had died in childbirth, the baby too. It was after that he'd taken to the drink.

He smiled at her. 'Why? Because you're special. If I give up the booze will you walk out with me, Meg Staley?'

She gaped at him. '*Walk out with you?* You hardly know me.'

'I've known you since you were a little 'un.'

Before Ben could speak again, she saw her brother and yelled across the street, 'You come here, our Shad.' When she pulled away from Ben he let her go, but she was conscious of his eyes following her as she and Shad started walking back up the hill. Giving in to temptation she turned round, but he hadn't moved, was still watching her, smiling as if he liked what he saw.

She tossed her head and didn't look round again. Drunks would say anything. He'd have forgotten all about it in the morning. Anyway, she didn't want to walk out with him or anyone else. He was years older than she was – twenty-four to her sixteen – though he was a nice enough fellow and had treated his wife well.

She sighed as her home came into sight. The only thing she really wanted at the moment was a bit of peace from her Mam's nagging . . . and more to eat.

But she wasn't likely to get either of those.

A few days later, after her shift at the mill ended, Meg slipped along to the outer edge of the reservoir and sank wearily down on the low wall that separated it from the moors, letting the chill, clean air fill her lungs. This was as far away from other people as she could usually get and was one of her favourite places. The remaining lights inside the mill shone across the water, but where she sat was in shadow. She didn't want to go home yet, couldn't face her mother's carping. There was always something wrong when she got back from work. It'd be better to wait until her brother Jack went home. Mam was never as bad when he was around.

Meg sighed as she wrapped her shawl more tightly round her head and shoulders, wishing she had some warmer clothing. But her mother held the purse strings and always had some excuse for not buying her anything new.

As she looked across at the mill Meg scowled. She hated working there, and thought it unfair to be paid only a few shillings for her fourteen hours a day. She wouldn't get a woman's wages until she turned eighteen in just over a year's time. They pretended she worked under the supervision of Jen Foster. As if she needed supervision! She was as good as any of the other women, quick with her fingers to piece together any threads that broke so as to keep the machines running all day – the weaving machines that made Mr Rishmore rich and young women like her so exhausted that by the end of the day all most of them wanted was to get home and sleep.

But where else was she to find work in a small town like Northby? She didn't know anything but working in the mill and if she didn't work, how would her family manage? Since her father's death, they were hard put to cope as it was.

She heard feet crunching on the frosty ground coming towards her, but didn't turn round. With a bit of luck, the person would walk straight past. When she heard the footsteps slow down and stop, she turned and glared at the man who had disturbed her peace. 'What do *you* want, Ben Pearson?'

'To see you, lass.'

She bounced to her feet. 'I've already told you, I don't make friends with drunkards.'

He put out a hand to stop her leaving. 'I haven't touched a drop since last time we met.'

She hesitated, finding this hard to believe.

'I'd do anything to make you think better of me, Meg.'

'I don't know why.'

He chuckled. 'Eh, you're a blunt one.'

She shrugged and folded her arms tightly round herself as she waited for him to answer. When he didn't, she asked again, 'Why?'

'Because of the way your eyes sparkle when you're angry. Because I think you're pretty—'

'Hah! That's a lie for a start. We both know I'm not pretty.' She looked down at herself scornfully. 'I'm too thin an' my cheeks are hollow.'

'Only because you work so hard an' don't get enough to eat.'

His sympathy made her feel uncertain how to deal with him and she could hear her voice coming out more softly. 'How do *you* know what I eat?'

'I know from what Jen's said the sort of thing you bring to work for your dinner. Poor pickings, that. An' everyone knows what your mother's like. She thinks the sun shines out of your Jack's backside. I bet it all goes to him, the good food. Does *he* know how little she gives the rest of you?'

'It's none of your business. Leave me alone!' She pushed past him, afraid his sympathy would make her cry. She hated people to see her cry.

'I'll not be drinking tonight,' he called after her. 'An' I'll not let you alone till you start walking out with me.'

She stopped dead on those words, then turned round and stared at him. 'You're just making mock of me.'

'I'm not. Never that.'

His gaze was level and steady this time and his voice wasn't slurred today. He had a nice voice, gentle and light in tone.

'Will you?' he asked.

'I don't know. We'll see how long you can go without the booze. A few days is nowt to a drunkard.'

'Hard words. I s'll prove you wrong, though.'

She moved away, feeling a warmth run through her. He hadn't forgotten and if he did give up drinking, if he really did . . . Well, other lasses had fellows, so why not her?

Ben stood and watched her till her outline blurred into the darkness as the last lights inside the mill were turned off. He sat down right where she'd been sitting, feeling it linked him to her. He was living in lodgings, sharing a room, and had little privacy there, so he understood the need to seek places where you could have a quiet little think.

He sighed. It was hard giving up the drink, much harder than he'd expected. Yesterday he'd got as far as the door of the pub before he came to his senses. The lads he usually drank with were teasing him about it at work, but he'd set his mind to it, so he'd do it. He'd do anything for Meg. He didn't know why he fancied her so much. He'd never felt this strongly about his wife, just married her when he found they'd made a child together. And she'd died so soon after he'd felt guilty, as if he'd killed her on purpose.

He smiled. There were other lasses much prettier than Meg, but somehow she made them seem like pale imitations. Her brown eyes glowed with such life when something made her angry, as it often did, that his breath caught in his throat to see it. And her eyes were nearly as dark as her hair, brown with golden glints. She must wash her hair more often than other lasses did, because it always looked nice. And that said something about her, because water had to be fetched by the bucket from the stand pipe at the end of each street to the tiny terraced houses Rishmore provided for his workers. It wasn't easy to keep clean. Ben had seen how hard it had been for his wife.

Jem Staley, Meg's father, had been killed in the machine-breaking riots – eh, that must be two years ago now! – and the eldest son had been transported. The mother had gone to pieces, leaving Jack to hold the family together – a sixteen-year-old lad at the time – helped by young Mr Rishmore's charity. He was a great one for offering charity Mr Samuel was, but cold with it, so that you'd rather not trouble him unless you had to.

Ben shuddered at the memories. He'd been too ill to join the rioters that night and considered himself lucky. The incident had shaken everyone in town. Northby folk weren't the sort to riot, not usually. And it had made no difference to the damned machines. There the new ones were, clanking and clattering all day, tended by poor slaves like Meg while other slaves like him tended the mill's horses and drays.

A sudden longing for a deep draught of beer and the warmth of the pub weakened his resolve for a moment and he licked his lips, imagining the taste of it. His friends would be there by now, they'd smile a greeting and . . . He shook his head, mouthing the word no. He wasn't giving in to it. Not any more.

But it was going to be hard.

Meg caught up with her brother Jack as he was walking home from work. He looked as tired as she felt.

'Had a hard day?' she asked, slipping her arm through his.

'Aye.'

'Me, too.'

When they got near the house, she grimaced. 'I hope she's in a better mood than yesterday.'

He didn't need to ask who *she* was. 'You shouldn't answer her back.'

'I've as much right to talk as she has – an' I talk a

lot more sense, too.' Meg shoved the door open with a muttered, 'Here we go.'

It was Friday, one of their two meat days. Not that there was much meat in the stew, but enough to flavour it. When Netta Staley began to dole out the food a few minutes later, she made sure Jack got most of the meat.

He looked down at the plate. 'What about the others, Mam? They've got no meat at all.'

'There's not enough to go round today. They've got the gravy, haven't they? There's many childer don't get even that.'

'I've told you before: we'll all share what there is.' He placed a piece of the stringy meat on Meg's plate, then gestured to Shad, Ginny and Joe to hold out their plates too.

'It's the breadwinner as needs that,' Netta said shrilly, reaching out to stop him. 'We can't afford enough for everyone.'

As he carried on sharing his food, she burst into tears and left the table.

For once he didn't follow. 'Eat up, you lot. It's a shame to let good food go cold.'

Meg cleared her plate quickly. It wasn't good food, because her mother was an indifferent and careless cook, but she was ravenous so ate without complaint. Luckily for them it wasn't one of Jack's nights for going out or their mam would be hitting out at them after he'd left. She seemed to enjoy slapping them or hitting them with her wooden rolling pin. No wonder Shad stayed out whenever he could.

I wish I could leave here, Meg thought as she lay sleepless under the thin blanket, cuddled up against her sister Ginny. If I could, I'd go away tomorrow.

Phoebe Dixon watched her husband choke and gasp his life away. Three days it took from when Hal fell ill, just three days to destroy her life as well as his. She didn't love him, but he represented the only security she'd ever known and they'd rubbed along together all right.

After she'd laid him out, she found the pot where they kept their savings and counted its meagre contents, much depleted by his long period of ill health, not to mention his spendthrift ways. She had just enough left to pay for a simple funeral. It would leave little for her, but Hal wasn't going to have a pauper's funeral, she'd promised him that and she always tried to keep her promises. Mr Pickerling, the Curate, would hold the funeral service. Well, no one expected the Parson to come out to a tiny hamlet like Calico, situated on the edge of the moors miles from anywhere – not for a mere alehouse keeper, or for any other reason if the Parson could help it.

The burial took place on a chilly day, with dark clouds threatening rain and a wind whining fitfully across the moors, sometimes blowing hard so that Phoebe's dark skirts flapped like crows' wings and the men had to hold tight to their hats. Some thought it wrong for women to attend funerals. She'd have thought it wrong not to go with Hal on his last journey in Ross Bellvers' cart.

When the service was over the Curate waited for his fee at the gates of the walled burial ground which stood on a slight rise next to the church. For two centuries the dead of Calico and an occasional beggar or packman who'd died within the parish had been buried here.

Phoebe paid Mr Pickerling, who said apologetically that he was very sorry to trouble her for this money. She smiled and shook her head. They all knew how poor he and his family were on a Curate's stipend. When he tipped his hat to her before walking off down the hill she stood watching till he was out of sight, not saying anything.

Even after he'd disappeared from view she couldn't move because now that she'd buried Hal, she didn't know what to do or where to go. At nearly fifty, with no children or living relatives, she could see nothing ahead of her but the poorhouse.

When Ross took her by the arm and led her back with them she went quietly, too tired to protest. The small group of men came with her into the inn she'd helped run for nearly twenty years. The Packhorse it was called, because once packmen had been its most numerous customers apart from the villagers. It stood on Calico Road itself, as most houses in the village did, and was a rambling old place.

The Curate said the rear part had been built even before Queen Elizabeth sat on the throne of England, built by monks to live in while tending their sheep. If he said so, Phoebe supposed it must be true. All she

knew was she never felt comfortable in that part of
the inn and avoided it as much as she could.

Back at the inn she found that the neighbouring
women had brought in plates of food to hold a burial
feast for Hal, which was kind of them. She smiled
and nodded to show her appreciation, but couldn't
eat, not a bite. All she could do was sit there and wait,
though she wasn't sure what for.

The group fell quiet when they heard a horse's
hooves. When a gentleman walked into the inn, all
finely clad, someone whispered, 'It's young Mr
Greenhalgh – Mr Jethro,' and Phoebe's heart began
to thud in her chest. If he came from John
Greenhalgh, the owner, he surely brought only bad
news.

The newcomer looked round the public room, not
appearing to like what he saw. 'We heard that Dixon
had died.'

Heads nodded but no one spoke.

'Which of you is Mrs Dixon?'

Someone pushed Phoebe forward.

'We're sorry to hear about your loss, Mrs Dixon.
We'll give you a week to move your things out.'

Tears came into her eyes. 'Move out?' She'd half-
expected this, but it still hurt.

He looked at her impatiently. 'Didn't I just say so?'

There were mutterings in the silence, not a word
clear but the tone angry like the distant buzzing of a
fly against a window pane.

She found the courage to ask, 'Can't I stay on, sir?
You'll need someone to run the alehouse and I've

been doing that for the past year while Hal's been ill. I know the work. I've proved I can do it.'

'Your husband might have been ill, but he was still there. My father doesn't believe in giving such responsibility to a woman. Besides, what would you do if someone was drunk and causing trouble? A woman on her own couldn't manage.'

He had raised his voice, though the group was so quiet he needn't have bothered, and when he stopped one man muttered, 'Does he think we're all deaf, then?' But luckily only the person next to him heard and dug in an elbow, making a shushing sound.

Jethro looked round. 'Until we find someone to run the Packhorse for us, is there a man in the village who can take over? We'll pay you, of course.' When no one spoke, he added, 'Otherwise we'll have to close the place down.'

There was silence. People looked questioningly at one another, shaking their heads very slightly as if to decline. But if the Greenhalghs closed this inn, where would folk go for a pot of beer? The Packhorse was the centre of village life, the only place they had to take their ease, because it was too long a walk down the hill to the next village.

As the visitor began to frown and tap his foot impatiently, one man took a sudden decision and stood up. 'I'll do it, Mr Greenhalgh.' He didn't address him as sir, a word he disliked, because he wasn't beholden to the Greenhalghs for anything, either his livelihood or his cottage, and glad of it, too.

'Who are you?'

'Ross Bellvers, smallholder.'

Jethro studied him for a moment, then nodded. 'Very well. See that you keep the place clean until we find a new man, and no drinking away the profits. My father will expect a full accounting.' He turned back to the widow. 'Mrs Dixon, a word with you in private.'

Phoebe followed him into the living quarters at the rear, noting how his lips curled in disgust at the poverty of the furnishings and the untidiness. She wished then that she'd not let herself go to pieces after Hal died, knew she looked more like a beggar woman than an alehouse keeper's widow today, and was filled with shame.

He held out a small purse. 'This is to help you on your way.'

When she didn't reach out for it, he tossed it on the table, turning to leave then stopping as if on an after-thought to ask, 'Did your husband ever say anything to you about why he was given the job here?'

She knew what to say to that one. 'No, sir. Never.' But of course she knew why Hal had been given this place. Even men as close-mouthed as him talked in their sleep or when they were ill, and wives slowly put the pieces of the puzzle together. She also knew better than to admit anything.

'And he didn't leave any papers?'

'No, sir.'

'You're sure of that?'

'Oh, yes, sir.'

Without another word Greenhalgh walked out of the alehouse and mounted his horse.

Once the hoof beats had faded into the distance, Ross went into the back room and found Phoebe sitting weeping.

'To throw me out!' she sobbed. 'He brought me in here to toss a purse at me. As if that'd make it all right! I've been here over twenty year now, Ross. It's my *home!* I don't have anywhere else to go.'

He patted her on the shoulder. 'That's a Greenhalgh for you. This is the only time one of them sods has visited Calico for years and . . .' He stopped, struck by that thought. 'How's he to know?'

'Know what?'

Ross grinned at her. 'Whether you stay or go. You look a right old mess today, Phoebe love. When you're back to your old self, he'll not even recognise you. *If* he ever comes here again, which he likely won't. We'll change your name, though, just to make sure.'

She looked at him, hope dawning on her face. 'What happens when they send someone to take over here?'

'Depends whether the fellow's married or not. If he isn't, you can ask him for a job. After all, you know the trade.'

'Dare we?' she whispered, as if afraid to speak out loud.

'Why not? You can run this place for *me* till the new man arrives, and if nothing else it'll give you time to make plans. Nay, what are you weeping for, lass?'

'Because you're so k-kind.'

'I'm not *kind!* I'm just being practical. For the sake of the village. What would we do if we didn't have this place?'

From his tone she might have been accusing him of a crime by calling him kind, and she knew better than to repeat it. Folk in Calico kept their feelings to themselves. Let townfolk gabble on about nothing, people up here knew better. You should only speak when you had summat worth saying – especially when there were strangers around.

And her Hal would have added: Especially when the strangers were Greenhalghs. He'd been afraid of them, no doubt about that, afraid they'd kill him if he didn't keep his mouth shut.

Jethro rode slowly back down the hill to Backenshaw. He hadn't enjoyed telling the woman to leave but his father had insisted she must go. And no one dared argue with John Greenhalgh, least of all his son. Perhaps, given the circumstances, it was for the best, but she'd looked so shocked and unhappy when he'd told her.

One day, though, his father would die and then Jethro would make his own rules about how he dealt with his dependants and employees. He'd not treat them softly – he was too much John's son for that – but sometimes he felt his father was unnecessarily harsh.

With everyone.

His own son included.

2

October

Toby Fletcher looked up when his workmate tapped him on the shoulder.

'Bob wants to see you, lad.'

Toby nodded and went to wipe his mucky hands on a piece of cotton waste, then walked across the big workshop into the room Bob called his 'office', which was just a corner cut off the main space. They made all sorts of bits and pieces here – furniture, gates and boxes, odds and ends for the house – and they did house repairs as well, for Mr Greenhalgh and for other employers. Toby was one of the more skilled workers, good with his hands and always had been. He knew Bob Taylor valued him as an employee and he respected Bob. This summons would likely be a repair job that needed doing in a hurry.

Bob greeted him with, 'Young Mr Greenhalgh just sent down word. His father wants to see you.'

'Then he can go on wanting. I've nowt to say to *him*.'

'Happen he has summat to say to you, though, lad. Word is, the old man's dying.'

Toby had already turned to leave but spun round

to ask angrily, 'Why should that make a difference to me?'

'It allus does an' well you know it. Go an' see him. Take my advice an' make your peace with him while you can or you'll live to regret it.'

For a moment longer Toby tried to hold firm to his refusal then he shrugged and left the office. John Greenhalgh owned half the small town of Backenshaw, nestled in the foothills of the Pennines, and although Toby didn't work directly for him, even he would hesitate to get on the man's wrong side.

Within minutes he was striding up the hill to the big house, having washed his hands and face but not bothered to change his clothes. If Old John wanted to see him, he could see him in his working clothes or not at all.

As he drew closer, Toby's steps slowed down and he sighed. What now? Everyone in the village knew that John was his natural father, but that hadn't made much difference to his mother's life – or to his, either. Marjorie Fletcher had come over from Rochdale way when Backenshaw was just a village. There was no sign of a husband but she was carrying a baby in her arms, a strong little fellow nearly a year old. She'd been met and given one of the new two-roomed cottages to live in, on the master's express orders, which had surprised everyone, but when folk asked her outright if Mr Greenhalgh was the father, she'd refused to discuss it.

Old John had had nothing to do with the two newcomers, not even speaking to Marjorie in the mill. He charged them the same rent as anyone else and left her to cope as best she could. He was, folk sniggered, too busy with his new bride and, ten months later, with his new son, to go after women as he had before.

Marjorie had continued to work in the new spinning mill Greenhalgh had built. Her hard work earned people's respect and, though she might have slipped up once, she never associated with a fellow again and was a regular attender at church. But she never talked about her past or her family, not even to Toby.

As the baby grew into a lad the resemblance to John Greenhalgh showed up so clearly that you couldn't doubt who'd fathered him – and the resemblance to his half-brother Jethro was remarkable. They could have been twins. So Marjorie explained to Toby that Mr Greenhalgh was his father too, but that he was bastard born and must never speak to the mill owner or expect anything of him.

Jethro, the legitimate son, was carefully guarded, though from what he needed protecting people never could work out. He went away to a fancy school for the sons of gentlemen when he was ten and he talked differently from the Backenshaw folk because of his lady mother. He kept away from Toby, even crossing the street to avoid him, but that didn't stop the resemblance between them from continuing to astonish other people.

Until today's summons John Greenhalgh had not even nodded to his natural son in the street, but the old man had attended Marjorie's simple funeral when Toby was eighteen, or at least someone from the big house had turned up in a shiny new carriage, sitting there with the blinds pulled down but not getting out to join the other mourners. Mind you, they could have just sent an empty carriage as a mark of respect. Toby wouldn't put anything past the tricky old sod in the big house. But at least they'd allowed him to keep the cottage which was the only home he'd ever known.

When he got to Parkside, the Greenhalghs' stone-built mansion, the young man hesitated for a moment then walked up to the front door. If Old John wanted to see him, he'd let him into the house this way or Toby wouldn't go in at all.

The maid who answered looked down her nose at him till he said who he was, then her frown turned to a more welcoming expression and she gestured him inside.

'They're expecting you, sir. If you'll just wait here in the hall for a minute or two, I'll send word up to the master.'

She'd called him *sir*, Toby thought with a wry grimace. Eh, he'd gone up in the world. No one had ever called him that before. Probably wouldn't again, either. Clutching his hat in his hands he stared round, taking in everything he could because it would likely be the only time he saw the inside of this place. It was just as people had said, a bloody palace. He felt angry at such a display of wealth. It wasn't right that one man should own so much when others were clemming for lack of food.

The maid came back. 'If you'll follow me, sir, I'll show you up to the master's bedroom. Shall I take your hat?'

'Nay, I can carry it mesen, thanks.'

He trod up the stairs in her wake, amazed by how soft and thick the carpet was – even his clumsy boots made hardly a sound – and how beautiful the woodwork was. It had a patina so fine he'd have liked to stroke the polished surfaces and examine the pieces of furniture he passed to see how they were made.

She opened a door. 'Please go in, sir.'

He paused to take a deep breath and square his shoulders before entering a room so big he was surprised to see it was only a bedroom. He and his mother had shared one only a quarter the size of this for years, dividing it with an old sheet hung over a rope, for modesty's sake. Since her death that bedroom had been his alone, which was something of a luxury in a village where ten people might have to share a two-roomed cottage.

When he looked across at the bed he forgot everything else in his shock. It was as if he was seeing the ghost of John Greenhalgh, so thin and white was the man lying there. The resemblance between Toby and his natural father had always been very noticeable, even when the old man was plump with good health. Now, it seemed to shout at him from that thin, pale face.

John stared back at him, eyes alive with intelligence though the rest of him lay so still you'd almost think he'd died already. His face was grey-white and his lips hardly marked by colour except for a faint bluish tinge.

'Toby Fletcher,' he said, the first words he'd ever spoken directly to his natural son.

Toby nodded but said nothing. He stayed where he was, uncertain what was expected of him.

'Come closer to the bed where I can see you properly.'

He moved forward, trying not to show how the room overwhelmed him, for it made him feel small, he who stood six foot three and was noted for his broad, muscular shoulders.

'Thank you for coming,' John went on in that husky thread of a voice.

'They said you were dying. I'd not have come else.'

A younger man standing in the shadows to one side of the bed let out an angry choke of sound at this bluntness and took a quick step forward. Without turning his head, John said, 'You'll stay silent, Jethro, or leave the room.'

Breathing heavily, casting a furious glance in Toby's direction, the man stepped back again.

His half-brother, Toby thought, surprised by a sudden feeling of amusement. A couple of years younger than him and a couple of inches shorter, but with almost the same face – a damned Greenhalgh face. This family looked down their noses at ordinary folk nowadays, though John's father had been a handloom weaver and there were whispers that John himself had not made his early money honestly. The mill he'd built had thrived, though, and he'd been a model citizen ever since he opened it. Backenshaw had thrived too, and was now almost big enough to be called a town.

'You're a Greenhalgh all right,' John said slowly, each word seeming an effort. He glanced sideways at his son, who was still scowling. 'No use denying what anyone with eyes can see, Jethro. You and he look so alike and—' He broke off, coughing feebly and gesturing towards a glass of water.

A manservant stepped forward to lift him up and help him drink. As he settled back against his pillows John gave Toby a wry smile. 'I asked you here because I've not long left to live. We all come to it. Neither rich nor poor can escape death.'

'It seems to me the rich escape it for longer than the poor do,' Toby said, remembering another death bed and a woman whose love for him had shone in her eyes until the light went out of them for ever.

John nodded agreement. 'You're right. But for all our money, we still come to it in the end. My money couldn't save my wife when she fell ill.' He paused to gather his breath. 'I brought you here because – I find I cannot die in peace unless I do something for you, Toby Fletcher. You are, after all, my son.'

Another mutter from behind him and Jethro scowled across the room at Toby, who scowled right back, before turning to his father and saying sharply, 'I need nowt from you. I can make my own way in the world. The only time I've wanted owt from you was when my mother lay dying. I knocked on that big front door of yours to seek help for her and got turned away.' He'd been distraught at the thought of losing her. Eh, to think she'd been gone eight years! But there wasn't a day passed that he didn't remember her fondly.

'I was in London, didn't find out about Marjorie until it was too late to help her. I'm sorry about that. I did attend the funeral.'

That silenced Toby. So it had been *him* behind the carriage blinds.

'It's I who need something from you now, Toby.'

He stared across at the bed in puzzlement then gestured round the room. 'How can someone like you need owt from me?'

The dying man was betrayed into a spurt of laughter, which made him choke so that he had to be given another drink of water. 'I was wrong to do nothing for you and Marjorie. I need to make up for that now – if I'm to go in peace. So I beg you to accept what I offer.'

Angry words of refusal welled up in Toby's throat, but the habit of years made him hold them back. Bastards like him soon learned not to make bad worse by taking offence easily, because unlike other lads they'd no father or brothers to stand up for them. And even when he'd used his superior strength to make his point, he'd got into trouble for it, which had upset his mother. So he'd learned to control his anger and use words and humour instead of blows to calm down a situation. 'What did you have in mind?'

'I'm thinking of giving you a piece of land and a small inn. Will you accept them from me?'

Toby waited. He wasn't going to leap at the offer like a greedy puppy snapping at food. Did the old devil really mean it? Eh, it'd have been sweet to toss the offer back and tell Old John to keep his bloody inn. But it'd have been stupid, too – and Toby had never considered himself stupid. This was his big chance in life, so he wasn't going to throw it away. It was an effort to force the necessary words out, though. 'Aye. I'll accept them.'

'I knew he would,' Jethro sneered.

'Then you knew more than me,' his father said. 'I'm pleased, but can I ask why, Toby? You've always been very independent and you refused my offer of a job in the mill.'

He shrugged and told the truth. 'I'll accept because I'm not a fool. Because it'll make me my own man, an' who'd not welcome that? Where is it, this inn of yours?'

'Up near the tops on Calico Road. The inn's called the Packhorse. The village is called Calico too because they used to weave the cloth there.'

Toby had heard of the place but never been there, for it was a fair distance from Backenshaw, two or three hours' walk.

'I warn you, it's a strange place,' John continued. 'The folk up there are independent to a fault and pride themselves on being moor folk and better than townies, so you'll have to earn acceptance by them.'

Toby smiled. 'I like it on the moors.' The space and freedom up there seemed to free his soul from the weight of other people and he often went for a walk outside the village on fine Sundays to breathe the tangy, bracing air, so different from the smoky air of Backenshaw itself. And if the folk at Calico were surly at first with him, he felt sure they'd accept him after a while because he usually got on well with people of all sorts, which was why his employer often sent him out to do repairs to the houses of the better sort of customer.

Eh, to be your own man, to call no one 'master'! Was it really going to happen to him?

For what seemed a very long time the man in the bed looked across at him and there was no reading his expression. Then he nodded. 'Good. Make something of the place. Make me and your mother proud of you.'

Toby chose his words carefully. 'I'll make good use of it, you can be sure.'

John sighed and closed his eyes. 'You'll need to see my lawyer. He's waiting with the papers in the library. Once you've signed them the place is yours. You can write, can't you?'

'Aye.'

The old man held out his hand.

Impelled by he knew not what, Toby went across to the bed, took the limp hand and held it in his for a few moments, before laying it gently down on the bed again. He didn't speak or look back as he left the room. What was there to say? They hardly knew one another and it was far too late now to remedy that.

You can write, can't you? The words rang in his ears as he went down the stairs and he could feel his cheeks going warm from shame. He knew the alphabet, could write his name and read a few simple words, but that was all. He was better with figures and could calculate how much wood was needed for a job as well as folk with fancy schooling, but he'd been too busy earning his daily bread, even as a small lad, to go to school regularly. That had upset his mother, but he'd been stubborn, going after money to put bread on the table because as she grew older she hadn't always enjoyed good health and they'd had some hard times.

He followed the same maid down the stairs and into a room lined with so many books that he stopped in astonishment near the door. He hadn't known there were this many books in all of Lancashire! A man clad in black looked up from a table near the window and gestured him across.

'You're accepting the gift from Mr Greenhalgh then, Mr Fletcher?'

'Aye.'

'You'll need to read this before you sign it.'

Toby took the folded piece of paper, looked at how long the words on it were and handed it back. 'You'll have to read it to me. I can read simple stuff, but I can't understand long words like those.' No doubt the man would report that to the Greenhalghs and then his damned brother would laugh at him. At that moment Toby vowed to learn to read properly and never shame himself like this again.

He listened to what the lawyer said, asking several questions till he thought he understood the meaning of the deed of gift. There was only one condition: he was to provide a free pot of beer for his half-brother every January. He'd have laughed at that piece of foolishness if the lawyer hadn't been so solemn-faced.

As he signed the papers, Toby felt relieved that at least he could pen his name without hesitation. He looked at the space where his father had signed, surprised as always by the way you spelled Greenhalgh. Why the 'gh' at the end should be spoken like 'sh' he'd never understood. He'd seen the word in big letters on the side of the mill all his life and when he started learning his letters had asked the teacher why, but the man had grown cross at being interrupted and said it wasn't for him to question how his betters spoke their names.

The lawyer cleared his throat and Toby realised he'd been lost in his thoughts. He put the quill down and sat back, watching as a manservant and the housekeeper were brought in to witness both signatures.

When he walked out of the house holding his copy of the deed to the inn, he held his head high, shame at his inability to read easily forgotten because he owned land now. It was probably stony and barren if it was up in one of the V-shaped valleys moor folk called cloughs, but it was land nonetheless. The inn was called the Packhorse. Toby liked that name and hoped it looked out over the lower valleys so that he could watch the world, not be hemmed in by other buildings as he was in Backenshaw.

As he got near the place where he worked he threw back his head and laughed, jeering laughter so harsh he quickly clamped his mouth shut to keep it back. *Make something of it. Make me and your mother proud of you,* John Greenhalgh had said. Well, to hell with that! Toby didn't intend to dance to the old devil's tune. He'd make no one proud unless it suited him to do so.

If his mother had lived it might have been different, because he'd have wanted to make *her* proud of him, not to mention earning enough to buy her every comfort possible. But she was dead, so he'd do as he pleased now, thank you very much, John Greenhalgh.

And the condition attached to the gift made no difference. Why would his half-brother want a free drink of beer every January? It didn't make sense for a man as rich as Jethro Greenhalgh would be once his father John died. Any road, Toby doubted his half-brother would bother to ride all that way to claim his beer, and even if he did, the arrogant sod would wait his turn to be served like any other customer.

When Toby had left the room, John gestured to his manservant to leave too and beckoned his son closer to the bed. 'That should get him out of your way. Calico is a good two hours' walk from Backenshaw.'

Jethro shrugged. 'Perhaps, but as I said when we discussed it last time, I'd have preferred to get him right out of the country. Up on the moors isn't far enough.' Not when the two of them looked so much alike. He'd hated that since he'd first seen Fletcher in the street years before and noticed people staring at them both – then gone home and examined his own face in the mirror again and again, finding it so like Fletcher's he'd been shocked to the core.

'I tried that . . . hired men to talk to him about Australia. They promised him a free passage and a good job when he arrived there, but he told them he'd never leave Lancashire.' John paused, staring into the distance before adding, 'And I found I'd no stomach for harming him, so that was that. Nor should you hurt him. He *is* your half-brother, after all.'

'I know he's my brother. That's the problem. But you surely don't think I'd harm him?'

'Who knows? But I want your solemn promise that you'll not hurt him in any way.'

'Oh, really, Father. Is this necessary?'

'I think so. Men can be pushed into doing things sometimes.' John paused to stare into a past about which only he knew the full truth, then jerked back into the present to say sharply, 'I not only want your promise that you'll not harm him, but that you'll not let him be harmed by anyone else either. I owe his mother that, at least.'

So Jethro gave his word, though it hadn't been

necessary. He wasn't like his father, whose ruthless-ness was a byword in the town.

'And I want your promise that you'll go up to Calico every year for that free pot of beer.'

Jethro stared at him, read determination in his father's eyes and shrugged. 'If you insist.'

'I do. You're to keep an eye on the place. And on Andrew Beardsworth. He's too close to it. I don't trust him. He knows too much, has too much to lose himself.'

As the silence whispered around them, broken only by hot coals settling in the grate and the clock ticking on the mantelpiece, Jethro asked suddenly, 'Why the hell did you do it, Father? I've never under-stood that.'

John stared into the distance. 'I'd no choice. Her brothers were threatening to kill me, had a knife to my throat. They meant it too. I was rather fond of living. Still am.' His mocking laughter at his own vulnerability turned into another fit of coughing.

This time his son held him up for a sip of water then laid him down gently on the soft feather pillow. The old man had always controlled his life too tightly and had a far harsher way of dealing with the world than Jethro would choose, but he found himself regretting the loss he would soon suffer.

The husky voice whispered on. 'The last of her brothers died only a few days ago. As far as I know, they all kept quiet about what had happened because I paid them well when my circumstances changed.

Now, let's forget about Tobias Fletcher. My conscience is clear. I've left him well provided for and I've arranged it so that he'll leave Backenshaw as soon as I'm dead. I just want to live my last few weeks in peace.'

But he died the next night, passing away in his sleep.

One Sunday Meg took a deep breath and announced to her family that she was walking out with Ben Pearson that afternoon. After a stunned silence, Netta let out one of her angry cries and bounced to her feet.

'I'll not have it!'

'How will you stop me – tie me down?'

Jack moved between them. 'But Pearson's older than you, love, years older.'

'He's been wed afore – he'll be after only one thing from a lass,' Netta sneered. 'And he's a boozer, too. You can never trust drunkards. I'm not having it. Jack, tell her not to go.' When he said nothing she started weeping loudly, calling his name again and again.

Jack looked at his sister. 'Why him, Meg?'

She hated to see that careworn air about him. Like her he was young, but unlike her he seemed resigned to living with their mother, being her support in a hard world, for he'd made no attempt to walk out with any of the lasses from the mill. 'Because I want a life of my own, Jack. As you should. And because I like Ben. He's kind.'

'What about his drinking?'

'He's given it up.'

Netta laughed. 'Hah! If you'll believe that, you'll believe anything. Once a boozer, allus a boozer.'

'Ben hasn't had a drink for weeks. I've checked. I wouldn't walk out with him till I was sure.' Meg went to cram the battered bonnet on her head, wishing she at least had new ribbons to trim it up. She heard her mother continue pleading with her brother to stop her walking out.

'No, Mam, she has a right to a life of her own.' Jack moved to stand between the two women.

'You'll be sorry, Meg Staley!' Netta screeched as she left the house, so Meg slammed the door behind her as hard as she could, something her mother hated. As she walked along the street she heard the door open again and knew Netta would be standing on the doorstep watching. She didn't turn round. Let her watch.

Ben was waiting for her at the corner. His face lit up at the sight of Meg and the hard angry lump inside her eased a little. He held out his arm and she took it, walking self-consciously up Weavers Lane with him, seeing people she knew staring at them. It'd be round the mill tomorrow: Meg Staley's walking out with Ben Pearson.

They went slowly up the hill past the rich folk's houses towards the moors and to her surprise she found herself enjoying his company. He spoke so gently to her and he'd even brought food for them wrapped in a clean cloth: new-baked bread and crumbly white cheese. When they sat on a wall to eat it, he told her again she was pretty, and though she shook her head at that, she knew she was at least looking her best.

'Shall we walk out again next Sunday if it's fine?' he asked as they came back down the lane.

'If you like.'

'I'll look forward to it. I'll see you to your door.'

She stopped. 'Better not. Mam's up in arms about me walking out with you and she'll only be rude.'

'It's better we do this openly. As long as *you* are kind to me, I don't give a damn what your mother says.'

Which made her like him even more.

When Meg went into the house, her mother was waiting for her and slapped her face before she could say a word.

'I'll teach you to cheek me, you young devil. And whatever Jack says, you're *not* going out with that fellow again.'

She raised her hand for another slap and Meg put up her own arm automatically to fend it off. Suddenly she had had enough of this sort of treatment. 'If you ever hit me again,' she shouted at the top of her voice, shoving her mother away so hard she bumped into a chair, 'I'll hit you right back.' Then she turned and ran out of the house, doing without food and slipping into the tiny chapel lower down the lane when it started to rain. She didn't go home until the service was over and then walked slowly back, knowing that at least her big brother would be there to protect her now.

★

Jack saw his sister come in and thought how tired she looked. The straw hat was bedraggled and Meg's hair was hanging in damp rats' tails down the sides of her face. When she raised a hand to brush it back, he saw the bruise on her cheek and knew their mother had been slapping her again. He'd tried to stop her hitting the children but in vain. She always turned it off with, 'Aw, it's only a slap or two. Keeps them in order.'

'Mam said you came back once. Where did you go afterwards, Meg?' he asked.

'Out on my own.'

'She's been back with *him* again,' Netta said. 'She'll come home with a babby in her belly at this rate an' shame us all.'

Meg rounded on her mother. 'I've done nothing wrong an' I won't. How can you even think that of me?'

Jack looked at her searchingly. 'Promise me you won't let him touch you.'

'I'll let him kiss me. Why not?' He'd done that already, a shy, gentle kiss, which had thrilled him more than her. It was the cuddle that went with it that had pleased her most. 'I won't let him do the other thing to me till we're wed, though.'

Netta bounced to her feet. '*Wed!* You can't go getting wed. We need your wages here. Jack, tell her!'

He pulled his mother down beside him and kept hold of her arm.

Meg spoke to him because she could hardly bear to look at her mother. 'She's not tying me to her for life. I'd rather throw myself in the reservoir. An' when I want to get wed, I shall.'

'Not without my permission!' Netta looked at her triumphantly. 'At your age you can't get wed unless I say so. Not till you're twenty-one, you can't. An' I won't let you.'

'Then I'll live in sin, big belly an' all.'

Jack shook his mother's arm slightly. 'Stop this. She's only walking out with him and she has a right to make friends. She wouldn't have run out again if you hadn't gone for her.' He looked at his sister pleadingly. 'Just take care, eh?'

Meg nodded, an unspoken promise to him. Then she looked at her mother, an angry glance that said just as clearly as words that she'd run her own life from now on.

When Netta burst into tears, Meg left Jack to comfort her and went upstairs to take off her best clothes, which were wet now. Ginny was still awake in the bed they shared and Shad whispered from the next room, 'She's been in hysterics since you left, our Meg.'

'Let her. I don't care.'

She hung the clothes on the nail in the wall then sat on the edge of the bed and tried hard not to weep. But though she stopped herself from sobbing aloud, she couldn't prevent a few tears from escaping and trickling down her face. She couldn't stand living like this much longer. She'd do anything to get away from her mother, anything!

Ginny reached out to pat her back and the touch comforted her.

'Why is Mam like that?' Meg asked, not waiting for an answer because there wasn't any explanation for sheer bad temper. 'She's got Jack doing what she wants. Isn't that enough for her? I tell you, I'm leaving home as soon as I can.' She meant it, too.

3

Toby made plans to go up to Calico Road on the following Sunday. He was reluctant to give up his job until he'd seen for himself that his father's legacy would support him. For all he knew, the land he'd been given could be a barren patch of moorland and the inn a ruin or a tumble-down little alehouse. He was quite sure there was some hidden reason for the gift John Greenhalgh had made. He'd racked his brains about it, but couldn't think what it might be. All he knew was: that man wouldn't do anything out of sheer kindness or Toby's mother would have had an easier life.

After some deliberation he felt obliged to attend his father's funeral on the Friday. He was too tall to avoid being noticed among the crowd of tenants and employees following the hearse, but stayed at the rear and did nothing to draw attention to himself. Unfortunately Jethro Greenhalgh spotted him almost immediately and glared at him, after which he avoided looking in his direction again.

That same evening the rent man turned up and gave Toby a week's notice to quit the cottage in which he'd lived since he was a baby.

'And my instructions are to make sure you leave it in good order, just as you found it,' the rent man finished.

Anger rose in Toby at the pettiness of this. 'I'll do just that, then, leave it *exactly* as my mother found it, bare of comfort except for the plank bed built into the alcove and the shelf over the fire.'

The other man looked round, frowning now. 'What are you talking about? There are plenty of shelves and fixings here.'

'Aye, because she and I made the place home-like. I put up most of these shelves myself with wood I got from work, and now I'll be taking them all with me seeing as Mr Greenhalgh wants everything left as we found it.' He hadn't meant to remove them – what were a few old shelves? – but after this summary dismissal he'd not leave even the hooks by the door.

When the rent man had left, Toby stood for a few moments feeling pain well up inside him. To throw him out like this! And for what reason? He didn't understand it, but he'd not forget what his damned half-brother had done.

Pulling himself together, he began methodically sorting through his possessions. Perhaps he'd find a thriving inn waiting for him. No, that wasn't likely. Folk as money-mad as the Greenhalghs wouldn't give something away unless it was near worthless. But if Toby could just win a living from the place, it would do him. He hadn't been ambitious before, but now had a strong urge to show his half-brother what he could make of himself.

He went round to his employer's house and explained the situation, arranging to stop work immediately and borrow the larger of Bob's two carts and the horses to draw it on the Sunday. Bob was very indignant at his being thrown out of his home like that and refused to take payment for the cart.

'I'll miss you, lad.'

'Aye. An' I want to thank you for all you've taught me. If you're ever up Calico Road, there'll be a pot of beer waiting for you.'

They shook hands, keeping the contact for longer than usual.

'Good luck,' Bob said at last, stepping back.

Toby went round to Rab Jervis's house that evening and offered him five bob to help load and unload everything on Sunday then bring the cart back. Rab agreed eagerly. He had a large family and was always short of money.

It was almost midnight before Toby went to bed on the Saturday, but by then he'd not only packed his things but done as he'd threatened and removed every shelf and hook from the cottage. After less than four hours' sleep he woke in the early morning to hear rain beating against the window panes and cursed it. But you couldn't change the weather so he got up, ate the bread and cheese he'd left ready in a cloth the night before, and put a sack round his shoulders to keep off the worst of the downpour.

By the time he got back with the cart, Rab was waiting for him inside the cottage. 'Sod of a day!' was his greeting, but for all his dour expression and sagging body, he was a hard worker and they were soon loaded and ready to go.

As they drove along Rab huddled under some sacks and said very little, which suited Toby just fine because he was finding it more painful to leave his home than he'd ever have believed possible. Damn Jethro Greenhalgh! Damn all of that name! He was glad he had a different name, though he wished he knew more about the Fletchers. He reckoned they must have disowned his mother when she bore a child out of wedlock, for she'd always refused to talk about them, wouldn't even say where exactly she came from.

It took longer than he'd expected to get up to Calico in such muddy conditions, but an hour and a half later the slow-moving cart reached a signposted turn which joined a wider road leading to Todmorden in one direction and over the tops to Halifax in the other. The road on to which they turned was one of a few ways across the tops from Lancashire to Yorkshire, not the main route but still one that was regularly used. It began to climb almost immediately and from time to time Toby got down to give the horses a lighter load, leaving them to plod along at their own pace, because they were a docile pair and he knew their ways. At such times Rab trudged along on the other side of the two animals. Like Toby, he was soaked through by now.

After a while they came to a sign reading *Calico ½ mile*. Ahead they could see a clough leading down from the tops. Trees were growing in the shelter it provided and as they drew closer they saw a narrow stream racing down one side of the road, swollen with rainwater. It passed under the main road at a low stone bridge just before they reached Calico itself, then tumbled off to the right down the slopes of the moors, heading for Yorkshire, Toby supposed.

Part of the hamlet was built along the main road, with other houses scattered in irregular fashion up the slopes nearby and the odd farmhouse showing at intervals across the fields.

'What the hell did they want to build a village right up here for?' Rab grumbled as Toby slowed the horses and began to look for the inn. 'Eh, I'm glad it's you as is going to live here not me, lad! It'll be a bugger of a place come winter.'

Toby looked for the inn but found nothing until he'd gone right through the village and rounded the final bend. A sign was swinging in the wind. The Packhorse, announced in faded letters, and there was a crude picture of a horse with its panniers laden with goods. He called out to his own horses and as they came to a halt in front of the inn, pulled off his hat, shook the water from its brim then wiped his forehead and eyes with the back of his hand. He was surprised to find the inn quite large, though the building looked very run down.

Was this really all his? Excitement began to rise in him. It wasn't a ruin but a proper working inn! Situated on the main road as it was, it must cater for travellers, though he couldn't see the gentry using such a shabby place.

'Eh, looks like you've fallen on your feet, lad,' Rab said.

The rain had eased off so Toby took a minute or two to study the long, sprawling building. The front part looked to be the most modern, built of stone with a slate roof that was dark and shiny from the rain. To the right of the inn he saw wheel ruts leading round to what were no doubt the stables and behind it sagging roofs suggested a jumble of sheds and outbuildings. The rest of the inn sprawled up the hillside and at the rear was a more solid building which looked far older than the rest. If he'd had to guess, he'd have said the rear part had been built first of all, then each section of the front added on carelessly, without thought to how the whole looked.

And this was all his!

How could so small a village have spawned an inn so large? Toby wondered. Pride of ownership filled him together with a sense of recognition, as if something in him knew this place, knew it in his very bones.

'Aren't we going inside?' Rab asked, breaking the spell. 'I could murder for a pot of beer.'

Hesitating a moment longer, then telling himself not to be so stupid, Toby took the sodden sack from his shoulders, flung it into the back of the wagon and pushed open the door. The horses could wait a minute or two to be fed and watered. They were tired and wouldn't budge.

A group of men sitting round the table nearest the fire stopped talking abruptly to stare at him as he went in, gaping in shock. His damned face again! Even up here they'd recognised it. After a minute they looked away again, all except one man, who heaved himself to his feet, his expression anything but welcoming.

'Who are you?'

'Toby Fletcher.'

'You look like a Greenhalgh to me.'

'I'm related, distantly, but that's not my fault, is it?'

The other man gave a reluctant smile. 'What d'you want?'

'Two pots of beer and to warm oursen up by yon fire.'

Going behind the counter to where a barrel stood on its wooden frame, the man took two earthenware pots from the shelf above it and drew a jug of ale, filling the pots so carelessly that beer splashed across the wooden counter top.

When Toby had paid, the man pocketed the money and slouched back across the room to his companions, but they didn't start talking again, only sat and watched him and Rab suspiciously. If this was how they greeted strangers in Calico, no wonder the alehouse had so few customers.

Rab didn't seem to notice the hostility but lifted his pot to his lips, smacking them in appreciation as he set it down. 'A good drop of ale, that.'

Toby had a taste, pleasantly surprised by the quality of the beer. He took another mouthful, studying the customers as openly as they were studying him. Who was that fellow to pocket the money from what was, according to the lawyer, Toby's beer? In fact, according to the deed of gift, he now owned everything inside the inn. He couldn't take that in properly even yet because everything was so much bigger than he'd expected.

'Aren't you going to tell 'em why you're here?' Rab whispered.

'Not yet. Let's see what happens first.' Toby took another sip then set his pot down and went to hold his hands out to the fire.

After watching him for a minute or two, the man who'd served them stood up and left, returning a short time later with an older woman. The minute she saw Toby she stopped dead, her mouth dropping open in shock as if she too recognised him. She took a deep breath and hesitated noticeably before coming across to them. 'I hope your beer is all right, sir?'

'It's good.'

'Terrible day to be out. Come far, have you?'

She waited as if expecting him to tell her his business, but Toby didn't say anything, simply nodding as he took another sip. When Rab drained his pot, Toby jerked his head in his friend's direction. 'Another beer for my friend, please. I'm all right for the moment.' He waited till she'd served Rab then asked quietly, 'Could I have a word with you in private, please, missus?' He was astounded to see stark fear etch itself across her face, making her suddenly look years older.

The man who'd got their drinks had been watching

and now came across to join them. 'Is something wrong, Mary love?'

'He wants a word in private, Ross.'

'You'll feel safer if I join you, then.'

Toby frowned at him. 'What do you think I'm going to do – hurt her?'

'Can't be too careful with strangers. Any road, Mary's my cousin. She's been helping out here for a while. I'm the one in charge till Mr Greenhalgh sends someone to run the place.'

'Well, in a manner of speaking, I'm that someone.'

'Thought so. Trust them to put family in here!'

Toby wondered why he sounded so bitter about it. As he looked round he saw that everyone in the public room was listening to their conversation with open hostility on their faces. He'd deal with that later. 'Are the stables round the back?'

The woman nodded.

Toby turned to his friend. 'Rab, will you go and see to the horses, please? Take them round the back. There are some nosebags of oats ready on the cart.'

'You'll be all right if I leave you, lad?'

Toby nodded. He turned to look questioningly at the woman, who led the way behind the counter and through a doorway which had no door to it, only a shabby curtain of rubbed and stained green velvet with fraying edges. The room behind was immaculately neat, but everything in it looked well worn. Toby took the seat indicated while Mary and the man who'd served him sat together on the opposite side of the table. Tired of beating about the bush he said baldly, 'I'm not here to run the place for the Green-halghs, I'm the new owner.'

'*Owner?*' The man gaped at him. 'They said nowt about selling the place.'

'They've only sold it to someone in the family,' the woman said in a tight, unhappy voice.

'I'm *not* a Greenhalgh!' Toby said firmly, wondering how many times he would have to repeat this before they believed him.

She looked at him sceptically. 'You're connected. It's written all over your face.'

'Aye, well, Old John was my father, if you must know, but he never wed my mother or did owt for me till he left me this place, so I don't count myself one of them. My name's Fletcher, not Greenhalgh. Toby Fletcher.'

She stared at him as if shocked afresh by that, studying his face. Then she got slowly to her feet. 'I'll go and pack my things, then. Do you want to buy my furniture? I'll have nowhere to put it now.' Her face was working with the effort not to weep and she turned blindly towards the staircase.

Toby quickly barred her way. 'Why should you leave? Because I've Greenhalgh blood in me?'

'That's one reason. Also you're a young man and you'll no doubt have a wife to help you here. The Packhorse doesn't bring in enough to hire other help, you know. If they told you different, they were lying.'

'I'm neither wed nor walking out with anyone.' Though if the lasses in Backenshaw had had their way he would be, only he'd never met one he wanted to spend the rest of his life with. 'Have you been working here for long, Mary?' Toby studied her. She was biting her lip, as if uncertain what to answer, which puzzled him. Surely it was a straightforward enough question? He waited for her to speak, studying her. She was a thin woman with greying hair and a pleasant face – or it would be pleasant if it wasn't creased with anxiety.

'For a while,' she said.

But she didn't explain further so in the end he said his piece. 'Look, I'm a carpenter by trade so I know nowt about running an inn. If you know the work, you can stay on and teach me.' He grinned suddenly. 'Though you'll have to tell me how much I can afford to pay you.'

The man leaned forward. 'Why did Greenhalgh sell you this place?'

'He didn't sell it, he gave it to me.'

'Greenhalgh did?'

'Yes. Surprised me too. But he was dying and I think he wanted to appease his conscience because he never did owt else for me or my mother. And I meant what I said: I reckon nowt to the Greenhalghs, whatever my face looks like, and whatever the old man gave me.' He turned back to the woman. 'Well, love, will you teach me the trade and run my home for me? I'm a hard worker and a quick learner.'

She burst into tears and Ross put an arm round her, patting her shoulders till she managed to stop weeping.

'Eh, look at me, skriking like a babby,' she said in a husky voice. 'An' all because you've offered me a job an' a chance to stay on here. I love Calico and can't bear to think of living elsewhere.' She blew her nose and gave him a teary smile. 'You'll not regret it, Mr Fletcher, I promise you. I'm a good worker.'

'Right, then, that's settled. So if you'll show me round quickly and say where I should sleep, I'll unload the cart and send Rab back with it. Oh, and I'd rather you called me Toby. I'm not used to *Mr* Fletcher.'

Ross threw him a dirty glance and laid a hand on Mary's sleeve. 'Whatever he calls himself, he's still got Greenhalgh blood in him an' I don't trust any of those sods. Maybe you'd be better making a new life for yourself somewhere else, love?'

She looked from one to the other then shook her head. 'I'd rather give it a try here first.'

Ross turned back to Toby, his expression grim. 'Then I'll tell you straight, Fletcher: if you harm one hair of her head, you'll have me to answer to. We look after our own here in Calico.'

'I've never hurt a woman in my life. But you seem to be looking after more than your own at the moment. You put the money I paid for the ale into your pocket an' I reckon that's mine by rights.'

Scowling, the man flung some coins on the table then turned and walked out, pausing in the doorway to say, 'I still think you're wrong, Mary.'

She watched him go, then looked at Toby. 'Don't make an enemy of Ross. They think a lot of him in the village and he's been very kind to me since my man died.'

'I never make an enemy of anyone if I can help it. But he did pocket my beer money.'

She knew Ross had been doing that quite often since Mr Greenhalgh put him in charge, because the takings were right down. Well, Ross had always made the most of every opportunity, he'd had to. And no one thought it wrong to rob a rich man like Greenhalgh.

She sighed as she came downstairs from showing Toby which bedroom to use. Things were allus changing, whether you wanted it or not. Look at the way Calico had changed since she and Hal came here. It'd been full of handloom weavers then, making a good living from weaving calico. But then they'd started weaving cotton in mills, producing better cloth more cheaply, and gradually handloom weaving had brought in less and less till the families in Calico had had to find other ways to earn their bread. Some had gone down the hill to work in the spinning mill at Tappersley – and regretted it because Andrew Beardsworth was a greedy, grasping devil, who treated his operatives badly – while others had simply packed up and left the area.

The families left were the stubborn ones and they were all very close. She knew they regarded her as one of them, and she felt this was her home.

But she liked the looks of the tall young man in spite of his Greenhalgh blood. He was strongly built and had a determined mouth, but he had gentle eyes and a warm smile. But strong or not, he was only one man and if the folk in the village took against him he'd be in trouble, whether he owned the inn or not.

And in that case so would she because she would be relying on him now for her job and to keep a roof over her head. So she'd have to help him if she could.

She would have done so anyway. He was Marjorie's son.

Toby had refused to take the front bedroom, which clearly belonged to Mary and looked as if it had done for a while. He found himself another room at the back which looked up the clough. That'd do him just fine.

She seemed so much at home here it puzzled him. How long had she been here, then? She'd said 'for a while' which could mean anything. And the furniture in the house place was hers. That was what she called the private living area behind the public part of the inn. Eh, he hadn't heard anyone use that term since his mother died. That was what she'd always called their downstairs room, too.

He made no comment about these puzzling matters, but helped Rab unload the cart and put his bed and personal possessions in his own room for the time being, leaving his other stuff out in one of the sheds.

Eh, there were so many rooms and outbuildings here, it felt like a palace to him. A dusty, echoing palace, though. His room was big but had had no furniture in it till he came. Surely an inn should have its rooms furnished for travellers to stay in?

When he went downstairs to the house place, he found Rab there, supping tea not beer now.

'The inn's bigger than I'd expected,' Toby said, smiling at Mary.

'We don't use it all, haven't for years. I'll show you round properly tomorrow,' she said. 'There are other rooms in the middle part and then there's *the back –*' she said it as if it was special or different in some way '– but there aren't many gentry stopping here nowadays, though we do get a few pedlars and packmen, people on foot or in carts. I know everything's in a sad state of repair. My husband wasn't much good at that sort of thing.'

'Well, if there's one thing I know about, love, it's house repairs,' said Toby with a smile, upset to see her so nervous with him still. Though what was the use of bothering about the empty rooms if there was no one wanting to hire them? He was beginning to wonder who exactly Mary was, but he was sure she meant no harm to him. She seemed a very honest soul.

As he went out to wave his friend off, Rab said, 'There's a horse in them stables an' a cart, too. I reckon they're yours now. The cart needs a bit of work, though.'

As Toby watched him pull away he felt a wave of loneliness sweep over him. Eh, pluck up, you fool, he told himself sternly. There was no time to waste on regrets. He needed to learn how to run an inn and look after the beer. It was lucky he had Mary to teach him.

When he went inside again he found her on her own preparing him some food in the house place. She had only an open fire to work with. He reckoned he'd make a start on the inside by putting in a proper closed stove. It had been all right for him to cook on an open fire, but you needed better equipment in an inn.

'Whose horse is that in the stables?'

She looked round and shrugged. 'Yours, I suppose. We bought it out of the inn's takings.'

'I'll pay you for it if you think that fairer.'

'All I really need, Toby, is to have a job and some-where to live.'

'This is your home an' I'll not be turning you out.'

She blinked her eyes rapidly and tried to smile her thanks, but a tear spilled down her cheek, so he didn't ask any more of the questions that were puzzling him but left her to recover. When he peered into the public room, he found it empty of customers. If they were anything like the folk in Backenshaw, they'd have gone off to spread the news of his arrival. There was another public room to one side, but it wasn't in use. He paced it out and checked the window that was rattling and had a loose catch. He'd have to sort that out.

'I've got some food ready for you,' she called.

When he went back to join her she set a plate of fried ham and potatoes down in front of him, looking at him anxiously as if worried by how he'd react to her cooking.

'Where's yours?' he asked when she didn't join

him. He knew, for he'd peered inside it, that the food cupboard was almost bare, but he'd brought enough bread and ham with him to last a few days, and other food, too, so there was no need for her to go without.

She avoided his eyes. 'I'm not hungry. I'll get myself something later.'

'I don't like eating on my own.' He went across to the dresser and took another of the old-fashioned pewter plates from it, scraping half his fried ham on to it and setting the plate down opposite his. Then he pulled out a chair and gestured to it. 'I'm not eating unless you do. The food I've brought is to be shared. Now, get yourself some bread and join me.'

Instead she burst into tears and when she showed no signs of stopping, he gave in to impulse and pulled her towards him, letting her weep against his chest. 'Stop crying, Mary love, and tell me what I've done to upset you?'

Her voice was muffled and she didn't try to look at him as she said, 'You've done nothing wrong, nothing! In fact, you've been kind to me and now you're giving me your food . . . only I've deceived you and I can't bear that.'

He frowned down at her head, seeing how soft the grey hair was as it curled from underneath the little lace-trimmed cap she wore. She was about the same age as his mother would have been if she'd lived and a pang shot through him to think of her being afraid of him. 'Tell me what the trouble is, then.'

The front door of the alehouse banged and a voice called, 'Shall I get my own beer, Mary?'

She pulled away from Toby, wiping her eyes on her apron. 'I'll get it for him. You're not used to drawing beer yet and I don't like them touching my clean taps and jugs with their dirty hands.'

As she moved swiftly through the doorway into the public room, Toby went to watch her, heedless of his meal going cold. She drew beer into the jug from the barrel and filled one of the earthenware pots. Unlike Ross, she didn't spill any. When the man paid she put the money into a little drawer behind the small counter.

She looked from him to the newcomer uncertainly. 'Jim, this is Toby Fletcher, the new owner. Jim's got a farm to the west of the village. His daughter Alice helps out here sometimes.'

The man threw a sour look in Toby's direction and jerked his head slightly in a way which could be taken as a greeting.

'Pleased to meet you,' Toby said, coming forward to stand behind Mary. 'Give him his money back. The first drink for my first customer is free, to cele-brate my taking over the inn.'

The man's face brightened a little and he held his hand out for his coin then raised his pot to Toby and drank deep.

She frowned and shook her head as if not pleased with this.

'Go and get your food while it's warm. I'll join you in a minute or two.' When Mary looked at him uncertainly, Toby pushed her gently towards the house place, then turned back to his customer. He'd been hoping for a chat but the man had gone to sit by the fire with his back to the counter, so Toby leaned against the wall and studied his new domain instead, debating how to start a conversation.

Quite a large room, this, with several tables, some benches and stools, and a few wooden armchairs. It was getting dark outside now and at the moment there was only the firelight to brighten the place. The counter was poorly made but well scrubbed and the pots waiting for use were clean. There was a tray for the dirty pots and a bucket for any slops.

He went to collect the pots the group of men had left behind on the table. 'Nasty sort of day, isn't it?' he offered as the customer looked up.

A grunt was his only answer, so Toby shrugged and went into the house place again.

Mary stood up when he entered. 'I'll go and mind the public room.'

'We'll hear if anyone else comes in. Sit down and tell me what you meant. How have you been deceiving me?'

She swallowed hard then said in a rush, 'My name's not Mary and I'm not Ross's cousin. I'm the wife of the man who used to run this place. Young Mr Greenhalgh told me I was to leave after Hal died, only I didn't. I don't have any family left, you see, so I've nowhere else to go. Mr Greenhalgh gave me some money, but what's money when you're among strangers? I've lived here for over twenty year now and it's my *home* and – and I don't *want* to leave. So Ross said to change my name and pretend I was his cousin and just – well, stay on. He didn't reckon Mr Greenhalgh would be back, so he'd never know I'd not done as he said. Only we never thought about them selling the inn to someone else.'

Toby smiled at her. 'Is that all you've done to deceive me? I don't reckon it's a hanging crime. What's your real name?'

'Phoebe Dixon.'

He studied her, head on one side. 'That suits you much better than Mary. Well, Phoebe, since I'm the owner now, it's up to me who stays or goes. So I'll ask you again: will you stay and work with me, teach me my trade, be my housekeeper and cook?' He waited, then burst out laughing, 'Oh, no, don't start crying again, woman!'

So she both laughed and cried, then wiped away her tears and gave him a wobbly smile. 'You'll never regret helping me,' Phoebe promised fervently.

The next day Toby got her to show him round the rest of the inn. Used to studying buildings, he could see that it had indeed been added to bit by bit – a room here, a room there – and some of the builders had been more skilful than others.

As they approached the rear of the building, however, Phoebe stopped talking and began to look faintly apprehensive. Toby had to bend his head to get into the back part, so low were the doorways, and yet once inside he found a huge room with a high ceiling. He stared round in astonishment at the manner of its building. He'd seen nothing like it before and wondered if this was how they'd built all houses in the distant past. There was one large room, with no ceiling but the underneath of the roof with all its beams showing, festooned by years of cobwebs. Several doors led off it to the rear and there was a door leading outside to the right. 'It seems more like a barn than a house,' he said, thinking aloud.

'The Curate came to look at it when he first arrived. He said it was very old and had probably been built by monks. It was a barn once, only later had someone turned it into a house and built those rooms on.' She waved a hand at the rear doors.

Toby went to examine the uprights, nodding approval. Good wood, well seasoned, and yes, it'd last a long time still, though the plastered walls needed attention and some of the small, old-fashioned bricks were fretting away. The builders had used massive trees as the frame of the building, ones with big branches that curved in the way they needed. They'd cut the trees in half and used each pair to form a rounded V-shape at the short end of the room. Then they'd connected them with cross-beams to give them stability.

The walls had been filled in by a series of oblongs separated by wooden cross-pieces. The bottom oblongs were filled by bricks, the upper ones plastered, so that the walls looked like an untidy patchwork.

Toby felt strangely as though someone was watching him, and turned to Phoebe to ask, 'Can anyone get into this part of the house? It seems very different from the front.'

She shivered. 'None of the villagers would even try to get in.'

'Then maybe there's someone lurking in one of the rooms.'

She looked at him solemnly. 'You feel it too, then?'

'Feel what?'

'Folk in the village say it's haunted an' I wouldn't be surprised if they're not right. It fair gives me the shivers an' I never come here unless I have to. Eh, the times I've had a quick check round to make sure there's no one here as shouldn't be – and there never is.' She shuddered. 'Let's get back to that warm fire.'

'I'll join you in a minute.' He peeped quickly into each of the three rooms at the back. Like the main chamber, they were completely empty. He'd examine this part of the inn properly later and do any necessary repair jobs because it was more important to get the front looking better. If this old part was unsafe, he'd either repair it or demolish it. But it didn't seem unsafe, just – well, there was no word for it but *strange*.

He walked back slowly, unable to believe he owned such a big place, feeling overwhelmed by his good fortune. Why had John Greenhalgh given it to him? It seemed so unlike the man.

That reminded Toby of the shame of having to ask the lawyer to read the deed of gift to him. He wouldn't forget his vow to learn to read and write properly, either. Jethro Greenhalgh wasn't going to get the chance to sneer at him again, and anyhow

Toby reckoned he'd need to be able to read easily
and cast proper accounts with a business to run.
He'd watched Bob write things down all the time and
his old employer had always said you didn't just hope
to make money from a business, you had to know
where each penny went and whether it was working
for you properly. And Bob was a rising man, so who
better for Toby to model himself on?

He would think it a shame not to take advantage of
all the opportunities he'd been given!

Humming happily, he went up to mend the catch
on his bedroom window and oil the squeaking hinges
on Phoebe's bedroom door. Then he went out to the
stables and sheds, amazed at how perfectly usable
stuff had just been left lying around in piles. He spent
a bit of time petting the old mare, who seemed glad
of the company, then he checked the cart, which was
in a sorry state.

He didn't reckon much to Phoebe's husband –
slack, he'd been, letting the inn go to rack and ruin
– but she was a lovely woman, and hardworking too.

Jethro was informed that Toby had left the
Backenshaw mill cottage and taken every stick of
wood from it, even the shelves and coat hooks which
he'd claimed were his.

'Shall I cry theft, Mr Greenhalgh?' the rent
collector asked eagerly. 'We can easily get someone
to swear the things were in the cottage when the
woman moved in, though I think he has the right of
it and the place was bare.'

'No. Why did you turn him out? I didn't tell you to do that.'

'Your father's orders. Said as soon as he was buried, I was to give Fletcher notice.'

Jethro felt anger rise in him, but it wasn't this man's fault that John Greenhalgh was trying to control things even from the grave. He dismissed the rent collector and went to sit by the window in the library.

Jethro didn't like the methods used, but admitted to himself that it was a relief to have Fletcher away from Backenshaw. But as long as the man lived he posed a threat and whether anyone else realised it or not, Jethro was only too aware of that because his father had taken him fully into his confidence when he'd realised he hadn't long to live.

Now it was a question of wait and see. If Fletcher did nothing to draw attention to himself, perhaps things would work out all right.

And at the moment Jethro had more than enough on his hands running the mill he'd inherited from his father because there were quite a few changes he intended to make there. He'd miss the old man's expertise, but he wouldn't miss being told what to do or the penny pinching when money needed to be spent on maintenance.

But as the days passed he found he couldn't get his bastard brother out of his mind and decided in the end that it wouldn't hurt to pay someone in Calico to report on what Fletcher was doing.

Jethro let out a sniff of amusement as he remembered the strange condition Fletcher had agreed to.

The free pot of beer to be provided every January gave him an excuse to go up there himself and check how things were. Was that why his father had made the condition? Surely the old man hadn't expected the two of them to get to know one another or act as brothers? It was the last thing either of them wanted. He'd never know now. All he did know was that his father had been a very devious man.

But Jethro would definitely find someone to spy on Fletcher for him. It never hurt to know what was going on. Jethro was his father's son where that was concerned, if not in other ways.

Ah, to hell with Fletcher! He had more important things on his mind. He needed a wife to run his home and provide him with heirs, and he wanted several children, especially a son to inherit the mill. He'd resisted marrying while his father was alive because he didn't want the old man picking out a wife for him. That was something he'd do for himself. His parents' marriage had been so cold, he had a fancy to marry not for money but from inclination. If he could find someone suitable.

He'd have to keep his eyes open.

By December Meg and Ben had spent several Sunday afternoons together because the weather had been fine if cold nearly every weekend. After their second outing he started waiting for her after work as well, walking her home, asking her how her day had gone, chatting gently.

At home, though, things had gone from bad to

worse. Her mother didn't speak to her any more, gave her the worst of the food and made her life difficult in many little ways.

One day, knowing Ben wouldn't be able to get away on time because they'd had a late delivery of cotton, she waited for him instead, feeling nervous of making this unspoken declaration, wondering what he'd say.

His whole face lit up at the sight of her standing by the gatehouse and he ran across to hug her. 'Eh, lass, I didn't expect to see you tonight!' He looked down at her, his face solemn, and kept his arms round her as he bent his head to give her the gentlest of kisses on the cheek. 'I'm right proud to have everyone see a lass like you waiting for me.'

Meg linked her arm in his, feeling happy, and they walked slowly home.

She had to put up with a lot of teasing about him from the women she worked with but didn't mind that. She did mind the barbed remarks her mother made when Jack wasn't around, though, and the lies Netta told. Only once more did her mother slap her and then Meg did as she'd promised and hit back.

Jack was reproachful when he found out what had happened. 'Nay, love, that was badly done of you. The Bible tells us to honour our mothers and fathers.'

'Them as wrote the Bible hadn't met *our* mother then. I'm not lettin' her thump me any more, Jack, an' that's flat.'

He shook his head then looked at her again. 'You look different lately. Happier.'

She nodded and couldn't hold back a smile. 'I am.'

'Because of Ben Pearson?'

'Yes. He's a lovely fellow an' he's not had a single drink since we started going together.'

'You're still too young to get wed, love.'

'I don't feel young.'

'And we do need your money. That's why Mam's so worried.'

Meg could feel the smile fading and her face stiffening. 'I'm not staying with *her* for the rest of my life, whether I get wed or not. She could have been married to Phil Gitten by now an' taken the burden off you. Did she tell you that? No, I thought not. Or she could get herself a job in the mill. There's some part-time work going, you know. Only she'd rather have *you* working for her, making her life easy. She'll never let you go, Jack.'

He sighed. He'd long suspected that, but if he left the children would be in trouble so he had to stay, whether he agreed with what his mother did or not. 'You won't run away with Ben, will you?'

'He hasn't asked me to wed him yet.'

'He will.' Jack had seen for himself the way the man looked at Meg.

As the winter grew colder, Ben bought Meg a new shawl, soft and warm and of a dusky pink colour that suited her to perfection, with her dark hair and eyes.

'You shouldn't have.' She stroked the wool, loving the feel of it. She'd never had anything brand new before.

'I wanted to. I've seen you shivering.' He hesitated, then said in a rush, 'Will you wed me, Meg? You know how fond of you I am.'

She'd already decided what her answer would be. 'Aye, I will.'

He nearly crushed her ribs, he hugged her so hard. 'Eh, lass, lass! I'm that pleased. I don't have much money, but I'll work hard an' you'll never go hungry as long as there's breath in my body.'

'There's just one thing. Could we leave Northby after we're wed, go and live somewhere else, do you think?'

He looked at her in surprise. 'I thought you'd want to stay near your family.'

She tried to laugh but it turned into a sob. 'What I want is to get as far away from *her* as possible. I could never be happy in the same town even, because she'd be watching me, telling folk I'm no good. She spoils everything, makes it feel dirty. I want us to be happy together, you and me.'

Ben suddenly guessed what lay behind this. 'Has your mother been saying things about me?'

Meg nodded.

'What sort of things?'

'Lies. I know they're lies so I'm not repeating them to you.' She knew he hadn't been drinking again because he wouldn't deceive her. Anyway, she'd overheard his friends teasing him, asking if he didn't get thirsty any more.

He took her hand and raised it to his lips. 'Whatever I was in the past, I'm not now. You've been the making of me, Meg. So if you'll wed me, I'll look for work somewhere else.'

She leaned against him. 'It can't happen too soon for me.'

'Let's go and see your mother about getting wed, then.'

She sighed. 'There's another problem, love. I'm not old enough an' she'll not give me permission. She's been taunting me with that already. We may just have to – you know, go away and live together.'

His face grew tight with suppressed anger. 'I don't want us to live together without being wed. You deserve better nor that.'

'Talk to our Jack, then. He's the only one who can make her do anything. But if she still won't agree, I'm leaving with or without you. I can't stand much more of her.' Her mother had deliberately torn her best skirt last week. Meg knew it was deliberate because she had seen the flare of triumph in Netta's eyes when she taxed her with it – though of course her mother had denied it, said she must have caught it on a nail.

Meg didn't tell Ben about the spiteful tricks her mother constantly played. He had enough to worry about without her adding to it. He said he'd talk to other draymen and drivers, ask them to look out for jobs for him when they delivered or picked up stuff outside Northby.

Toby listened carefully to Phoebe's ongoing explanations about running a pub, and particularly the difficulties of brewing the beer yourself. You had to pay duty on malt, beer, and even on the hops you used. It made his head spin to think of it.

'I used to enjoy brewing,' she said wistfully. 'Me an' Hal allus worked together and if I say so myself, we made decent beer. He liked that side of the job best. But when he fell ill, I just didn't have the time or the strength to do it all myself so we started buying from Gib Travis, the landlord of The Three Tuns over Todmorden way. He sells to quite a few small places now and he's an honest man who brews good beer.'

'Makes sense to continue doing that. I know less than nowt about brewing.'

'You'd better go over and see him then. We need to order some more anyway. Oh, and he'll want paying on delivery, mind. He doesn't give credit and I don't blame him. My Hal let some of his friends put things on the slate and at times we were hard put to find the money for new barrels.'

'Do they still owe us money?'

She nodded.

'Why didn't you tell me before?'

'I thought it'd do more harm than good if you want to be accepted here.'

It only took a minute's thought to realise she was right. 'Well, you know Calico folk better than I do. But no more. If people can't pay, they can't drink.'

After some thought he asked her if there was someone who could take over the inn for a few hours, so that she could go with him to The Three Tuns the first time and introduce him.

'Alice Bent comes in sometimes, when they can spare her on the farm. She's only fifteen, but she's got her head screwed on right.'

'Then get her in.'

Toby drove them over to see Gib Travis in the cart, feeling almost in holiday mood. Although it was cold, the sun was shining and that always cheered you up. He was getting to know the ways of Bonnie, the old mare he'd inherited with the inn. Although she didn't like to hurry, she was a strong and placid animal, which was a relief because he hadn't had much to do with looking after horses before and had had to ask Ross for help and advice.

Gib Travis seemed a pleasant fellow. He was so thin Toby couldn't help wondering if he ever touched his own brew. But he drew himself a pot when he gave one to Toby to test and drained it with every sign of enjoyment.

Phoebe went to chat to Mrs Travis after she'd made the introductions and the two women seemed to find a lot to talk about.

On the way back Phoebe looked at Toby and smiled. 'You did all right there.'

'Thanks to you, telling me what to say and ask for.'

'Eh, it's the least I could do. I owe you a lot, lad.'

He smiled back at her. 'Let's just say we work well together.' He noticed a frown slide across her face briefly. 'What are you worrying about now?'

'What'll happen when you marry.'

'I'm in no hurry to wed and I'll never turn you out of your home, Phoebe. That I swear.'

So of course she was in tears again. Was there ever such a woman for weeping, and as often from joy as from sorrow, he thought as he watched her mop her eyes.

But it was good to have company in his daily life again. He'd never stopped missing his mother.

And best of all, he loved being his own man, whatever his father's reasons for giving him the inn.

PART 2

1828

4

One day in early January Jack came home from work feeling exhausted. His heart sank as he heard from down the street his sister and mother screaming at one another. It embarrassed him to see the neighbours out on their doorsteps, listening and grinning.

He ran the last few yards and burst into the house to find Meg quivering with rage, clutching her precious pink shawl to her bosom. It was dirty at one end and there were muddy threads of pulled wool trailing from it. He knew she wouldn't have worn the shawl to work because it was such a treasure to her that she kept it for best, hanging out of harm's way on a nail he'd hammered in for her 'specially in the girls' bedroom.

He had to shout to make himself heard. 'What's happened?'

Meg held the shawl out for his inspection. 'She wore my shawl. Look at it! It's all mucky an' there are pulled threads.' Tears rolled down her cheeks as she held the soft wool against her cheek.

He looked at his mother and for a moment saw shame flicker on her face – or hoped he did, because it was dreadful of her to have damaged Meg's most precious possession.

Then Netta tossed her head, staring at him defiantly. 'I only borrowed it to go down to the shops. It's not my fault if I fell, is it?'

'You damaged it on purpose,' Meg shouted, 'I know you did. I hate you, you wicked old hag!'

Netta went puce with fury, picked up the nearest object, which was a wooden bowl, and hurled it at her daughter, catching her on the temple.

The sobs cut off abruptly and Meg tumbled to the ground like a rag doll, lying still and frighteningly silent.

Jack rushed across the room to kneel and cradle his sister in his arms. *'What have you done, Mam?'*

'She should have lent that shawl to me when I asked. I'm her mother and . . . *Jack!'*

But he wasn't listening. He was holding his sister close, watching the blood run down her temple and praying she wasn't badly hurt.

To his relief, her eyes fluttered open but she looked up at him as if she didn't know where she was, her expression that of a child puzzled by the unkind world around her. He remembered suddenly what a bonny, mischievous little girl she had been. She wasn't bonny now, she was gaunt, and her eyes had a bruised look to them, as if the world was dealing harshly with her. Well, it was. It had dealt harshly with all of them since his father's death. But their mother didn't make it any easier.

As she realised where she was, Meg's vague

expression vanished to be replaced by one of deep sadness. 'I can't stand any more of this. I'm going to ask Ben to take me away. Even if she won't give permission for us to wed, anything will be better than living with *her*.' She put up her hand to her forehead. 'It hurts, Jack. Everything hurts.'

Determination to help her rose in him. She, at least, should escape the unpleasantness their mother seemed to generate. He helped Meg sit up, then went and poured some clean water from the bucket into a bowl, dampening a rag in it and wiping away the blood. After the wound was clean, he picked his sister up, ignoring his mother's wailing and shaking her off as she tried to hold him back at the foot of the stairs.

'What about me, Jack? What about me?'

'You're not the one who's hurt.' As she tried to push in front of him, he nudged her out of the way with his elbow and carried his sister up to her bedroom, setting Meg down gently on the bed next to Ginny. He took her hand and patted it as he said quietly, 'There's no need to run away, love. I'll make sure she gives permission for you to marry Ben.'

'She won't do it. She's told me that, taunted me about it.' Meg lay back and let the tears run down her cheeks, making no attempt to wipe them away.

'She *will* give permission because if she doesn't, I'm leaving too.'

'She'll know you don't mean that.'

'But I do.' His voice was quietly emphatic. 'You're not the only one who's sick of all the upsets she causes. Why can't she be happy like other women?

We've enough to eat, haven't we? A roof over our heads? What makes her so miserable?'

Outside the bedroom door Netta pressed one hand to her mouth and crept back downstairs.

Jack bent to kiss Meg's cheek. 'Leave it to me, love.'

When he'd gone, Ginny tugged Meg's arm. 'Our Jack won't really leave us, will he?'

Meg leaned closer to whisper, 'No. But don't tell Mam that or he'll never get her to do anything.'

When Jack went downstairs he found his mother sitting by the fire, shoulders hunched, staring into it. She didn't look up as she said, 'Meg was only knocked out for a minute. I don't know what you're making such a fuss about. It was just an accident.'

He sat down opposite her and said severely, 'It wasn't an accident and you well know it. You *meant* to hurt her and you're making her life miserable, so I need to make a fuss about it. I'm the man of the house and it's up to me to see that things are done properly in our family. I've decided it'll be best for Meg to leave and make a new life for herself. The two of you are never going to get on. If you don't give her permission to wed Ben Pearson, she'll run away. And if that happens, I'll leave too.' He met her eyes steadily as he added, 'I mean that. We can't go on like this.'

Netta chewed on the knuckles of one hand, looking sideways at him and trying to gauge whether he really meant it. 'We can't manage without her money.'

'We can and will. You save money each week, I know you do, even if it's only a penny or two. If we can't save for a while, it won't matter.'

'An' if I let her marry that tosspot, you'll stay with me, our Jack? Promise.'

He nodded. He knew he had no choice but to stay, no choice but to deny his own wish to go out walking with a certain pretty lass. His mother's strident tones made him wince and her next words only made it more vital that he should help Meg get away from her.

'That sister of yours is no good, you know. She'll come to a bad end, you mark my words.'

'Meg's just a lass like any other, Mam. All she wants is to marry the fellow she loves. What's so wrong with that?'

Netta began to sob noisily but he didn't try to calm her down as usual, couldn't bear to touch her if truth be told. Instead he took down the book Parson had lent him, lit an extra candle with a splinter of wood and set it down beside him. He started to read, though the words were meaningless. He heard his mother's sobs falter to a halt and forced himself to finish the page before glancing up. She was scowling across at him, so he turned to the next page and bent his head over it, listening, waiting.

For a moment there was silence then she yelled suddenly, 'Oh, very well! Let her get wed. She'll soon find out marriage isn't a bed of roses. And we'll be better off without her. She's setting them childer a bad example, egging them on to be cheeky to me.'

Jack stood up, setting the book down carefully on the mantelpiece because it was unthinkable to damage such a precious object, and blew out his reading candle. 'We'll go and see Parson about it this very evening.'

'I can't go tonight. I . . .' Her voice trailed away at the anger on his face.

'No more excuses, Mam. Get your shawl.'

'It's old an' matted an' I'm 'shamed to be seen out in it. No one gives *me* pretty new shawls.'

'Are you coming or not?' When she didn't speak, he reached for his book again.

'Oh, all right!'

When they got back, the wedding was booked and he'd paid for a special licence to hold the ceremony on the following Saturday afternoon because he was afraid his mother would change her mind if things were left longer. He went up to tell Meg but found her asleep, her long dark lashes still wet with tears.

Ginny stared at him from the bed. 'She were crying,' she whispered. 'Our Meg doesn't usually cry. An' look at her forehead. It's all bruised.'

He leaned forward to ruffle his little sister's hair and, when her arms came up for a hug, he drew her to him and kissed her cheek before whispering back, 'Meg won't be crying when she hears my news in the morning. Now, get yourself to sleep, young lady.'

As he went down he told himself he was doing the right thing, that without him Ginny and Shad and Joe wouldn't have a proper home. But that didn't stop his desperate longing for a life of his own, a woman of his own to love – and a little peace in the evening after a hard day's work.

Netta refused to go to the wedding but Jack took the children along to watch his sister make her vows to Ben Pearson. To his mother's fury he had dipped even further into their small pot of savings to buy Meg a new outfit from Roper's pawn shop: a skirt in a rich maroon colour and a bodice of a soft pink.

She washed and mended them carefully after work, drying them in front of the fire. He'd seen his mother eyeing them with a sour expression and had warned her not to lay a finger on them.

The ceremony was brief but the happiness in both bride and groom's faces warmed Jack's heart. He kissed Meg, wished her happy and shook Ben's hand, then went to his reading classes while the children ran off to play. They all spent as much of their free time out of the house as they could.

Arm in arm, the newly weds walked back to pick up Meg's clothes. They found them scattered on the doorstep, trailing in the muck of the street. Ben looked at his wife in shock, seeing the happiness fade and tears well in her eyes.

Her voice was tight with pain. 'I'd folded them up neatly. Now I shall have to wash them again.'

He helped her pick up the pieces of clothing, surprised by how little she owned. He didn't know how to comfort her. 'Eh, she's a nasty old bitch, your mam.'

'Why do you think I'm so glad to be leaving?'

He looked at her anxiously, blurting out the question that had occurred to him more than once.

'You've not wed me just to get away from her?'

'Of course not.' But she did sometimes wonder if she'd have married him otherwise – or at least, so quickly. He was a kind fellow but he didn't make her pulse beat faster. She'd heard the other lasses talking and they seemed much more taken with their young men than she was with Ben. Oh, she was being silly! Asking for the moon. He was a good man who worked hard and she was lucky he wanted her.

Together they carried her bundle back to the lodgings they'd rented from a fellow Ben knew. They had the front room downstairs of a two-up, two-down house near the lower end of Weavers Lane and that'd have to do until they could afford something better or he found a job elsewhere. Meg was still determined to leave Northby and, until they managed that, she'd carry on working so that they could save some money and buy a few things for the house. All they owned now was a bed, two rickety old chairs, a table and a few dishes.

When they went to bed that night Meg felt so nervous she didn't know what to do with herself until Ben gathered her in his arms and laughed softly in her ear.

'What do you think's going to happen, lass? I'm going to love you, not beat you senseless.' He trailed one finger down her cheek. 'I'll be gentle, I promise. You might even like it.'

He was gentle but she didn't really enjoy the love-making. At least it was over quite quickly and didn't hurt as her mother had told her it would. Ben enjoyed it, though, so from then on Meg pretended to like it, which seemed to make him happy.

What *she* enjoyed most was the way he held her in his arms afterwards and talked about his dreams for their future. He filled her so full of hope. Surely life couldn't help but get better now that she was married and away from *her*?

Toby looked round the tap room, trying not to let his feelings show on his face. So far the folk here in Calico weren't giving him a chance to settle into the community and make friends. They were polite enough, but conversations stopped whenever he went near a group and no one ever made a real attempt to chat to him, even when he was alone in the bar with a customer. At Christmas they'd been cool with him, though many of them had grabbed Phoebe and planted kisses on her cheeks in honour of the season.

She said it was early days yet and you had to give folk time to get used to you, but he wondered if she knew more than she was telling him.

So he thought, to hell with it, and went for a stroll round the unused and dilapidated part of the house. The rooms in the middle area were as dusty and depressing as ever. Some contained a few pieces of furniture, though they were heavy and old-fashioned, covered in thick dust. If there'd been any demand for bedrooms, he'd have got some of them cleaned out and ready. But there wasn't.

The better class of traveller, whether in their own carriage or on horseback, mostly went straight past the inn. It was a good thing in one way because the stables were run down and there was no spare fodder for customers' animals. When he asked Phoebe what she and Hal had done if someone had a horse, she frowned for a minute then said, 'Sent for some fodder off Ross or Jim. Eh, it's a long time since that happened.'

'Well, I think we'll buy a bit extra in, just in case.' Toby was finding he had a shilling or two to spare each week and was saving his money carefully, making do with the wood that was lying round when he wanted to do repairs, making every nail count.

The less affluent travellers sometimes called in for a drink and often wanted food. Phoebe always managed to find them something, telling Toby many a time how much easier her life was with the new stove to cook on and provide her with hot water by simply turning on the boiler tap. To her it was the most marvellous thing he'd done, putting in that stove.

During the warmer weather he'd do something about the outside of the house, he decided, but in the meantime he'd continue checking the place over. It stood to reason that he needed to keep it weather-proof. He found a room in the middle part where rain was getting in through a warped window frame and another where there were water stains on the ceiling. When he went outside he could see slates hanging awry on a small sideways sloping piece of roof. He climbed up and fixed them. Such a small job. Why the hell hadn't Hal Dixon done things like that? What had been wrong with the man?

'I'm going to work on the back part of the house today,' he said to Phoebe one morning, once the front and middle were fully weatherproof. Alarm flickered in her eyes, he could have sworn it, but she didn't say anything.

As she watched him gather his tools, she wrapped her arms round herself and continued to look worried.

'You don't like me working on the back part, do you?' he ventured, hoping to draw her out about it.

'No, I don't. I've told you, it fair gives me the shivers.'

He waited but she didn't elaborate and he decided not to push her for an explanation. She was a lovely woman, like an aunt to him now, but everyone had their secrets and he didn't feel he had a right to pry into hers.

Jethro was sitting in his carriage, being driven home after visiting a machinery manufacturer, when the carriage slowed down to negotiate a bend and he saw her. He stared out of the window as the horses clopped past the formal gardens of a large house which he knew belonged to the Goddbys, an old-established county family who, if rumours were true, had fallen on hard times. She was standing by the gate, laughing at something another young woman was saying. Her brown hair was gilded by the sun, her face so plump and pretty he could feel something inside him yearn to touch her. But mostly it was the warmth of her smile that attracted him.

Afterwards he sat lost in thought. He couldn't have said what the other woman looked like, but he remembered every detail about *her* – couldn't get the lovely image of that laughing woman out of his mind.

As the carriage pulled up in front of his house he started, like someone jerking out of a dream, then opened the door and jumped out without waiting for the groom to do it. The front door was opened before he got there but he didn't look at the maid who'd performed this service, just went into the library, shut the door on his staff and began to pace up and down thinking . . . remembering her . . . *wanting her*.

After a while he stared round like someone waking from a deep sleep, scowling at what he saw. The place seemed so empty and quiet without his father. No voice booming out commands or yelling at the servants, no one to eat dinner with or talk to. It was time, more than time, for him to marry.

What had been holding him back was the problem of how he was to meet suitable young women. He felt himself to be neither fish nor fowl in Backenshaw. It had been the same for him at school, where the other boys came from much grander families, and the lesson had only been reinforced once he returned home to work in the family business because he couldn't make friends with the operatives in the mill, even those he'd played with as a lad.

His father had never cared about socialising with

his neighbours when he could be working and earning more money – which had made Jethro's mother's life very lonely. No wonder she had died so young. Jethro only remembered her as a pale, apologetic woman who never spoke above a murmur. His father had even resented having to give the operatives at the mill Sundays off and hadn't attended church regularly, thinking it a waste of time and the Parson a fool who had no right to tell *him* how to live his life.

The Greenhalghs weren't gentry as the other county families saw it, so the only recognition Jethro ever got from those few families who lived nearby was a cool nod in passing, even the ones whose sons had been at school with him. There was no one of his own kind and age in Backenshaw with whom to make friends, even had his father encouraged the making of friends.

The young woman came into his mind again. Who was she? One of the Goddby family or a visitor? Suddenly it was vitally important to find out so he walked across the mill yard to see Barney Spencer, the overlooker. Barney was very good at finding things out, or dealing with delicate problems, and no one was more loyal to the Greenhalghs, for the man owed his rise in the world to old John.

Two days later Jethro had the information he required. The young woman was indeed Sophia Goddby, the younger of two sisters. Her brother Peregrine had inherited the estate a year or so ago, but was a dreamer who seemed to have little idea of how to manage his inheritance, for he was more often to be found on the moors collecting rare plants or just walking about, no one could understand why, even in the depths of winter when there were no flowers to be found.

Jethro and Barney laughed together at the stupidity of this. Still, it might be a way of meeting the fellow: 'Find out where he goes and when. I'll try to bump into him by accident. And see if you can find out more about his sister, the younger one.'

Barney cocked one eyebrow at him. 'Interested in her, are you?'

'Might be.'

'It's common talk down the valley that she's courting young Easdale. Folk are predicting a marriage.'

'Are they indeed?' Oswin Easdale had been one of Jethro's chief tormenters at school. To take Sophia away from *him* would add spice to this chase.

The following week one of his gardeners guided him up on to the moors behind his house. 'Mr Goddby usually comes this way, sir.'

Jethro pushed a coin at him. 'Good. Get yourself off home, then.' He found himself a rock to sit on, one sheltered from the wind but which gave him a good view of the path that had been pointed out to him.

To his surprise he found the peace of this place more attractive than he'd expected. Sitting quietly in the fresh air was something he hadn't done much of. A pale winter sun lit up the landscape, while clouds cast moving patterns of shadows across the gentler slopes of the tops. In the valley below, where Backenshaw sprawled, smoke rose steadily from his own mill chimney. In fact he had never really seen his mill from here and felt proud of the way it dominated the village, with the rows of workers' dwellings lined up neatly around it.

Suddenly he saw a figure coming towards him, pausing to take a flask out of his pocket and raise it to his lips, only to find it empty and stuff it back with a curse. The man started walking again, not noticing Jethro, his footsteps weaving a little.

It was Goddby and he was drunk, by God! Jethro grinned. Well, well. This might turn out to be a very useful encounter. People often said more than they intended when they were in their cups. As the other man would have passed without a word, he called, 'Good day to you, sir! It's a fine day, isn't it?'

Goddby stopped, stared at him owlishly, then shrugged.

'I'd welcome a little company.' Jethro gestured to the rock he was sitting on and pulled out the flask of brandy he'd brought in case he felt the cold. 'May I offer you a nip of brandy? Nothing like it to warm you up on a cold winter's day.' He watched the other man's face brighten and Goddby held out his hand for the flask, immediately taking a big swig.

'I don't believe we've met before, but I recognise you by sight. Goddby, isn't it?'

'Aye.' He wiped his lips and let out a sigh of satisfaction. 'But my friends call me Perry.'

'I wouldn't presume – we are, after all, from rather different circles.'

'Who am I to set myself above anyone? You're Greenhalgh the millowner, I know, but I don't know your first name.'

'Jethro.' He held out his hand and they shook solemnly. 'What are you doing out here on the moors, if I may ask?'

Peregrine Goddby sighed. 'Wondering whether to put a pistol to my head and end it all.'

'My dear fellow, that's a bit drastic, isn't it? Are things really that bad for you?' Jethro waved one hand towards the flask in a permissive gesture.

'Worse than bad. Thanks.' Goddby took another pull of brandy then scowled into the distance. 'It's all right for you millowners, you're used to dealing with business matters and know how to make money, but I wasn't raised to it and I can't do anything right. I'm even worse than my father at managing, and God knows, he lost big chunks of the estate.' Pain shadowed his face as he added softly, 'Places I used to play in as a lad, streams where I used to fish for tadpoles – all gone.'

Jethro waved away the return of the flask and watched as his companion downed another mouthful. 'Is there anything I can do to help? I hate to see a fellow gentleman in trouble.'

'Hah! Not unless you'd care to give me ten thousand pounds and . . .' He bit back further confidences. 'Sorry. Shouldn't trouble you with my problems.'

'Why not? I have problems of my own. It's good sometimes to share things with a friend.'

'Not business problems, I'll wager.'

'Hardly. As you say, I was bred to it, for all they sent me away to school for a few years. No, I've just lost my father and am finding the house a bit –' Jethro hesitated delicately '– lonely. I came up here to think about taking a wife. Only trouble is, I don't know any suitable young women.' He sighed and gazed out across the landscape, hoping his companion wasn't too drunk to take the hint. 'The matter is quite urgent. I need someone to run my home, be there in the evening.'

'Well, I've got two highly suitable young women at home,' Perry said, his words slurred and his eyes hard with anger. 'My sisters. Trouble is, I can't give them dowries and m'mother's not stopped complaining about that since she found out. And although chaps are interested enough in them, they're all demanding dowries. Hell, I don't even know how I'm to pay the tradesmen's bills next quarter, let alone provide for my sisters.' He looked sideways, squinting in his efforts to study Jethro's expression. 'Would *you* require a dowry?'

'Not if I really liked the woman in question. I have more than enough money for both of us.'

'Sophia's already courting but Harriet is still available.' Goodby hesitated and a calculating look came over his face.

Jethro hid his amusement at the other man's transparency and waited for the offer.

'Why don't you come and meet her? Come to dinner tomorrow?'

'Are you sure?'

'Of course I am.' He tried to stand up and failed. 'Had a bit too much to drink,' he confided in his slurred, upper-class drawl. 'Would you give me a hand, old fellow?'

So Jethro took him home, fussed over him and sent him back to Goddby Manor in his carriage.

But Perry wasn't too drunk to remember his invitation or to say as he was helped into the carriage, 'Don't forget! Tomorrow for dinner. And you'd better stay the night. It gets dark devilish early at this time of year and there's no moon.'

Jethro smiled as he ate his solitary meal that night. It couldn't have been easier. Now all he had to do was woo the young woman – woo or coerce, whichever was necessary. Not Harriet, though. Definitely not the older sister.

'Sophia.' He said the name quietly and with great satisfaction. He even liked the sound of her name.

5

As the days passed Toby began to understand the workings of the inn and to admire Phoebe's skill at managing the beer, the customers, and even cooking for the odd traveller wanting food. It'd be a while, though, until he could improve the place enough to attract the custom of passing gentry.

He'd tramped the five acres that went with the inn and found only rough fields, suited perhaps to sheep, but he knew even less about sheep farming than running an inn. Still, it gave him a warm feeling to walk across the land and think: *This is mine!* However, when Ross Bellvers asked if he could pasture some sheep on that land, Toby settled down to a haggling session and came away with the satisfaction of earning money without doing a hand's turn for it.

One day a pedlar arrived at the inn, cold and angry, leading his donkey and asking if he could put the poor creature in the stables because an axle had broken on his cart about half a mile back. 'If you have a handcart you could lend me, I'll go back and get my goods off the cart and store them here too,' the man went on glumly. 'I'll be lucky if no one steals them meanwhile. The cart's just sitting there by the road, all of an angle. And I'll have a quick pot of ale while you're at it.' He drained it rapidly, his mind still on his problems.

'How big is your axle?' Toby asked. 'It's just that there are a few oddments of wood here and we might be able to cobble together a makeshift axle and bring the cart back here. Then you could get it repaired properly or buy a new one. I was a carpenter before I inherited the inn and I've not forgotten my trade.' He offered his hand. 'Toby Fletcher.'

'Bram Craven.' The pedlar looked more hopeful already. 'I'd be grateful for your help.'

'Let's give that poor creature of yours something to eat and drink first. It looks exhausted.'

When the donkey had been made comfortable, Toby put the tools he thought he'd need into a canvas bag and fetched the small wheeled barrow he'd cobbled together for taking his wood and tools round the house, placing a few longer pieces of wood into it. The barrow was sturdy enough to use outside, he was sure. 'You lead the donkey and I'll push this.'

Wind was whistling around them as they walked back along the road, sucking away their body warmth relentlessly. The sky was heavy with clouds which seemed to get darker and hang lower by the minute.

'It's going to snow soon, I reckon,' Bram said gloomily as they reached the lopsided cart. 'Then I'll be stuck here good and proper.' He checked his goods and heaved a sigh of relief. 'Well, at least no one's come by and stolen my stuff.'

Toby looked at the broken axle. 'I think I can fix it

well enough to get us back to the inn.' Whistling cheerfully he began work and soon had the cart repaired enough to be driven slowly back.

By the time they got back, the makeshift axle was squeaking and groaning, and the cart was looking shaky again. The first flakes of snow drifted lightly down on them as they trundled the cart into the stable yard.

Bram scowled up at the sky. 'Look at that! I'm going to be stuck here for a day or two now, I reckon.'

'I keep some hay and feed so your donkey will be all right and we can push the cart into this space, so it'll be out of the weather and safe enough.'

'How much am I going to owe you for the help and for staying the night?' Bram asked, stuffing his hands into his pockets and shivering. 'I've just stocked up on goods, you see, and I'm a bit short of money. If you could take some of the payment in goods, I'd be grateful.'

'Got any nails?'

'Aye.'

'Well, I'm needing a few bits and pieces like that, so we'll discuss it later. You see to that animal of yours now.'

He'd hardly finished explaining to Phoebe what had happened and asking her about a room for Bram than a carriage drew up outside. From it descended a plump, middle-aged man with a sour expression on his face. His bad mood was explained when his wife was helped from the carriage and proved to be so ill she couldn't stand without help.

'I'd hoped to get her home,' the man grumbled to Toby, 'but she's been weeping and saying her head hurts and she can't take the jolting a minute longer. Do you have two bedrooms, landlord – for I'll get no sleep if I'm in with *her* – and a place for my coachman and horses?'

'We can find something, I'm sure. I've only just taken over here, so things aren't in proper order yet, but we've plenty of rooms.' Phoebe was already helping the lady inside and Toby asked her if she could find the necessary accommodation. By that time the snow was whirling down thickly outside.

'My name's Madson, Hugh Madson, merchant of Halifax.'

'Toby Fletcher.' He settled his unexpected customer in front of the fire with a pot of mulled ale, which seemed to cheer him up a little, then went up to see how he could help Phoebe, who was looking harassed.

'If they're to stay, I'll need some extra help, Toby love. Alice Bent will come in, I expect. Winter isn't a busy time of year on a farm.'

'All right. Go and get her.'

'Can you do it for me? I don't like to leave this poor woman on her own. She's not at all well and her maid isn't with her.'

'All right. The farm with the white gate, isn't it?' He checked that the Madsons' coachman had everything he needed in the stables and strode off through the snow, smiling to himself at this sudden turn of fate. Bad weather could obviously be good for trade in an isolated place like this.

Toby knocked at the farm door and Jim opened it wearing his usual surly expression. After Toby had explained that they had a couple of days' work for young Alice, however, her father's face brightened and for the first time he gave Toby a genuine smile. 'She'll be there in a few minutes.' He hesitated, then added, 'Thanks.'

Toby strode back, rather enjoying this emergency in spite of the cold and the snow.

It was two days before any of his unexpected guests could leave. Madson was in a foul temper much of that time, but Bram helped out in the inn and was cheerfully resigned to staying put.

When they heard he was there, several of the women from the village came to buy bits and pieces, which further cheered up the pedlar. 'I'll stop whenever I'm passing now,' he said as he got ready to leave. 'You can tell folk to watch out for me, Toby lad.'

Mr Madson said little as he paid his bill, but his wife was very grateful for Phoebe's care of her and slipped her a half-crown in gratitude.

'We'll get a couple of bedrooms sorted out properly,' Toby told Phoebe. 'I don't want to be taken by surprise again. Alice lass, how about you coming for another day to help with the extra cleaning?'

She beamed at him. 'Dad will be ever so pleased.'

He hadn't realised until now how carefully the

local folk had to scrimp to make ends meet, because the men always seemed to find the pence for a pot of beer, even if some of them had to make it last longer than the pots of their more fortunate neighbours.

The day after their meeting on the moors Jethro had himself driven five miles down the road in the last of the daylight to visit his new friend Perry. He didn't notice the cold as he sat in the carriage with hot bricks at his feet and wearing a heavy overcoat with caped shoulders. Beneath it he was wearing a black cloth coat with a velvet collar and dark grey trousers strapped under his shoes, the colours sombre because he preferred dark colours rather than in deference to his recent bereavement. He couldn't see that it made any difference to the dead what you wore. His shirt collars were modest because he couldn't abide high ones that stuck into your neck and chin. Anyway, he wasn't a fashionable fribble but a millowner and man of business. If Goddby's family weren't prepared to take him as he was, then to hell with them. A smile curved his lips briefly. They needed him more than he needed them.

He was greeted at the door by Perry, who was, Jethro noted cynically, very effusive in his welcome. After his overcoat had been taken away by an elderly manservant he was ushered into the drawing room to be introduced to Goddby's womenfolk. The room was overheated for his taste and so full of ornaments and knick-knacks that Jethro moved across it very carefully. Before he could bow over his hostess's hand he had the opportunity for a better look at the two sisters. Seen up close in the full light of the lavish display of candles they were elegant creatures, clad in frills and silks, sitting modestly on the sofa. But the plumper woman was still the one who caught his eye. There was more character in her face and, he was sure, more fire within that chaste bosom. And a very nice bosom it was too.

He turned his attention back to the old dame, who greeted him with as much enthusiasm as her son had, bobbing her head so much it set the lace and dangling ribbons on her enormous cap fluttering. She had sleeves so wide it made him blink in surprise for a minute and her blue silk gown gave no hint of the family's lack of money. Good silk, it was, he could tell that at a glance.

'Mr Greenhalgh, I'm *so* pleased to meet you at last. We've heard a great deal about you from dear Perry.'

Jethro took her hand and bowed slightly over it, knowing full well Perry knew little about him other than his name and that he was a rich millowner. The old lady's looks had faded but she had clearly been a beauty once. It must be from her that her daughters got their looks because Perry was a plump fellow whose hair was already going thin on top and whose teeth stuck out and gave him a strong resemblance to a hare. Old Goddby had looked much the same, from what Jethro remembered, though he'd never spoken to the father, only passed him in the street.

'Do let me introduce my daughters, Harriet and Sophia.'

As the two young women stood up and dropped slight curtsies, Jethro made no bones about studying them again. His glance lingered on Sophia so long that a brief frown replaced the calm expression on her face and Harriet glanced quickly from one to the other of them, as if annoyed.

Well, he didn't care what the older one thought. The younger sister was definitely the one for him. Oh, the other was bonny enough but lacked spirit, or so it seemed to him. He wanted to be the man who fanned that spark in Sophia's eyes into a flame, who took that lush body into his bed and taught it to know a man's needs.

And he was going to, whatever it cost him to buy her.

He couldn't have said afterwards how the evening went, because all he remembered was Sophia, sitting opposite him as they ate, shooting him uncomfortable glances as he continued to focus all his attention on her. She said little, ate only lightly and retired to bed early, together with her sister who was making no attempt to hide her annoyance at his lack of interest in her.

He feigned tiredness when they'd gone and let Perry show him to his bedroom where a fire was burning brightly and all was arranged for his comfort. He stood looking down into the flames for a while, thinking about *her*, then got ready for bed, sleeping soundly as always.

The following morning Sophia wasn't present at breakfast. Jethro didn't comment on that, spoke to the older sister when he had to and took his leave of his hostess soon afterwards.

When Perry saw him to the door, Jethro invited his host to come and dine with him the following week. 'I have something to discuss with you. I think you'll find it worth your while.'

As Sophia went up to her bedroom after the interminable evening ended she let the anger out. Dreadful man! Who did he think he was to stare at her like that? When her father was alive, they'd never have invited someone like him to dine, never!

Harriet came through the connecting door and they unpinned each other's hair. 'What did you think of him, then?'

'I disliked him.'

'He didn't seem too bad to me. He's quite good-looking, really.'

'Well, you can have him then.'

'I would, but it's you he's interested in.'

There was a pregnant silence then Sophia shook her head. 'Well, he can't have me. You know I love Oswin.'

'But old Mr Easdale has already said his son can't marry a woman without a dowry.'

'Oswin loves me, though, he told me so. It's his father who won't allow the marriage and who holds the purse strings – what he doesn't gamble away.' Sophia's voice was bitter. 'Why have we all been cursed with fathers who've done nothing but lose the family money?'

'Mr Greenhalgh has plenty of money, Perry says.'

'I don't care. I'm *not* interested in him.'

On the second Sunday after her marriage Meg opened the front door and found her mother standing there.

'Well, aren't you going to invite me in?' Netta demanded.

Meg wanted to say no but didn't dare, afraid her mother would make a scene in front of the new neighbours. Oh, she didn't even want her in their room! If only Ben had been here, he'd have protected her.

Netta stopped in the doorway and fired her first shot. 'Is this all the furniture you've got? He's not a very good provider, is he? My Jem took me to a proper house when he wed me.'

'This is just for the time being. Would you like to sit down?' When her mother was seated, she asked nervously, 'Can I get you a cup of tea?'

'Yes. And a piece of cake if you have one.'

'We haven't. It's just the tea.'

'Poor fare for guests.'

Meg bit her tongue. They'd never had cake at home, so she knew her mother was deliberately goading her. She went to put another piece of coal on the small fire and swing the kettle over it, feeling reluctant to turn round again. But her mother had to be faced so she busied herself setting out their two cups and the chipped teapot she'd bought from the pawn shop.

'And how are you enjoying married life?'

'Very much. Ben's a good husband.'

Netta pulled a face as if she didn't believe this. 'We'd expected you to come round to see us.'

'We've been busy and I'm at work all week.' Meg had no intention of going back to the house that carried only unhappy memories for her since her father's death. She wished now that she'd told her mother to go away, was sure Netta was only there to poke her nose into their business then gossip about it in such a way as to blacken their names.

When she served the tea her mother sipped disdainfully. 'Cheapest sort. Can't you afford better than this?'

'No, we can't.'

Ben came back just then from seeing to the horses, stopping dead in the doorway when he saw who was there.

'My mother came to see us,' Meg said, hoping she didn't look as unhappy as she felt.

He stared from one woman to the other then back at his wife, his expression turning grim as if he could tell how she was feeling.

'There's some tea in the pot,' Meg said as the silence continued. 'You can use my cup.'

'Poor sort of home where there's not even a spare cup,' Netta said at once, smirking. 'But then, our Meg never was much good in the house. She'll not know how to make the best of the money you provide. You'd better keep an eye on her.'

Meg watched Ben's mouth drop open in shock.

She was used to her mother's nasty comments, if you could ever be said to get used to unkindness, but she had never seen him look as angry.

'You'll regret the day you married her,' Netta went on. 'Let alone she's too young, she's lazy.'

He stood up and walked across to take the cup from his mother-in-law's hand, setting it down so carelessly on the table that it overturned and the remaining tea spilled out. 'If that's the way you talk to my wife – *your daughter!* – in her own home, then you're not welcome here, Mrs Staley.' While she was still gaping at him, he pulled her to her feet, put a hand on the small of her back and propelled her towards the door.

As he pushed her out into the street, Netta shrieked with fury and began to weep loudly, which brought the neighbours running. Sobbing as if her heart was broken, she pointed her finger at him and cried, 'See how he's treating me! Throwing me out of my daughter's house. What sort of a son-in-law is that?' She turned a malevolent gaze on Meg and continued, still at the top of her voice, 'And *she* lets him. Yes, she does! It's a sad day when a mother's treated like that.'

Ben's friend, who had rented them the room, came to stand behind him at the front door and mutter, 'By hell, you've getten yoursen an old tartar of a mother-in-law there. I don't envy you, lad.'

Ben raised his voice. 'She'll not be coming here again if she knows what's good for her.'

A woman moved forward from the crowd, giving

Ben and Meg a dirty look as she put an arm round Netta's shaking shoulders and led her away. He turned round to find his wife in tears.

'She did that on purpose. She hates me! Take me away from Northby . . . please take me away.' And then Meg was weeping against him.

That evening Jack came round. Ben answered the door and gave him a stern look. 'If you've come to upset my Meg, you can just go away again.'

'I'd never do that. I've come to see how she is and find out what really happened.'

Ben gestured him inside and he saw Meg, sitting red-eyed near the fire, huddled defensively into herself.

'I'm sorry she upset you, love,' Jack said at once, going across to give her a quick hug.

'I should have known better than to let her in, but I thought she'd make a scene if I didn't. Only she made a scene anyway.' Meg sniffed and wiped away a tear with the back of one hand. 'I shouldn't let her get at me like this, should I? I ought to be used to it by now.'

'You shouldn't have to get used to it,' Ben snapped. 'No one should.'

'Tell me what happened,' Jack said.

She explained and he looked from her to Ben in consternation. 'I'm sorry, more sorry than you can know. Mam seems to hate anyone else being happy, as Meg clearly is with you.'

Ben put his arm round his wife. 'Well, I'm looking for a job somewhere else. Anything will do. In the meantime, I'm not having my lass upset like this again, so you'd better tell your mother to keep away.'

Jethro went about his business as usual, showing nothing of the seething emotions that filled him. He had learned as quite a young boy to hide his feelings from the world, and especially from his father who always seemed to exploit any weakness.

But whatever he was doing, Jethro kept seeing Sophia's face: in the morning when he woke, in his dreams, even when he was walking round his mill – something he did every day, though he left most of the supervision of the operatives to Barney Spencer under the new and more lenient rules he'd instituted. Barney said the operatives were producing as much cotton as before, so it just went to show that being too severe with them did no one any good, in Jethro's opinion.

He set his lawyer to make discreet inquiries about the state of the Goddbys' finances and what he was told made Jethro smile.

On the day appointed for Perry to dine with him Jethro came home early and took his time getting ready. He sat and waited in the drawing room, a stark place compared to that in the Goddbys' house. He would have to do something about it, he decided, but didn't want it so full of frills and fuss he was afraid to move around in it.

When he heard a carriage draw up in the driveway, he said, 'Ahhhhh!' and sat up very straight, listening to the maid showing his visitor into the house. He hadn't invited the fellow to stay the night because, if things did not go according to plan, it'd be too uncomfortable the following morning. Anyway, the moon would be nearly full tonight.

Only when the door of the drawing room opened did he rise to his feet and move across to greet his guest. 'My dear Perry! I'm so glad you could come.'

The two men shook hands then Jethro gestured to the seat opposite his and moved towards the tray of drinks. 'Care for a glass of brandy before we eat?'

'Happy to.'

Jethro was surprised by how quickly the brandy vanished down Perry's throat. Without comment, he took the decanter across and refilled his glass. They talked of the weather, and of the stupidity of trying to build a tunnel under the Thames where several men working on it had died when it collapsed. Afraid his guest would grow too drunk to talk sense, Jethro rang to tell the maid they would eat now and led the way into the dining room. A plain dinner of roast beef, fried chicken pieces and boiled potatoes drenched in butter awaited them, followed by Jethro's favourite plum pudding with sweet white sauce.

'We'll serve ourselves if you don't mind,' he said to his guest, 'then we can talk privately. This is a bachelor establishment so I don't have all the frills that you're used to. Here, let me carve you some beef.' He had deliberately not provided wine with the meal.

By the time his guest professed himself satisfied, Jethro had come to the conclusion that the man was greedy. No wonder he was so plump. Well, greedy men wanted many things, not just food. Money would surely tempt this one?

It wasn't until the pudding had been cleared away and a decanter of port brought in that Jethro raised the question he'd been itching to ask.

'And how are your sisters? Beautiful women, both of them, but I found Sophia rather more – shall we say, appealing?'

Perry choked on his wine. 'Oh. Ah. Yes. Sophia.'

'They are both unmarried and unspoken for, are they not?'

'Well, er – that is – in short, yes.'

'Good. Then I'd like to ask for Sophia's hand in marriage.'

Perry set down his glass and swallowed hard. 'You're quick to make up your mind.'

'I had already seen her and felt attracted to her. That feeling only intensified when I saw her again.'

Avoiding his host's eyes, Perry stammered, 'Well, the thing is, Sophia has been – that is, she's not exactly spoken for, but she's been seeing a lot of young Easdale. Only there are some difficulties with his family because there's no dowry . . .'

'Then she must find a husband who doesn't require one.'

Perry bent his head and fiddled with his glass. 'Trouble is, she's devilish stubborn. Thinks she's in love with Easdale. I had a few words with her before I came – in case you expressed an interest. Have to be practical, don't we?'

A man less practical than this one would be hard to find from all accounts, Jethro thought, already tired of beating around the bush. 'We should indeed be practical, so I'll lay my cards on the table. On the day after I marry Sophia, you will receive a draft for five thousand pounds. What's more, as my brother-in-law, you can always be sure of my advice. I can, if you like the idea, help with your family's finances or even take them over from you. I can assure you that you'd continue to benefit from our association.'

'Five thousand!'

It took Perry a minute or two to pull himself together so Jethro took a tiny sip of port – he had never been a heavy drinker – and waited.

'You couldn't . . . consider Harriet instead, could you?'

'No.'

'Ah.'

Jethro forced himself to smile. 'I am, as I said, very attracted to Sophia.'

'I see.'

'Why do you not think about it, talk to her, then let me know what she says?'

'Yes. Yes, I can do that.'

The conversation limped on for another half-hour, then Perry asked for his carriage and took his leave.

The man's a fool, Jethro thought, as he listened to the sounds of horses' hooves and rattling wheels fade away into the night. We'll see if his sister is also stupid. She didn't have a stupid face.

In the meantime, he had a fancy to go and claim

his pot of free beer up the Calico Road before the month was up. Jethro's father might have been sanguine about what Fletcher would get up to, but he intended to leave nothing to chance. He wanted, no needed, to see for himself. In the hands of a man of sense that inn could be made into a thriving establishment – only was his bastard brother that sort of man? Jethro hoped not. He didn't want a man with a face so like his own getting known as a local innkeeper. Why the hell did the two of them have to look so alike? And why did Toby have to be taller than he was?

Sophia stared at Perry in horror. 'I hope you told him no? As if I would allow myself to be bought by a man like him!'

He glanced sideways at his mother, who wore the glassy smile with which she usually confronted trouble. No help to be had there. Taking a deep breath, he explained to Sophia how bad things really were, how only the five thousand pounds Mr Greenhalgh had offered as a marriage settlement would allow the family to stay in their home, and how, if Jethro Greenhalgh made good his additional promise of helping them manage their finances better, they might even be able to provide a dowry for Harriet later on.

He watched as the bad news sank in and Sophia sat staring at her clasped hands, every inch of her body betraying her unhappiness. Impatience at her stupidity made him snap, 'You have no choice but to accept his offer.'

She raised her eyes to his. 'How can you do this to me? You know my affections are already engaged.'

'*I* didn't do it; Father did. He lost more money than we realised in his foolish investments. And I've no turn for business, know no way to pull us out of the mire without this marriage and, we hope, a similarly advantageous one for Harriet.'

'Then let *her* marry Mr Greenhalgh.'

'He doesn't want her. I suggested it.'

She swallowed back the tears that threatened. 'I must see Oswin first. I can't accept Mr Greenhalgh's offer until I've seen Oswin.'

Her mother cleared her throat. 'You'll see him here, well chaperoned. We daren't risk anything else at this stage.'

Sophia looked from one to the other, then rose to her feet. 'I'll write him a note.'

'I'll take it over to him,' Perry said at once.

She had the note written within minutes, but had to wait three hours for Perry to return with an answer. Her heart sank when she saw that he wasn't accompanied by Oswin.

She walked slowly downstairs as her brother came into the hall. 'Was he not at home?'

'Yes, he was.'

Sophia's final hope vanished and she felt sick to the soul.

'I gave him your note and explained what had

happened, about the offer you'd received. Oswin said to tell you his father is obdurate and won't countenance a marriage with you or any other penniless female. He sent his regrets and his best wishes for a happy future.' He wrinkled his brow in thought for a moment, then added, 'Says he'll always remember you fondly.'

The words came out in a whisper. 'Couldn't he even come and tell me that himself?'

'I suggested it. I'm not quite as heartless as you think, old girl. But he refused. Said there was no point in it. Sophia, wait!'

But she had gone running up the stairs, skirts flying, one hand pressed to her mouth to hold in the sobs.

And when Mrs Goddby went up to offer her daughter what comfort she could, she found the door locked.

Sophia did not emerge until morning, sitting in icy silence over breakfast, saying nothing but, 'It seems I have no choice but to accept Mr Greenhalgh's offer.'

Her mother and brother sighed loudly in relief. Harriet glared at them all.

6

Jad Mortley, the overlooker at Beardsworth's mill, was in a foul temper that day and when one of the children couldn't keep up, beat her until she could only moan, after which he threw a bucket of water over her and ordered her to get back to work. Only she couldn't move. When he dragged her to her feet, she gave one thin scream and fainted.

The women working in that section muttered under their breath but didn't dare raise their eyes. Only when the overlooker kicked the child did one woman break ranks and run forward to stand protectively in front of her daughter.

'Leave her alone! You've beaten her till she's near out of her senses. She's nobbut eleven. Do you want to kill her?'

For answer he clouted her about the ears. 'Get back to your work. You'll be fined for this. How I deal with the young 'uns is my business. Doesn't matter what their ages are. If they don't do their work properly, they're in trouble.'

But the mother wouldn't, couldn't, move and crouched to cradle her child in her arms.

He laughed and sent for the husband. 'Your wife

and daughter won't work. See if you can do better with 'em. I'm only giving you this one chance. I want both of them back at work in five minutes.'

The man looked down at his sobbing wife, saw his daughter's bruised and bloody back and attacked the overlooker. It took three men to pull him off, for all he was much smaller than Mortley.

'I'm calling in the magistrate and having him arrested for assault.'

'It'll be the last thing you ever do then,' a voice called from the back, artificially high to disguise the identity of its owner.

Another high, unnatural voice repeated the same threat from a different part of the big spinning shed.

With a curse the overlooker turned to the trio, the man now with his arm round his wife and a bruise darkening his cheek where Jad had punched him. 'It's not worth bothering with the magistrate. You and your family are to be out of your house by nightfall.' He raised his voice to add, 'Anyone as gives you shelter will be thrown out as well. Now get back to work, the rest of you.'

As they did so, the man picked up his daughter and carried her home.

In spite of the overlooker's threats, help was given as the family made frantic preparations to leave. A handcart was found in which the child could lie on top of their bedding. Pennies were collected to give them a start and the general advice was to get across the moors and as far away as possible.

They all knew that Jad Mortley would go after

them and exact revenge one way or another because it had happened before.

'Take the Calico Road,' people said. 'If you can get there, they'll help you. They're good folk in Calico.'

Toby was locking up for the night when the group came round the corner into his stable yard. A man, a woman and six children of differing heights, all shivering. A groan drew his attention to the cart and to his horror he saw a thin girl lying in it on her front, exposing a bloodied back.

'What happened?'

'Mr Beardsworth's overseer beat her senseless. He likes beating childer, Jad Mortley does.'

The woman said, in a voice ringing with pain, 'He went mad today. Doesn't usually hurt 'em this bad because they can't work afterwards. I couldn't let him go on kicking her, so I left my work and went to stand in front of her. He threw us all out. Only he comes after you, if he's angry enough. Other folk have disappeared.' She looked over her shoulder as if she expected to see the overlooker appear any minute.

Toby closed his eyes for a moment, sickened by what he saw, then opened them again and said briskly, 'You'll need somewhere to spend the night then, and I've got just the place for you. Wait there.' He went into the house and called for Phoebe, explaining what had happened, then he took the family through to the back place. 'No one will know you're here and you can stay till the lass is fit to travel. Mortley will have stopped looking for you by then.'

'Mr Beardsworth will go mad if he finds out you've given us shelter for so long. The pair of them will come after *you* then,' the man said. 'If we can just stay this one night, that'll be enough.'

'You'll stay till she's better. And I'll feed you while you're here.'

There was a hue and cry up the hill the next day for a family who were supposed to have stolen goods from their employer.

Toby went into the public room, listened to the tale being spread by two brutish-looking men and shook his head as if disgusted. 'I've not seen them here, but then, they could have passed through during the night and we'd not have known. Would you like a pot of beer to set you on your way?'

Beardsworth's men nodded enthusiastically and Toby stood chatting to them while they drank then escorted them to the door, watching to make sure they didn't try to search his outbuildings.

Only when he came inside did his face show what he really thought of them. A pair of ruffians if ever he'd seen any.

Ross Bellvers came up to him. 'Can I have a quiet word about this?'

Toby took him into the house place. 'Yes?'

'You've seen that family, haven't you?'

'Why do you say that?'

'I saw Phoebe's face and the way she slipped in here to get out of them two's way.'

'If you'd seen the child's back, the way she's been beaten, such a little lass too . . .'

Ross laid one hand on his arm. 'It's happened a couple of times before. I gave one lot shelter myself. Only it was a young woman who'd been raped that time. Mortley did it. The man's vile.' He nodded to Toby. 'I don't think anyone else noticed Phoebe and I shan't let on that you're hiding anyone. What's more, I'll set my son to watching out for them two sneaking back.'

Toby looked at him, then nodded. 'Good idea.'

'I knew the family must be here still when they weren't found.'

Toby let out a sigh of pure relief. 'Yes.'

'Where have you got them?'

'Up the back.'

'They'll not like it there.'

'They do. Said they slept well, even that poor child.'

'Too tired to notice, I expect.'

Toby stared at him. 'Notice what?'

'That the back part is haunted.'

'I've never seen any ghosts.'

'Neither have I. But I've *heard* 'em and so have others.'

Toby shrugged.

'Will that family be staying long?'

'A few days. The little lass is bad.'

'I'll send across a sack of potatoes to help feed 'em.' He clapped Toby on the shoulder again and went back to his pot of beer.

Which all surprised Toby greatly.

A week later he got out his cart, sure now that the

inn wasn't being watched, and drove down the hill at dusk to set the family well on their way. He'd done all he could for them and only hoped they'd get clean away.

After that incident he found Ross more friendly and the other folk in Calico took their lead from him. When Toby mentioned this to Phoebe, she just smiled and said, 'I knew they'd take to you.'

Jethro rode up to Calico one day after Goddby's visit, having decided that he might as well deal with the other matter that was preying on his mind while he was waiting for a decision from Sophia. He shouldn't let the thought of his bastard brother irritate him like this, but it did. Calico wasn't nearly far enough away from Backenshaw for him to feel comfortable.

It was a cold day but fine, and once he'd pushed the thought of his brother to the back of his mind, Jethro found himself enjoying the outing. He should ride out more often. He enjoyed the exercise and, unlike his father, didn't intend to spend every minute of his life attending to business.

He took his groom with him, as he did every time he rode out any distance. Peter had been with him for several years and was a powerful man. Not that Jethro thought his bastard brother likely to attack him, no, but there were sometimes desperate men on the tramp and he preferred to be careful. Two men were less likely to be attacked than one.

Peter was as near to a friend as Jethro had, given the way his father had insisted they live. The man had been his mother's groom till her death, and then Jethro's own from when he was twelve. His father had always paid more attention to making money than to his only son, so it had sometimes been Peter who'd comforted the boy over things which troubled him, as they did most lads at times. And it was Peter more than anyone who had helped him understand the vagaries of the world in which he lived, usually while the pair of them were sitting on a bale of hay out in the stables.

The Packhorse looked as ramshackle and inhospitable as it had the previous time he'd visited and Jethro felt reluctant to enter it, as if to do so would change his life. Indeed, he almost turned back without going in, which was a strange fancy, most unlike him. Shrugging off the idea, he dismounted and handed the reins to Peter. 'Walk him up and down. I shan't be long. We'll stop for refreshments elsewhere on the way back.'

As he was straightening his clothing he looked down the side of the building and saw Fletcher and another man, shouting and waving their hands around. They looked as if they were about to have a fight, but suddenly the man stepped backwards, clearly unwilling to take on such a well-built opponent. Fletcher spoke briefly then went back into the building, slamming the door behind him. The other turned on his heel and came stamping along to the front of the inn, stopping when he saw Jethro watching him. His scowl deepened. He muttered something and went striding down the road, turning off almost immediately on to a rough track.

Jethro watched him for a moment, wondering what that was about, then went inside.

Phoebe, who was wiping tables, clasped the wet cloth to her bosom in shock when she saw who had just come in, but to her enormous relief he didn't seem to recognise her.

'Fetch your master.'

'Yes, sir.' She ran to the middle part of the inn, heading for the sound of hammering. 'It's young Mr Greenhalgh. He wants to see you, Toby.'

'Oh, does he!' He slung down his hammer, sorry not to be able to work off his anger. Cully Dean had been asking yet again for credit to be extended so that he could continue drinking a few pots every day. Well, he could ask all he liked. Toby wasn't giving credit to anyone, however much the regular drinkers disliked that. Hal had allowed his cronies to have their drinks chalked on the slate and they'd rarely paid off their debts, apparently, because every now and then, in a magnanimous drunken gesture, he had wiped the slate clean, literally, and then the heavy boozers had started building up their debts again. Toby had removed the piece of slate from the public room.

No wonder the place hadn't been making the profits it should, he thought.

He didn't want to see or serve his half-brother. He'd hoped Jethro wouldn't bother to take advantage of the clause charging Toby to provide a free pot of beer every January because he'd reckoned it was simply an excuse for his half-brother to poke his nose into Toby's affairs. He didn't like the thought of that, not at all. The inn was his now, his to do what he wanted with. The lawyer had assured him of that. Muttering in irritation, he rubbed the sawdust off his hands and untied his leather apron.

'I'd rather not go back into the public room until he's left, if you don't mind,' Phoebe said in a voice which fluted with nervousness. 'I don't think he recognised me and I don't want to jog his memory.'

'He has no right to order you off *my* premises, Phoebe, so you've nothing to be feared of now. He's not the King of England, after all.'

'Rich folk can do anything they like, whether they're kings or not. And the Greenhalghs are known for getting what they want by any means they can.'

But Jethro *had* recognised the widow and was feeling angry that she hadn't obeyed his order to leave the district. After all, she might know more than she had claimed and he didn't want her telling his family secrets to the bastard. He began pacing up and down the public room, wondering what was keeping Fletcher.

Footsteps approached, echoing on the wooden floor and not hurrying. Irritated, Jethro swung round to watch the fellow saunter in.

For a moment they stood there eyeing one another, so alike in appearance that no one could ever doubt they were brothers. Except that Toby was a couple of inches taller and more heavily built.

Damn him! Jethro thought. And damn his father too, for siring the fellow.

Toby moved towards the barrel of beer, taking the initiative. 'You'll have come for your free drink.' Before Jethro could protest, he'd filled a fresh jug from the barrel and poured out two pots, waiting till his half-brother had picked one up before raising his own. 'Here's to good ale. There's nowt like it.'

Jethro sipped then took a proper mouthful, surprised by the excellent quality of the beer. 'Actually, I didn't come for the beer, Fletcher, but to offer to buy this place back from you. I didn't agree with my father letting it go out of the family so I'll give you two hundred pounds for it.'

Toby stared at him, surprised but hoping he hadn't shown it, then raised his pot for another sip to buy more thinking time – though he didn't really need to consider his answer, so why pretend? 'I don't want to sell, and if you're worried about keeping the place in the family, there's no need. After all, I'm family myself, even if I was born on the wrong side of the blanket.' He grinned at the look of outrage on the other man's face.

'Two hundred and fifty, and that's my final offer.'

'The money won't change my mind because I *don't* want to sell. I like it here. Nor I don't see why you'd want the inn back anyway. A fine gentleman like you . . .' he let the words hang in the air for a minute, then continued in the same mild tone ' . . . would be out of place serving in here.'

'Damn you, fellow, I don't want to run it, just to—'

Jethro broke off, annoyed with himself for having nearly betrayed his reasons.

Toby took a step forward. 'And damn you, *brother*, I know exactly what you want. To get me and this,' he pointed to his face, 'out of the district. Well, I'm a fair distance from Backenshaw and have no need to go there for owt, so let it content you that I'll stay away from there. That'll suit me just fine because I've no desire to see *your* face, either. It reminds me of your – *our* – father, and how badly he treated my mother.'

Jethro choked back the rage that filled him at this impudence and slammed down the pot on the counter. 'You'd better think about it more carefully. Selling could save you a lot of – shall we say – *unpleasantness* in the future.'

'If that's a threat, I'll tell you to your face that it won't make me budge an inch. I'm here and I'm staying. Remember that.'

Jethro glared at him. 'Then just make sure you don't come anywhere near Backenshaw and remind me of your existence. And tell that old woman to get out. I've warned her once and given her the money to get her back to wherever she comes from.'

'She's going nowhere. Let alone I need her here, this place has been her home for over twenty years and there's no reason for her to leave it.'

For a minute their eyes met, glowing with anger and challenge. Then Jethro slammed down his pot, swung on his heel and stormed out.

Toby stood behind the bar with anger boiling up in him, all the stronger because he was still annoyed by his earlier encounter with Cully Dean. Who did Jethro Greenhalgh think he was to tell Phoebe to leave the place she loved? Dammit, what an arrogant sod the man was! Toby would rather be related to anyone else than him. Well, almost anyone else.

He couldn't help wondering why Greenhalgh should want Phoebe out of the district. Frowning, he considered what this might mean. Did she know something about the Greenhalghs – or had her husband known something?

Toby's rage soon faded because he was not one to dwell on problems. He smiled as he looked round. He loved the inn. Whatever the reason for its being given to him, it was his now and Greenhalgh had better not try to take it away from him or he'd find himself with a fight on his hands.

He went into the house place to see Phoebe standing at the foot of the stairs which led to their bedrooms. 'You heard what he said?'

She nodded. 'Toby, he was offering you a lot of money. Maybe it'd be more sensible to sell and—'

'I'm *not* selling. I like it here.'

She still looked worried. But he had that stubborn expression on his face that she was beginning to recognise, so she didn't try to reason with him. He was more of a Greenhalgh than he'd admit, though he had a kinder, gentler side to his nature which must come from his mother's side and for that she thanked God every day. Without his kindness she was quite sure she'd have died of grief at leaving this place. It was her home, the only real one she'd ever known.

And Toby, dear Toby, was like the son she'd always wanted.

As Jethro rode away from the inn, still simmering with anger after his encounter with Fletcher, he saw a figure he recognised working in a field and reined in his horse to stare at the man. Surely that was the fellow who'd been arguing with his damned brother? He sat thinking for a minute watching the man slam the spade into the ground behind the house, anger in every line of his body. There was a small cottage at the far end of the field, and everything there looked ill-tended and untidy.

Jethro turned to his groom. 'Go and tell that fellow I want a word.'

When Peter accosted him, the man left the spade standing in the ground, rubbed his hands down the sides of his breeches and followed Peter back to the drystone wall that bordered the road. The groom clambered over it; the man stayed on his own side, surly, suspicious.

'Wait for us along the road a little,' Jethro said softly, and paused until Peter was out of earshot before turning back. 'What's your name, fellow?'

Cully scowled at him and considered telling him it was no business of his, then remembered who this man was and thought better of it, giving his name reluctantly.

Jethro pulled a coin from his pocket and held it out. 'Would you like to earn this?'

Cully moved forward because his eyesight wasn't

the best except close to something. When he saw what the coin was, he nodded eagerly.

'Then climb over the wall and we'll talk. I'm not standing up here in this cold wind much longer.' He waited until Cully had clambered over the drystone wall then led his horse back down to the partial shelter of a dip in the road.

'You're interested?'

'How would I have to earn it, sir?'

'Am I right in thinking you bear no love towards Toby Fletcher?'

Cully spat on the ground to show his disdain. 'He's no right to come here changing things.'

'I agree absolutely. In fact, I'm a bit worried about how Fletcher will manage the inn. I feel responsible for it since my father gifted it to the man. A village needs an inn. Where would you all be without it? What if it closed down?'

His companion looked alarmed at the mere thought of that, then folded his arms in the attitude of one prepared to listen while giving nothing away.

'I'd be happy to pay for information on what Fletcher is doing – say, every month. My groom could meet you somewhere convenient.'

Cully wrinkled his brow. 'What sort of information would that be?'

'Just keep me informed of what the fellow's doing, how business is at the inn – that sort of thing.'

'That's easy enough.'

'You'll do it?'

'If you'll pay me for it.' Cully grinned. 'You don't

like Fletcher even though he's your brother. Well, neither do I.'

Jethro's voice became icy. 'What I like or don't like is none of your business. And what's more, if anyone finds out about what you're doing for me, our agreement will end and you'll find yourself in hot water. I have a lot of friends in high places and can cause you a great deal of trouble if I so choose.'

The man's grin had vanished and a look of anxiety replaced it. 'I'll say nothing, sir, I promise.'

'Where can you meet my groom? I don't want people noticing, mind.'

Cully pursed his lips in thought, then nodded as the solution came to him. 'In Todmorden, first Thursday of the month. Market Day, it is, stock markets too. I allus see my cousin, have a drink at the White Hart Inn, so I won't be doing owt different.'

Jethro nodded, pleased by this sign of cunning. He looked towards his groom and beckoned, explaining what he wanted, then dismissed Dean with a jerk of the head and rode off.

Cully watched them go, then grinned and went back to his digging. He'd fallen lucky here. And if he was even luckier he'd be able to do Fletcher a mischief. Teach the bugger to change things when folk didn't want 'em changing! Teach him to screw every last halfpenny out of poor folk as needed their pot of beer to stop their aches and pains.

Sophia sat nervously in the parlour awaiting the arrival of Jethro Greenhalgh who was coming today to propose marriage formally. She had tried to talk to her sister about the unfairness of the sacrifice she was being called on to make, but had found little sympathy there. Harriet considered Jethro Greenhalgh a good catch, said Sophia was a fool to complain of becoming a rich man's wife, and was bitterly resentful that his fancy hadn't settled on her. She had even accused her sister one day of setting her sights on him from the first and they'd had a short, sharp quarrel over that.

The sound of horses' hooves and carriage wheels on the gravel of the drive made Sophia sit up very straight. She had vowed not to betray her unhappiness at the prospect of marrying him, but to receive him calmly and live with him calmly afterwards, too. If she maintained her dignity and self-respect through all this, and reminded herself that at least her family would benefit from the marriage, then she could cope.

She wouldn't marry Oswin now if he asked her. To send a message, not to come to see her . . . the thought of that still made her angry, as well as hurt.

Jethro was shown in and stopped briefly in the doorway, staring across at her with what could only be described as an avid expression on his face. It made her feel nervous but she rose and waited for him to come to her, holding out her hand to create a barrier when it seemed as if he intended to embrace her. She couldn't have faced that, not yet, not till she was more accustomed to him. 'Do take a seat, Mr Greenhalgh.'

He shook her hand, retained it when she would have pulled back, and smiled at her. 'Annoyed, aren't you, Miss Goddby?'

She could only gaze at him in shock, and stammer, 'I don't know what you mean.'

'Of course you do. And *I* would rather we spoke frankly about our situation.' He let go of her hand and waited until she'd sat down on the sofa before sitting next to her.

He was too close but she didn't like to edge away. When he reached out and took hold of her hand again, she was startled and tried to draw back but he merely tightened his grasp.

'I've come to ask you to become my wife, Sophia. Will you marry me?'

So blunt. Had he no manners, no tact? Clearly not. She took a deep breath and forced out the words she had rehearsed so carefully. 'I'd be honoured, Mr Greenhalgh.'

'Jethro.'

'Yes, of course. Jethro.' He pulled her into his arms and started kissing her before she had realised what he intended. She tried to put up with it but didn't want a stranger's lips on hers, and in the end heard herself whimpering a protest as she struggled to pull away.

He laughed and let her go. 'Not bad for an unwilling bride. You'll grow used to my embraces, Sophia. I'll make sure of that.'

'I'm not unwilling. It's just that I hardly know you.'

'It's just that you're still besotted with Oswin

Easdale.' He clicked his tongue and shook his head in mock reproof. 'Don't lie about that. Everyone knows you've been seeing him. But I'll tell you now: I was at school with the man and he's stupid, however good-looking he may be – and what's more, he's a bully. You're far too intelligent for him. He'd not have made you happy.'

She stared at him in amazement. This was the last thing she'd expected to hear him saying. 'Aren't you disturbed about my – my previous feelings?'

'No. You'll get over that. What *would* upset me was if you didn't see the sense of marrying me, because that'd mean you were as stupid as him. I want you, Sophia, and have done ever since I saw you talking to your sister at the gate a week or two ago.'

'You're surely not pretending to have fallen in love with me?' she asked, unable to hide her scorn.

'I'm not pretending anything. I don't believe in *falling in love*. All I know is, I want you to wife and have found a way to achieve this.'

She didn't know what to say so bent her head, only to jerk it upright again when he continued to surprise her.

'I thought we'd get married next month. March is a good time for weddings, don't you think?'

It was out before she could prevent it. 'So soon?'

'Oh, yes. The sooner the better. In fact, now I come to think of it, your brother's case is desperate, so maybe we should get a special licence and marry next week?'

She heard herself begging, 'I pray you, give me the month, Mr – um – Jethro. We hardly know one another as yet.' She knew she couldn't marry him so soon, just couldn't do it.

He looked at her, his eyes narrowing, then nodded. 'I will, if you'll give me your solemn word not to see or speak to Easdale in the meantime.'

'That's easily done. He wouldn't come and see me, not even to say farewell. I wouldn't want to see him now.'

'Doesn't surprise me that he wouldn't come. He never did enjoy unpleasant scenes.' Jethro studied her flushed and unhappy face. 'I'll make you a far better husband than he would. I'll be faithful, for a start. He's not stopped his trysts with maidservants and tenants' daughters while courting you.'

'I don't believe you! He *wouldn't*!'

Another of those confident smiles of Jethro's. 'I don't need to lie about that because it's the simple truth. I could find you a dozen witnesses if you wanted to make your feelings public.'

Hot shame scalded through her. Somehow Jethro's words rang true. She had believed Oswin loved her. Surely a man in love with one woman wouldn't . . . couldn't . . . do that with another?

There was a tap on the door and Perry and her mother came in, looking questioningly from one to the other.

Jethro pulled Sophia to her feet and stepped forward, keeping tight hold of her hand so that she was obliged to go with him and remain close to him.

'I'm delighted to inform you . . . Mrs Goddby . . . Perry, that Sophia has done me the honour of accepting my proposal of marriage. We intend to marry as soon as the banns can be called.'

'My dear girl.' Mrs Goddby stepped forward for one of her brief embraces. 'I'm so happy for you.' She turned to their visitor. 'But I'm afraid we can't possibly be ready that quickly, my dear Mr Greenhalgh. There are the bride clothes to make, everything to arrange . . .'

'We'll be married as soon as the banns have been called,' he repeated. 'I don't care if she comes to me with only the clothes she stands up in, as long as she comes.'

He smiled at Sophia in the way she was coming to recognise, a tightly possessive smile, then turned back to her brother. 'I'll need a word about the business side of things before I leave, Perry. And Mrs Goddby . . . Sophia – I hope you'll come and dine with me on Sunday, shall we say to arrive at noon? You'll want to look over the house. Parkside needs a lot doing to it, I'm afraid. It's spacious enough, but has never known a woman's touch and the furniture is old-fashioned and uncomfortable.'

Mrs Goddby inclined her head graciously. 'We shall be happy to visit you, Mr Greenhalgh.'

'Good. And where is Miss Goddby today?'

'She's not feeling well,' Sophia said hastily.

'But I shall see her on Sunday, I hope?'

It was an order couched as a polite wish. Sophia bent her head in agreement. She had quickly come to realise that her betrothed was a forceful man who made other people do as he wished. After a careful sideways glance at him she decided that she would save rebellion and protest for the things that really mattered to her, things she could and would change.

A shiver ran through her as she saw his eyes rest on her again and that half-smile appear on his lips. Jethro was a good-looking man, but so tall and well-muscled he made her feel nervous. Physically she would be like a child in his grasp, without any physical power at all. She would have to find ways of standing up to him, though, have to learn to manage him, because she didn't intend to become a subservient creature who rushed to obey his every whim and command. That wasn't in her nature. Sophia raised her chin and gave him a cool glance. He would find that out after they were wed.

Her calm lasted until she'd waved him goodbye at the front door, then she ran upstairs and shut herself in her bedroom, locking the door and pressing her hands to her flushed cheeks, telling Harriet when she knocked that she needed time to compose herself.

What would it be like being married to such a man?

The mere thought of it terrified her – and yet she found it excited her, too.

7

Jethro had himself driven over the tops to see Andrew Beardsworth who had been a friend and business associate of his father's. He'd been promising to do this for a while. Andrew was always very pleasant and had put some useful business his way recently, though he was a harsh master in his own mill.

It was annoying that the quickest way to get there was to drive past the Packhorse. Jethro studied it, noting the repairs that had been made and the small cart that drove straight round the back, as if this customer was familiar with the ways of the place. He'd rather Fletcher had proved lazy like Dixon had been, and that the inn had remained little frequented by the gentry.

There was another man visiting Beardsworth so they sat and drank a pot of tea together, since none of them was the sort to drink wine in the daytime.

Hugh Madson looked at Jethro. 'Have any trouble coming across the tops?'

'Not on a day like this.'

'We had some trouble a while back. It was snowing and my wife fell ill, so we had to stay at that little inn in Calico.' He looked at Jethro. 'That's where I've seen you before – or rather a face just like yours.'

'The landlord's a distant connection.'

'Looks very like you. Could be your twin brother.'

'Indeed.' Jethro kept his expression calm, glad he was able to do this however he was feeling, for he was in fact furious at the mere thought of people connecting him and Fletcher like this. 'How did you find the service there?'

'Better than I'd expected. The new landlord did his utmost to make us comfortable, though he's still refurbishing the place. I shall have no hesitation in recommending his inn to others.'

When he'd gone Andrew Beardsworth cocked one eyebrow at Jethro. 'Sounds like your half-brother is improving matters.'

'Yes. I'd rather he failed, though. One reason for my visit is that I'm getting wed and wanted to invite you to the wedding. It's to Sophia Goddby, actually.'

'County gentry, no less. You've done well for yourself.'

'Or she has. They're in a bad way financially or they'd not be letting her marry me.'

'I'm thinking of getting wed again myself. Life's a lot easier when you have someone to warm your bed for you.'

'Do you miss your wife?'

Andrew pulled a face. 'Not exactly. I just miss *having* a wife. They're damned convenient. You'll have to keep your eyes open for someone for me.'

Jethro nodded. 'I'll do that. Now, about those new

machines you've seen . . .' It was a relief to turn the conversation to the main reason for his visit. He didn't like discussing his personal affairs with anyone.

In March Ben came home one Saturday after work with a broad smile on his face. He gathered Meg into his arms, swinging her round exuberantly. 'I've done it! I've found mesen a new job. It's over in Rochdale. One of my old mates spoke up for me, the one as knows my cousin, an' he sent me word to get over there as fast as I can. I sent word back I'd take it.'

They stood together for a few moments with his arms round her and her head resting against his chest, but curiosity got the better of Meg's love of cuddling and she pulled away from him. 'What's the job?'

He hesitated, then admitted, 'It's in a brewery, looking after the horses an' driving a dray. Same as I do now.'

'Ben, no! Not a brewery.'

'It's a right good job, love. Much better pay than in the mill stables.'

'But you'll be working with beer. How will you stand it? Oh, Ben, I don't want you turning into a drunkard again!'

'I'll not let the drink get to me, not with you to come home to, I promise.'

She wasn't sure of that and didn't want to spoil his joy but couldn't hold back some words of caution. 'Maybe you should wait and find another job?'

He shook his head, his expression determined. 'I'd never find one as good as this. An' if we stay here, who knows what your damned mother will say about us next?'

'Say about us?'

'She's been tellin' lies again. Eh, it's first one thing then another with her.'

Meg's heart sank. 'What's she saying now?'

'Nothing you need to hear, but I'd be a poor husband if I didn't get you away from the owd besom.'

'All right. We'll go to Rochdale.'

But she wept against him in bed that night and it took Ben a long time to comfort her. How could a mother hate her own child like hers did? she asked.

He couldn't answer, only cuddle her against him and shush her.

The following week they left Northby. It was sad saying goodbye to Jack and her brothers and sister, but Meg had never been away from her birthplace before and all she saw was so wondrously new to her that she soon cheered up. She couldn't help exclaiming and pointing, asking questions one after the other as the carrier's cart jolted along a rough moorland track, then down into Rochdale itself.

Ben's friend had even found them a house to rent, only a one-up, one-down house in a terrace that stood back-to-back with another terrace of similar dwellings, but after their previous one room in someone else's house, it seemed more than enough.

And to have a proper cooking fire of her own was bliss to Meg, who had found that she enjoyed cooking and could produce far nicer meals than her mother ever had.

Once they had arranged their few pieces of furniture, however, she wished they had more because the rooms looked so bare.

'I'm off to meet my new employers now,' Ben said.

When he'd left she decided to go out and explore the town. It was far bigger than Northby, so she stayed near the centre, where the streets sloped down to a river. That helped her get her bearings. She didn't want to get lost.

It seemed strange to see so many people walking about and know none of them. As she strolled she found fine buildings alternating with areas that had narrow alleys and shabby houses crammed one against the other.

Surely in such a big place she could find herself a job of some sort? Ben might be bringing in enough money to support her, but they didn't have children yet. It would be foolish to sit at home when she could be earning.

She got back before him and made herself a cup of tea with some carefully hoarded tealeaves that had only been used once, sipping the warm liquid with pleasure. She kept jerking round every time someone walked past the window, but it wasn't her husband. What was he doing? Why was he staying out so late when he hadn't even started work yet? She began to feel neglected and a bit worried. What if he'd been hurt? People wouldn't know who he was or how to find her. It was after dark when he did come home, by which time she was feeling aggrieved.

'Why haven't you lit the candle?' Ben demanded. 'We can afford a light of an evening. And it's cold in here. Why've you let the fire burn so low?' He went across to the hearth and poked up the coals so that the flames rose higher.

'There was no need for lights or a fire. I wasn't doing anything, just sitting here waiting for you. And don't waste that coal. We've only got a few pieces till we can order some in.'

He straightened up and put the poker down. 'Where do you think I've been? Looking round the brewery and talking to Mr Brooks and the other fellows I'll be working with. I couldn't get back any sooner, love. Don't I even get a hug?'

Suddenly it seemed silly to sulk so she ran across the room to him and put up her face for his kiss. But his breath smelled of beer and she jerked her head back, pushing him away with both her hands on his chest. 'You've been drinking!'

'Just a couple of pots.'

'You promised me you wouldn't drink again, Ben, promised faithfully!'

'Mr Brooks gives everyone a drink or two at the end of the day. There's no harm in just a couple.' He caught hold of her and pulled her back into his arms. 'Stop that, Meg! It's my living now, beer is, an' think how bad it'd look if I refused to sup with the other fellows.'

She sagged against him. 'Oh, Ben, I don't like you drinking. Dad got loud and noisy when he drank and I've seen you myself staggering along the street when you used to drink too much.'

'Well, you won't see me in that condition again. I'm a sober married man now. But I'm not giving up my entitlements. It's good beer and I shall enjoy a couple of pots after a hard day's work – free ones, too.'

Nothing she said would change his mind on this and they had a short, sharp quarrel, something that was rare for them. But after they'd sat in silence for a while, one on either side of the table, fiddling with the bread and cheese which neither of them had any appetite for, he said, 'Don't let's fratch over this, love. I promise you I won't get into drunken habits again.'

And Meg was more than ready to make it up.

That night when they'd made love, she lay on the scratchy straw mattress which was all they owned, unable to sleep for worrying. She knew, she just knew somehow, that beer wasn't good for her Ben. It turned him into another person entirely. Even tonight he'd spoken more sharply to her than usual and they'd quarrelled. Tears rolled slowly down her cheeks, leaving cold trails behind them, but she could see no way to stop him working at the brewery. You had to earn money if you wanted to eat, especially when you were in a strange town where you knew no one.

The following morning Ben went to work before dawn, because it was part of his job to feed the horses and clean out their stables before the working day began. As soon as it grew light Meg went out looking for work. She found her way to two mills, but the gatekeepers said they weren't taking anyone on because work was short, so she went searching elsewhere. There must be some way to earn money, even if it was only by scrubbing floors. Two wages made a big difference when you were trying to set up a home and she hadn't fallen for a baby yet, to her secret relief.

It came on to rain while she was near the top of the hill, so she ran to take shelter in the porch of St Chad's church, which looked down upon the river and the town centre. She shivered, feeling cold now and wishing they'd stayed in Northby. But after a minute or two she told herself not to be silly. She'd escaped from her mother, hadn't she? That was the main thing. She'd soon get to know a few people. And she'd find work as well, of course she would.

She found it on the third day of her search, a curious sort of job to one who had only ever worked in a mill. She called in at a pawn shop, thinking the owner might know where there was work going. The woman behind the counter was massive, hard-faced, and stared at Meg so closely she began to wonder if she'd got muck on her face or something.

'I might know something for a lass as is prepared to turn her hand to anything.'

'Oh, I am! I'd be that grateful for a hint or two.'

The woman relaxed and leaned on the counter. 'It's more than a hint. I decided last night that I need some help here. I want someone as'll do owt that's needed: cleaning the house, cooking, shopping, and later, when she knows the trade better, serving customers. Think you can do that?'

'Oh, yes! Please give me a try. I'm a hard worker, I promise you.'

'If you're not, you'll be out on your ear. I work hard mysen an' I'll expect you to do the same. All right, you may as well start now. Come through.' She held up a flap in the counter and Meg followed her into the back room. 'I want this place cleaned up and the floor scrubbed – properly, mind – then you can come and help me clear up the shop. Ten bob a week to start off an' midday meals found. I'm Peggy Clarke, by the way.'

Meg nodded. 'Meg Pearson. Pleased to meet you.' She couldn't keep her eyes off the big metal contraption that was standing there instead of a fireplace.

Peggy smiled. 'I see you've noticed my stove.' She rapped on its black metal side. 'This is the boiler, so any time you need hot water, just turn this tap. Well, as long as the fire's lit an' you've kept the tank full, there's hot water. You fill it here.' Another rap of her fist. 'Now *there's* progress for you.' She also explained about the oven and cooking hob and Meg watched in fascination as Peggy enthusiastically demonstrated its features.

Afterwards Meg set to, scrubbing the floor with a will. She was aware of her new employer peering through the doorway from time to time but didn't say anything, just carried on working.

When she'd finished Peggy came in, her eyes hard and assessing, then nodded. 'Well, you know how to scrub, any road, an' you don't miss out the corners. Now, afore you start cleaning the shop, I need some things from the market or I'll have nowt to eat tonight.'

'Would you mind if I bought a couple of things for me an' Ben while I'm there?' Meg asked nervously. 'It'll not take me a minute, only I didn't know I was starting work today, so I've got nothing in.'

'As long as you're quick about it. If that husband of yours is as bad as mine was, he'll be demanding food on the table the minute he gets through the door, an' thumping you if it's not ready.'

Meg smiled. 'Ben's allus hungry when he gets back but he's never laid a finger on me.'

'If he ever does, hit him straight back, that's my advice to you.' Peggy spoke in the voice of experience. 'If you once let 'em start, they never let up on you. I fought back, but mine was a big sod an' he allus got the better of me in the end, though I reckon he'd have been worse if I hadn't stood up to him. I were glad when he died. I never wept a tear for him, not a one. An' I do better nor he ever did with this shop.' She stared into the distance for a minute then jerked into action again, arms waving, finger pointing. 'Right then, we can't stand gossiping all day. Go and get that shopping, then we'll make a start on cleaning up the shop.'

When Meg finished work at eight o'clock she rushed home, tired but triumphant, knowing she'd only just get there before Ben. She'd started cooking their tea when he came through the door, again smelling of beer. But his speech wasn't slurred and he was steady on his feet, so maybe he would be all right with just a drink or two. She prayed he would.

'I got mysen a job today,' she announced, beaming at him.

'An' does that stop you from giving me a hug?' he demanded, pretending to be vexed.

'I can't put this frying pan down now, it's red hot.' When she'd finished she set it down on the pair of bricks she'd stood on the table and gave him a hug. They ate the ham with thick slices of bread cut from a loaf also bought at the market, sopping up the grease and murmuring with pleasure at the taste. In between bites she told him about Peggy and the shop, explaining that she'd have to work late on Fridays and Saturdays.

'Eh, you're a clever lass. I'm proud of you.'

'We'll be able to buy some more things for the house now an' get some savings behind us for a rainy day.' Meg was eager to make it a proper home because she couldn't get her mother's scornful remarks out of her mind. And she never wanted to be without a shilling or two extra put by; never wanted to be like the women who came to the pawn shop, haggard and desperate to feed their children.

'There's only one thing I need in my house,' Ben said, his voice going husky and his gaze leaving her in no doubt of his desire for her, 'and that's you, Meg lass.'

She fell asleep with a smile on her face that night.

It was so wonderful to be wanted like that, to be loved and appreciated. And she was earning again. What more could she want?

The next day Peggy showed her new employee the little parlour at the side of the kitchen. It was clearly her pride and joy and had real velvet curtains with net ones as well to prevent people from looking in as they walked along the pavement outside. 'I sit here of an evening – when I've time, that is. And I'm in here on Sundays, of course. I paid for every stick of furniture, every ornament, mysen. *He* would have drunk the money. You're to dust in here every day an' clear out the grate when I've had a fire lit. An' don't you go breaking owt or I'll take the cost from your wages. I'm not runnin' a charity here.'

Meg looked round in amazement. 'It's a palace,' she said, her voice hushed. 'I've never seen anywhere like it. Oh, Peggy, it's lovely.'

Two days later a drunken man came into the shop and asked to redeem the things his wife had pawned the previous Monday. When Peggy got out the bundle of clothing, he snatched at it and tried to run out without paying, but she'd seen that trick before and kept hold of the knot at the top of the bundle. Jerking it away from him, she surged out from behind the counter, massive and fearsome in her rage.

The man backed away, stammering something.

Peggy snatched up the stout stick she kept handy and set about him with it, driving him yelping out of the shop and down the street. 'I'll teach you to steal from a woman as works hard while you're out swilling ale!' she roared, and the stick thwacked down on his back again.

She then returned to her doorstep, still yelling insults after him. Once he'd rounded the corner she came inside again and picked up the things that'd dropped out of the bundle. 'Rotten thieving sod. This stuff's not worth much, I only took it to do his wife a favour, because the poor bitch had no food in the house.'

'Are you all right?' Meg gasped, still upset by the scene.

''Course I am. I've never yet had a man come through that door as I couldn't best, except for my damned husband. They're nervous when they come here, you see, however much they pretend not to be.' Peggy grinned. 'But it doesn't hurt to yell and shout so that everyone knows I'll take no nonsense.' She winked at Meg. 'You remember what you saw today an' start as you mean to go on. Don't ever take any lip from any of the customers an' allus keep hold of stuff until they've paid what they owe on it.'

'Does that happen often?'

Peggy shrugged. 'No, but they've all sorts of ways of cheating. I'll learn you about 'em or you'll be no use to me. There are a few women I don't trust, but it's usually the men as give me the most trouble.' She made a scornful noise in her throat. 'Ach, I've no time for men. Lazy buggers the lot of 'em. I'd never marry again. My hard work goes on my own comforts now, no one else's.' Her clenched fist thumped down on the counter to emphasise this. 'As long as you work hard, you'll be all right with me, but don't ever try to cheat me.'

Meg stood up straight and looked her employer in the eye. 'An' don't you try to cheat me, neither, Peggy Clarke.'

After a minute of astonished silence, Peggy roared with laughter. 'That's the way. Stand up for yoursen. To everyone.'

It was a fine day and people were walking or riding across the moors and past the inn. The few periods of better business in the winter, usually caused by bad weather or accidents to people's carriages or carts, had made Toby realise how lacking his place was in the basic comforts the better-off customers expected of an inn. He'd managed now to get all the central portion of the house weatherproof, so they could use the bedrooms there for travellers, but they still didn't look very welcoming. He was going to whitewash the walls as soon as the weather grew warmer, and he was going to turn the small room that led off the public room at the front into a private parlour where the gentry could sit.

'Did you have many people staying the night?' he asked Phoebe as he looked longingly at the sunshine outside.

She hesitated. 'At first we had quite a few, but Hal said it was too much trouble and he could make enough to live on just by selling beer. He could be a bit grumpy at times and gradually word got round.

The better sort of folk stopped coming here.' She sighed. 'He was allus lazy, but he was never well, either, not for years, and towards the end it tired him to do anything. So he left more and more to me. We managed, but only just sometimes.'

'And you wanted more?'

She shrugged. 'I had hopes when we got this place, but nowt ever came of them.'

'I've got hopes too. But I'm not getting into debt to do the inn up, so we'll take our time.' Toby was feeling happily settled here now that people in the village were more friendly.

He looked at the sunshine then forced himself to concentrate on what he'd planned for the day. 'I think I'll go up to the back today and see what needs fixing there. You can't do anything with a place till everything's waterproof and all the windows and doors shut properly.'

Phoebe looked at him anxiously. 'We've never needed the back part. I should leave it if I were you. Let's get the rest ready first.'

He frowned at her and decided to speak frankly. 'Why do you always look uncomfortable when I mention the back, Phoebe love? Why don't you want me to work on it?'

She hesitated, then made a helpless gesture with her hands. 'Because it makes me feel uneasy to go there. It allus has done. I doubt visitors would be happy staying there, either. If we even had enough visitors to use all the other rooms, which we don't.'

'That family didn't seem to mind it there, though.'

'They thought they were in heaven after working for Beardsworth.'

Toby didn't admit that he too had felt strange when he first went into the old part, with its high ceiling and uneven stone walls, but had later begun to feel as if the presence he sensed there was a welcoming one. Indeed, he was still drawn back there from time to time, simply to walk round or sit for a while on a bench he'd built from some old lumber and put in there. If there was a ghost it meant him no harm, he was sure, though he couldn't have said why he felt so certain of that.

'It's such a waste to have all that space doing nothing, bringing in no money. The building's pretty sound. If we can't fill it with visitors, maybe we could rent it out to someone to live in.'

Phoebe's voice was sharp. 'No one from the village would live there.'

'Why not?'

She let out a great sigh of mingled annoyance and anxiety. 'You know why: because it's haunted. Everyone knows that.'

'That's nonsense! I don't believe in ghosts.'

But he decided to leave things be for the moment. He had enough work to do getting the front of the inn ready for use. Another glance out of the window at the spring sunshine decided him. It was far too fine today to stay indoors. He felt like getting out of doors, doing something different. But what?

Suddenly he remembered his wish to better himself by learning to read and write properly, and smiled. Calling to Phoebe that he was going out for a walk, he left the inn and turned up the hill towards the tiny village church. He'd been to the services, which were held on alternate Sundays by the Curate who visited a small church in Tappersley the other weeks, borrowing Ross's horse to do so. The Parson didn't deign to waste his own precious time on such small congregations even though they were part of his parish. He left all that to his Curate.

The church at the far end of the village was not only old but the smallest Toby had ever seen. There were no signs of any attempt to heat the place and the Curate had shivered his way through the winter services, gabbling off a short sermon then speedily sending round the collecting box, though it was never very full when it was returned to him.

Toby strode along at a rapid pace, eager now to do something about learning to read properly, not to mention writing and ciphering, casting accounts – all the things that a successful innkeeper needed to know. And who better to teach him than the Curate, since there wasn't a school or teacher in Calico? Surely Mr Pickerling would agree.

Church Cottage stood next to the church, of course. It was larger than the dwellings nearby but just as shabby. Mrs Pickerling opened the door, stared at Toby and held her floury hands in the air as if eager to dash back to her baking. 'Yes?'

'I'd like to see Mr Pickerling, if you please.'

'He's writing his sermon.'

'I won't keep him more than a minute or two.'

A baby started to wail from the rear of the house and children's voices joined in a quarrel about who should pick it up. 'Well, come in quickly. Don't let all the warm air out.' She threw open a door to the left of the entry, called, 'Someone to see you, Cornelius!' and hurried away towards the rear.

Mr Pickerling looked up from his desk, keeping one finger on his book as if to mark his place. 'How may I help you, Mr Fletcher?'

'I need someone to teach me to read and write better, and I thought of you.'

The Curate frowned. He was even thinner than his wife and looked as if he never had a good meal.

'I can pay you,' Toby added.

The Curate's wary expression changed to a smile and he abandoned his book, standing up and coming round the desk. 'My dear fellow, I should be delighted to teach you. But I would have to charge sixpence an hour.' He looked anxiously at his visitor. 'Would that be all right? Only there's the paper and books and . . .'

'That'd be fine. I could come three times a week and mornings would suit me best.'

Mr Pickerling sucked in his breath audibly and pumped Toby's hand. 'A perfect time, absolutely perfect. Can you read at all?'

Toby could feel himself flushing slightly. 'Not very well. I know my letters and I can read simple words, but I never had much chance to get any real schooling. I'm bastard born and I had to help my mother and earn my bread from an early age.'

Cornelius blinked at this frank speech. 'Ah, um, yes. I see. Then we shall start with the children's primer and see how we progress. When would you like to begin?'

'Could you spare an hour now or are you too busy with your sermon?'

'I can spare an hour, two even. I'm delighted to have the chance to teach you because I'm a strong believer in universal literacy.' He saw that Toby didn't understand the words and added, 'I mean that I believe in everyone learning to read and write. Parson doesn't agree with me but I stand by my beliefs.'

Universal literacy. Toby mouthed the words to himself two or three times so that he'd remember them. Educated people spoke differently from others, using longer words, and he wanted to do the same.

Cornelius pushed some papers aside, dragged a second chair up to the desk and gestured to his new pupil to sit down, saying in that breathless voice of his that barely carried across even a tiny church, 'I'll just go and tell my wife what's happening so she'll see we're not disturbed.'

When Toby got back to the inn and told Phoebe what he'd done, she smiled. 'I'm so glad. That poor man has six chidren and must live on a pittance. His wife can barely make ends meet, for *he* must dress as a gentleman to conduct the services, however hungry the little ones are. Three sixpences a week will make a big difference to Decima Pickerling.'

'Decima?' Toby queried. 'I've never heard that name before.'

'It means tenth child, she told me once. Eh, those two may be gentry by birth, but they're poor as church mice. Folk leave presents secretly at the back door – a few eggs or apples and suchlike.'

'Can they not give the food openly?'

'If they gave it to *him*, it'd count as offerings to the parish and that greedy Parson would get most of it. I don't think *she* mentions the gifts to her husband but some days she looks very thankful, I can tell you.' She saw that Toby was amused by this and added sharply, 'We look after our own up here in Calico, as you'll find out if you're ever in need.'

'Am I one of you now?'

She nodded. 'I think so. You've made a good start anyway.'

He smiled. Not only did he live now in a place that felt like home, but he was going to learn to read properly. You couldn't ask much more of life.

8

To Mrs Goddby's dismay, Jethro insisted on helping organise the wedding celebrations and, as he was paying for them, she could hardly refuse to involve him. He checked the list of people she felt must be invited and immediately pointed to the Easdales' names.

'Not them.'

'But I can't leave the Easdales out,' she pleaded. 'They've been friends of ours for a long time.'

'They're no friends of mine, though, and I think you'll agree that the less Sophia sees of Oswin from now on the better.'

'Oh. I hadn't realised that you . . .'

He turned the conversation firmly to the refurbishing of his house, but even here Mrs Goddby couldn't prevail because Sophia refused to let her mother help her do anything with it, saying she would know better what she wanted once she'd moved into Parkside after her marriage.

On the wedding day itself everything went smoothly, and if people were there more to take a look at the groom than to wish the young couple well, it was only to be expected given the circumstances.

Andrew Beardsworth had made the effort to attend, but spent a lot of time on his own because people seemed to want to keep their distance from him in a way they didn't from Jethro. Beardsworth didn't seem put out by this, but watched the ceremony and the gathering afterwards with great interest.

Jethro asked both Harriet and Perry to see that his friend wasn't left on his own too long and was glad to see that they each made an effort to spend a few minutes with him and introduce him to their neighbours.

As soon as he could without giving offence Jethro took his bride away, waiting impatiently as she went upstairs to put on her outdoor things. He'd had enough of these people who considered themselves well-bred but looked down their noses at him without troubling to hide their scorn. He didn't call that good manners! And it certainly didn't prevent them from eating the refreshments he had provided and guzzling down the wine he'd paid for.

As he waited for his bride to come downstairs again, he overheard two people telling one another that poor Sophia had been sacrificed and was still in love with dear Oswin. He turned round to see who they were, so that he'd know them for future reference. They'd not be invited to his house.

Harriet came down the stairs and across the hall. 'Sophia's nearly ready.'

She had been very quiet all day and there had seemed to be an air of tension between the two sisters. Jethro studied her closely and took a guess as to what was upsetting her. 'Your turn next, eh?'

'If anyone ever asks me. *You* didn't, even though I was heartfree. Why didn't you? What's wrong with me?'

'I wanted Sophia. I hope you haven't been taking out your disappointment on her?'

'Of course not!'

'If you want a husband so badly, I'll find you one.'

Harriet blinked then asked hesitantly, 'You can do that?'

'As long as you don't look down your nose at money without county connections.'

'Who am I, a mere spinster, to look down my nose at anyone?'

But he had seen Sophia coming down the stairs and forgot about his companion as he moved forward to greet her. 'You look beautiful, my dear.'

Harriet stood watching them, embarrassed that she had betrayed her feelings. When her sister turned at the door for one last look back at her old home, Harriet rushed forward impulsively to hug her.

'Sorry I've been so irritable today. I was jealous. I hope you'll be very happy, love.'

Sophia hugged her back with her usual vigour. 'You'll come and visit me soon?'

'If that's all right?' Harriet's eyes went to the man standing behind her sister, who nodded as if in approval of their conversation. Two months ago they'd never met him. Now he ruled their lives, it seemed, for Perry had handed over all business matters to him.

After the newly weds had left, an old friend of the Easdales came up to Harriet, trying to find out why they had not been invited. She said only that her brother-in-law had not been on good terms with Oswin at school and had wanted nothing to spoil his special day.

'Your sister was on *very* good terms with Oswin, though,' her companion said with a nudge.

'We've all been friends with the family, Sophia no more than the rest of us.' Harriet turned away and went to talk to someone else.

After the guests had left she was able to retire to her room and stand staring out across the valley. She envied her sister. Could Jethro really find her a husband? She wanted very much to get married and no one from the county families had shown an interest, not really. Even today a few people had been wanting to know if she would now have a dowry, though of course they hadn't asked her outright, just hinted. All they cared about was money because rents were low and some of them had suffered a drop in their income. Well, she'd look for a richer husband than an impoverished land-owner. She didn't want to spend the rest of her life in genteel poverty.

But even as she thought that, Harriet sighed. It seemed neither she nor her sister was destined to marry for love, as they'd once hoped.

She might mention the possibility of finding a husband to Jethro again when she knew him a little better, or get her sister to do so. From things that had been said it was already clear that her mother was thinking Perry and Sophia would be the ones to marry, while Harriet would stay at home to look after her.

Never! she vowed. Behind that fussy exterior her mother was a tyrant.

In the carriage Jethro allowed Sophia to sit in the far corner from him and made no attempt to touch her. Time enough for that when they reached his house.

'It went well, don't you think?' she asked as the silence between them dragged on.

'Aye. But if that's county society, they're shockingly inbred. Not an intelligent face among them, and the women are nothing compared to you.'

Sophia was pleased by his compliment, having learned by now that Jethro said nothing unless he meant it. She suspected that his praise would never be couched in flowery terms, but it was nonetheless welcome because her mother never praised her daughters for anything and they always failed to live up to her expectations. Though she had been pleased that Sophia had 'caught a rich husband'. Ha! It was, in fact, the other way round: Jethro had caught her.

Feeling weary after a very early start to the day and having been on her feet for most of that time, Sophia closed her eyes and leaned back.

Her new husband's voice was quiet and deep, rather soothing, as he said, 'You look tired.'

'I am. Aren't you?'

'No. I was bored towards the end, but that's different.'

She opened her eyes and said thoughtfully, 'Not inviting the Easdales caused a lot of talk.'

'Let it. I'm not having anything to do with them. And nor are you.'

'You're very quick to give me orders.'

He shrugged. 'Only about things that matter to me. The rest of the time it's you who'll be giving the orders. I'll allow you a free hand with the house. Money's no object, but good taste is. I don't have that. The only thing I couldn't abide would be to have the rooms crammed with too much furniture.'

She was betrayed into a genuine smile. 'Like Mama does?'

His cool, controlled expression almost slipped into a smile as he nodded agreement.

'That's not to my taste either,' Sophia told him, 'which is why I waited until after we were married to make a start on the house. She won't be able to interfere now that I'm out from under her thumb. I shall enjoy my task.'

'Good.'

When they arrived at Parkside he helped Sophia from the carriage, tucked her arm through his and led her inside. The servants were lined up to greet them: three women who worked indoors and two men from outdoors. Jethro had asked if he should hire more staff but she'd told him it'd suit her better to choose her own servants. Sophia nodded and smiled at them all, then followed her husband into what he called the parlour, her mouth dry with apprehension at the way he was looking at her now, not hiding his desire for her.

He surprised her by saying, 'I'm not going to kill or torture you tonight, you know.'

She didn't like the way he seemed able to read her mind. 'It's natural for a bride to be a little nervous, is it not?'

'We can get it over with now, if you like? Then you'll see you've no need to worry about being bedded.'

She gasped and took an involuntary step backwards. *'In the daytime?'*

'You can do that sort of thing at any time of the day or night, you know.'

'I'd rather not! What would the servants think?'

He stepped forward and took her arm. 'To hell with what the servants think. I don't run my life to suit them. We'll go upstairs now.'

'Jethro, no!'

But he only chuckled and used his physical strength to force her to go with him.

'Please don't do this,' Sophia begged in a low voice, trying to pull back as they reached the landing. But she could do nothing against his superior size and strength.

'I'm not sitting round watching you work yourself into a state over something that's perfectly natural. Besides, I've waited long enough for you.'

They found the youngest maid unpacking the

mistress's bags. He said curtly, 'Do that later, Betty. We don't want to be disturbed.'

Her face completely expressionless, the maid bobbed a curtsey to her new mistress and left.

Sophia stood by the bedroom door, unable to move, her heart pounding. He pulled her further into the room and locked the door.

'I've been looking forward to undressing you,' he said, his tone mild but his eyes glittering with anticipation.

'Jethro, don't! Please wait until later.' She backed away a step or two.

He followed and put one fingertip under her chin so that she had to look him in the eyes. 'Don't try to deny me, my dear wife. I intend to be master in my own bed.' He slipped off his coat and waistcoat, untied the simple neckcloth with a muttered, 'Damned choking thing!'

Then he looked at her, standing rigid, fear in every line of her body. 'Come to bed, Sophia. I'm not going to hurt you.'

But she couldn't move, so he came across to pull her towards the bed. She fought him then, struggling wildly but in silence, for fear of the servants overhearing them. As he removed every single item of her clothing, his eyes raked her body and his fingers lingered on her most intimate parts until she thought she'd die of shame.

When he let go, she whimpered and hid under the bedclothes, but he made short work of removing the rest of his clothes and then came back to her, pulling away the sheet under which she'd huddled and saying conversationally, 'Now, Sophia, your most important lesson as a wife really begins . . .'

To her surprise he was gentle from then onwards, soothing her with murmurs, caressing her lightly at first and praising the beauty of her body. The fear subsided a little and she stilled, letting him do as he would. This was, after all, the price all women had to pay for a man's protection.

But he wasn't satisfied with her quiescence and stopped his ministrations to say, 'I'm not having you lying like a piece of dead wood beneath me every night. I'll not finish this till you respond to my touch.'

Then he began to kiss her in a far less gentle way. She was afraid to give in to the strange feelings that were now running through her and tried very hard to hold out against his skilled hands and her own traitorous body. But she couldn't and as she began to respond and move with him, finally, with a soft laugh, he took her to wife.

Afterwards she lay there in his arms, bewildered. 'Jethro, I—'

'What?'

'They told me it would hurt.'

'Only if the man's a fool and takes no care for the woman's needs. I prefer it if we both enjoy the act of love.' He threw the covers off and stood up. 'You'll want to wash now and so do I. Then we'll go down and have something to eat. I'm hungry even if you aren't.'

She watched him walk into his dressing room, naked and seemingly unashamed of that. She wished he'd stayed with her longer, talked, explained – oh, she didn't know what she wished!

She wondered if she'd ever understand him. He seemed a mass of contradictions. The last thing she'd expected today was tenderness in bed. Indeed, he'd been kind to her in his own rather direct way about several aspects of their marriage and life together, and she wasn't sure she welcomed that because she didn't *want* to like him. It would make her too vulnerable. She'd found that out with Oswin, had vowed never to trust a man again.

But still, today had been – exciting. And he had made her enjoy it.

What else would surprise her in this strange marriage of theirs?

As the weeks passed Meg grew used to her job in the pawn shop and found she enjoyed it far more than working in the mill. Peggy didn't soften towards her in any way and never stopped emphasising that she would keep the job only as long as she gave satisfaction, but Meg knew why she was doing that so it didn't worry her.

On the third day, Peggy said, 'I can see I'll have to teach you to cook. You've no idea how to get the best out of food.'

'My mother wasn't a good cook, but I'd love to learn.'

'Well, I'm a good one, or would be if I didn't have

a business to run. And I like to enjoy what I eat. I work hard for it, after all.'

She was also a good teacher, seeming to enjoy showing Meg how to cook a whole range of simple but tasty dishes. And in spite of her harsh words, Peggy allowed her new employee first chance to buy things from the shop that hadn't been redeemed, letting her have them cheaply as long as there was still a small profit involved for herself. So Meg was able to buy more crockery, a stewpot and even a wooden settle. She loved owning things, loved surprising Ben with some new item for their home.

He often told her how happy he was with her, but she knew he was sad that she hadn't fallen for a child yet. Well, she wasn't! She was relieved about it. That sort of thing could wait until later. She didn't hanker after children and if that made her strange, then so what? It certainly made their life easier. Her mother had said Ben would land her with a houseful of kids and then she'd find out what hard work really was. Yes, and misery, for you always lost one or two.

So it was with a sense of shock and disbelief that Meg waited in vain for her monthly courses in October. They just didn't arrive. She was sure she wasn't expecting because she wasn't sick in the mornings and everyone knew that was one of the first signs. She felt just the same as usual so pretended to Ben that she had her courses, which gave her a few days without making love. It wasn't that she minded him touching her, just that he wanted her too often for her own taste and she never liked to refuse in case she drove him to drink more heavily.

Weeks passed and nothing happened. The baby didn't seem real. Her breasts felt a little tender, her waist was a little thicker, but that was all. She managed to hide her condition from everyone for three months, not buying things now, but saving every farthing she could.

'I want us to have some money behind us,' she said to Ben.

'Whatever you want suits me, lass, as long as you don't stint on the food. A man gets hungry after a day's work. Though you're turning into a good cook these days.' He worked long hours because he couldn't come home till the horses were settled for the night, and there was no such thing as a day off because every day the horses always needed feeding and the stables cleaning out. Though, of course, Sundays were shorter days for him with no deliveries to make.

Christmas came and went. They celebrated in their own way, eating a small chicken that Meg picked up cheaply at the market when she was shopping for Peggy. She made it last for several meals, of course, but still, it gave a wonderful flavour to the potatoes they ate in such quantities. Most folk lived mainly on bread or oatcakes, but an Irish neighbour said potatoes were cheaper and better for the children, that they didn't get scurvy if they ate lots. The woman even went so far as to show Meg how to use the potatoes properly, cutting out the green bits, which weren't good for you and just scrubbing the skins before cooking great pots of them. If you had a little butter or suet you could fry them with chopped onion and that was delicious. If you had a little meat you could have gravy with them. After years of her mother's eternal stews, which were pallid from lack of meat, Meg was enjoying cooking the different dishes Peggy and her neighbour showed her, and Ben certainly appreciated her efforts.

But she had a new worry as well as the thought of the coming child. He had started drinking more after work, she could tell. Oh, he was never drunk, but he slurred his words slightly sometimes and laughed too readily. When she taxed him with having had more than a couple of pots, he always denied it and got angry with her.

She didn't know what to do, found herself lying awake after he'd fallen asleep, worrying about what she would do if he turned into a drunkard again. The only consolation was that he got his beer free from his employer and still handed her his full wages, so at least she wasn't going short of money because of the drinking, as many women did.

Meg continued to conceal her condition from Peggy as well as her husband. She didn't want to lose her job and knew her employer wouldn't make any allowances.

But the time was coming when she'd not be able to hide it any longer because she had suddenly started to put on weight, especially around her waist and breasts. Ben would be pleased but Peggy might dismiss her and then what would she do? Deep inside herself Meg felt a terrible craving for money and security. She'd seen how the lack of money had warped her mother, made her cling to Jack, and didn't want to become like that.

Meg wrote once to her family, but didn't give them her address and didn't write again. She couldn't face what her mother might say about Ben's increased drinking and the coming child.

One day in late October when the rain was pounding down and the coldness of the wind was a sign that winter wasn't far away, Toby decided to do a tour of his domain to check that all was still weathertight for the coming winter. He wandered through the middle area, where two bedrooms now stood ready for chance travellers, then opened the door into the rear building and went quietly inside.

He always felt a sense of wonder as he entered this ancient place, and couldn't help speculating about the many people who must have lived here over the centuries. Mr Pickerling had told him something about the history of England and had come to examine the back part of the inn, getting excited about it all over again, as he had the first time he'd seen it. Words tripping over one another, he explained that an order of monks had probably built the rear part. He'd been thrilled to see what he called the cruck method of construction, using whole trees as the framework, which he'd only read about before.

Apart from Toby's bench, the back stood empty

still because they had no use for it – no furniture except for the bench, no shelves, nothing but bare walls and flagstone floors which made his footsteps ring out more loudly. Even his breathing seemed to send echoes round these rooms. And yet that didn't worry him. Phoebe might feel nervous about coming here, but he found it peaceful and it always left him feeling more relaxed. Perhaps the monks had left some of their peace behind them, embedded in the stones, and it rubbed off on later visitors. Toby pulled a wry face at his own imaginings.

It seemed such a waste to leave it unused, though. Should he try to find someone to rent it? He frowned. He wasn't sure he really wanted other people living here. *Don't be daft!* he scolded himself. *Of course you'd rent it if it brought in more money. You need to refurbish the front of the inn.*

When Ross came in for a drink that night, Toby offered him a pot of beer in return for some advice.

His neighbour grinned. 'I never turn down a free drink.'

Toby explained and watched his companion frown, as he considered the idea.

'Folk hereabouts don't like the back place. They think it's haunted.'

'Rubbish.' But a shiver ran down Toby's spine even as he mocked the idea because he knew there was *something* there.

'Mind you, I do know of a young couple as are looking to find somewhere to live when they're wed. He's the only son of one of the farmers further down the valley on the Lancashire side and they won't be short of money. I'll ask the father if they want to have a look. The lass doesn't get on with his mother and refuses to get wed till they can have a cottage of their own.'

At a nearby table Cully had been listening, scowling at the thought of that bugger getting even more money in his pockets when hard-working men like Cully were scratching to find enough for a single pot of beer. As he considered what he could do to get back at Fletcher, a slow grin spread over his face. It'd take a bit of trouble, but it'd be worth it.

Two days later the young couple came to inspect the rear building.

'Goodness, this room is huge!' she exclaimed, but looked over her shoulder uneasily even as she spoke.

'There are three others as well,' Toby reminded her. Many young couples managed to live in only one room for years, some for their whole lives, and not rooms this size, either.

Suddenly there was a quavering wail and a barn owl flew down from the rafters, swooping round and sending the girl screaming into her young man's arms.

'It must have got in through the air vent above the door!' Toby exclaimed as he ran to open the side door. 'Stand still and stop your screeching or it'll never find its way out.'

After a few swoops the bird flew outside and the girl gave an elaborate shudder, staying within the safety of her beloved's arms.

'Bad luck, owls are, when they come inside houses,' she said. 'There'll be a death for someone connected with one of us now.'

'Nonsense!' Toby retorted. 'The poor thing just got in through some hole and couldn't find its way out again. I'll go up and check the roof tomorrow, block the hole up. It won't happen again.'

As they went into the first of the two smaller rooms, there was a low moaning sound from somewhere nearby.

The girl stopped dead, turning white. Even the young man was looking worried now.

Toby went across to the window but could see no sign of anyone. 'Probably just a lad playing tricks on us,' he said bracingly.

As they entered the other bedroom there was another low moan and this time Toby went outside to check properly. Someone must be there and he'd give them what for if he caught them.

But there was no sign of any children running away. Indeed, the village children always gave the back place a wide berth during their brief periods of freedom, preferring to run wild across the open spaces of the moor. He couldn't understand it.

When he went back inside, the young man said, 'I'm sorry, Mr Fletcher, but my Mary doesn't like it here, says it gives her the shivers. We'll have to look elsewhere for a cottage.'

When they'd gone Toby went round the place again, but couldn't find anything to explain the low moaning noise. It was exactly the sort of sound any lad would make when playing ghosts – or perhaps it was the wind blowing through some twisted hole. The wind could play strange tricks on you, especially up here where it blew fiercely sometimes across the wide spaces of the moors. Only he couldn't find any holes except for the air vent above the outside door and that had never made sounds before, even in the highest winds.

He wandered round, running one hand along the wall and counting his paces – fourteen one way, eight the other. Such a fine, big room!

He looked at the four doors along the wall, three of them leading to smaller rooms in the lean-to section along the back, which had been built at least a hundred years later than the main part, Mr Pickerling said. The second door from the left opened on to a big cupboard. He paced out the smaller rooms as well, thinking to have all the facts at his fingertips next time he talked to someone about renting it. But he stopped dead as the sums came together in his head and looked round again, whistling in surprise that he hadn't realised it before . . . 'They don't fit!' He thumped his clenched fists against the sides of his body. 'Those damned rooms don't take up the whole space on this wall. Why the hell did I not see that before?'

He walked slowly along the wall again, counting his paces with even more care and trying to make them all the same length. Then he went into each of the rooms and counted once more. No, he hadn't been wrong. The three little rooms didn't take up the whole space. They were about two paces short. He peered inside the cupboard and even thumped the back wall, but it seemed solidly built.

When he opened the door that led to the front part of the inn, he nearly bumped into Phoebe.

'I heard they didn't want to rent the place,' she said.

He ignored that in favour of the more important subject. 'Why didn't you tell me about the secret room, Phoebe love?' He cocked one eyebrow at her and waited, watching tears well in her eyes then over-flow.

'I didn't want to deceive you, Toby,' she said in a rush. 'Truly I didn't. But I was afraid to say anything. I know you say you're not a Greenhalgh and you've been kind to me, very kind indeed, but it could be dangerous for us both to speak about that room. So I thought: better to let sleeping dogs lie.'

'*Dangerous?*' That was the last word he'd have expected her to use.

She nodded.

'Why dangerous?'

'Because it concerned old Mr Greenhalgh. I don't know what his son's like, but his father was a ruth-less man, fair used to terrify everyone. My Hal took care how he dealt with him, that's for sure, and my Hal wasn't afraid of many people.'

Still trying to digest this information, Toby said firmly, 'Show me the hidden room.'

'We'll need a candle.'

'I'll fetch one.' He ran to fetch it, lighting it at the

kitchen fire and guarding the flame carefully as he walked back through the building. Phoebe was still standing near the door and hadn't moved any further inside.

Sighing, she walked across to open the cupboard, taking down a key from on top of the inside lintel of the door, a very small, narrow key. 'I was afeared you'd find it sooner or later. Hold the light so that I can see inside. The holes aren't easy to find.'

What he at first took to be a knot hole in the wood at the top of the door turned out to be a keyhole; there was a similar keyhole near the bottom. When she'd unlocked them, Phoebe hesitated, then pushed open the back of the cupboard.

As she went inside he followed her, holding up the candle so that he could look round. He thought for a moment that she was laughing softly but it must have been the sound of the wind outside. 'Do we need to prop the door open?'

'Hal never did. Said it was the best-made door he'd ever seen, perfectly balanced and not inclined to swing about.'

The hidden chamber was as deep as the other rooms, but only two paces wide. Furniture and other objects lined one wall, piled one on top of the other. The air inside felt stale and some of the contents were covered in dust and cobwebs, as if no one had touched them for a very long time. Others had clearly been moved but not in recent months, he'd guess, because the dust was starting to build up on them again.

'When Hal was sick, I came in and looked at some of the things, which he'd never let me do before. Then I thought I heard noises and ran out. I didn't come back again.'

Phoebe was whispering, though there was no need. Who was there to hear them?

'These are some of my husband's things – well, his family's things really. I heard him talk about them when he was delirious. He kept saying he should have burnt them, that it'd have been safer, but he never could bring himself to do it.'

'Why should he have burnt them?'

'Because . . . I think he wasn't entitled to them. They belonged to his sister and when she died he just took them. Hal wasn't always – well, honest.'

Toby looked round again, frowning as he tried to take this in. He didn't like the thought of having stolen goods around, that was sure.

'Later on, when he was too weak to move much, I asked Hal what I should do with this stuff if anything happened to him. He said to keep it because we could sell it if we fell on hard times, in case he never got better enough to run the inn. There was a certain person who might pay a lot of money for some of the items to prevent them from falling into the wrong hands, Hal said. He always thought he was going to get better, right till the very end, though I knew he wouldn't.'

Toby went to inspect a gate-legged table in dark wood. 'It's old-fashioned furniture but good quality.'

Phoebe hesitated then said, 'There's a picture and

a sketch done by a travelling painter. They're not very good but Hal said they were the most valuable pieces of all – and the most dangerous.'

'Did you ever find out why he said that?'

Another hesitation while she avoided his eyes. 'Better you don't know, Toby love, for your own safety.'

'I think you should tell me.'

'No. I won't do it, not even if you throw me out for it.'

He could make a fair guess, though, given who had set Hal Dixon to run the inn. The pieces must be connected with the Greenhalghs.

Phoebe's lips quivered and she asked fearfully, 'Are you angry with me? Are you going to turn me out?'

'Of course not. How would I ever manage without you?'

'You'll get married one day, then I'll have to leave.'

'If I do marry – and I'm in no hurry – it won't make any difference to you.' He put an arm round her shoulders. 'You're like an aunt to me now, Phoebe. I'll never turn you out.'

She reached up to pat his cheek. 'You're a kind man, Toby Fletcher.'

'You'll tell me the rest of the secret one day, though.' He didn't know why he believed this so strongly, but he did.

She pushed him away. 'No, I won't. I think too much of you. You'll *never* persuade me to tell you. And if you try to force me, I'll run away.'

She was so agitated he patted her shoulder and spoke soothingly. 'Well, give me the key and go back to the public room. We don't want customers helping themselves to the beer, do we?' A thought occurred to him before she'd gone more than a few paces and he stuck his head out of the secret room to call, 'Wait a minute. Would you let me sell a piece or two of this furniture in Halifax? We need money to pay for proper refurbishments so that the inn can flourish again. I'll pay you back later, I promise.'

She looked at him and shrugged. 'I don't mind what you do with it, Toby love. It's doing no good here, is it?'

'Thanks.'

He watched her go, then went back to study the contents of the secret room. This could help a lot. Not that he was doing it to make his damned father proud, no, it was because his mother would have liked to see him do well. And because of his own pride in doing everything as well as he could.

As Toby walked slowly down the narrow storeroom, he lifted dust covers to reveal small pieces of furniture, old-fashioned but beautifully made, with inlay work on some pieces. These were definitely the sort of things rich people owned. He could have used them in the rooms set aside for the gentry, only . . . someone might recognise them.

He found the pictures Phoebe had mentioned, hidden under a pile of table linen. They were quite small, so how could they be the most valuable things here? The painting showed a young man and woman, arm in arm, dressed in their best finery. The man was tall and dark-haired, but the artist couldn't have been very good because in Toby's opinion neither of the faces looked like real people's. The sketch showed a young woman sitting staring across the moors, and he guessed it must have been done by someone else because it was much better than the painting. She was pretty and smiling, younger than he was now, perhaps even the same woman as in the painting. He'd have liked to meet her.

Well, he'd probably never find out who she was so no use wasting his time staring at her. With a shrug he put the pictures back and closed up the storeroom. As he came out into the big room the wind seemed to blow more loudly, rattling the window panes and whirling dust and debris about outside. Maybe there was a storm brewing up.

On second thoughts he decided to leave the things where they were for the time being. There must have been some good reason for Phoebe's husband to hide them here and until Toby knew what it was, he would do nothing.

Ben was jubilant when he found out about Meg's condition. 'Eh, we've done it, lass! We've made our first babby. When will it be born?'

'In July, near as I can work out.'

He paused, counting on his fingers. 'Why didn't you tell me afore?'

'I wanted to be sure.'

'Well, I suppose it doesn't matter – women get

strange fancies in their heads when they're expecting – but tell me straight off next time, love. It'll be better to have the babby in the summer. Makes it easier with the washing. They use a damned lot of clouts at first.'

Meg burst into tears. 'I didn't want a baby yet! I wanted to save some more money.' She looked round. 'I've spent too much on furniture. I wish I hadn't now.'

He put his arms round her. 'Don't be silly. I'm earning enough to keep you and the babby. And you'll love it when it's born, see if you don't. They're grand little creatures, babbies are.'

She watched his expression grow sad. 'It must have been hard to lose your wife and child like that.' He nodded, his lips going into a thin, tight line. She'd already found that he didn't like to talk about his loss. 'My mother says you shouldn't love babies till you're sure they'll live.'

'She would, the old witch! I don't reckon she loves anyone but hersen. Any road, you allus lose some of the childer. Life's like that. But you can love 'em while you've got 'em, can't you?'

Meg shivered, then grew angry. 'Don't talk about losing them, Ben! It's asking for trouble.'

'Sorry, lass. But it's best to face facts. Any road, we might not lose any of ours. Some folk don't. You're a strong, healthy lass. My first wife were allus sickly, even afore the child. No, we'll be all right, you and me.'

But she knew he was just saying that to keep her

happy. Every family lost a child or two. Even her mother had had other children, one born dead, one losing its life after a few months. Was that what had soured Netta, or had she always been so unkind?

Well, *she* intended to be kind to all her children, loving them equally. She'd never treat one as she'd been treated. Even now, months before it was born, Meg was starting to love the child lying so cosy in her belly. That had surprised her.

PART 3
1829

9

May that year was a month of contradictions, warm days followed by cool, rain and on one memorable occasion sleet, which brought people gaping to windows and doorsteps, and played havoc with the tender young plants.

The first week of June showed little improvement and everyone kept saying how poor spring had been, that summer was shaping to be the same, that the weather hadn't been as chancy as this when they were young.

Ben's hands had been raw and chapped all winter, and he'd grumbled about the snow and frost which he hated with a passion. He'd started to drink more heavily, giving as his excuse that a man had to have something inside him to keep the cold out, his eyes daring Meg to answer him back. She'd have spoken up if she'd felt it would make any difference, but she knew it wouldn't. The more she nagged him the more he drank, so she'd learned to keep quiet.

But she felt cheated after all his promises, and his drinking made her even more determined to continue working. She made sure her employer could never say that her condition affected her work but some days she grew so tired that when she got home she spent the whole evening lying on some sacks in front of the fire huddled in a blanket, too exhausted even to think properly let alone prepare a meal.

Ben grew increasingly worried and began urging her to stop work, but she refused. She hadn't told him but was still hoping to return to work soon after the birth. With only one child, that should be possible, surely?

As the baby was due within the month she would have to speak to Peggy about it and beg her mistress to continue employing her. Surely she had given enough satisfaction to merit that? Peggy would easily be able to find someone temporary to help her out for a few days till Meg had recovered from the lying-in because there were always people seeking work.

She'd have to find someone to look after the baby but Meg thought Rhona next door might do it, because she had a baby of her own – though Rhona wasn't as careful with her child as Meg would have liked. But everyone in their road was short of money and glad of a chance to earn a penny or two extra. Meg didn't know her other neighbours very well because she worked such long hours, just enough to nod to or pass the time of day mostly. She ought to make a bigger effort to talk to the other women in the street and would do if only she wasn't so tired all the time.

She was serving a customer when a man rushed into the pawn shop, calling, 'Come quick, missus, your man's hurt!'

After a startled glance at Peggy, Meg ran after him, snatching her shawl from the hook as she passed it because it was another cool day.

'What's happened to Ben?' she called to the man, who was already hurrying off.

He turned to look at her, hesitated, then said brusquely, 'He's had a fall. Hurry up! Mr Brooks said to fetch you quick.'

She couldn't keep up with him. He kept looking back at her impatiently and urging her on, but in her condition she couldn't move any faster and soon had to stop for a moment, panting and bending over as she got a stitch in her side. 'Where are we going?' she asked when she could gather enough breath to speak.

'To the brewery.' He set off walking again.

She followed, but more slowly this time. 'I thought Ben was delivering on the south side of town this morning?'

'He got back, didn't he? Needed to fetch another load. Now save your breath and get a move on!'

So Meg forced herself onwards, stumbling, trying to ignore the stitch in her side and the increasing heaviness of her legs.

There was a crowd of people at the gates of the brewery, peering into the yard and talking excitedly to one another. They parted when they saw her coming and she heard mutters as she passed through the gap.

'That's the wife.'

'She's only young.'

'Eh, poor thing, she's expecting.'

Meg slowed down, as much from fear as from lack of breath now. Why were they calling her 'poor thing'? Inside the yard she saw a group of men behind one of the drays, with the owner of the brewery standing a little apart from the others and looking unusually solemn.

When Mr Brooks saw her he hurried across. 'Your Ben's bad, Mrs Pearson. He fell off the dray backwards and hit his head. He's still unconscious.'

She blinked and the words began to repeat themselves inside her head, though without real meaning. *Fell. Hit his head. Still unconscious.* She couldn't utter a word so pushed past Mr Brooks. The men parted to let her get to her husband, who was lying frighteningly still on the ground.

She knelt beside him. 'Ben?' She shook his arm but his eyes were closed and he wouldn't look at her. *'Ben, wake up! Ben!'* She could smell beer on his breath and asked, 'Had he been drinking?'

The men muttered to one another and when she looked at them, avoided her eyes. She knew then. Knew what had caused Ben to be careless. She pressed her lips together to hold back the red hot wave of fury. Drink! She hated it.

Then she looked back at her husband and the fury faded, leaving only pity. He was pale and still, his breath hardly stirring his chest. And he was a kind man in spite of the drinking, had never laid a finger on her, didn't deserve this.

The bystanders started muttering again but none of their comments made any sense to Meg because she had suddenly caught sight of the blood on the setts below his head. Ben's blood. A whole puddle of it. She moaned, pressing one hand to her mouth and collapsing across his body, sobbing, begging him over and over again not to leave her, to wake up, come back to her.

They had to pull her away when the doctor arrived. He conducted a cursory examination and shook his head as he stood up. 'There's very little we can do for the injuries to his head, I'm afraid.'

'But he's not dead?' Mr Brooks asked. 'Surely there's a chance?'

The doctor shrugged. 'There's always a chance as long as they're breathing. You can never tell with head wounds. Has he moved at all? Moaned? Twitched?'

'I wasn't there when it happened.' Mr Brooks looked at the men, who shook their heads.

'Then it's just a question of wait and see.'

As soon as the doctor stepped back, Meg flung herself down by her husband again.

'Nay, we can't leave her there.' A man bent to tap her on the shoulder. 'You'll have to get up now, missus. We need to move your husband. We'll bring him home to you and you can look after him.'

The doctor looked at her and stepped forward. 'Is this the wife?'

'Aye. Not long wed.'

'She looks very close to her time.' He raised his voice, speaking slowly and loudly, as if to an idiot. 'How long until the child's due, Mrs . . . um . . .'

He looked round for enlightenment on her name.

'Pearson.'

'Thank you. How long now, Mrs Pearson?'

She replied without taking her eyes off Ben. 'Just under a month, doctor.'

He spoke to the men again. 'She can't look after him, not in that condition. He's too heavy. And as you can see, she's taking it badly, not thinking clearly. It's her condition. Childbearing affects the female brain.' Once more he raised his voice, 'Are there no relatives to assist you, Mrs – um – Pearson?'

She shook her head, feeling impatient with his questions, wanting only to be with Ben for when he regained consciousness.

He turned to the men and said in a low voice, 'Dealing with the weight of a man's inert body could bring on the birth too suddenly and that might be dangerous for both her and the child. You'd better take him to the Spotland Workhouse. They'll see to him. Tell them I'll call in later to arrange admission.'

There was silence at this. The workhouse was a place of last resort for old folk who had softening of the brain or lunatics or those dying of a growth. Most people would do anything rather than go in there, although the overseer at Spotland was a decent man, at least, and looked after his charges better than most folk in his position did.

'I'll fetch my wife to help her,' Frank said suddenly. 'Livvy's good when there's trouble.'

The doctor nodded. 'I'll leave you to take him to the workhouse, then. I have other patients to see. I'll

call in there on my way home to check how he is.'
After another glance at Meg he left, shaking his head
and looking solemn as he walked across the yard with
Mr Brooks.

It was ten minutes before Frank returned with his
wife, minutes during which it began to rain. After a
hurried consultation, the men persuaded Meg to
move away and carried Ben into one of the sheds on
an old door.

She followed, weeping quietly but with such a tone
of despair in those soft sounds that the men shuffled
from one foot to the other, each wishing another
would think of something to say to comfort her.

When Livvy Price pushed her way through the
group, plump and capable, there was a collective sigh
of relief.

She pulled Meg gently to her feet and put an arm
round her. 'Eh, this is a bad business, it is that.'

But Meg didn't even look at her.

'See how she's shivering, poor lass!'

'I think we should get her home,' one man said.
'Stands to reason she'll be better off there.'

Like the doctor, Livvy raised her voice slightly
when addressing Meg, who didn't seem to understand what was going on round her. 'We'll have to get
you home and warm, love, or you'll hurt the babby.'

At last the words sank in and she shook her head.
'I'm going with Ben.'

Livvy looked round questioningly. 'Where's he
going?'

Her husband supplied the information. 'Doctor

said to take him to the workhouse, said she can't look after him in that condition.'

'Then why is he still lying here on the ground? Why haven't you taken him?' Her voice was filled with scorn.

Someone went to consult Mr Brooks, who had retreated to the warmth of his office, then they came back and lifted Ben on to a small cart belonging to the brewery.

Meg wouldn't leave his side, or even consider returning home.

'We'll ride with him on the cart then,' Livvy said in the end.

At the workhouse the overlooker received them, gazing at Ben's inert body then back to Livvy, who seemed to be in charge. When told the doctor had ordered the man to be admitted, he sighed and showed them where to carry the unconscious figure.

'You'll have to leave now,' he told Meg. 'We'll see to your husband, don't worry.'

'Wait outside for us,' Livvy hissed to the men who'd brought them. 'She's in no state to walk home.'

'I want to stay with him,' Meg protested.

The overlooker shook his head. 'Sorry, love. No visitors are allowed until the doctor has examined the patient and given his instructions.'

'But the doctor's just seen him!'

'Well, he hasn't given *me* any instructions, and anyway we only allow visiting in the mornings except for the dying.'

'You need to get home and warm yourself up,

love,' Livvy interrupted. 'Think of the babby if you won't think of yourself.'

Meg found herself without strength to resist any longer and walked out with her companion. At the gates she turned round to look at the workhouse and the high walls that surrounded it, with the River Spodden flowing behind. 'I don't like to think of him shut in there.'

'You can't look after him yourself, you know you can't. Come on. We'll take you home.'

But when Meg tried to walk pain shot through her and she doubled up, crying out and clutching her belly.

Livvy put a hand on her abdomen and felt its rigidity. 'Dear Lord, she's started having the baby! It's the shock that's brought it on.' She looked round. 'Maybe we should take her back inside.'

Meg wasn't so far gone in pain that she didn't understand this. 'I'm not having my baby in that place! I'm having it in my own home.'

Livvy sighed in resignation. 'I don't blame you. I wouldn't, either.' She turned to the two men from the brewery. 'Help me get her on the cart.'

Meg didn't notice the journey back, too caught up with the pain that was tearing her body apart. She clung to the older woman, groaning as the contractions racked her.

'Eh, she's coming on fast,' Livvy worried. 'Can't you get that horse to move any more quickly?'

'No, missus.'

'Where does she live?'

'Moss Row.'

When they reached the street, the men denied any knowledge of the house number so Livvy shook Meg to get her attention and, when she indicated the house, the men carried her inside. They stood just inside the door, still holding her, looking round uncertainly.

'Well, get her upstairs!' Livvy ordered. 'Can you think of nothing for yourselves?'

They rolled their eyes at one another then went up the narrow stairs, grunting with the effort. After laying Meg down on the bed they turned round, eager to get away.

But Livvy was barring the doorway. 'One of you fetch a neighbour. I can't do this on my own.'

'Right.'

'And the other one can light the fire for me and get some water on to boil.'

The man nearest the door edged outside with a quick, 'I'll go and find a neighbour to help.' The one left behind clattered down the stairs to the kitchen, looking anxiously back over his shoulder because Meg was crying out in pain now.

Shaking her head at the cruelty of life and the help-lessness of men when faced with a birthing, Livvy turned to deal with Meg, who had forgotten her worries about her husband as her body's needs took over.

One morning in May Sophia Greenhalgh found her head swimming when she tried to get up, so let it drop back on the pillow. A wave of nausea overtook her and she pushed aside the bedclothes in frantic haste, running to vomit into her washbowl. Shivering, she crept back to bed and rang for her maid.

'Eh, shall I send for the master?' Betty asked.

'No, you shan't.'

'But you're ill. He'll kill me if I don't tell him.'

'I'm not ill. I'm expecting a child, that's all! And I don't want him told about this yet.'

'I'm sorry, ma'am, but for the life of me, I dursn't keep it from him. He'll turn me off if I do.'

So Jethro was sent for and came back from the mill, striding into the bedroom he'd left two hours previously. 'What's wrong, Sophia? They said you weren't well.'

She glowered at Betty, who shuffled her feet and avoided her eye. Waving one hand in dismissal, Sophia waited until the maid had slipped out of the bedroom before turning to her husband. 'I'm not ill. I think I'm having a child, that's all.'

'Ah.' He looked at her with immense satisfaction.

Sophia was aching for a cuddle or some sign of affection at this important moment in their lives, but he made no move towards her and she soon dismissed that foolish hope. Who should know better than she that the only affection Jethro showed was in the marriage bed? And that was probably only to help satisfy his own needs.

'We'll have the doctor over to examine you,' he said.

'What on earth for? I'm not ill, just having a baby. It's perfectly normal to be sick in the mornings from all I've heard.' And she'd heard a lot since she got married. It was as if she'd joined a club and the other matrons spoke quite frankly in front of her now.

'Nonetheless we'll let him check you. No need to take risks.'

Sophia glared at him, but he wasn't looking at her.

He moved across to the window. 'You'll not go riding until after it's born. And you'll do no physical work. Are you sure we have enough servants? Do we need to hire more?'

'I don't do any physical work now and of course we have enough servants.'

'Good. But we must make sure you lead a quiet life.'

She sighed and leaned back, closing her eyes. To her astonishment he came across to the bed then and pressed a quick kiss on her cheek before moving away, avoiding her eyes again as if he'd done something to be ashamed of.

'I'll leave you to rest. You should stay in bed till the doctor has seen you.'

Sophia said nothing. Better to get up after he'd left than to defy him openly or he'd order the servants to keep her in her room. She had already learned how ruthless Jethro could be when he wanted something – or perhaps ruthless was the wrong word? He wasn't a cruel man. Adamant or determined might be better ways of describing him when he wanted something done a certain way. The servants and mill workers always rushed to obey his orders.

In fact, he wasn't at all the kind of man she'd thought him when they married, but a much more complicated creature.

She sometimes wondered what it would have been like to marry Oswin. Would he have been so firmly in charge of their lives or would he have left things to her? Probably the latter. She had come to the conclusion that Oswin always took the easiest route and Jethro the most direct. And Oswin had lain with other women at the same time as he was courting her. She hated the thought of that. She knew now that many men, sometimes highly respected men, were unfaithful to their wives, but for some reason felt certain that Jethro wasn't. He wasn't the sort of man to flirt idly and, besides, he wanted her nearly every night. When would he have found time for others?

Would the child make a difference to her, to them? Would being a mother help her to settle down and find some measure of personal happiness?

Her brother had never been as content as he was now, pursuing his interest in botany and leaving the estate management to Jethro. It made her angry to see Perry so heedless of his duties. Her mother was delighted to have the burden of debt lifted from her shoulders and now asked her son-in-law's advice about everything she did, so afraid was she of ever being short of money again. That utter dependence irritated Sophia.

Only Harriet was unhappy because she desperately wanted a husband and home of her own.

It was all too much. Sophia closed her eyes, and the

next thing she knew Betty was waking her up because the doctor had arrived. He hovered a short distance away asking detailed questions, phrasing things delicately, as if she didn't understand what was happening to her own body.

As she'd expected he pronounced her to be in excellent health, though how he knew that without even touching her, she couldn't work out. And he spoke to her as if she'd lost half her wits.

When Jethro came up to see her after the doctor had left she was still furious about that and told him so in no uncertain terms.

He grinned at her. 'I don't like him either, but he knows more than I do about looking after women in your condition.'

'How can he when he didn't even touch me? I think any midwife would know ten times as much as him.'

Jethro went away looking thoughtful.

Sophia got dressed and made it very plain to her household that she was still in charge and didn't intend to lie in bed till the child was born.

After the birth was over Livvy said, 'It's a girl, Meg love. Eh, you were lucky it all happened so quickly. There's some as take days to give birth.'

Meg lay there exhausted, eyes closed, trying to take in the fact that she had a daughter. She opened her eyes to see Rhona shaking her head and exchanging glances with Livvy as they looked down at the child cradled in Livvy's brawny arms.

Terror shot through Meg. 'What's wrong with her?' She pushed herself up on one elbow but had to repeat her question before they'd answer.

It was Livvy who said gently, 'Not wrong exactly, but she's not a strong baby, Meg love. She came a bit early, didn't she, and she's quite small? It's always harder to raise them when they come early.'

'Give her to me!'

They passed over the bundle and she had her first sight of her daughter's face, such a bonny baby with fine, wispy blonde hair and blurred-looking blue eyes. But she was also wan looking and much smaller than other babies Meg had seen. In fact, the poor little creature looked downright weary. Well, Meg felt tired herself. She'd like to sleep for a month! It was hard work birthing a child.

With a sinking feeling she suddenly remembered Ben. How could she have forgotten? 'Have you had any word from the workhouse?'

'No, love.'

Poor Ben. He might never see his daughter. It took all Meg's strength of will not to dissolve into tears at that thought, but she knew the baby had only her to rely on so she daren't give in to her anxiety. She bent to kiss the delicate forehead then said in a low voice, pausing a couple of times to swallow the sobs that were nearly overwhelming her, 'I'm going to call her Helen – for Ben's mother. It's the name he wanted if we had a girl.'

'It's a pretty name. He'll be glad about it when he gets better.'

Meg grasped Livvy's arm. 'You do think he'll get better?'

'Eh, what do I know, love? Even the doctor didn't know. But Ben's alive, so you have a chance at least.'

'Yes. There's a chance, isn't there?'

'Now then, stop worriting and let me clean you up. You've a daughter to care for now as well as a husband. Life has to go on.'

Meg allowed them to treat her as they would. She was sore, exhausted, could feel the blood trickling from her as it did during her monthlies. They'd found rags for that.

When Livvy finished she asked, 'Is there someone who can come in to help you?'

Meg shook her head. 'I'll manage.'

'You should stay in bed, for the first day at least.'

Meg looked down at her daughter. 'How can I? She only has me. And anyway, I have to go and see Ben.'

'You can't! It's a long walk out there.'

'I have to.'

'I'll do your shopping for you tomorrow,' Rhona offered. 'I can fetch what you want when I'm buying my own stuff. You can go and see Ben in a day or two when you're a bit stronger.'

'Thanks.'

Livvy stood up. 'I have to get back now to see to my own family. Rhona will drop in later. Just put the babby to the breast when it wakes up. They don't need showing how to suck.'

The infant was lying asleep beside her so Meg allowed herself to drift off into sleep too.

She was woken by the baby's thin crying but it stopped almost immediately as if the effort had been too tiring. Meg listened but there was no sound from downstairs, so she supposed she must be alone. For a moment fear filled her. How could she possibly manage this without help, without a husband? Then the baby whimpered and that sound helped her to pull herself together.

Picking up her daughter, she bared her breast, putting the little mouth next to her nipple and waiting for the infant to start sucking. But the tiny baby didn't seem to know what to do and her whole face screwed up again as another thin, drawn-out wail issued from her mouth and stuttered quickly into silence.

'Come on now, love, drink your milk,' Meg whispered, running one fingertip down the child's soft cheek and over her lips. And to her delight it happened: the child opened and shut her mouth once or twice, then fastened on the nipple and began to suck.

Tears of joy welled in Meg's eyes at this miracle and the feeling that ran through her as she felt the soft little lips taking their milk from her breast. She bent to plant the lightest of kisses on the child's forehead. 'I love you, Helen.'

She frowned down. The name they'd agreed on didn't sound right, was far too grown-up for such a tiny infant. 'Nell, then. I'll call you Nell.'

But that didn't sound right, either. Very tentatively she tried 'Nelly.' And it sounded perfect. 'My little

Nelly,' she repeated, kissing the nearest cheek. 'That's what I'll call you. You can save Helen for when you're grown up.'

And whatever those women said, her daughter *was* going to grow up. Meg would make sure that her Nelly grew big and strong like other children, if she had to work her fingers to the bone to pay for good food and warm clothing. Her child wasn't going to want. And Ben was going to get better. He must. They both needed him so badly.

The following morning Meg got ready, wrapped the baby in layers of clothes and an old shawl she'd bought from the shop, and went outside.

Rhona appeared at her door, gaping. 'Whatever are you doing?'

'Going to see Ben.'

'But the workhouse is over a mile away.'

'I'll manage.' Meg set off, not wanting to waste her energy on arguing.

She was exhausted by the time she got there, but straightened her clothing and shushed the baby, who was a bit fretful, before knocking on the door.

A woman opened it and told her she couldn't go in, so Meg pushed her aside and went in anyway.

They brought the overseer to her and he sent for the Matron, who tutted at them all and asked if they had no kindness for a woman who'd borne a child only the day before?

'Your husband's still the same,' she said. 'Eh, you

look that pale, lass. Have you eaten owt this morning?'

'I forgot.'

'Then you'll have summat afore you see him. You'll do no one any good by fainting from hunger.'

She sat the young woman down and insisted she drink a cup of tea and eat a piece of bread and butter before going any further.

This simple act of kindness brought tears to Meg's eyes and she said, 'Thanks,' in a husky voice before eating the bread, suddenly ravenous.

'Can I see my husband now?' she asked the minute she'd finished.

'I'll take you up.'

They went into a narrow room even smaller than their bedroom at home and Matron waved her hand at the bed on which Ben lay. 'As you can see, we're keeping him clean and warm, but the doctor says there's nowt else we can do. We must let Nature take her course.'

'Can I stay with him a bit?'

'Aye. I'll send someone to fetch you in half an hour, then you'd better get yoursen home and have a lie-down.'

So Meg sat beside Ben and took hold of his hand. It seemed natural to talk to him. 'I've brought your daughter to meet you, Ben. I do hope you'll hurry up and wake. She's so lovely and we really need you.' She gulped back the tears that threatened and went on talking to him, but he made not a single sign of hearing or understanding and eventually her voice tailed away. His face had a pale, waxy colour and his breathing was so shallow she had to lean forward to make sure he was still alive.

When Matron came for her, Meg was glad to leave. The silence in the little room made her feel as if she was alone.

It seemed a very long way home again and when Rhona saw her, she exclaimed in dismay and made Meg go straight up to bed. 'I'll leave you to sleep, but I'll be in again later to see if you need owt.'

But Meg wasn't able to rest until she'd fed Nelly and the baby kept stopping and having to be coaxed into feeding again, so that took a long time. In the end, Meg changed the wet clouts and let her daughter sleep, falling asleep herself out of sheer exhaustion, not even attempting to get anything to eat.

10

Although he was still tempted, Toby did nothing about the things he'd discovered because he was afraid of getting Phoebe into trouble. He locked up the secret chamber and rarely went into it, though for some reason he had a hankering every now and then to see the sketch of the young woman.

Phoebe still refused to say who she was and wept when he pressed her.

Sometimes it felt as though he could hear echoes in the big room – soft footsteps, the faintest of far-away singing, a door closing.

It made him smile wryly. He was getting altogether too fanciful! It was likely all the new knowledge that was stirring up his brain, because learning to read and write properly was taking up an increasing amount of his energy and attention. Even running the inn couldn't compete with the fascination of learning about other countries, other people's lives, the history of his own country. So many things he hadn't known. So many things still to learn.

Just to dip his quill into the ink pot and write words that made sense and looked neat and orderly thrilled Toby, and as for ciphering . . . well, he found that easiest of all. Once you'd learned how to write the numbers and recite the multiplication tables, suddenly you could do a whole host of calculations with the greatest of ease.

Other men in the village made fun of him for wasting so much of his time with the Curate and spending good money on lessons and books, but Toby didn't care.

Mr Pickerling said it was a sheer pleasure to teach such a willing and able pupil. Toby suspected that the Curate was lonely, because there was no one else of his station in the village. Yet although they were gentry, the Pickerlings were as poor as anyone else and couldn't afford to visit people outside Calico, even if the Parson who employed Cornelius had been friendly enough to invite them to dine, which he wasn't.

Toby had met the old Parson when he came for one of his rare visits to the village and had been affronted by the patronising tone of his voice and the sneering expression on his face.

Well, what did he care about the Parson? The inn was bringing him in enough to live on and a bit to spare, and that was all Toby needed. His previous ambitions for the place had faded somewhat in comparison with the intense pleasure of learning. Buying his first book gave him more joy than higher takings from the inn ever could. He had never thought to own a book and now intended to buy others, and newspapers too.

Ross popped into the inn regularly. He would sip

his ale slowly, not being the sort to get outright drunk, and chat to his friends, but always made time to talk to Toby as well. The other men took their lead from him, all except Cully Dean who seemed to have found the money to buy his drinks these days, but who was as surly as ever. In some ways Toby felt himself to be still an outsider, not truly one of them. Well, hadn't he always been an outsider, bastard born and an easy target for bullying until he grew big enough to stand up for himself?

When you had a book to read, though, you had a friend who didn't look down on you.

One morning Phoebe found him reading in the back part of the inn. She sat down beside him and took the book from him. 'I've been wanting to talk to you for a while, Toby love.'

'Can't it wait till later?'

'No. Later there'll be people wanting drinks and we'll be interrupted.' She clutched the book to her chest, then took a deep breath and said in a rush of words, 'Toby, an unmarried young man like you ought to be courting. I want you to have a happy life, and that means a family of your own.'

He looked at her cheekily. 'Will any woman do or can I wait till I find one I really fancy?'

'Toby, I'm being serious!'

'I know you are, but—'

'I've never had children of my own, always regretted it, and you will too if you don't do something about it. Besides, if you had some children, I could be a sort of grandmother to them, couldn't I?'

Her wistful, hopeful tone came nearer than anything else to convincing him, but somehow he couldn't bring himself to marry just for the sake of it. If he found a woman he couldn't live without – and he didn't see that happening – things might change. 'I'm sorry, Phoebe love, but I doubt I'm the marrying sort.'

'Have you never fancied courting anyone?'

'No.'

'You don't – dislike women?'

'Of course not.'

'I mean, you don't dislike the idea of bedding them? Some men do.'

His big hand covered hers and he said gently, 'I've bedded one or two over the years, but I didn't want to wed them any more than they wanted to wed me. Leave it be, Phoebe. I'm not looking for a wife.'

But she began introducing him to young women from the neighbourhood and in the end he had to be rude about that to her – and to them – before folk would leave him alone. Why was there such a conspiracy to get young fellows wed?

For a time he took up with the widow of a man in the village because his body had its own needs and these could be urgent. He enjoyed Jenny's body if not her conversation. The books and reading suffered, as did his hours of sleep, since Jenny didn't want her relatives knowing about them, he had to creep out to see her after the inn had closed.

Phoebe guessed what was happening and didn't

know whether to be glad or sorry. Jenny wasn't the sort of woman she wanted for her Toby. She suspected that the widow was simply looking for another husband and Toby was the best prospect in the district. But somehow Phoebe didn't dare interfere.

When, after a few weeks, Toby started going round with a scowl on his face and making sharp remarks about widows who wanted to trap a man into marriage whether he was interested or not, she guessed that he had been given his marching orders. And sure enough, there was no more creeping out after the inn had closed – as if she hadn't heard the stairs creaking!

A month later the eager widow married a man from Todmorden and moved away from the village. Toby bought some more books and read half the night as well as the day, using up good candles as if the cost meant nothing.

Phoebe tried to take her comfort from the fact that he was happier again and that, even without his taking a deep interest, custom from passing travellers was picking up a little. Word was getting out about her cooking, the quality of the beer and the comfort of the beds. She knew, because friends further down the valley had told her that.

One night more fugitives from down the valley appeared and this time Ross and Toby worked together to hide them and then get them away safely. That gave Phoebe fresh cause for concern. She didn't want her Toby getting on the wrong side of

Mr Beardsworth. Toby might be big and able to defend himself, but Mr Beardsworth was both rich and ruthless.

Eh, why couldn't life be calmer? Why did there always have to be something to worry about?

Ben Pearson didn't regain consciousness after the accident and faded away before Meg's eyes. She went out to Spotland to visit him every day and each visit found him looking thinner, frailer, his breathing so faint and slow you had to bend ever closer to hear it. At first she'd clung to hope, but it faded and now all she had was the desperate need to be there every morning because it was the only thing she could do for him.

They'd tried dripping water into his mouth, but he made no attempt to swallow it. They didn't even try to feed him.

One day the doctor was there when Meg arrived and took her aside. 'I'm sorry, but it can't be long now, Mrs Pearson.'

She held Nelly tightly, glad to have something warm to cling to, until the baby protested with an angry little mewing sound.

Matron said she should stay there that night, and she did. They brought her food and were kind to her, but she couldn't eat, knowing that Ben was literally starving to death.

Just after the moon had risen he stopped breathing. Meg knew at once that he'd gone because the room seemed to be filled with a special stillness, and with echoes of sadness and regret as if he was sorry to leave her. She didn't call anyone but sat on, knowing that they would take the last of him away from her when they found out he was dead.

In the morning Matron came in, saw what had happened and drew her to her feet. 'I see he's passed away, love. He has a more peaceful look on his face now, doesn't he?'

Meg could only nod. Her voice seemed drowned in tears.

'What about the burial? We can see to that for you, love, if you like.'

Meg shook her head vigorously. 'No! He's not being buried in a pauper's grave. I'll pay for a proper funeral.'

'How?'

'They took up a collection at the brewery so I have some money.'

'You'd be better spending that on yourself and the baby. You've lost weight. You aren't eating properly, are you? Eh, you need to keep your strength up for the baby's sake.'

Meg couldn't seem to think about herself, not yet. 'My Ben has to have a proper funeral,' she insisted.

'But he's beyond knowing, love,' Matron said gently, 'an' you have a child to look after now.'

'He's having a grave of his own an' that's flat.' Meg looked pleadingly at the other woman. 'Can you bring his body home to me? Please? I want him to lie in his own home one last time.' She looked round sadly and added, 'Not here.'

The funeral took place the following day. Meg insisted on attending and taking her baby too, though Rhona had offered to look after the child. 'Thank you, but Nelly will be glad one day that she was there at her father's funeral, I know she will.'

Rhona rolled her eyes and said no more. As if an infant would remember!

The coffin was carried from the little house to the church on a brewery dray and some of the men were given an hour off to walk behind it with Meg, because Mr Brooks prided himself on doing things properly where death was concerned.

The wooden box looked small sitting in the middle of the dray where the two slightly upward-sloping halves of the floor met in a lower channel at the middle. No chance of the coffin bouncing off, Meg thought as she walked behind it, because the dray had been designed to keep barrels of ale in place safely.

Nelly was asleep against her. She wished the child would wake. No, she didn't. She wished *she* could sleep like Nelly. But she'd hardly slept a wink last night and today her mind kept drifting. Just put one foot in front of the other, she told herself. That's all you need to do.

Inside the church someone led her to the front where she sat on her own. The Curate came to take the service, gabbling the words so quickly she wanted to call out to him to slow down, to remember that in that coffin lay a man who had a right to be treated with respect. But she didn't dare so the service went on at breakneck speed. Nelly slept the whole time.

Afterwards the men from the brewery lifted up the cheap coffin and carried it out to the hole that had already been dug at the back of the graveyard, a place where there were no fancy headstones and statues, just plain strips of stone lying on the ground in squares that framed the graves, with the names of those buried there carved in their sides.

'Oh, no! I forgot about a stone,' Meg exclaimed.

Mr Brooks, who had also attended, said brusquely, 'I'll get one made. Now, Mrs Pearson, let the Curate finish.'

When they'd lowered the coffin and thrown in some dirt, the men from the brewery obeyed a jerk of the head from their employer and moved away, muttering, 'Sorry about your loss, missus.'

Mr Brooks cleared his throat and took Meg's arm. 'Let the gravediggers do their work now, my dear.'

She stepped back, thinking of poor Ben lying there under all that damp earth, then became aware that her companion had pressed some coins into her hand.

'Just a little extra to see you and the baby through till you're on your feet again,' he muttered, tipping his hat and walking away.

She looked down at the coins. There weren't many. Was that all a man's life was worth? But most employers wouldn't have been half as generous so she shouldn't complain, because the men had taken a collection so this must be from Mr Brooks himself.

The gravediggers paid her no attention. It was a

cool day with rain threatening and she was damp and
shivering, but she stayed there until they'd filled in
the hole, saying farewell to Ben inside her head
before making her way home.

Nelly was crying by the time she got back and
needed feeding and changing. Afterwards Meg
collapsed on her chair, exhausted. She hadn't had
Ben's support since the birth but knowing she never
would now made everything feel far worse. She was
alone. There was only her to raise the child. The
dampness of her clothes made her shiver suddenly
and she laid Nelly down on a piece of sacking while
she got the fire burning up again. Oh, but she felt
weary to the core! If only she could lie down and rest!

It seemed to take for ever to feed the baby.

Afterwards they both slept, Meg with her head on
the table, Nelly curled up in the warm nest of her
mother's lap.

The following day Meg had to buy some bread so
decided to call at the pawn shop while she was out.
She'd sent a message to Peggy that she'd be back as
soon as she could and had half-expected her
employer to come round to see her or at least send
someone to ask how she was.

When she went into the shop she found another
woman behind the counter.

'Yes?'

'I'm Meg Pearson, I work here.'

'Used to work here,' the woman said. 'She's took
me on now.'

'Can I see her?'

'I suppose so. It won't do no good, though. She's promised me I can stay.'

Peggy came into the shop and stood behind the counter staring at Meg. 'You look poorly,' she said abruptly. 'I'm sorry about your husband. Bad luck that, because he was a good provider.'

'I came to ask if I can have my job back.'

Peggy shook her head at once. 'You'll not be able to cope and I won't pay someone as can't be relied on. I'm a woman on my own and I have to have reliable help.' She fumbled in the drawer under the counter and produced some coins. 'I owe you some wages though. I'll not have anyone saying I've treated you unfairly.'

When Meg didn't hold out her hand, Peggy slapped the coins down, then turned to her companion. 'Go and see to the kitchen fire and push the kettle on to the middle of the hob.'

Meg stared at the coins then looked at Peggy. 'You could at least have given me a try.'

'They say your Nelly's sickly. Bad enough to have a baby allus wanting feeding, but to have a sickly one – no, it'd never do. I'd not have kept you on anyway after it were born.'

It took Meg a moment to gather her strength and move forward to take the coins. She had a sudden urge to hurl them back at Peggy, but couldn't afford to give in to it so put them carefully in the drawstring purse hanging underneath her skirt then left.

She remembered to buy a loaf on the way home

but she didn't remember how she passed the rest of the day.

The following morning she woke to hear Nelly wailing beside her in the bed. Her first thought was that she had no way of earning money now and no one to turn to for help. Beyond tears, moving mechanically, she tended her daughter and let the day pass as it would.

After all, she had some savings still and would surely find another job before the money ran out . . . when she was just a little stronger . . . when she dared leave Nelly with someone else . . . when she was a little less tired.

Meg lived as frugally as she could but the coins in the pot grew fewer and fewer. She found an occasional job here and there, mostly scrubbing, washing or cleaning out shops, but couldn't settle into permanent work because of Nelly.

The first time she came home to find her little daughter ill and Rhona gloomily predicting that the baby would die before her first birthday as so many children did, Meg nearly fell into despair. But by the time she'd carried Nelly home and got a fire burning brightly in the grate, she found anger taking over from the despair.

As the days passed she needed to cling tightly to that bright spark of anger because Nelly was very poorly, coughing and shivering, so restless that Meg could only sleep in snatches. The baby didn't feed properly and seemed to grow frailer by the day.

Meg slept very little, her eyes always burning with the need for sleep. When she did take a nap she always woke with a jerk and a terrified look at the child lying beside her. She had to coax her daughter to suckle. When the baby was restless she rocked and cuddled her, singing to her until her voice was hoarse.

And somehow, very slowly, the child pulled through.

When the money was almost used up Meg took some of her meagre possessions to the pawn shop, refusing to deal with the woman who had replaced her and entering into a spirited bargaining session with Peggy. She got more than had at first been offered for Ben's chair and was glad to be rid of it, for it had been a silent reminder that there used to be two of them.

'Don't think you'll keep getting the better of me!' Peggy warned her as she passed the money over. 'It's because you were a good worker that I've been soft with you this time. I shan't be so soft next time.'

Next time! The words seemed to echo in Meg's mind all the way home. There would be a next time, she admitted that to herself. The best she could hope for was to eke out her money until Nelly was stronger then find a proper job. The worst . . . she didn't like to think of the worst. She was *not* letting anyone put her and Nelly into the poorhouse.

In the meantime she rented out the upstairs room to a young couple and their money helped a little.

Jane was a colourless woman and Timmo a dour

fellow. They were incomers to Rochdale like she was and kept themselves to themselves, except for using the downstairs fire for cooking, as agreed.

When Meg needed to sell the settle, Timmo offered to help her carry it to the pawn shop for a penny. He was short of work that week and had been prowling round the room upstairs, she'd heard his footsteps going to and fro. He'd been in and out of the house a few times seeking work, but in vain.

Jane said she'd keep an eye on Nelly while Meg and Timmo carried the settle to the pawn shop. She was good with the baby, often watching her wistfully when Timmo wasn't around.

In the shop he hovered behind Meg while she argued with Peggy, which made her uneasy, but he didn't say or do anything.

'Got yersen a new fellow?' Peggy asked when the bargaining was over.

'New fellow? What, Timmo? No, he and his wife have taken my upstairs room. He was just helping me carry the settle.' And had asked payment for doing it, which wasn't a neighbourly thing to do.

It was a lovely day so Meg waited till Timmo was back upstairs then put the coins in the money pot on the mantelpiece and went outside. She met Rhona standing on her doorstep and paused for a brief chat, explaining that she was taking Nelly out for a walk outside the town, which would be a treat for them both.

As she walked, she held the baby in her arms and enjoyed seeing her little daughter watching the world wide-eyed. She also felt pleased to see Nelly's cheeks grow slightly pink in the rare autumn sunshine.

The outing did them both a world of good.

When Meg got back she found that her room had been ransacked and the money stolen. She pounded up the stairs but the room was bare, with no sign of Timmo and Jane or their meagre possessions.

She stood there in deep shock for a few moments, unable to think or move, then went running next door to ask Rhona if she'd seen anything.

'I saw them move out. They said Jane's mother was ill over in Todmorden. She was crying the whole time they were bringing their stuff down, so I thought nowt of it. Any road, I had to go out to the market or we'd have had nothing for tea.'

'How did they take their stuff away?'

'It was Bill Pargin who took it, so they must've sold it to him. I kept an eye on them when I got back in case they were making off with some of your things, but they only took their own stuff, I made sure of that.'

'They stole my money from the pot, though!' Then the tears came, floods of them. Rhona called in the watch. An old man came, stared round the upstairs room, then said there was nothing much he could do, but he'd ask around.

He came back a few days later to say that Timmo and Jane had vanished completely and no one could be found who had seen them leave town.

Meg had gone to see Bill Pargin herself, but he insisted he knew nothing about her money. And since the young couple had sold him only their own possessions, he was entitled to keep them.

After that things went from bad to worse for Meg. The weather grew swiftly cooler as September turned into October. The money she'd carried in her purse ran out and when she couldn't pay the rent, they turned her out of the house and sold up the rest of her things, except for a few bits and pieces that she'd slipped out under her skirt and left with Rhona.

Her neighbour came in to say 'the mester', as she always called her husband, would let Meg use a corner of her downstairs room, but just till she got on her feet. Only she couldn't get on her feet, could she, because she could still only work part of the time.

And then Meg's milk dried up and she had to feed Nelly on cow's milk with sops of bread in it. The child started to fade again, which made her mother's heart go chill with terror. If she lost Nelly as well as Ben, she would kill herself. She would!

Rhona faced her one day after her husband had left for work. 'The mester says you've to move out now.'

Meg blinked at her in bewilderment. 'Why does your husband want me to go?'

'Says he likes having his house to hissen. I daresn't argue with him. He can turn reet nasty if I don't do as he says.'

Meg was so hungry she couldn't think straight, had no money left and only a small crust of bread to feed Nelly with softened in water. It wouldn't be enough. The child was hungry and needed milk. It puzzled her why she wasn't hungry herself because she was eating very little in order to keep most of the food for Nelly.

She'd beg for bread in the streets if she had to. She'd do anything for her child. But if they had no roof over their heads, how would they manage? Overcome by her troubles, she began to cry and Rhona came to put an arm round her shoulders.

'You'll have to go on the parish, love.'

'No!'

'You've got no choice. I can't let you stay on here. The mester would beat me black and blue if I tried to go against him.' She sighed. 'I'm sorry, love. I know you're having a bad time, but it's for the best. They'll look after you both in there, feed the child.'

After a sleepless night Meg walked slowly to the poorhouse in Spotland, which brought back agonising memories of Ben dying. The overseer shut the gate behind them with a dull, threatening thump that seemed to echo in her head and took her inside, calling out for someone to fetch the matron.

They both sat there and looked at Meg. In the end it was Matron who spoke. 'Now, Mrs Pearson. Tell me what's happened to bring you here. I thought you had some money left after your husband's funeral. Could you not find work?'

So she told them about the theft and how sickly her baby was.

'You're not from Rochdale. Where exactly do you come from?'

She explained about her brief marriage and leaving Northby. It seemed so long ago now, all that. It was a different person who'd been so happy.

Matron looked at her in surprise. 'You have family there still?'

Meg nodded.

'Why don't you go back to them, then? Why come here?'

She scowled at them both. 'Because I hate my mother.'

The overseer intervened. 'That's a child's reasoning, Mrs Pearson. You'd be better off with your family than in here, you know you would, and we'd be better off without another two people to feed.'

'But how could I get back to Northby?'

'We could make you a small payment, enough to get you a place with a carrier going in that direction. It'd save us the cost of looking after you, you see.'

Beside him, Matron nodded.

The overseer spoke more sternly. 'You'll have to go back to your family, willingly or unwillingly.'

Meg pushed herself to her feet, gathering Nelly close, wrapped in the ends of her shawl. 'I'll need to think about it.'

Matron walked with her to the gate and slipped a coin into her hand. 'You really will be best off with your family. In the meantime, buy yourself summat to eat, love. You'll think more clearly with food in your belly.'

The small act of kindness made tears rise in Meg's eyes and she brushed them away with the hand not holding Nelly. As she walked back, she was blind to the crisp beauty of the late-autumn day. Her gaze was more often on her daughter's face than on where she was placing her feet, so that she stumbled and once fell.

A woman picked her up but Meg couldn't find words to do more than thank her, so set off walking again.

When she got back she hesitated at the door, took a long, shaky breath and walked inside.

Rhona was waiting for her. 'Well? What did they say?'

She explained.

'Why didn't you tell me you had family?'

'I'm not sure they'll take me in. I don't get on with my mother.'

'Of course they will! Families allus look after their own. You'd be a fool to go to the poorhouse when you can stay outside and be free.'

Meg supposed Rhona was right but she knew how her mother would crow if she returned to Northby destitute. It wasn't freedom to be beholden to a woman she detested.

Only what else could she do?

And at least Jack would be there.

The thought of him made all the difference. Suddenly she longed to see her brother, a longing so intense it hurt. He was a loving, kindly man and would help her and Nelly, she knew he would, though she hated to place more burdens on his shoulders.

But she wasn't going back to the poorhouse and asking for her fare. If she did that, she'd be returning to Northby as a beggar.

She was going home through her own efforts or not at all. It was the only way she could face doing it.

Sophia looked out of the window at the driving rain and sighed. She walked across the room, then walked back again, so restless and bored she could have screamed. Jethro had forbidden her to go out in such inclement weather, even in their own carriage, even just down the valley to visit her mother and sister.

'Send the carriage for them instead,' he told her. 'They'll not object to coming here, knowing your condition.'

Of course they wouldn't dare object to anything *he* proposed! She was angry enough to say sharply, 'Yes, but what sort of mood will they be in if we seem to be ordering them around? It's like rubbing their noses in the fact that you hold the purse strings.'

He stared at her, eyes narrowing and lips pressing together into a thin line. 'Is your sister saying spiteful things to you?'

'No, of course not,' she said quickly.

'You don't usually lie to me.'

His tone was mild. It was always mild with her these days, whatever she said or did. She shrugged. 'It's only natural that Harriet should be a bit sharp sometimes. No families are sweet and loving all the time.'

'What that young woman needs is a husband.'

He didn't say any more but those words left Sophia

prey to more worries. Surely he wasn't going to force Harriet into marriage? If he did, her sister would never speak to her kindly again.

That evening as they ate their meal in the soft glow of several ornate colza oil lamps, Jethro asked suddenly, 'Are you well enough to entertain visitors to a meal and an overnight stay?'

'Yes, of course.' Suddenly she could hold the words back no longer, even if she angered him. 'You keep trying to protect me and I keep telling you I'm feeling well. It's the *boredom* which upsets me more than anything else. I think I'm going mad lately because you won't even let me leave the house half the time.'

Another of those long, level looks then Jethro said quietly, 'Well, this'll give you something to do for now and we'll think about other ways of occupying you afterwards. I want to invite my father's friend Andrew Beardsworth to visit us. He came to the wedding, but I don't think you really talked to him. He's another who has risen in the world. And best of all for our purpose, he's a widower looking for a wife. So we'll invite your sister too.'

'Harriet?'

'Do you have any other sisters?'

Sophia was struggling to understand this new turn of events. 'You're trying to find a husband for her?'

'Why not? I've heard her say she wants to wed, heard it more than once. I won't force her into anything, but the connection with Andrew Beardsworth would be useful to me.'

'I wish I could remember him better.'

'He's a little shorter than your sister, I should guess, and owns a thriving mill so he's very comfortably circumstanced. I don't know him very well, though, because he was my father's friend rather than mine.'

'How old is he?'

'Forty. He has two children of twelve and ten. Daughters. Very polite children. He keeps them in order, as I shall keep ours. His wife died eighteen months ago and I know he'd like a son and heir before it's too late.' Jethro paused, steepled his fingers and looked at her again in that assessing way. 'Do you want me to tell your sister about him or shall you do it?'

'Let me.'

He inclined his head and picked up his knife and fork again.

'What would you do if I had hysterics, ranted at you, threw things?' Sophia demanded suddenly. This eerie calmness of Jethro's annoyed her sometimes. Most of the time, actually. It was as if, outside their bedroom, he wore a mask. She still didn't feel she really knew him. Oh, she knew his body – knew it well – but she had no idea what went on inside his mind.

'If you had hysterics I'd probably empty the water jug over you.'

'And suppose that didn't calm me down?'

'Then I'd slap your face.' He put down his knife

and fork and stared at her. 'Is this a serious question? Do you feel hysterical?'

'No. Just bored.'

'Yes. So you said. I will do something about that, I promise. Your fretting could upset the child growing inside you.'

What about me? she wanted to scream at him. Don't you care about upsetting me, or is it all for the child?

But she didn't say it. She had just enough self-control left to keep those words inside her head. Jethro was, by everyone else's standards, a very good husband and provider. Was she wrong to want more from him?

After some thought Sophia sent a message to Harriet asking her to come and visit, staying overnight. She mentioned that a friend of Jethro's would also be visiting them but didn't include their mother in the invitation or mention the reason for the visit.

She found herself pacing up and down the parlour as she waited for her sister, feeling unaccountably nervous. When the carriage drew up outside, all mud-splashed, she muttered, 'At last!' and went out into the hall to welcome her.

In the parlour Harriet went to warm her hands at the blazing fire. 'It's cold out. Winter is upon us now.' She pulled a wry face at her sister. 'I can't tell you how glad I am to get away from Mother for a few hours. She fusses over things till I could scream.'

Sophia was impatient of this small talk. 'I've something to tell you.'

'Oh?'

'Sit down and listen.' She explained rapidly about Jethro's friend and the possibility that this Andrew Beardsworth was looking for a wife.

Harriet grew thoughtful.

'Well, have you nothing to say?'

'What is there to say until I've met him? I only vaguely remember him from your wedding. If he's at all presentable, I'd be very amenable to considering marriage. There's no one suitable in our acquaintance, and anyway, your Jethro is right. They *are* inbred. This might be a golden opportunity for me, though I'm sorry he already has children, even if they are only girls.'

'Hasn't *anyone* ever asked you to marry them, Harriet? I'd have thought the dowry Jethro could provide would have made a difference.'

'Oswin asked me.'

'What? When did he do that?'

'A month after your marriage. Once word got round that there might be a dowry attached to me now. Though actually, Jethro hasn't provided anything yet except the promise of one.'

'Why didn't you tell me about Oswin before?'

Harriet shrugged. 'It might have upset you and I didn't think Jethro would like that.'

Sophia threw up her hands in despair. 'Can you do nothing without his approval? *You* aren't married to him, after all.'

'We're dependent on him and I wouldn't care to cross him. He's very – forceful.' She frowned at her sister, and after a moment's hesitation asked, 'What's it like, being married to a stranger? What's it like in bed?'

Sophia gaped at her, feeling a hot blush rising up her neck and face. 'What sort of question is that?'

'The sort I've been wondering about for a while because I've been considering whether to ask Jethro to find me a husband. He did half-promise to once, after all.' Harriet waited, head cocked on one side, then prompted, 'Well, what *is* it like?'

'Jethro is very – um – considerate in bed. I think other men aren't always like that. He's polite and – and kind to me outside the bedchamber, too.' In spite of herself, Sophia added, 'But I still don't feel I know him. He keeps his thoughts to himself most of the time.'

There was silence while she tried to recover her composure and Harriet stared thoughtfully into the fire.

'I shouldn't mind not knowing my husband very well,' she said eventually. 'It'd be a small price to pay for being married and having a home of my own. I hate it when people pity me for being unmarried at twenty-six.'

They were interrupted by a maid bringing in a tray laden with tea things, followed by another carrying plates of small cakes and scones.

When Sophia had served her sister, she asked hesitantly, 'What shall I tell Jethro?'

'I'll tell him myself that the idea of marriage pleases me. I loathe living with our mother, especially now you've gone, and I'll do anything to avoid having to spend the rest of my life serving her.'

'She speaks as if it's settled that you'll stay with her.'

'Yes. But I won't if I can help it.' Harriet smiled suddenly. 'We'll leave your Jethro to deal with her if anything comes of his plans because I'm sure she'll object to the mere idea of my getting married. But she won't dare go against him. For the moment I'll just say I was invited to dinner tonight to make the numbers even and let her think there were other people here as well.'

Meg left for Northby early the following morning, on foot, carrying Nelly and a pitifully small bundle of clothing for the pair of them. She was ashamed to go home with so little, but she'd be even more ashamed to be sent home by the poorhouse guardians.

The weather was bitterly cold but she had Nelly wrapped up warmly in her pink shawl and she hoped to get a ride on a farm cart for part of the way at least. But no one stopped for her although she called out to them, so she continued to set one foot in front of the other.

The first evening she had a bit of luck. A woman about to turn into a lane stopped to greet her, studied her shrewdly then asked if she'd eaten that day. She was surprised when the bundle Meg was carrying in her arms moved and a baby peered out.

'Nay, lass, were you intending to keep walking all night? What about the babby?'

Meg looked at her, so cold it took her a minute to think out an answer. 'I have to get to Northby. No one would stop for me. So I've kept on walking.'

The woman clicked her tongue in dismay. 'Here, give me your other bundle. You can sleep in my kitchen tonight and I'll find some milk for the babby.'

It was like going to heaven to sit in front of a warm fire while Nelly smiled and cooed at the old woman who had taken them in.

'I'm grateful,' Meg said, surprised at how faint her voice was. 'Very grateful indeed.'

'If we can't help one another, we're poor sorts. I haven't much, but I've enough to share with you tonight.'

'I must leave early in the morning, make the most of the daylight.'

The old woman nodded. 'I s'll pray for you – and for your little lass.'

The second day Meg felt a little better and she now had some bread for Nelly, at least. The old woman had said it was for both of them, but Meg would happily do without for the pleasure of seeing her child fed. Only one cart stopped for her, and the driver could only set her a couple of miles along her way, but it was a help. After that she hardly saw a soul, but managed to keep walking for most of the day.

That night she sneaked into a barn and lay in the warm hay till morning.

When the farmer found her he chased her away, called her a 'dirty beggar'. But when Nelly cried in terror at the loud voice he stopped, muttering, 'And a baby too! Shame on you.'

Meg was ashamed. Deeply. But what else could she do now?

After that it was just a matter of grim endurance, putting one foot in front of the other. As it grew dark she was surprised to realise she recognised this place. Northby, the top end, near the mill where she'd once worked.

She'd made it!

'I got us here, Nelly,' she whispered in a hoarse voice, shaken by a bout of shivering. 'Just another few minutes an' we'll be there.'

When she stood outside the house, though, she hesitated, suddenly afraid to knock. But it had to be done, so she raised one hand, letting the bundle of clothes slip. The knock didn't sound very loud. She waited but no one came to the door. Maybe they hadn't heard. Raising her hand again, she did her best but hadn't the strength to knock really loudly.

This time it opened and Jack stood there. She said his name then blackness took her and she knew no more until she regained consciousness lying on the rug in front of the fire, with him holding her in his arms.

She let them do as they wanted with her then. They fed the baby and they fed her some broth. Even her mother spoke gently to her.

When she'd finished her tale, Jack said, 'Nay, why

should you go into the poorhouse when you've allus got a home with us? You did right to come here.'

Then Meg knew she and Nelly were truly safe and could let herself slip into sleep.

It took a while for Meg to regain her energy, even though she was eating regularly now. She and her daughter were living in the front room and she spent a lot of time just lying on the bed in there, too weary to do much but care for her child.

But gradually she started to feel better and began helping with the housework or going for short walks on fine days with Nelly in her arms. Most of the time her mother ignored her, hardly saying a word unless she wanted a job done, and that suited Meg just fine. Jack talked to her in the evenings, though, and she to him. Those gentle conversations made the heaviness in her chest lighten, the pain of her husband's death start to fade and gave her hope for the future. Eh, he was a wonderful brother, Jack was!

In mid-December her mother started making sharp remarks about having to stretch the food to fill two more mouths. It had surprised Meg that no such remarks had been tossed at her earlier, but perhaps even Netta could tell when something was impossible.

If she was to start work her mother would have to look after Nelly, something that worried Meg greatly. Even though Nelly too had recovered and was at a delightful age, gurgling and waving her fists at anyone who paid her some attention, Netta never picked her up voluntarily. Ginny, Joe and Jack were always cuddling her though, and the baby got excited at the mere sight of them. Even Shad deigned to stop and have a word with his little niece every now and then.

Meg agonised about leaving Nelly in her mother's care but felt she had no alternative. She would have to stay in Northby to get the help she needed, but more important, she wanted her daughter to be near the rest of the Staleys. A person could be killed in a snap of the fingers, it seemed, so there had to be other family around – just in case – for Nelly's own sake.

One day Meg waited till everyone had gone to work or school then asked her mother to sit down and talk to her.

'I can't sit and gossip like some do,' Netta said at once.

'It's important.' Meg hesitated, then asked right out, 'If I find myself a job, will you look after Nelly for me?'

'What other choice do we have? But I'll only do it if you hand over your money to me like the others do.'

There was silence then Meg nodded – reluctantly.

Netta's expression brightened but quickly grew sour again. 'They're not taking anyone on at the mill.'

'I know. I've already asked about that. I thought I'd walk round Northby today and see if I can find another sort of job, only I need you to mind Nelly while I do that. Folk don't like to take you on if you've a baby in your arms.'

'You're right there. Eh, you'd have been better not marrying in the first place, but would you listen to me? No.'

Meg drew herself up. 'Let's get this straight. I don't regret marrying Ben, because he was a good husband to me and best of all he gave me Nelly. That child is the sunshine of my life and I intend to do my best for her.'

'You still had to come home for help.'

Meg bit off an angry retort. It was never any use arguing with her mother. Netta didn't listen to any arguments or points of view except those inside her own head. 'Well, now I'm trying to find work and earn some brass, so what are you complaining about? Will you look after Nelly or not? If I have to find someone else, there won't be as much money for you.'

'I've no choice, then.'

Meg knew this was the best she could expect from her mother, so cleaned up her daughter, set the baby clouts to soak then got ready to go out.

Leaving Nelly was harder than she'd expected and she turned back at the door to give her another kiss. She didn't think her mother would hurt the child, because of the extra money Meg would earn for the family, but she also knew Nelly wouldn't get any hugs or cuddles, wouldn't even be talked to.

'If I don't come back,' she said as an afterthought, 'it'll be because I've found a job and have to start straight away. Don't forget to feed Nelly.'

'I brought up six of my own. You don't forget that

sort of thing.' Netta sniffed scornfully. 'And if you do forget, they soon start skriking and letting you know.'

'Nelly doesn't cry much and she has to be persuaded to eat half the time. If anything happens to her, if she doesn't thrive, I'll leave again. I promise you that.'

The two women stared at one another then Netta shrugged. 'I know how to look after a babby. It's only five year since I had our Joe, three year since your Dad were killed.' She sighed.

As Meg walked slowly down the long main street, she marvelled at the changes there had been in Northby even in the time she'd been away. More houses were being built on the higher ground to one side of the street, with much banging and shouting. Another terrace of dwellings for workers at the mill, no doubt. There was a new wall round the church, brick, very neat. Square setts had been used to pave more of Weavers Lane, which was still the main thoroughfare – not the shabby part at the bottom end, but the middle and upper end.

Eh, she'd never expected to be back here, never wanted to return either. But you did what you had to, especially when you'd a child dependent on you.

When she reached her destination, Roper's pawn shop, the moment couldn't be put off any longer. This was her main hope for a job. Taking a deep breath, she pushed open the door.

Roper came out of the back room at once, looked at her empty hands and frowned in puzzlement.

Meg stared round, seeing the chaos and muddle

she had glimpsed from outside. Peggy would have gone mad to see such a mess. 'I've come to ask for work.'

He looked at her in surprise. 'Meg, isn't it? Meg Staley?'

'It's Meg Pearson now, but my husband died so I came back to Northby. I was working in a pawn shop in Rochdale.' She let her eyes move quickly over the jumble of bundles and objects. 'I can see your business is doing well, but you need help.'

He scowled. 'Well, I can't afford it.'

'You can and we both know it. What's more, I know the job and you'll make *more* money with me sorting this stuff out an' maybe washing some of it if you're going to sell it.' As he screwed up his mouth, clearly about to refuse again, she added quickly, 'I did some housework and cooking for my last employer as well.'

'Cooking?'

She knew then that she had caught his interest and let her breath filter out slowly as his expression grew thoughtful.

'I could give you a try, I suppose,' he said, 'let you prove what you say. In fact, you can start straight away.'

She nodded. 'All right. And the wages?'

'You need to have a job afore you talk about wages.'

'I'll work this one day just for my food, but I won't do owt else till we agree about wages.'

'All right. You can start by getting me summat decent for my dinner and tea. I'm nearly out of food.'

'I'll need money if I'm to go shopping.'

With a deep sigh, as if it hurt him, he went into the back room and came back with two shillings which he slapped on the counter in front of her.

She didn't pick it up. 'Let me see what you've already got in first, so I know what to buy. You wouldn't want me to waste your money, would you?'

He shuddered visibly at the thought.

It was a big enough house to have a separate pantry but the shelves contained more objects from the shop than items of food. 'You've hardly got anything in at all, Mr Roper, so two shillings won't be enough. If you want me to do a stew, I'll need to buy meat and taties and onions. If I could get a bit of suet, I could make a few dumplings to go with it.' She watched him lick his lips at the thought. 'You need a loaf, too, and I could get the stuff to make some drop scones – if you have a griddle?'

'I've got a griddle somewhere. I'll fish it out while you're shopping.' He fumbled in his pocket. 'How much more will you need?'

The world seemed brighter as Meg walked down the street. She had a chance of a job and was hopeful that she could persuade Mr Roper to keep her on, if only for her cooking.

She worked hard all day, producing an excellent dinner for them both at the end of the morning and making sure her portion was visibly smaller than his, though she'd had enough tastes of the stew while cooking to make up the difference. She always seemed to be hungry these days.

Roper spooned up his stew eagerly, dunking the bread into it and dripping gravy down his chin. After the meal he tried to fumble with her breasts as she passed him. Meg snatched up the chopping knife and threatened him with it.

'I only—' he began in an aggrieved voice.

'I don't allow touching and I get *very angry* if anyone tries to maul me around.' She looked down at the knife then back at him. 'I've learned to defend mysen, Mr Roper – you have to when you're a widow – an' I know where a knife can do most damage to a man.' She glanced at his crotch, saw him wince and move his hand instinctively to cover his privates. 'If you want me to work here, you'll not try that sort of thing again.'

He scowled. 'Who needs you? I can get a woman any time I want.'

'As long as it's not me.'

She caught sight of herself in a specked mirror hanging on the wall. Her face was flushed, her eyes hard. She looked far older than her nineteen years and vicious with it – felt vicious too when men tried to take advantage of her, as a few had.

'I'll go back into the shop while you clear up,' he mumbled, his eyes on the knife in her hand. 'I've still not decided whether I want to employ you, mind. I'll have to consider it again if you're going to threaten me with knives.' He hesitated, caught sight of the empty dishes and licked his lips.

Meg considered her own situation as she worked. She wanted this job, really wanted it, but she'd upset him. Remembering how he'd gobbled down the stew, she set about cooking some drop scones. Waiting till the shop was empty she took him one 'just to try'. It was still warm and she'd put butter on it, which was melting.

His eyes lit up and he took a huge bite, chomping loudly, then finished the rest, wiping a trickle of melted butter from his chin with one dirty fingertip. Afterwards he stared at her, his eyes narrowing as he licked the last of the grease off his fingers. 'You're a cunning bitch.' A slow smile lifted the corners of his mouth and for just a minute made him look more kindly. 'But that's not a bad thing in my business.'

'I'm a good cook.' Thanks to Peggy.

'What else can you cook?'

She listed some of Peggy's favourites.

He gave a few slow nods, kept her waiting for an answer then gave her another sly smile. 'You'd not have got a job with me three year ago, but I'm better set up now than I were then. I can afford to hire you – an' I can afford the money for good food. See that you give it me.'

She nodded. 'I will, Mr Roper. But you'll find me a big help in the shop too. And don't worry, I've learned not to be soft with customers.' She knew better than to be soft with anyone these days. 'What hours?'

'As long as I'm open.'

She shook her head. 'You're open from early till midnight an' you live on the premises. When would I get any sleep if I had to walk home afterwards?'

His tone was aggrieved. 'I'm not asking you to work longer than I do.'

'I don't mind working till late because if you're anything like my last place, you'll get most of your custom in the evenings, but I want to start a bit later in the mornings. I'll have to do your shopping on the way here as well, don't forget.' She waited, tapping her foot impatiently, then burst out, 'Aw, you know you need help – an' you like my cooking. I'll be worth it.'

'Aye, but you're a cheeky young madam.'

'I'll need to be, working here.'

'Must you allus have the last word?' He let the silence stretch, then waved one hand. 'All right. Fetch me another of them scones then get off home to your babby. An' here's some money for tomorrow's food. Mind, I want an accounting of what you spend. No keeping the change for yoursen!'

'As if I would.'

Outside she sagged against the wall for a moment or two, feeling shaky with relief. She'd done it. She'd got a job.

Meg was bone tired by the time she opened the front door but felt triumphant. Then she heard Nelly grizzling, sounding unhappy, and her own happiness vanished as she rushed to pick her little daughter up. She watched as the child recognised her and stopped crying, then dropped a kiss on the little cheek, which was still damp with tears.

'You got a job, then?' Netta demanded, interrupting her murmurs to the child.

Meg nodded. 'At Roper's.'

'How much is he paying you?'

'Ten shillings a week, plus my dinner and tea. I'll keep two shillings of that for myself and give you the rest.'

'You should give it all to me.'

Jack intervened. 'Eight shillings is more than fair. After all, Meg will get two of her day's meals at work so she won't cost you much for food.' He turned to his sister. 'I don't like you working for that man, though, love. He has a bad reputation with women. What if he tries to have his way with you?'

Meg laughed, a sound so harsh she surprised herself. 'Just let him try! Just let *anyone* try!' She had proved her ability to defend herself that very day, but she wasn't going to worry her brother by telling him that. 'I know what I'm doing, Jack. It's a lot better than working in the mill an' I'll make sure I get first pick of owt that's being sold.' She watched her mother's face brighten again and added, 'Best of all, I start later than other folk, because I'll be working in the evenings from now on, so I'll have time to be with Nelly before I leave for work.'

Sophia watched from her fireside chair as Jethro brought in Mr Beardsworth to be introduced. She remembered the man now, though she hadn't done more than greet him at her wedding. He looked very self-assured and by the way he was studying her sister, knew exactly why Jethro had invited him there.

When the men had left to go and talk business in Jethro's office, Sophia asked, 'Well?'

'I don't find him repulsive. There's something about him, an aura of power, that men like Oswin lack, however confident they seem.' Harriet paused, head on one side. 'But I don't think I'd like to cross him.'

Sophia knew what she meant. She wasn't sure about Mr Beardsworth but couldn't put her finger on what exactly was making her feel uneasy.

They dined in state in the rarely used dining room, which Sophia was still in the process of refurbishing. She watched as Harriet conversed with their guest and he openly appraised her, nodding his approval of her sensible answers.

After they'd eaten dessert, Sophia stood up to lead Harriet out, but Jethro held up one hand.

'Stay with us, ladies. We're not going to get drunk on the port. We leave that sort of behaviour to the *superior classes*.'

She knew by now how low an opinion he had of idle gentry, and also of people who let themselves get the worse for drink.

'It's been a pleasant meal,' Beardsworth said, raising his glass to study the colour of the port, then setting it down untasted. 'I've enjoyed the company.' He looked sideways at Harriet then his gaze moved to Sophia, eyes resting with approval on her swollen belly for the coming child could no longer be hidden. 'I can see already that you've made my friend Jethro happy, Mrs Greenhalgh. I envy him.'

'Thank you.'

He picked up the glass and took the tiniest of sips, pursing his lips as he rolled the port round his tongue.

'A bit too sweet for my taste, but a pretty colour.'

When they got up to move back to the parlour, Jethro took Sophia's arm and led her quickly out. To her surprise the other two didn't follow them.

'What's happening?'

'He's asking her.'

'Already?'

'Aye, why not?'

In the dining room Harriet stared at Mr Beardsworth in surprise as he put out his arm across the doorway to prevent her from following her sister.

'You know why I've been invited here tonight, Miss Goddby.'

She nodded.

'I prefer to speak frankly. I won't waste my time coming here again if you aren't interested in marrying me.' When she didn't speak, he prompted, 'Well, are you?'

She swallowed hard. She'd already found out that her brother-in-law believed in plain speaking. Mr Beardsworth, it seemed, was even more blunt, even about something as delicate as this matter.

'I wouldn't have come here if I weren't interested in finding myself a husband,' she managed. But although she prided herself on her sensible attitude to life, she was feeling flustered at how quickly this was happening.

'And?' he asked.

'And . . . well, I'd not be . . . averse to . . . to taking matters further.'

He gave a smile of pure triumph. 'Good.' Taking her hand, he raised it to his lips, a gesture which surprised Harriet, as did the shiver that ran through her at his touch. Again, she had the thought that he seemed very masterful and she would never dare go against his wishes, but at the moment it mattered less to her than getting away from her mother and her own idle, useless life. She realised he was speaking and turned her attention to what he was saying.

'We'd better do the thing properly. You must come over to visit me, see my house, meet my daughters, then we'll talk again before we make any announcements.' He offered her his arm.

It felt strong and well-muscled. As the shock of what had just happened began to fade, Harriet was able to speak with her normal calmness. 'I should like to come and visit you, Mr Beardsworth.'

'Andrew.'

When they rejoined the others she heard him issuing an invitation to Sophia to come and visit, bringing her sister.

The two women exchanged glances, Sophia's questioning. Harriet nodded.

Sophia turned back to their visitor. 'We'd be delighted, Mr Beardsworth.'

'Good,' said Jethro. 'I'm glad that's settled. We can all go to bed now.'

Only when she was getting ready for bed did Harriet feel panic shiver through her. What had she done? Could she really be considering marriage with a man she had only just met? She knew so little of him.

Then the thought of living for ever with her mother made her stand stock-still, clutching her nightgown to her breast. She would do anything to avoid being left a spinster. Life with him surely couldn't be worse than her present existence.

As she donned the nightgown and brushed out her hair Harriet grew thoughtful. It wasn't going to be easy. There was something about Andrew Beardsworth, something very sharp beneath that polite, pleasant behaviour. He hadn't made his fortune by being soft, she was sure. How softly would he treat her? She didn't want to escape one tyranny only to fall under another.

Only – there was no way of finding out. She would have to take the risk. Whatever he was like to live with, it was better to be a wife than remain a spinster. No one had any respect for unmarried ladies, not even their own families.

Beardsworth left Parkside very early the next morning before the ladies got up, spent most of the day doing business in Todmorden, then set off for home mid-afternoon. On the way across the tops there was a loud cracking sound and the carriage jerked about violently before coming to a halt, tilted at an angle. He clambered out with some difficulty. One of the wheels had broken. No one could have foreseen the accident, but he nonetheless berated his coachman about it, ending his tirade with, 'Well, what are you going to do about it?'

'There's an inn only a few hundred yards along this

road, sir – the Packhorse. It's respectable enough, though a bit run down. The gentry don't use it much, but you could wait there while Sam here tries to find someone to repair it.'

Beardsworth nodded, but his expression grew tighter. If there was one inn at which he wouldn't have chosen to stop, it was this. However, he didn't intend to stand by the road getting wet while the groom went for help, so he set off walking, with Sam following a few paces behind him.

He stopped for a moment when he was nearly there to study the inn more carefully than he ever did while driving past on his way to Northby. The same huddle of buildings straggled along the road and back up the slope to a very old part that he'd have knocked down straight away if it had been his. Someone had recently painted the doors and window frames near the main entrance but the rest of the place still had a dilapidated air to it.

Phoebe was serving a customer, but when she saw that a gentleman had entered, she abandoned Johnny to hurry forward and greet the newcomer. 'Can I help you, sir?' Then she recognised him and her breath seemed to stop in her throat. Andrew Beardsworth!

He didn't notice her reaction, thank goodness, because he was looking round.

'Do you have a private parlour in this place?'

Toby heard his loud, arrogant tone from the back room and went into the public room at once. 'I'll deal with the gentleman, Phoebe.'

Gratefully she returned to her other customer, but listened carefully to what was being said.

Andrew Beardsworth stared at Toby as if he couldn't believe his eyes. 'Hell, they said you looked like him, but I didn't realise—'

'I've been told before how closely I resemble a relative who is in better circumstances than I am.' Since Toby didn't like being known as Jethro Greenhalgh's bastard half-brother, he'd decided to claim no more than a distant connection to the family whenever he could. Useless to deny the relationship completely because his face betrayed him immediately to those who knew his brother.

He waited to discover what had brought Beardsworth here, but the man just stood there, his eyes unfocused as if he was lost in his own thoughts, with a frown showing that these weren't pleasant. In the end he shook his head, muttered something and turned back to Toby.

'Well, *landlord*, my carriage has a broken wheel and I'd prefer to sit and wait for it to be repaired in more privacy than your public room can afford.'

'That's easily provided, sir.' He gestured to a door to one side of the public room. 'Though you'll have to forgive us for the chill in there. We only light the fire when it's occupied. But it's already laid and will soon warm the place up.'

'I'll go and do that now,' Phoebe said quickly. 'I'll bring a shovelful of hot coals and soon get it blazing.'

'Thank you, Phoebe.'

Andrew hadn't really looked at her before but at the sound of her name glanced quickly across the room. Yes, it was definitely Hal's wife. What was she doing still here? Jethro had said he'd told her to move away from the district. 'And my wheel? It'll need to be repaired. Is there a wheelwright in this village who can do it?'

'I'm afraid not, sir.' Toby looked across at the group of drinkers. 'Johnny, can you go and ask Ross to send down the road for help for Mr—?' He saw from the expression of apprehension on their faces that they both recognised and disliked this traveller and turned back to his guest with a questioning expression, not willing to continue until he knew who the fellow was.

'The name's Beardsworth.'

Toby had learned to conceal his real feelings as a lad and to use words as a shield and weapon, but even so it was all he could do to hide his anger and disgust now. So this was the man who let little girls be beaten within an inch of their lives in his mill, the man whose reputation made mothers threaten to send naughty children to Tappersley. But in his position he didn't dare offend Beardsworth so merely nodded.

In the back room Phoebe was taking some glowing coals from the fire with a small hearth shovel. As Toby came in and said, 'Let me do that for you,' she started and dropped a red hot coal on the rug, letting out a muffled shriek.

He took the shovel of live coals from her, glad of a minute to pull himself together and suppress his own feelings. He watched her shake the hot embers from the rug into the hearth and spread it out again. 'Are you all right?'

'Yes. I was just . . . worried about something.'

'About our new customer, perhaps?' He scowled. 'I'd rather not serve a man like that myself.'

'Don't let him see how you feel! And be careful what you say to him. He can be a dangerous enemy.'

Toby walked into the private parlour, shutting the door behind him and the gentleman.

'What's that bugger doing here?' one of the men in the public room asked Phoebe when she went across to see if they wanted anything else.

His neighbour nudged him. 'Shhh, you fool!'

'Anyone else need another drink?' Phoebe asked to change the subject. Two men held out their empty pots and she went to collect them.

No one said another word about the man in the next room, though occasionally someone would glance towards it and scowl.

Their unwanted guest made a thorough nuisance of himself, ringing for refreshments, then ringing again a short time later to ask how long it was likely to be before his carriage was repaired.

'I can't tell you, sir,' Toby answered smoothly. 'I'm not a wheelwright. We've sent someone down the hill and your groom's gone with him.'

When Sam came back and went in to see his master, Toby deliberately stood nearby. He was annoyed to hear how roughly Beardsworth spoke to his servant. You'd think the accident had been the man's fault to hear him.

'So the wheelwright can put on a temporary wheel to get the carriage to his workshop, sir, then he'll finish a wheel that matches properly tomorrow. But it mustn't be driven with any loads on it while the temporary wheel is in place.'

'Well, make sure he takes care with my carriage. I don't want the paintwork scratching. And he's to do my work first. Are you *sure* he can't repair it tonight?'

'Certain, sir. No one could. It takes time to make a wheel that fits exactly.'

'Get on your way then and send that landlord to see me.'

'Yes, sir.' Outside, the groom showed no surprise at the sight of Toby standing there. He rolled his eyes and gestured to the room, whispering, 'He wants to see you. And he likes folk to look lively when he gives an order.'

Toby grinned and went back to wipe the counter, taking his time about it.

The groom grinned despite himself then shook his head and went outside.

When Toby judged he'd kept his unpleasant guest waiting for long enough, he went and knocked on the door.

'Come in!'

The man's voice was irritable. Toby kept his face expressionless, but mentally doubled what he'd intended to charge.

'It seems my carriage won't be ready till tomorrow.

Do you have any other conveyances here, Fletcher? I'm a busy man and have better uses for my time than sitting around in your miserable excuse for an inn.'

'Only a small cart and an old mare, sir. Hardly a suitable conveyance for a *gentleman* like you, especially as it looks like rain.'

Beardsworth went to the window, looked out and turned back to scowl at Toby. 'Rain or not, I'll hire your damned cart. Do you have someone who can drive me?'

'I'll do that myself.'

'How much for the hire?'

'A guinea, sir.'

'That's outrageous!'

'I'll need to hire someone to take my place here. And it'll be another half a guinea for the use of this room and the refreshments.' Leaving the millowner sputtering with indignation, Toby went off to let Phoebe know what he was doing. Outside he harnessed the old mare to the cart, talking to her softly as he worked so that she nickered and nudged him with her head, waiting for the carrot or wrinkled apple he usually gave her.

When Mr Beardsworth came out he looked round the stable yard with a sneering expression before asking, 'Where's that idle groom of mine?'

'He went back to your carriage, I believe, to help get it on the road again. If you'd like to climb up beside me, we'll set off.'

They drove mainly in silence because Toby had no desire to initiate a conversation with this man and

Beardsworth spoke only to give directions. When it began to rain, Toby was glad to see the sour expression on his customer's face grow even sourer, feeling actual pleasure when he saw his passenger shiver. He rarely felt the cold himself so began to whistle cheerfully, sure it would irritate his companion.

'Stop that damned noise!'

Toby grinned.

'What are you laughing at?'

'Nothing in particular, sir. I'm just a happy sort of person, I suppose.'

When they got to Beardsworth's house an hour later, he made no offer of refreshments, tossed the money at Toby so carelessly that the coins fell to the ground and went inside without a word of thanks or farewell.

Toby bent to pick up his payment then stared at the house, which stood to one side of a large mill. By the bright lights of the mill he could see that it was a small village, not much larger than Calico. Tappersley was just off the main road, one of the many settlements that had grown up where there was a stream with enough force to turn the waterwheel that had powered the machinery in the early days. He'd seen the sign to it, knew about the terrible conditions at the mill there, but had never visited it before.

It looked stark and grim, not at all like Calico, and consisted mainly of terraces of tiny dwellings clustered round the mill. They looked shoddy places, smaller than the ones in Backenshaw and sagging already. Beardsworth was using steam power to turn the machinery now, of course, and the tall chimney was belching black smoke into the air, adding to the general gloom of the scene.

There weren't any children playing in the street or women gossiping on doorsteps. In fact there was no one to be seen. It was as if they were all hiding from their terrible master.

It would be interesting to find out if Phoebe knew anything else about the damned fellow. He was sure she did – but would she tell him?

Even though it was still raining, once he was out of Tappersley, Toby's spirits rose and he felt as if he could breathe more easily. He let the horse find its own way up the hill through the darkness and once back at the inn he unharnessed the tired animal and wiped her down before going inside.

Phoebe came out to the stables and hovered, as she did when she needed to tell him something that she didn't really like discussing.

'Well?' he asked in the end. 'Aren't you going to tell me what you know about that fellow?'

'It's been a long time since I saw him, but he and Hal had dealings just before we married. I don't know exactly what they were. Hal told me to keep away whenever Beardsworth was around, so all I know is bits I overheard by chance.'

'And what did you overhear?' he probed patiently.

'Talk of thieving, I think.' She hesitated, then added quickly, 'But I don't know any details.'

'All right.' He heard her walk out, finished settling the old mare for the night and went into the inn. The usual regulars were drinking in the public room, his meal was ready, Phoebe was teasing someone about a puppy. It was all very normal.

Only . . . there was something about Andrew Beardsworth that left him with a bad feeling. Toby hoped the man would never come into his inn again.

And if anyone else sought help in escaping from him, Toby would give it willingly. He hated to see weaker folk bullied and ill-treated. Hated it with a passion. People had bullied him till he grew tall and strong. He'd never forgotten how it felt to be thumped and not be able to thump back.

Jethro received a letter two days later, delivered by Andrew's groom.

> *Delayed by broken wheel on way back. Spent some time at the Packhorse. Met your half-brother. Can we not buy the fellow out and send him to the colonies – or else do something more permanent about him? He's got an insolent look to him and we don't want him poking and prying into our affairs. What's more, he's got Dixon's wife working for him. I don't like that.*
> *Andrew*

Jethro re-read the epistle, then screwed it up and threw it into the fire. He'd had a careful eye kept on Fletcher and the man was showing little enough ambition these days, spending a lot of his time reading so he'd heard. His lip curled into a pronounced sneer at that thought. Who did the fellow think he was to sit around reading, like his betters?

Should he do something about Fletcher?

No, he'd promised his father to leave the man alone.

And anyway, he didn't like breaking the law. His father had always been scornful of this, but Jethro felt the law was what held society together, lifted them all above the level of savages.

He'd make sure his carriage was in good repair if he travelled in that direction, though. That road was the quickest way over the moors to Tappersley, and if Andrew married Harriet, they would inevitably have a closer association and drive across to see them quite often.

Jethro hadn't told Sophia that he had a bastard brother. Why should he? It wasn't something to be proud of.

But he'd continue to have a watch kept on Fletcher. The money it cost was irrelevant. What mattered most was his peace of mind and the security of his family.

Jethro took Harriet and Sophia to visit his friend, as arranged, amused by how mildly Andrew spoke in the women's company, how he fussed over the lady he was planning to marry. Not like him at all. He was usually brusque and to the point. Was he the right husband for Harriet? Who could tell? But at least his mill was doing well and she'd be secure. And away from her mother. Jethro had never seen anyone as keen to leave home as she was.

'The village is very ugly and the house a bit small,' Harriet said when they got back to Parkside and the women were alone, 'but it's very new and modern inside, and I like that.'

'Shall you marry him, then?'

Harriet nodded. 'Yes. He's to come and speak to Mama and Perry, though we both know they won't refuse his suit, not if your Jethro approves of him.'

'There's still time to back out if you have any doubts. Jethro won't force you, not if I ask him not to.'

Harriet looked at her. 'What do you mean by "have any doubts"?'

'Well, his daughters were very subdued. It seemed to me that those girls were afraid of him. And his servants seemed cowed too.'

'I don't want uppity step-daughters, and I prefer servants who know their place.'

'I see you're determined to see no fault in him. Very well.'

Harriet went to hug her sister. 'Please understand, this is my chance to escape from Mama and spinster-hood.'

'There are other men.'

'Why haven't they approached me then? It's as if they've been warned off – since Oswin. You don't suppose your husband . . . No, of course he wouldn't. Anyway, I shall get what I want out of this marriage and I hope I can give Andrew the sons he wants.'

*

The wedding took place a month later, during the whole of which interlude Mrs Goddby complained or wept or raged at her ungrateful daughter, saying she didn't know what would become of her, left alone in her old age. Almost as an afterthought she kept insisting it was impossible to be ready for a wedding in such a short time and made little effort to arrange things.

'You won't be on your own, you'll have Perry to look after you,' Harriet kept repeating, though she was growing very impatient with her mother.

'A son's not the same. There was no *need* for you to marry, Harriet, no need at all.'

'But I want to.'

'"Marry in haste, repent at leisure." You hardly know the man. And he has mean eyes . . .'

After the ceremony Harriet climbed into her husband's new carriage and sat back to enjoy its comfort. His daughters were to stay with Sophia and Jethro for the night and Andrew would send the carriage for them the next day. He said little on the way back and it was getting dark by the time they arrived at Tappersley. He ushered her into the house and a maid came to take her cloak.

'We'll retire at once, Nan,' he said to the servant.

Harriet looked at him in surprise, wondering why he hadn't asked her what she wanted. But she said nothing. If he wanted to consummate the marriage straight away, she wouldn't protest. She was rather nervous of sharing his bed, if truth be told, so the sooner she found out what this mysterious act was like, the better.

In the bedroom, he waited while maids brought up bedwarmers and hot water. When they were alone her husband looked at Harriet in a way that made her heart lurch in sudden panic.

'Take off your clothes, but don't bother with a nightgown. I'd only rip it off you.'

She stared in shock at this blunt speech. 'Is there a dressing room?' she asked, feeling even more nervous now.

'No. We dress and undress together.' He moved across and unfastened the pearls he'd given her as a wedding present, then squeezed one breast hard and pinched the nipple, so that she let out an involuntary whimper of pain. 'Well? What are you waiting for? Take them off or I'll do it for you.' He stood back to watch her undress.

Hands trembling, she began to unfasten her clothes. When she would have needed a maid's help, he stepped forward and dealt with the laces and ties.

As she stood there clad only in her chemise and the last petticoat, Harriet looked at him pleadingly. 'Please let me get into bed before I take these off, Andrew. I feel embarrassed and you're still fully clothed.'

He laughed. 'I won't be for much longer.' Reaching out, he pulled the clothes roughly from her body.

She cried out once in shock, then pride made her bite back further protests and she forced herself to stand still as he ran his hands down her body, then pushed her towards the bed and began to take off his own clothes.

'You *are* still a virgin?' he asked conversationally.

'Yes, of course.'

'Good. There's nothing I enjoy so much as deflowering a virgin.'

She didn't enjoy the experience, which she found painful and humiliating, but tried to do as he wished.

When it was over he rolled off her, saying, 'You were telling the truth anyway. That's a good start.' Within seconds he was asleep.

Harriet didn't fall asleep till after the clock in the downstairs hall had struck midnight.

Was she to face this every night? It was a higher price to pay for being a married woman than she'd expected. A tear trickled down her face. She'd loathed every minute of it, loathed the roughness, the touch of his hands, even the smell of him.

Oh, dear God, how was she to endure a lifetime of this? And how could Sophia possibly *enjoy* it?

The following afternoon Harriet met Andrew's children and their governess, Miss Swainton. Kate and Marianne were the quietest, most subdued girls she had ever met, hardly opening their mouths and mainly confining their answers to her questions to a yes or no.

'How did you find my daughters?' Andrew asked over their evening meal.

'Very quiet and polite.'

'Good. That's what I want. I'd beat them myself if they were impudent or disobedient.'

She blinked in shock at the callous way he had dismissed the girls. 'I wondered if they should join us for the evening meal sometimes?'

'No. They do all right as they are. Don't try to inter-fere in their upbringing.'

'I thought you'd want me to act as a mother to them.' She had been looking forward to it, Harriet realised.

He gave her a long, level look. 'No. I want you to give me a son. That's the main reason I married you.'

'I see.'

He resumed eating and she didn't try to introduce any further topics of conversation. Didn't dare.

PART 4
1831

12

September – October

Meg stood in the hall, listening shamelessly while her brother admitted to their mother that he'd proposed marriage to Emmy Carter – and been turned down. When she heard Netta making threats to leave if he married the girl, she could stand it no more but joined them and begged Jack to pay no attention. He loved Emmy, had done for a long time. He should ask her again, refuse to take no for an answer. 'If you want to get wed, you do it,' she told him. 'Life's too short to waste a chance of happiness.' Which of course brought her mother's wrath down on her as well as him.

Later she found the marks of a slap on Nelly's arm, for the child bruised easily, and threatened her mother with retaliation in kind if she ever found her beating her granddaughter again. 'I'll hit you back twice as hard . . . take a stick to you if I have to. Fancy taking out your anger on a two-year-old child!'

Her Nelly was such a quiet, good little thing, playing on her own in a corner or trying to help with simple tasks. There was no need whatsoever to beat the child.

After he found that Emmy had left town secretly,

poor Jack grew even quieter. Meg saw him several times taking Emmy's dog for walks, which seemed to lift his spirits a little. He even brought it round for the children to play with and suggested adopting it, but of course their mother wouldn't agree to that.

Then Meg met Liam Kelly one Sunday when she was taking Nelly for a walk. After that, what the rest of the family did became less important to her. Liam was her own age, a sunny-natured young fellow who clearly found her attractive and with whom Nelly lost her usual shyness.

They met a few times and when they did they talked easily, laughed and were happy together. Hope began to rise in Meg that something would come of their friendship, that because of it she'd escape from the misery of her mother's house, she and Nelly both. It seemed the only way to escape.

Then one day Liam failed to turn up for their prearranged meeting, something so unlike him that she went round to his house to ask if he was all right. She'd not yet met his family but he'd talked of taking her home and introducing her so she plucked up her courage and knocked on the door, worried about him.

There was a scuffling and whispering inside the house, then the door was opened by an old woman who stood there unsmiling. 'Yes?'

'I'm Meg Pearson. Is Liam here?'

'He's busy.'

'He was supposed to meet me, so how can he be busy? Can I speak to him, please?'

The woman folded her arms across her body and

scowled. 'No. And he won't be meeting *you* again, not after your mother's visit.'

'*What?*'

'You heard me. My Liam would never take up seriously with a girl who had a mother as nasty as that one.'

'Let me talk to him, *please!*'

She shook her head. 'He doesn't want to, not now. And none of us wants him to, either. You know what they say: look at the mother before you marry the daughter.'

'But I'm not like—'

The door slammed shut and Meg walked away, anger seething within her. Why had her mother done that? But the anger was soon replaced by the pain of rejection and Meg went to her old haunt by the reservoir to weep for a hope destroyed.

And of course her mother was unrepentant, saying she wasn't having a daughter of hers marrying a Catholic, and from a low Irish family too. After that Meg could hardly bear to speak to her. If it hadn't been for Nelly, she'd have left long ago. Oh, the things you had to bear for your child!

Only Jack understood how upset she was and scolded their mother for interfering. He'd long suspected that she lay behind Emmy's refusal of him. But it was too late for Meg to mend her fences with Liam. Was she never to find happiness?

Then Nelly fell ill of a fever, as so many young children did, and Meg forgot everything else in her worry for her child. She didn't dare take time off work because she was afraid Roper would replace her as Peggy had, but she was worried sick about how carelessly her mother nursed the child. Nothing Meg did or threatened seemed to make any difference. Her mother simply insisted she was doing all anyone could.

On the fourth day of the child's illness Meg nearly didn't go to work, but Nelly seemed quieter, more at peace when she kissed her goodbye, so in the end she tore herself away. She knew that her daughter would need extra delicacies to help her recover, delicacies that only her money could provide, so forced herself to go out.

When Jack came into the shop that afternoon and told Roper that Meg was needed urgently at home, terror froze her in place for a few seconds. Then she pulled herself together, snatched her shawl and followed him outside. He was avoiding her eyes, so she grabbed his arm and forced him to stop. 'What's wrong? What's happened?'

He stood rigid, saying nothing, but a tear rolled down his cheek.

'Jack? *Tell me!*'

'I'm sorry, love, but Nelly died this afternoon. Mam sent our Joey to fetch me, but it was too late to do anything by the time I got home . . .'

Only then did he try to put his arms round her.

She shoved him roughly away. 'Why didn't she send for *me?* Why did she wait so long? She must have known Nelly was worsening.'

'I don't know. But I doubt you could have done anything even if you'd been there. You know how easily children can slip away and Nelly wasn't strong.'

'I'll never forgive *her* for this.' Meg turned away, staring blindly into the distance. Nelly gone. Her little daughter dead. She should have stayed home, spent those last hours with the child at least. She would never forgive herself for that.

Now she had nothing left.

And her mother hadn't even sent for her! That added further to the pain – and made up Meg's mind for her. As soon as she'd buried her child she'd leave Northby so that she never had to see her mother's face again.

They started walking and Jack tried to offer her words of comfort but Meg didn't listen to them because there was no comfort possible. She kept seeing Nelly as she'd left her that morning, first flushed then pale, barely aware of what was happening around her, but smiling faintly when Meg had kissed her.

When Jack stopped her, raised his hand and brushed at her cheek she realised she was crying, silently, hopelessly. His cheeks were moist too.

At home she stopped outside the door, closed her eyes for a moment to gather from somewhere deep inside her the courage to do this, then slowly walked inside. Nelly was lying on the settle covered by a piece of ragged cloth. Netta was sitting by the fire, stretching her hands out to its warmth, with a cup of tea beside her.

Meg couldn't even bear to look at her mother, so uncovered the child's face and kissed her, then picked up the wasted little body and carried her daughter into the front room, the place where the two of them had slept, the only place she had any privacy or peace.

Gently and carefully she undressed and bathed her daughter, preparing the thin body for burial, fetching water from the kitchen but not speaking to anyone.

When her mother came to the door and started to say something, Meg glared at her and said, 'Get out!' in a voice that cut the air like a knife. She didn't need to look into the mirror to know that the vicious expression was back on her face.

She heard hammering in the back yard and a little later Jack brought in a coffin he'd made. The wood looked hard and full of splinters so she put her pink shawl in it and laid Nelly on its softness, wrapping the ends tenderly round the child.

'I've arranged the funeral for tomorrow,' her brother said. 'I'll take time off work to be with you, to carry the coffin to church.'

She nodded, but couldn't speak or she'd have started screaming and never stopped.

Later Ginny came to tell her the evening meal was ready but Meg shook her head. 'I don't want anything.'

Her sister hesitated before saying, 'I'm that sorry, our Meg. She were a lovely little kid, our Nelly, an' I'll miss her. So will our Joe. He's crying now.'

Meg could only nod.

When everyone else had gone to bed Jack came to sit with her for a while, not saying anything, just being there. His presence was as near to comfort as anything could be. He made them some tea and she drank it thirstily, but she couldn't eat, not a crumb.

Eventually he had to go upstairs and get some sleep.

Meg didn't feel sleepy, didn't want to lose a minute of her last hours with her daughter.

In the morning the children came to say goodbye to Nelly before they left the house, but when her mother would have followed them into the front room, Meg stopped her at the door. 'Get away.'

'But I'm her grandma.'

'I remember you slapping her face last week. It makes me want to slap yours now. And I will if you don't stay right away from her.'

Netta gaped at her for a moment then made an angry noise in her throat and went back into the kitchen.

'I don't want *her* coming to the funeral,' Meg told Jack. 'I'll go for her if she comes near my Nelly again.'

'All right, love. Whatever you want.'

In the end there was just Jack and her to bury her child. He carried the tiny coffin through the streets and Meg walked beside him, heedless of who saw her weeping.

Parson spoke the words of burial gently and she was grateful for that. Her Nelly had been a gentle soul. Meg didn't believe what he said about the life hereafter, didn't believe in anything any more, but she did want Nelly to have a proper funeral, so sat there motionless and let the words flow past her.

Afterwards she didn't linger by the grave, not wanting to see them pile black earth on her darling child. She turned and walked away as fast as she could.

When Jack caught up with her she thanked him and persuaded him to go back to work. She didn't tell him what she intended to do because she knew he'd try to stop her.

Her mother wasn't at home, which made things easier. Meg pulled up the floorboard in the corner and took what she considered to be her share of the family's savings. No more, no less. Then she made her clothes into a carrying bundle, Nelly's too because she didn't want to leave those for her mother to pawn.

She didn't look back when she walked out of the house, striding swiftly up Weavers Lane towards the moors. She had done with Northby, was never coming back, not even to see Jack. Never, ever!

As she walked, the wind blew her along and clouds raced across the sky. The wildness of the weather suited her mood. At first she debated whether to kill herself. She could go back after dark and tie bricks to her body before throwing herself into the reservoir, as other desperate souls had done. Or else she could find a high point on the moors and leap off it.

But for the moment it all seemed too much trouble, so she just kept on walking through the rest of the day and far into the night.

★

When Sophia found she was expecting her second child, she was pleased. Secretly she was hoping for a girl this time but Jethro had been jubilant about the son she'd presented him with a year ago and said openly that he hoped this one would be another boy.

To her surprise, he was a good and caring father, going to the nursery every day to see his son and play with him, something she'd not expected of a man so guarded. But with Martin, Jethro's mask of cool reserve vanished and he even laughed aloud as he played with his son.

Jethro looked at her across the bed as he was getting undressed. 'I'm pleased about the baby.'

'Good.' She was exhausted, wanted only to sleep as she had done last time she was in this condition.

He blew out the candle with his usual care, lifted the covers at his side and joined her in bed. No separate beds for them, he'd said early on in their marriage, though she would have welcomed a little privacy sometimes. 'You're a good wife, Sophia.'

She was startled. He so rarely gave compliments that she treasured each one. 'I'm glad you're happy with our marriage.'

'Aye, I am that. Pity your sister hasn't presented Andrew with a child yet. He's not best pleased.'

'Did he tell you that?' She was worried about Harriet, who had grown very quiet since her marriage and who refused point-blank to discuss what was wrong, as something surely was. 'He didn't need to. I can guess from what he says, how he looks at her. He's deep down angry.'

'From what I hear about making babies, the more he fusses about it and makes her anxious, the less likely it is that she'll start one.'

'Where did you hear that?'

'From Tettie.'

'Oh.'

She smiled in the darkness. Jethro set a lot of store on Tettie and her knowledge of children and birthing. He'd searched everywhere for a good nurse and when he'd found Tettie, had brought her back in his carriage, treating her with every courtesy, so highly was she recommended. And indeed, Sophia too had soon grown to value their son's nurse, who had helped her with the birthing and been of great comfort.

The woman was now devoted to little Martin, who was rosy with good health and laughed often, something Sophia believed to be important. She had been burdened even as a small child by her mother's expectations and desire for her to mind her manners, never to run, shout or play loudly. She had vowed that her children would be happy and carefree when they were little – though of course they must learn to behave politely in company.

She hadn't discussed her views with Jethro, who left what he referred to as 'women's matters' in her hands as long as their daily life went smoothly, but she'd made her wishes plain to the servants and above all to Tettie, who shared her beliefs about happy children thriving more than others.

'Are you tired tonight?' Jethro asked just as she was about to drop off to sleep.

Sophia knew what that meant. 'I am a little, but if you want me . . .'

'I know you're tired, but it's been a few days since we've lain together. I'll be quick.' He took her rapidly, expertly, with the minimum of fuss, then sighed into sleep.

She lay awake for a while, grateful for his consideration in bed. She was always very careful to tend to his needs, even now, because she didn't want him lying with other women. Tettie had told her about the diseases men could catch from loose women and pass on to their wives. Besides, Sophia liked the fact that Jethro was coming to depend on her in small ways, though she wasn't sure he realised how much yet. Not for her the quarrels that had often erupted between their parents or the cold silences that they witnessed between her sister and Andrew.

She wanted a happy home – even if her husband still didn't confide his thoughts and worries, or talk about his youth. What a reserved man he was! Would she ever penetrate the façade he presented to the world? She knew what he liked to eat and wear, how he preferred his home life arranged, what made him happy in bed. But she didn't know what went on behind those dark eyes and the imperturbable expression he donned like a coat each time he left their bedroom.

Did she want to know more about him? Wasn't it safer to continue living calmly like this? She sighed.

It might be safer but she did want more from him, much more. She wanted him to love her, then she would dare let herself love him. Was that too much to ask?

Toby stood by the window of the front bedroom next to Phoebe's and looked down the road that led eventually to Halifax. Narrow, twisting its way across the moors and down into the valleys, it was an important if minor route connecting Lancashire and Yorkshire, and it carried traffic most days. He'd hoped for better things for the inn because of its being on this road, but although business had improved, he still didn't get much carriage trade unless travellers had a problem. You'd think even the gentry would want to eat and refresh themselves. Perhaps they'd found Hal Dixon so unwelcoming they'd decided never to stop there again.

Oh, he should be satisfied with what he had, he knew. It was more than he'd ever dreamed of previously. But he wasn't. In fact, he felt downright restless today and was half inclined to go for a tramp across the moors. It was cold but not raining and . . . No, he couldn't. They'd be delivering the new barrels of beer today and it was better if he was there to keep an eye on things. Not that Gib's men were likely to be dishonest. He'd been dealing with Gib ever since he took over the inn and he trusted the man. But trust or not, you had to be seen to be in charge.

Besides, Phoebe wasn't well and he wanted to keep

her in the house place as much as possible near the warmth of the fire. If he went out today, she'd be down in the cellar supervising the placing of the new barrels. She hated to lie in bed, but that's what she really should be doing. The severe head cold that had laid her low a week or two ago had settled on her chest and she hadn't picked up again, still wheezed and coughed when she tried to talk.

It was time – more than time – to find a maid to help about the place, but he'd put it off, not wanting to disturb their peaceful life together. There was no one suitable in the tiny village, though Alice Bent came in regularly to help out. But Alice was courting and would soon marry, then what would they do?

Any permanent maid they hired from outside the district would need to live in but there were plenty of rooms.

He'd go into Halifax the very next week and visit the agency which found servants for people. Surely they'd be able to help him?

In Halifax Toby was walking along the street minding his own business when a woman, a lady by her clothing, stopped dead in front of him, her face turning white, her eyes revealing deep shock. He tried to move round her but she put out an arm to stop him.

'Excuse me, sir, but you're so like my husband – Jethro Greenhalgh – I can't believe it. You could be brothers. Twins even. Are you related to him?'

She had a pretty face and kind eyes, wasn't

looking down her nose at him however finely she was dressed, so he stayed to answer her question.

'I am distantly related, Mrs Greenhalgh, yes.'

'Why have I never met you, then?'

'Because I was born on the wrong side of the blanket, ma'am. The Greenhalghs don't recognise me.'

'What's your name?' Sophia didn't know why she wanted to know but she did. And if he was a relative, it was foolish not to recognise him. It was one of her minor regrets that neither she nor Jethro had any close relatives and therefore Martin had no aunts, uncles or cousins.

'I'm sorry, ma'am, but I don't think your husband would approve of our meeting. Better we ignore one another in future.'

'But—'

He shook his head, gave her a regretful smile and walked away. At the corner he stopped and turned round to watch her covertly from behind a cart. He saw another woman who resembled her come out of a shop, smiling and waving a small parcel, saw that Mrs Greenhalgh was still frowning and looking in his direction.

Damnation, what ill chance had brought her here today? He came to Halifax so rarely, mainly to buy books.

He was very sure that his half-brother wouldn't like it when he heard of the encounter and rich men could so easily cause trouble if they wanted to.

Well, just let the arrogant sod try!

Only Jethro hadn't seemed quite as arrogant last January when he came in for his free pot of beer. Toby was always surprised he bothered. But this time he'd talked a little, stiffly, then softening as he spoke of his son.

On that thought Toby frowned. He'd been a bit slack lately, spending more time than he should have done with his books. Thinking of possible trouble made him realise how easy it would be for someone to break into the inn. Maybe he should do something about that, put in a couple of stout doors between the various sections, with bolts on them? It wouldn't cost a lot.

They'd have to kill him to get him out of his home now. He loved it there.

But Jethro's wife had a bonny face. In other circumstances Toby would have liked her, he was sure. And she'd looked happy, which said something for his brother's behaviour as a husband.

Eh, what did he know about that? He'd still not met a woman he wanted to wed, to Phoebe's immense disappointment.

There must be something wrong with him.

Days blurred into one another for Meg after she left Northby. Sometimes she found shelter for the night; sometimes, if it was fine, she lay behind a wall or in a crevice in the rocks. She didn't seem to feel the cold any more, or care if her clothing grew sodden with rain.

When people tried to speak to her she turned away,

not wanting anything except the wildness and space of the moors. The only time she went willingly to settlements was in search of food. She preferred to sneak into a barn or make a nest in a haystack on rainy days.

A man tried to rob her once and instinct made her pull out the sharp knife she carried in her pocket and threaten him. He laughed at her, so she slashed his face for him. Then he stopped laughing. She wasn't afraid of him, taunting him as the blood ran down his face. 'Come at me again and I'll cut you to ribbons.'

He could have taken her still, for he was stronger than she was. But he didn't. He backed away then strode off along the path.

Once she came to her senses, she realised the risk she had taken. But at the time she'd felt quite confident about her own power to defend herself and so had driven him away. What the incident did was make her realise she wasn't going to kill herself – not yet anyway. Perhaps not ever. If she did, who would remember little Nelly? It seemed very important that she keep her daughter's memory alive.

Occasionally Meg found her senses for long enough to realise that this life couldn't go on, that winter would come and with it snow and cold. Then something would remind her of Nelly and the wildness would flow through her again, sending her striding off across the hills.

On one of her more sensible days she sat down to count her money, dismayed to find how few coins were left. She didn't even know where she was and sat gazing round in puzzlement. Where had she been? What had she spent the money on? She had only the vaguest of memories of the past few days – or was it weeks? And even those memories were as grey and shifting as dream images.

She became aware that it was raining and that she was soaked to the skin. Her bundle was heavy with moisture. But she couldn't seem to move on, just sat there in the rain, her face lifted and her tears mingling with the water falling upon her.

Toby was driving back from Halifax after a fruitless search for a maid when he saw a woman sitting huddled on a rock a little way off the road. He'd normally have passed by because you couldn't help every penniless vagabond you met, but something about her reminded him of his mother, he couldn't say what, just that there was a resemblance. Perhaps it was because they were both thin and dark-haired, or perhaps it was the way this woman held herself. Something, anyway. So he reined in his horse and called, 'Are you all right?'

But she didn't seem to hear him. He studied her, noting the sodden clothing and distant expression on her face. Was she a madwoman? He opened his mouth to tell the horse to walk on, but at that moment she shook her head in exactly the same way his mother had always shaken hers when she was puzzled – and he was lost, knew he simply couldn't pass this particular beggar by.

He secured the reins and put a nosebag on the

mare. There was nothing to fasten the cart to, not out here on the tops, but Bonnie wouldn't move away if she had something to eat. She was a plump greedy animal, given the chance, and he knew he spoiled her. But he enjoyed having an animal of his own. He spoiled the stable cats too, putting food down for them in the winter.

When he got closer to the stranger he saw she was weeping soundlessly, pain in every line of her body. 'What's the matter, love?' he asked gently.

She blinked and very slowly turned her head towards him. 'She's dead. My little Nelly's dead.'

'Your child?'

She nodded and gulped, making such a sad sound in her throat that he had to put his arms round her and pull her to him, had to. 'Eh, I'm sorry about that.'

He felt her sag against him, limp and boneless suddenly, and when he looked down he saw she'd fainted. How thin she was! How sharp her features and sunken her eyes! Everything about her was cold and wet. How long had she been out here in the rain?

He talked as he picked her up. 'You'll catch your death of cold sitting out on the moors on a day like this, lass. Come home with me and do your weeping by my fire.'

She didn't respond so he started walking back to the cart, astounded to discover how light she was. He tripped once in the rough tussock grass and nearly sent them both sprawling. 'Hey up, lad!' he admonished himself. 'Slow down or you'll hurt her worse.'

But what could be worse than to lose a beloved child? Not much!

When he laid her in the back of the cart she sighed and opened her eyes, but closed them almost immediately.

'I'm so cold,' she said in a rusty whisper of a voice. 'So very cold.'

'Lie still and I'll fetch your bundle, then we'll get you to a fire.' He raced over the uneven ground and came back again with the dripping bundle, his own hair and clothes wet now. Putting up the tailgate, he snatched the nosebag off the horse and tossed it into the cart anyhow in his haste to get the woman back to the warmth of his inn.

Clambering up on the driving bench, he picked up the reins and shouted at Bonnie to walk on. When she set off at her usual amble, he shook the reins to make her move more quickly. She hardly increased her pace so he took the whip and cracked it in the air over her head. Surprised by this, she picked up speed at once and within a few minutes they were home again.

The rain was still coming down heavily, beating at him as he picked up the woman and carried her into the house place by the side door.

Phoebe stood up and gaped at him. 'What's happened?'

'I found her on the moors. She's just lost a child, I think, and she's half-crazed with grief.'

'Then she needs to be put in the poorhouse. That's where—'

'*No!* We can look after her here, surely? I'll just see
to the horse and come back. Can't leave poor Bonnie
standing out in this.'

'What's got into you, Toby Fletcher?'

But he was gone.

Phoebe looked at the waif he'd brought in and
clucked in dismay at how wet and thin she was. She
began to strip off the sodden clothes, then carefully
edged the woman's unconscious body down on the
rug in front of the fire.

By the time Toby came back in she had the
stranger wrapped in a blanket, had pulled out one of
the bricks they always had heating at the back of the
oven for travellers and wrapped it in a piece of old
blanket before putting it at the stranger's back. The
kettle was just on the boil and the teapot was out on
the table.

'Shall I carry her up to one of the bedrooms,
Phoebe?'

'No. We need to get her warm again. Best to leave
her here by the fire for a while.' Then she became
aware of how wet he was too and began to scold him.
'You go and get those wet clothes off at once.'

But she was coughing even as she scolded and he
was worried about leaving her to nurse the woman
from the moors. He changed his clothes, went to
serve the customers in the public bar, but sent
everyone home earlier than normal. And whenever
he could, he went into the house place to help
Phoebe.

The stranger regained consciousness but was so

feverish she didn't seem to know where she was or what was happening to her. She drank the broth Phoebe urged on her spoonful by spoonful, though, and her colour was definitely better.

But Phoebe was looking so exhausted now that Toby insisted she go to bed and leave everything to him. It didn't take much persuasion to make her do that, which showed how bad she must be feeling. He brought down his own blankets and a quilt to lie on, then stretched out on the floor near the woman. Best keep her next to the fire where she would stay warm.

He grinned as he pulled the covers up and settled himself for sleep. He had all those rooms and several spare beds, and here he was, sleeping on the floor.

But he had to be there in case the poor creature regained her senses.

13

Meg woke and at first couldn't think where she was. This wasn't a new experience, it had happened a few times since she'd left Northby, so she didn't panic. That's how she always said it to herself, 'left Northby', because she had trouble even thinking about why. It could send her into that black place where there was no light, no hope.

Today curiosity pushed that thought away and she raised herself on one elbow to stare round. She was inside a house this time, lying near a fire wrapped in blankets, wonderfully cosy blankets. There was a lamp burning low on a scrubbed wooden table and although the fire had died down the room was still warm. Stretching, she let out a long sigh of sheer relief. She felt quite safe here.

There was a sound behind her and she rolled over quickly to see a man lying on the floor on the other side of the fireplace, wrapped in blankets like she was. Even as she watched he opened his eyes and looked at her. He had such a kind face she still didn't feel any sense of panic.

'How are you feeling now, lass?'

'Who are you? Where is this place?'

'I'm Toby Fletcher and you're in my inn. I found you out on the moors yesterday when I was on my way home from Halifax. You had a fever but that seems to have burnt itself out during the night. I looked at you once or twice and each time you were more peaceful and your forehead was cooler.'

'Oh. Thank you.' She became suddenly aware that she was naked under the covers and pulled them right up to her chin. Had he undressed her? Touched her?

'It's nearly morning and Phoebe will be down soon.'

As his face creased into a smile she lost more of her nervousness. A man with such a warm, friendly face surely couldn't mean her any harm.

'We didn't like to move you away from the fire or leave you on your own, and Phoebe's not so well, so I stayed down here to keep an eye on you.' He stretched again and gave a rueful grimace. 'It's not the softest bed I've ever slept in, though.'

'Is Phoebe your wife?'

'No, she's a sort of aunt. She helps me run my inn.'

He threw off the covers and she couldn't help shrinking, drawing back from him, though he was fully dressed.

'Nay, lass, I mean you no harm. But I need to get that fire burning properly again.'

He stepped across her and adjusted the damper of the stove so that the faint red glow at the centre of the fire began to brighten and spread. All the time he continued to talk soothingly, though she couldn't seem to concentrate on what he was saying. She liked his voice, though, because it was deep and gentle, reminding her of her father's when he was playing with tired little children before carrying them up to bed.

When she felt herself drifting towards sleep again she didn't even try to fight it. She was so very tired.

Toby turned round and smiled to see her fast asleep again, her face as peaceful as a child's, her hair in a tangle and a couple of curls looping down over her forehead. He bent to push them back and feel her forehead again. It was no longer burning hot nor was she sweating.

Who was she? he wondered. And if she'd lost a child, where was her husband? Didn't she have one or was it just a story she'd made up? No, surely not. You couldn't feign grief so deep. Moving quietly, he got himself a hunk of bread and slathered butter on it then poured a glass of milk out of the crock on the stone shelf in the pantry. Sitting down, he settled into enjoyment of his simple breakfast.

He was just finishing when Phoebe came down, looking pale and rumpled.

'How is she, Toby?'

'A lot better. She woke, talked sense, but fell asleep again quite quickly. And her fever seems to have abated.'

Phoebe bent to check the stranger and nod agreement. 'I wonder who she is?'

'I've been wondering that, too.'

'We'll leave her there for the time being. I can make a start on cleaning the public room.'

He watched her indulgently as she fussed over the closed stove. She took great pride in any improvement he made to the place and kept saying so, but most of all the stove with its capacity for heating water so easily. He sometimes felt he should do more to the place, but then he'd buy a new book, start reading it and go across to discuss it with the Curate. After that any improvements he'd been considering seemed unimportant as he considered the new ideas Mr Pickerling had planted in his mind.

When the weather was warm enough he'd go and sit in the back place with a book on his lap, often not reading it, just enjoying having it with him. He didn't light a fire in the big fireplace at one end of the main room there because it'd have taken too long to warm the place up and he could rarely snatch more than an hour for himself. They'd strung up ropes for the winter, so that Phoebe could hang things to dry there when it was raining, but she always whisked in and out quickly.

It sometimes seemed to him that the peace he found in the ancient building seeped into his very bones and he would come back to the inn seeing no need for anything but a quiet life earning his daily bread, not being greedy for money, helping others when he could, as he'd helped several sets of fugitives now. He often wondered what had become of the first ones, though. So many children for that poor couple to tramp the roads with. He hoped they'd found a home.

He went out to tend the mare and check the cart, finding the stranger's sodden bundle lying in the back of the latter. Oh, dear! He should have remembered that last night. He took it in to Phoebe, who opened it and made a sad sound as she found a child's clothing inside as well as the woman's, and a small child's at that.

'Eh, the poor lass!' she said quietly. 'And to think of her keeping them. She must have loved her daughter very much.'

They both contemplated the little garments, then Phoebe looked at the clock and gave him a shove. 'Look at the time. You'd better get on with things, Toby love. We're late starting today.'

Once or twice as he worked he remembered his encounter with Mrs Greenhalgh in Halifax and wondered what his dear brother would say to that. Well, let him say what he would. Toby had more or less promised Jethro Greenhalgh to stay away from Backenshaw, even though he missed his old friends, but he wasn't limiting where else he went. He had a business to run, Phoebe dependent on him – and now a stranger to look after, too. He must be free to do the best he could for them and go wherever he needed to.

He paused, puzzled. Why had he included the stranger in his responsibilities? He didn't know. But he certainly wasn't turning the poor woman out into the wintry weather so he'd have to look after her for a while. How she'd survived so far was a mystery to him – and probably to her as well.

Jethro sat in his carriage on his way to see Andrew. The latter had summoned him urgently but hadn't revealed why in his hurried note. Jethro was growing a little tired of these summonses, because he was enjoying the simple pleasures of living with his wife and not having his father ordering him around. And he enjoyed the happier atmosphere in the mill, too. He felt no need these days to be always seeking more ways to make money. The mill and a few other business investments produced more than enough for a sane man.

But Andrew seemed driven in the same way Jethro's father had been, always seeing trouble, always dissatisfied and wanting to make more money. He could never have enough and kept coming up with new and more grandiose plans to make their fortunes. John Greenhalgh would have been interested in such plans, but Jethro wasn't, especially when they broke the law.

There was nothing like marriage and fathering children for sobering a man down, he decided with a wry smile at himself.

When he arrived in Tappersley, Harriet came out to greet him and ask after her sister.

Andrew pulled her back roughly. 'Get about your business, woman! He's come to see me on a matter of urgency, not to tattle over teacups with you.'

Jethro saw her eyes fill with tears and looked at his

host in disapproval. He had felt guilty for a while now because each time he saw her, his sister-in-law looked more subdued and downtrodden. As the two men went into the mill office, Jethro said mildly, 'I was surprised to hear you speak to Harriet like that. Are the two of you not on good terms?'

'You know what's wrong. She's not done what I wanted her for, not produced a son for me.'

'That's still no reason to treat her like that.'

'Mind your own business. My private life's my own.'

Jethro could feel himself stiffening. 'It *is* my business. She's my wife's sister, for goodness' sake. If you make Harriet unhappy you make my wife unhappy too. Besides—' He broke off, not sure whether to proffer advice or not.

'Besides what?'

'If you want to get a woman with child, Tettie says you should make sure she's content. The unhappier the woman, the less likely she is to conceive.'

'Have you been discussing my affairs with your damned nursemaid?' Andrew thumped the desk, his face flushing with anger.

Jethro could feel the muscles in his own face growing rigid, could always tell when he'd donned that expressionless mask he saw sometimes in the mirror. Well, with a father like his, it'd sometimes been extremely important not to betray his true feelings. 'Certainly not. I consulted Tettie when I wanted to get *my* wife with child and followed her advice –

with the results you see. One son born, another child on the way.'

'Sophia's breeding *again*?'

'Yes.'

'Congratulations.'

He sounded, Jethro thought, as if the word had nearly choked him.

'But you can still keep out of my affairs. I treat my wife as I see fit. I don't believe in pampering women. They're there to serve us, not the other way around.'

Jethro said no more, could only hope the seeds he had planted would take root. He was feeling guilty now that he'd matched Harriet with Andrew, but hadn't previously realised how badly his fellow millowner treated women because Andrew had been more his father's friend than his and Jethro had not often come here in those days. He changed the subject because he knew when it was unwise to pursue a point. 'You said you had something urgent to tell me?'

'Aye. Your bastard brother has been seen in Halifax.'

'Well, it's only to be expected that he'll visit nearby towns.'

'He was seen there by our wives.'

'Ah.'

'And *your* fool of a wife accosted him, asked him who he was.'

Jethro paused for a moment to control his reaction to that way of describing Sophia, then managed to ask quietly, 'Did she now? And what did he tell her?'

'Said he was a distant connection, according to Harriet. She was full of the resemblance between him and you, couldn't stop talking about it till I shut her up.' He let out a little growl of anger and the quill he'd been fiddling with snapped suddenly. 'Did your precious Sophia not tell you about the encounter?'

'No.' And he'd have words with his wife when he got back about that – no, not 'have words' but ask her gently. In her condition he didn't want to upset her.

'I think we've no choice but to get rid of Fletcher now. An accident, perhaps. Your spy can arrange something, no doubt? I gather that fellow will do anything for money.'

Jethro didn't even need to consider this. 'No.' The word was flat and very emphatic.

'Why not? Surely you've not grown squeamish? You're John Greenhalgh's son, for heaven's sake. He'd not hesitate to rid himself of a problem.'

'He never touched Fletcher, who was always a risk. And when he was on his deathbed my father made me promise not to harm the man. I see no reason to kill my half-brother just for existing.'

'What happens if someone recognises him, knows the story, lets the secret out?'

'I think if that were going to happen it'd have done so by now.'

'It can still happen at any time, as I keep damned well telling you!'

'Well, if it does, we'll deal with it then. After all, it's me who'll be affected not you.'

'If one secret comes out, others will follow. I've no mind to have *my* past raked over in public.'

'Then let sleeping dogs lie.'

Andrew spent half an hour trying to change his companion's mind, by which time each man was holding his temper on a tight leash.

Tired of arguing, Jethro stood up. 'This is getting us nowhere. If that's the only reason you brought me here, then I'll get back home. I do have a mill to run and a family to care for. That's enough for me these days – and should be enough for you too. What do you need more money for anyway?'

'To rub in the faces of the county set. To make them recognise men like us.'

'A waste of time. They'll never treat us as equals, however rich we become. Who cares what they think anyway?'

'I do.'

Jethro waited impatiently for his carriage to be brought round, refused an offer of refreshment that was made grudgingly and was relieved to get away from a man who increasingly irritated him. All he regretted was that he'd not managed to speak to Harriet. He'd ask Sophia to question her sister, find out why she looked so unhappy.

On the way back he saw the Packhorse in the distance and on a whim stopped there for a drink and something to eat. He might as well see how things were for himself.

To his surprise he was served in a side parlour clearly set aside for the better class of customer, and the dish of stew was very palatable indeed, though Dixon's wife who served him didn't look well and apologised for coughing.

His half-brother came to stand in the doorway.

'You didn't come for your free pot of ale this year.'

'I was too busy.'

'We'll not charge you for the meal, then. After all, you are a relative.'

Jethro looked at him and decided to speak openly. 'I have to thank you, I believe, Fletcher, for telling my wife that you're only a distant connection.'

'It suits me better. I'm not proud to have my name linked with yours.'

'What's wrong with the name Greenhalgh?'

'It's associated with harsh treatment of the folk who work for you and bring in all that money.'

'I think you'll find that things have changed since my father's day.'

'Pity they didn't change before *my* mother worked herself to death in that mill.'

Anger sparked briefly in Jethro but he held it firmly back. He had to admire his half-brother's calmer demeanour, even if reluctantly. 'How is business?'

'Adequate for my needs. Excuse me.'

Someone had come into the public room and Jethro listened to Toby exchanging greetings with a regular customer, who teased him for buying more books. Jethro was surprised about that. He hadn't figured the fellow for a reader. The lawyer had said he could barely sign his name on the deed of gift.

When he'd finished his meal Jethro rang the hand

bell and thanked Phoebe, then asked for his carriage to be brought round.

As he went out into the public room one of the other customers goggled, looking from him to Toby and back again.

'We're distantly related,' Toby said, with a grin in Jethro's direction. 'Hardly even know one another but the Good Lord made a mistake and gave us the same face.'

'Very distantly related,' Jethro confirmed. He didn't like the way the other men were staring at him as if they resented his very presence. People were too independent up here on the tops. Even since the decline of the handloom weaving that had given the district its name, most of them managed to earn a living without calling any man master.

As the carriage bounced along the road again he decided there was nothing to worry about with Fletcher. The man was minding his own business and living quietly. He didn't know why Andrew was creating such a fuss about what was mainly a Greenhalgh concern.

But he did wonder why Sophia hadn't mentioned the encounter with his half-brother.

That night was the first time Andrew gave Harriet a serious beating. He'd thumped her before, but not actually beaten her. When he started raining blows on her, she tried to shield herself, but he wouldn't stop, couldn't. It infuriated him to see her bear the beating stoically, making no sound loud enough to be heard outside the bedroom. That made him unleash the full fury of his fists on the tender parts of her body that no one but him would see. He wanted her to scream for mercy as his first wife had, but she didn't.

For some reason he couldn't get that damned nursemaid's advice out of his mind and drew back, breathing heavily, hearing Harriet whimper as she moved her sore body, all the time watching him warily.

When he reached out to touch her shoulder, she yelped and jerked away from him, saying, 'In God's name, no more! What have I ever done to deserve this?'

What *had* she done? he wondered suddenly. Nothing, really. He was subject to these fits of rage and always took them out on the nearest person. Shame mixed with the anger still simmering in him and he surprised himself by muttering, 'I'm sorry,' into the shadowy darkness left by a single candle burning on the mantelpiece.

And he *was* sorry, for the beating had done no good to either of them. He was still anxious about Fletcher and still concerned to get himself a son. 'I shouldn't have done that. I won't again.'

Harriet said nothing, but she didn't believe him and lay awake for most of the night. She hated him now though she didn't dare show it because she was trapped. What a fool she was to have rushed into marriage so quickly. Even life with her mother would have been preferable to this.

The following morning her face bore the marks of a blow or two that had been meant for her body and he was appalled by how dark the bruises were. 'I think you'd better stay in bed till your face recovers.'

'Who will run your house for you if I do?' She looked at him coldly from across the bedroom. 'If you will beat me, we must both face the consequences of your actions.' She was out of the room before he had his new surge of anger under control.

So he turned his rage on another object. Toby Fletcher. If Greenhalgh was too weak to act, then he wasn't. By hell he wasn't!

When Meg next woke she saw an older woman stirring something on the stove. A vague memory surfaced of a man with a kind face. He'd talked about someone called – she searched her mind for it and felt pleased when she remembered. 'Phoebe?'

The woman turned round. 'You're awake, are you? How do you feel?'

'A lot better, thank you.'

'I have the clothes you were wearing washed and dry, and you'll want to use the privy, I should think.' Phoebe came to help her up, but was caught by a bout of coughing. 'Sorry. Had a cold and can't seem to shake it off. The coughing makes me dizzy.' She leaned against the table.

Meg wrapped the sheet round herself but then had to clutch the table because she still felt a bit dizzy. 'My legs feel very weak. We make a good pair, don't we?'

'Yes.' Phoebe smiled at her. 'You look a lot better than yesterday, though. You've got a bit of colour in your cheeks now. I'll show you where to go but you'd better get dressed quickly before Toby comes back.' She passed over a small pile of clothing, turned her back for modesty's sake, then showed the lass where to go, thinking that her clothes were little better than rags, all stained and tattered around the hem.

Toby came in soon afterwards. 'Well, Greenhalgh has driven off now. I hope he'll stay away this time.'

'There's nothing you can do to stop him coming here. It's a public place, an inn. What does it matter anyway? Most of the folk round here know about the connection between the two of you. Word usually gets out, however hard you try to keep things secret.'

'I don't like being reminded of who my father was.' He looked at the empty nest of blankets. 'She's awake, then?'

'Aye. And in her senses. Seems a nice enough lass.'

'Shall I pick up the blankets or will she be lying down again?'

'I'll not be lying down. I have to get on my way.'

He turned to see her standing in the doorway, but for all her brave words she was using the door frame for support and looked as if a few steps were all she'd be able to manage. Her face wasn't pretty, too thin for that, but her eyes were bright with intelligence and life.

'There's no need to leave yet. You'll need a day or two to recover,' he told her.

'I don't want anyone's charity.'

'If that's all that's worrying you, you can help Phoebe to pay for your food – which is all your staying on will cost me. She's not well, as you can see.'

'I keep telling you I'm all right,' Phoebe protested, but her pallor betrayed her as did another bout of coughing that had her doubled up.

'And I keep telling you that I'm not blind,' Toby said, still in the same mild tone. He bent to pick up the blankets and when he started trying to fold them, the stranger took hold of one end and they managed the task more easily between them.

'Thank you.' He watched her sit down afterwards as if the effort had exhausted her and laughed suddenly.

'What's so amusing?' she asked, not used to people who laughed and smiled so much.

'I was thinking that you and Phoebe between you probably make up one whole woman.'

She found herself smiling and admitting in her own mind that he was right. 'Well, then, as long as I'm of some use . . .' She looked questioningly at the older woman.

Phoebe smiled at them both. Trust her Toby to ease the situation. 'I'd be grateful for your help. What's your name, lass?'

'Meg.'

'Just Meg?'

She nodded.

'Then let's get some of my good stew into you if you're to help me. You look like you need feeding up.'

Someone called from the public room and Toby left to serve a customer.

Phoebe looked at Meg. 'I can see from your face that you've had some hard times . . .'

'I don't want to talk about them!'

'Not to me, not now when I'm still a stranger. But later, when you know me better, if you ever want to tell me about it, well . . . people say I'm a good listener. I've not had an easy life myself so I don't sit in judgement on other folk.' She set a bowl of stew in front of the young woman, cut her a slice of bread and turned back to her cooking.

Meg ate slowly, enjoying every mouthful because the food had been given to her in kindness.

After a while Phoebe had to sit down, shaking her head. 'I'm that weak. Can't seem to shake this off. Would you keep an eye on that kettle for me? Push it to the side of the hob when it boils. I'll just lie down on the sofa for a minute or two.'

Within seconds she was sleeping so Meg finished eating her food, cleared her bowl away into the scullery she could see through an open doorway, and came back to pull the kettle to one side and stir the stew which was starting to simmer gently now. When Toby returned, she put one fingertip to her lips and gestured to Phoebe.

He nodded in understanding and sat down at the table, saying in a whisper, 'I wouldn't mind a bowl of that stew myself.'

'I'll get it for you.'

She did that but he could see that like Phoebe she

was quite weak so gestured to a chair at the table. 'Have a rest now. It takes time to get over a fever and I doubt you've been eating properly for a while.'

She didn't protest. 'I do want to work for my keep, though. I've vowed never to be beholden to anyone again.'

'That's all right. Just do what you can and we'll all help one another.'

He watched her when she wasn't looking in his direction. She was stick thin but had lost that sallow waxy look at least. He wondered yet again what had brought her to this, but knew better than to ask. You got to know people when you were working in an inn, which ones wanted to talk and which didn't. She definitely wasn't the sort to tell her private affairs easily to a stranger.

Rain began falling again during the late afternoon and when the customers left, Toby closed the inn earlier than usual.

'We're all tired. Let's go to bed.'

'We'll find you a proper bed tonight, love,' Phoebe said. 'You can have the bedroom next to mine. It's small, but we cleaned it out for a maid so we only have to make up the bed.'

'I'll help her do that,' Toby said. 'You look asleep on your feet, Phoebe love.'

They two were so comfortable together, Meg envied them. 'I can do it myself.'

'Quicker with two of us.' He smiled at her. 'Go up with Phoebe and I'll fetch some sheets from the linen cupboard.'

When he joined her in the bedroom, she had her arms wrapped round herself and was staring out of the window.

'What can you see?'

'Rain beating against the panes, darkness, nothing really. I'm glad to be inside tonight. It's hard sleeping out when it's wet.'

'Must be.' He pulled back the blankets and shook out one of the sheets. 'You look tired out. Catch hold of that end. We'll do this more quickly together.'

Within a few minutes the feather mattress had been shaken into softness and the sheets put on the bed. He stepped back and looked at her. 'I'll just go and fetch you up a hot brick, then I'll get off to my own bed.'

He was back within the minute, carrying a brick wrapped in flannel. 'There. That'll warm you up.'

She hadn't tried to get into bed, not till she was sure she was safe with him. She watched him tuck the brick into the bed and move back to the door. He didn't look at her in *that way*.

When he'd gone she set the chair back under the door handle so that no one could sneak in without her hearing. He seemed nice, hadn't tried to touch her while they were making the bed, but you could never be too careful when you were a woman on your own. Then she took off her top and skirt and crawled into bed.

She was so bone weary she'd expected to fall asleep immediately. But she lay awake for a while because she had recognised a new feeling. The first tiny tendril of hope had crept into her mind – hope that she would find something to do with the rest of her life, hope that the future wouldn't be as bleak as this past few weeks had been, hope that her little daughter was sleeping peacefully somewhere kinder than this life had been to her.

Jethro arrived home and went to find Sophia. 'Why didn't you tell me?'

'Tell you what?'

'That you'd seen my damned half-brother in Halifax and—' He cut off further words, horrified that he'd betrayed his secret to her.

She moved across the room to him and laid one hand on his arm. 'I'd guessed he was your brother, Jethro. The resemblance is too strong for a distant relationship. That's why I said nothing. I didn't want to upset you.' For once his mask of imperturbability wasn't in place and as she looked up at him she saw how conflicting his emotions were. 'Do you want to tell me about it – or shall we not mention it again?'

His hand came up to clasp hers and with a tense exhalation of air he drew her across to sit on the sofa. 'I used to see him in the street when I was a lad, but I didn't find out much about him until I was nearly grown, then my father told me. And I was angry, because Fletcher is older than me – and I don't like him to wear my face. Does that sound stupid?'

'No, of course not.'

'I wanted to send him away and my father tried to fix things . . . paid men to persuade him to go to

Australia or America, the further away the better. Only he wouldn't leave, said he belonged here in Lancashire.'

'Who was his mother?'

'A woman who worked in the mill. She came to Backenshaw from somewhere else after the baby was born, though my father never had anything to do with her again because he'd married my mother by then. The woman died a few years ago but *he* stayed on in Backenshaw, working for a carpenter. He's good with his hands everyone says. Well thought of too, but I always hated him. Still do.' He paused for a moment, wondering if that was true and amended it to, 'Well, not hate, but I don't like the fact that he exists.'

'That's sad, if you're brothers.'

'*Half*-brothers.'

'It's still a close relationship.'

'Not for me.'

'What does he do? Where does he live? In Halifax?'

'Why do you need to know?'

'If I'm to avoid him, it'd be useful to know where not to go. But if you don't want to tell me, I won't ask again.'

He shrugged. 'Fletcher lives in that inn on the tops, the one on the road to your sister's, the Packhorse. My father gave it to him just before he died. I was against that and tried to buy it back, but Fletcher wouldn't sell, said he liked living there.'

'He's far enough away from Backenshaw now, surely?'

'Not for me.' Jethro leaned his head back against the sofa and sighed. 'I have to go across to Halifax occasionally, or to see Andrew. Every time I pass that inn I think of Toby Fletcher and grow angry.'

She shook her head. 'I can't imagine feeling like that about my sister.' When she said that she saw a look of anxiety cross his face. 'What is it? What's the matter with Harriet?'

'Nothing.'

'Don't lie to me, Jethro.'

He turned his head to look at her. 'I think I've done your sister a disservice, introducing her to Andrew. She's not happy and he's – well, too abrupt with her.'

Sophia looked down at her skirt, tracing the edge of a frill very carefully. 'I know she's unhappy, but she won't talk about it.'

'Oh, hell!' He pulled her into his arms and, for the first time since their marriage, embraced her openly, in daylight, outside their bedroom in a place where any of the servants could have seen them. 'I'm sorry, Sophia. I meant it for the best. She seemed so eager to get married and move away from your mother, and he wanted a wife.'

'I don't blame you. There was no way you could have known he'd be unkind to her. But I can't help worrying about her.'

'No use dwelling on it. The deed is done now. Well, I'd better get back to work.'

She watched the bland expression settle on his face again and was sorry, but once he'd gone she smiled.

She'd seen behind that mask today. It felt like an important step for both of them.

As for the brother, it seemed strange to think of Jethro having one, especially one who looked so like him. But if he wanted to keep his distance from the fellow, then she'd do as he wished.

14

In the morning Meg woke and stretched luxuri-
ously because this was the most comfortable bed
she'd ever slept in. She was feeling so much better
today, warm and cosy and – oh, dear, she'd promised
to help out in the inn in return for her food and keep!
What was she doing lying in bed like this when it was
full daylight already? She threw off the covers,
finding the November morning very cold.

There was water in a pretty jug sitting on a
polished washstand. She couldn't resist stroking the
flowers on the jug and running her fingers over its
shiny surface. She listened but could hear no sounds
of movement so risked taking off her underclothes
and giving herself a quick wash all over. What a
pleasure that was! If only she'd had prettier clothes
to put on afterwards, not her ragged old things. By
the time she was dressed again she was shivering but
didn't care. It was worth it.

From the top of the stairs she heard someone
moving about in the house place and hurried down
to join Phoebe – but it was Mr Fletcher who was
riddling the fire to get rid of the night's ash.

He turned as he heard her come in. 'Phoebe, can

you – oh, it's you, Meg. Have you seen Phoebe this morning? She's usually down before me.'

'No, I haven't. Shall I go and knock on her door?'

He looked down at his filthy hands and back at her. 'Would you? And if she doesn't answer, just peep in and check that she's all right. I'm a bit worried about her.'

'Yes, of course.' She ran back up the stairs, happy to be of use. When she knocked on the bedroom door, she heard a sound from inside and peeped in. There was enough daylight coming round the edges of the curtains for her to see that Phoebe was lying in bed with her eyes closed, looking pale, her breath rasping in her throat.

As Meg tiptoed across to stand by the side of the bed Phoebe opened her eyes. 'What time – is it?'

'I don't know but Mr Fletcher said you were usually up by now and he was worried, so he asked me to come and see if you were all right.'

Phoebe tried to sit up but after a brief effort let her head drop back on to the pillows. 'I feel dreadful,' she admitted in a croaky voice. 'But he needs me. Will you help me up? I'll manage all right once I get going, I'm sure.'

'I don't think you should even try. You look really poorly. Besides, he's got me to help him today, so he won't be on his own.'

'But you're ill too.'

'Weak, not ill. And I'm a lot better this morning, thanks to you two.'

Phoebe stared at her then tears welled in her eyes. 'I hate to let him down.'

'You can't help being ill. Look, shall I bring you up a cup of tea and something to eat? You may feel better after you've eaten.'

Phoebe grimaced. 'Just the tea, please. I don't think I can eat anything. It hurts to swallow.'

So Meg went downstairs again to relay the news, which made Mr Fletcher so anxious he washed his hands and ran upstairs to see for himself how Phoebe was.

It was lovely to see how he cared about the older woman. Sighing, wishing she had someone to care for her, Meg turned to study the stove, which was a bigger version of Peggy's. The fire was burning up now so she checked that the kettle was full and moved it across to the hottest part of the blackened iron hob.

Footsteps thumped down the wooden stairs again, heralding the return of Mr Fletcher.

'I've told her to stay in bed. Do you think you'll be well enough to help me today? I'll get Alice from the village to come and do the scrubbing and heavy work, but I really need someone to do the cooking. Can you manage that, do you think?'

Meg nodded. 'Yes. I'm quite a good cook, actually, Mr Fletcher, or so my last employer told me.'

'Call me Toby or you'll make me feel ancient.'

She looked at him and nodded. 'All right.'

'What was your work? Were you really a cook?'

'I wasn't exactly a cook. It was a mixed-up sort of job, really. I worked in the pawn shop part of the time and as a maid to the owner the rest, doing Mr Roper's cooking and seeing to his washing and other stuff.' It seemed a very long time ago and she felt as if she was speaking about someone else not herself, but she was glad to see Mr Fletcher's – no, *Toby's* – face brighten.

'Eh, it's a relief that you can cook because we provide food for customers sometimes. We don't prepare much, just one hot dish usually, stew or roast meat, chops, things like that. But if any gentry stop at the inn, which they don't usually, they want better food and then Phoebe fries them some ham and onions, and potatoes as well. She calls it a fricassée. Oh, and she usually does some scones or griddle cakes too. We can always eat them up ourselves.'

He beamed at her and before she knew it Meg was smiling back at him. When had she last felt like smiling? She couldn't remember. Not since before Nelly died. To her surprise he came to stand closer and laid his hand on her arm.

'Don't,' he said softly.

She blinked up at him. 'Don't what?'

'Look so sad.'

She turned away, spreading her hands helplessly.

'I know you've had a terrible loss – you told me about your daughter dying when I found you and – '

'I did?'

He nodded, his expression solemn now.

'I don't usually mention that.' She hadn't said a

word to anyone else about it since she'd left Northby.

'How long ago did it happen?'

Meg shook her head, not seeing the room now or the glowing fire, seeing only the hole in the ground and the little coffin being lowered into it. 'I don't know. A few weeks ago, I suppose. I don't even know what date it is now. I've been too upset to notice. I've just been wandering, sleeping rough or in barns. I don't remember much about it except that the freedom of the moors seemed to draw me on.' She made a huge effort not to cry or lose herself in her grief, because he was being so kind and he needed her help. It felt good to be needed again. 'I was lucky you found me, took me in.'

'You were. There aren't many people travelling along Calico Road at this time of year.'

'Calico Road?'

'The village is called Calico, because they used to weave it here before the machines took over most of the weaving, so the road hereabouts got the same name. You can still see the old looms in some of the attics and a few folk still weave their own cloth, just for them and their families. In the old days, of course, they wove wool from their own sheep and then later on cotton which the putter-out supplied and—' He broke off. 'Sorry. I get carried away sometimes. I like reading, you see, and finding things out.'

'It was interesting.'

'And if we're talking about folk being lucky, well, I was too. With Phoebe ill, I'd have been lost if I hadn't found you. I can't cook, that's for sure, except to fry up a bit of ham and an egg or two. We've been meaning to get a maid and I wish we had so Phoebe wouldn't worry about . . .' His voice trailed away and he looked at Meg speculatively. 'You wouldn't be wanting a job, would you?'

Everything went very still in the kitchen as if the world had stopped dead for a moment. *A job,* she thought. *Yes, of course. I do need a job now.* 'Do you really mean that?'

He nodded. 'You'd have to live here, though. It's a bit lonely, only a small village. Would you miss living in a town?'

'No. Not at all. I've found the moors – comforting.' She managed a wobbly smile. 'But you don't know whether I'm a good worker or not.'

'You don't know whether I'm a good employer or not. I may be so nasty to you that you'll run away again.'

He tried to look severe and failed. He'd done it again, made her smile. She shook her head at him. 'We'll give it a day or two and see how we get on, then we'll both decide. But I'm happy to cook something for you today, and perhaps—' She broke off, noticing that he was holding out his hand to her.

'I usually shake hands to seal a bargain.'

So she let him clasp her hand in his big warm one, smile down at her again with those kindly eyes, and somehow it put heart into her. She could feel the touch of his fingers for a long time afterwards, kept looking down at them, but of course he'd not left a mark. He was a big, strong man, you could see that, but so gentle with it. She'd never met a man quite like him.

If he really meant it, she thought she might find a measure of peace working here on the edge of the moors. The spaces and the sense of freedom seemed to give her strength, help her to carry on. Just as he did. He seemed so reliable.

Then she remembered that it was an inn. She'd be selling beer, watching men getting drunk, making fools of themselves. She wasn't sure she could do that. Not after what the drink had done to Ben.

Cully pocketed his monthly payment after reporting on Fletcher and when Peter had left, called for a third pot of beer. As he was about to drink it another man sat down opposite him.

'My master asked me to speak to you, Cully Dean.'

Cully recognised him at once, in spite of his bad eyesight. Jad Mortley had a streak of white hair at one side of his head and a gravelly voice that you never forgot once you'd heard it. 'Why?'

'He wants a little job done. And he'll pay well for it, too. You do like earning extra money, don't you?'

Cully licked his lips and nodded. Yes, of course he did. But if the other folk in Calico found out he was working for Beardsworth, they'd never speak to him again. Still, more money would be good. 'What exactly does he want me to do and how much is he paying?'

'He'd like to get rid of your friend Toby Fletcher.'

'Ha! Who wouldn't? That one's no friend of mine!'

'Exactly. So you wouldn't be sorry to see him under the ground?'

Cully stared in shock as the words sank in. Surely he didn't mean . . . 'Nay, I want nowt to do with murder.'

The stranger leaned across and grabbed him by the front of his clothes, pulling his body half across the table so that their faces were very close, and betraying a strength that made the smaller man tremble to feel it. 'You could get rid of him easily. Drop a little poison in his beer or arrange an accident. An accident would be best so no one need ever know it was done on purpose. My employer will pay you ten guineas if you get rid of him.'

As he let go, Cully dropped back on to the bench. He glanced from side to side but the room was a blur around him, as usual. He could only pray no one was close enough to hear. He moved and the coins chinked in his pocket. Already he had more money in his pocket than he'd ever seen in his life, and in spite of using it regularly to buy his beer at the Packhorse still had some safe in the leather draw-string bag he'd hidden in the shed to keep it from his wife. Ten guineas on top of this would – no! He suddenly realised the regular monthly money would stop if Fletcher died. 'I'd need more than that because if I kill him, my other money will stop.'

'Twenty guineas, then. But no more, and you don't get paid until he's dead.'

'I'll – see what I can do. How do I let you know if I – succeed?'

'I'll find out, don't worry. Just do it and you'll be paid.' Jad slipped a coin into the other man's hand.

Keeping it hidden in the palm of his hand, Cully raised it to his eyes and squinted. A whole guinea! He breathed deeply. You could buy a lot of beer with a guinea.

'That's just to get you started. One guinea extra to show my master's good will.'

'I'll do it.'

As he drove his rickety little cart home Cully alternately smiled and frowned. He wasn't sure about this. Didn't really like the idea of killing someone – not to mention hanging for it if they found out.

But he did like the idea of earning twenty guineas – that was a fortune to a man like him. If he had that much money he could leave Calico, which was a miserable place to live, and he wouldn't take his bloody wife and brats with him either. He could open a little shop or run an ale house, perhaps, find himself a new woman, one who didn't nag all the time and didn't keep having brats who needed feeding . . .

A carriage stopped at the inn that day and a gentleman helped a lady out of it, both of them shivering in the icy wind.

'Are you sure this place is respectable?' she asked, hanging back for a minute and staring at the Packhorse.

'I've heard so. Anyway, this morning's delays mean we haven't eaten since breakfast and I'm damned if I'm going on until I've had something to eat, even if it's only bread and cheese.' He tugged at her arm and with a little grunt of annoyance she moved forward, turning up her nose as they entered the public room and saw the group of common men drinking.

Toby hurried forward to greet them, hoping their coachman could deal with their horses. If he had more carriage trade, he'd hire a man for the stables, but he didn't have enough work to offer and couldn't afford the extra wages just now. 'Welcome to the Packhorse, sir, madam. Let me show you into the private parlour.'

The lady looked round the side room with a disdainful expression, though Alice had scrubbed the floor and dusted everything only that morning. But the fire's warmth drew her across and she held her hands out to it with a sigh of relief. 'Do you have a wife, landlord?'

'Er – no. But I have a cook if you need a woman's help?' He knew what such requests usually meant and didn't ask any further questions.

She inclined her head. 'I do.'

The man said, 'I'm glad to hear you've got a cook, for I've not eaten in six hours and I'm famished.'

'This woman only started work here today,' Toby warned, 'but she's prepared a very tasty stew and some scones. It's simple food, I know. Would that do? As you'll understand, we don't get the custom up here to cook fancy food every day just in case someone stops.'

'Stew will do me fine. Just fetch it out, and plenty

of it too. Oh, and give my coachman and groom something to eat as well, will you?'

Toby hurried into the house place and told Meg what had happened. 'The lady probably wants to use the chamber pot. You just have to take her up to the big front bedroom and wait outside, then I can empty the pot later.'

Meg looked at him in dismay. 'I can't go and talk to gentry dressed like this!'

He studied her ragged clothing, still with mud stains round the hem, then his eyes fell on Phoebe's 'company apron' as she called it, a huge white garment with frills over the shoulders. She always donned it to serve the gentry. He nipped it off the hook and beckoned to Meg. 'Put this on and they'll not notice what's under it. Phoebe always wears it to serve folk like these. I have to go out and tell his servants to look after the horses themselves, for I haven't the time to do that.'

'Can't Alice see to the lady?'

The girl looked from one to the other of them. 'I'm not waiting on 'em. It fair frits me, speaking to gentry does. Anyway, I have to get home now and help my ma, Mr Fletcher, you know I do.'

'All right, love. And thanks for coming.' He gave her the money she'd earned and Alice beamed at him as she tucked it inside her clothing.

Once they'd gone, Meg tied the apron strings carefully, smoothed out the front and summoned up all her courage.

By the time she'd escorted Mrs Glossop upstairs,

listened to her peeing like any other human being, then escorted her down again, she had lost a lot of her fear. And as she served them with the stew, Mr Glossop stole a taste with his spoon and smacked his lips just like her brother Shad did, so she felt even less in awe. He finished eating it quickly – if he wasn't a gentleman you'd call it gobbling – and called for another bowlful and some more bread, though the lady only ate one helping. Meg had never seen anyone eat like him, never! No wonder he was so fat, the lucky fellow.

When she went back to clear away the dishes, they were all empty and the gentleman was leaning back in his chair, smiling.

'Good food,' he said cheerfully. 'But I've still got a corner to fill.'

'I've scones, sir, baked fresh today, and there's butter and bilberry conserve to go with them, if that suits?' It had amazed her how many jars of conserve Phoebe had lined up on the shelves of the big pantry.

He nodded. 'It certainly does.'

She hurried out again.

When the satisfied customers had left, Toby went into the kitchen and found Meg standing staring at something in her hand.

She turned to him and held it out. 'They gave me this. It must be meant for you.' In her hand were two silver half-crown pieces.

He closed her fingers round them. 'That's your tip. They enjoyed the food so they gave you a bit extra to say thank you. Five shillings. That's what the gentry do.'

She stared at him in amazement, then opened her hand and smiled at the coins. 'I've never earned money so easily in my whole life.'

'Let's hope you earn a lot more the same way then, lass. Now, you look tired, so I think you should have a sit-down. I'll go up and see how Phoebe is and—'

'I nipped up not long ago. She's sleeping. She hasn't eaten anything but she's drunk three cups of tea.'

'Then you should definitely take a rest. You're not fully recovered yourself yet.'

Meg sank on to a chair. 'I am a bit tired, I must admit. I'm not usually so lazy, I promise you.'

'It's not lazy. You've been –' he searched for a tactful word to describe the state in which he'd found her and the reason for it, but only came up with '—unwell.'

'Out of my mind with grief,' Meg corrected him flatly. She didn't pretend, not even to herself, but stared blindly across the room, thinking of Nelly again, not noticing what he was doing until he set a cup of hot tea down in front of her.

'Here you are. Drink that.' He squeezed her shoulder, a gesture of comfort that made her look up at him with a half-smile. Eh, he wished he could offer her real comfort but only time would do that.

As she lifted the cup to her lips Toby went to peep into the public room, saw that everything was quiet then got himself some tea as well.

'I thought you'd drink beer, since you work in an inn?'

'I'd be drunk as a lord if I kept drinking my own beer. No, I may have a pot or two in the evening but I'm no toper. I prefer a good cup of tea most of the time or water from a moorland stream, pure and sparkling.'

'My husband used to booze,' she volunteered suddenly. 'He gave it up, then he started again. I think that's why he fell off the cart and was killed. He'd been drinking. I hate drunkards.' She didn't know why she was telling him this, but there was something about Toby Fletcher that made you trust him.

'I don't allow anyone to get blind drunk in my inn,' he said gently, 'but there are a few heavy drinkers. As long as they don't fight or vomit over my clean floor, I can hardly stop them drinking because that's how I earn my living.'

'No, I suppose not.'

'Does the thought of helping men to drink upset you?'

She nodded.

'I hope it won't stop you from working for me. You're a good cook and Phoebe's getting older. She really does need some help about the place.'

Meg had said it before she realised. 'No, it won't stop me from working for you.'

He beamed at her. 'That's good. Phoebe was saying last time I went up that you're a godsend.'

'Is that what I am?' She found herself smiling again, just a little smile but it felt strange as if her face wasn't used to doing it.

Someone called for a beer from the public room and Toby went to get it.

She sat there for a while because she was exhausted. What was there about her new employer that made her tell him things, that made her *want* to work for him? she wondered.

When she'd rested for a while she went up to see Phoebe, feeling guilty for neglecting her. She found the older woman feverish, her words muddled. She didn't even seem aware of what was happening around her.

Worried, Meg hurried to fetch Toby and together they studied the sick woman.

'I'll sit with her tonight,' he decided.

'She'll not want you tending her personal needs,' Meg said. 'I'll stay with her. I can snatch some sleep on the rug but I'll hear if she wakes, don't worry. I'm a very light sleeper.'

He looked at her. 'And definitely a godsend.'

She felt warm inside with so much praise today, hadn't felt like this for a long time. Well, praise wasn't something that had come her way very often.

Phoebe slept only fitfully, so Meg was up and down, giving her drinks, ministering to her needs, so tired she could have wept. But the old woman in the bed had been kind to her so whatever she could do, she would.

There was the sound of the bedroom door opening and she spun round, relieved to see it was only Toby. She didn't know why she should feel anxious about that. Who else could it be out here in this little village?

'How is she?' he asked.

'Very restless.'

'Have you had any sleep at all?'

'No.'

He brought his candle nearer to study her face. 'You need to get some sleep now or you'll be ill yourself. Go to bed and get a few hours. I'll wake you if I need you. Phoebe will be all right with me, I promise. I nursed my own mother when she was ill.'

She couldn't hold back a yawn. 'I'm sorry not to be of more use.'

'You've been a great deal of use, lass. Now, go and get some sleep.'

So Meg stumbled off to her bedroom, spilling hot wax from her candle on to the back of her hand when she yawned again. The sting of that woke her enough to get across to the bed, but she didn't remember getting into it.

In the morning she didn't wake up until someone shook her.

'It's morning, lass, and I'm afraid I need your help now.'

She blinked up to see Toby leaning over her. 'How's Phoebe?'

'A little better, I think.'

'I'm glad. What time is it?'

'Nearly nine o'clock.'

She sat upright in shock, then squeaked and pulled the covers back over herself because she was only wearing a shift, and a ragged one at that. 'Why didn't you wake me before?'

'You needed your sleep. Anyway, Alice has come to help out. I didn't even need to send for her today. She told her mother Phoebe was ill and they sent her over again. Folk are like that in Calico.'

He moved back towards the door. 'I'll leave you to get dressed. There's some food waiting. Alice's mother sent over a fresh-baked loaf.'

Suddenly Meg was hungry, ravenously hungry for the first time in ages. She found herself humming as she had a quick wash. It was a while before she realised what the noise was, though, because she hadn't sung or hummed for a long time.

15

Cully Dean woke the next morning, rolled out of bed and yelled at his wife because she hadn't got the fire going properly yet. Then he went outside to relieve himself and scowl at the weather. Raining again. It never stopped bloody raining up here. He shambled inside, found where his wife had hidden the last crust of bread and ate it as he sat wondering what to do that day.

Fletcher. He could go and have a look round the outside of the Packhorse. He still couldn't think how to get rid of the innkeeper but he'd have to find some way to do it because he didn't dare upset Beardsworth and his henchman.

'Can't you shut that brat up?' he yelled at his wife.

'No, I can't. She's hungry and there's nothing to eat. If you don't give me some money, there'll be nothing for you to eat later, either. You just ate the last of the bread.'

'Tell me what you want. I have to go down the hill so I'll bring something back.'

She immediately began listing things. Bloody women! Always spending your hard-earned money. Still, he didn't intend to go hungry, and if he left the brats without food they'd skrike half the night and drive him mad.

He went out of the house and fed the donkey. It was better company than women, didn't drive you mad always wanting things. He fiddled around in the shed for a while, still wondering how to get rid of Fletcher, then harnessed the animal and set off down the hill. After some consideration he bought a loaf and some cheese, remembered that *she* wanted potatoes and, since he liked them himself, went to Ross Bellvers to buy a whole sack. That'd keep her quiet for a long time. They couldn't usually afford that many.

'Come into some money?' Ross asked idly.

'No, I bloody haven't. This is to shut *her* up.'

Ross watched him go, still wondering where Cully Dean had found all this money recently. The man didn't usually feed his family; Ross had lost count of the times neighbours had slipped a slice of bread to one of the four hungry Dean children. He'd done it himself a time or two as well. The youngest was so thin and hungry-looking it nearly broke his heart to see her watching people eat with those big eyes full of longing.

While Cully was out, his wife sent little Sairey to the Packhorse because she knew Phoebe was a kind soul and often slipped the children something to eat. Sairey was particularly good at winning them food.

Meg opened the door and nearly died of shock because she thought for a minute Nelly was standing there. Only it wasn't Nelly, she realised, patting her own chest and blowing out a few breaths of sheer relief. 'Oh! Oh, you gave me such a shock. Do you want something, love?'

Sairey looked up at the stranger and said the magic word. 'Hungry.'

Meg stared down at her. The child was older than her Nelly, she could see that now, but so undersized that she wasn't much bigger than Nelly had been. Meg couldn't, just couldn't send her away hungry, but she didn't have any food of her own. 'Come in. I'll see what I can find.'

The child clearly knew her way inside the house place and went to stand by the bread bin.

'Wait there.'

Meg went into the public room and saw Toby in conversation with a man. She waited for him to finish, getting a little impatient because he went on and on. In the end the man nudged Toby and pointed in her direction.

With a smile, her employer came across. 'Is something wrong, love?'

'Can I have a quiet word?' She led the way behind the small counter and said in a low voice, 'A child came to the side door. She seems to know her way in. She's hungry.' She fumbled in her pocket. 'If I pay for it, can I give her some of our bread?'

He looked down at her, wondering what had made her so agitated. 'Who is she?'

'I don't know.'

He went across to the opening, lifted the curtain

and looked inside, then turned and beckoned to Meg to follow him.

'Hello, Sairey lass,' he said. 'When did you last eat?'

'Yest'day, Mr Fletcher. Piece o' bread.'

'And now you're hungry again?'

She nodded.

'Hasn't your Mam got any food?'

She shook her head. 'Dad ate it.'

'Let's find you something then.' He went and cut off a slice of crust, slathering on some butter. When she held out her hand for it, he kept hold. 'You're to eat it here.'

'Da says I've to take owt you give me home.'

'Not this time.' He'd heard Cully boasting a few days previously about how they could get food out of him for nothing. 'You eat it here or I'll eat it for you.'

Tears filled Sairey's eyes. 'He'll hit me when he finds out.'

'I know and I'm sorry, but I'm still not letting you take it home. Will you eat it now?'

She nodded, eyes still fixed on the crusty bread and the gleaming golden butter.

Toby pulled out a stool and sat her on it, then set the bread in front of her. Sairey fell on it like an animal, cramming it into her mouth and hardly waiting to chew before swallowing the mouthful. Almost inevitably she choked but as soon as she could breathe properly again, she went back to gobbling down the bread. When she'd finished he gave her a glass of milk, watched her drink it, then said, 'If your mother or sisters come here, I'll give them some bread, but they'll have to eat it here too. Do you understand that?'

She nodded.

'Get off home now, Sairey.'

When the child had gone he turned to Meg, who'd been watching what he did and who still looked as if something had shocked her to the core. Surely she'd seen hungry children before? She was so white he took a step towards her, then ran across because she was swaying. He caught her as she would have crumpled and held her in his arms as she began to sob quietly against him, then to let out thin wailing sounds like a soul in torment. He looked towards the public room not wanting them to hear this, for her sake, then picked her up and carried her out.

They passed Alice coming down the stairs and he said curtly, 'Keep an eye on the public room for me, will you, love? Something's upset Meg.'

It seemed the natural thing to do to carry her right through to the old part of the house. He'd found comfort there a few times himself, though he'd never worked out why.

When he carried her in, he made his way to the bench he'd put at the other end, which was the part of the room he liked most anyway, near the empty fireplace. Sitting down on it he cradled Meg like a child, rocking her slightly and murmuring, 'Cry it out, lass. Cry it out.'

And she did.

He'd never seen anyone cry so hard or heard such

naked anguish. It made tears well in his own eyes. All he could think of was to hold her close, rock her from time to time and make comforting sounds, though he doubted she heard them.

As she went on weeping he sensed the presence that sometimes seemed to linger in this ancient place, could swear he heard faint, far-off chanting and simply let the peaceful sensations flow over him. The very air seemed to quieten around them and gradually Meg stopped weeping so hard. Her breath was still catching on sobs and she hadn't opened her eyes, but she'd ceased the bitter keening that tore him apart.

Even as he looked down at her, her eyes opened and she blinked up at him, her lashes wet with tears, her cheeks streaked with drying trails of moisture.

'What is that sound?' she whispered.

'I don't know. Monks used to live here once and all I can think is that they left some of their peace behind them and – well, echoes of their singing.'

His words came out softly because he didn't want to break the spell, because that feeling was still enclosing them. Perhaps the stones were filled with it and gave it off in times of need.

She stared round, not afraid but wide-eyed as a child. 'Is this place haunted?'

'Not exactly. At least, I've never seen any ghosts. It's just – a place of ancient peace. That's how I think of it. I sit here sometimes.'

'It feels wonderful.' Meg sighed and leaned her head against his chest and they stayed where they

were, not speaking, not moving, just sharing that
feeling of comfort.

After a while she opened her eyes again and looked
at him. 'Thank you, Toby.'

'What upset you, Meg love?'

'That child – she looked so like my Nelly. I thought
my heart would burst with the pain of seeing her, of
knowing that Nelly would never grow up and Sairey
would.'

'Eh, lass, lass, I don't know how to help you.'

'You have done. You're the kindest man I've ever
met, Toby Fletcher. You held me when I needed it
so desperately. Only my brother Jack's held me since
she died – and I walked out of town after she was
buried, so no one's touched me since. I haven't even
wanted them to.' She put one hand up to clasp his as
it lay round her shoulders. 'You've touched me a few
times. You always feel warm. You make me feel
warmer, too. I've been cold, Toby, so very cold.'

He shook his head, feeling his own tears overflow
and not caring that she saw this weakness in him. 'I'm
glad I can help, though I think it's only time will really
cure your pain. And never quite. I still miss my
mother greatly, though it's been years since she died.'

'You understand, then.' She gave him one of her
almost-smiles then looked around. 'Can we stay here
for a while? Can we just – sit here quietly?'

'Aye, lass. I'd like that.'

She didn't leave his lap, didn't seem to realise how
intimately they were sitting, but he was only too aware
of it. He didn't know how long it was before she

stirred again – long enough for him to realise how fond he'd grown of her, even in such a short time. Long enough for him to stare into the distance and wonder if it would ever be possible for her to grow fond of him in return. Had she loved her husband? Did she still grieve for him as well? He didn't know, because she'd not talked about him much, but he intended to find out.

Eh, his mother had always said that love took you by surprise, and when he'd mocked her for believing that, she'd laughed back at him. 'One day you'll meet a woman you want to marry, Toby Fletcher, then you'll move heaven and earth to win her,' she'd said. She'd been right in that as in most other things. A wise, kindly woman, his mother.

When Meg stirred and got off his knee, blushing slightly, Toby made no attempt to detain her. He could see how embarrassed she was, so spoke quietly of monks and their ways, pointing to the huge beams that still bore the shape of the trees they'd once been. He explained that they'd been there for hundreds of years and described how this place had been built.

Then he showed her the secret room, watching indulgently as she grew excited by it, forgetting her grief as she examined some of the items inside it.

When they'd finished, he took her hand and looked down at her earnestly. 'Any time you feel the need, you come up here to the back, lass, and just sit for a while.'

'I will.' She stood on tip-toe and pulled his head

down till she could plant a kiss on his cheek. 'Thank you, Toby.'

The imprint of that kiss sat there like a warm shadow for the rest of the day, though it had been as simple and chaste as a child's.

Andrew was in a very bad mood for days after his encounter with Jethro. Although he didn't beat his wife again, he slapped one of his daughters, knocked the youngest maid flying when she dared to drop an item from a pile of washing while he was passing her on the stairs, and had his mill hands tiptoeing around in terror of offending him and losing their jobs and homes.

He'd taken the first steps to get rid of Fletcher, which should also get rid of Dixon's wife because no one in their right minds would employ an old hag like her. Once she was on the road, looking for work, they'd get rid of her too. He wasn't quite sure how much she knew about his past. Dixon had sworn he'd told her nothing, but still Andrew felt uneasy about her. And Jad was sure Fletcher was helping his mill hands run away, and that definitely had to stop. If they made an example of him, the other rogues in Calico would be a bit more careful what they did in future. It was like having a nest of vipers looking down on you. He hated the damned place.

It was taking longer than he'd expected to get rid of Fletcher, though, and that irritated him. He knew the anger that was simmering inside him wouldn't go away again until the man was dead. All right for

Jethro to play the honest man now, but *he* hadn't been involved in their early doings and his father was dead so had escaped the penalties the law imposed.

One day as they were having their midday meal, Harriet asked quietly if she might visit her sister.

He walked round the dining table, ignoring the way she flinched from him, and lifted her chin to study her face. 'In another day or two, when those bruises have gone completely.'

'Thank you.'

He noticed how her hands were shaking and that pleased him. Women should be afraid of their husbands. How else could you keep them in order?

Harriet watched him go out to the mill, still feeling shuddery inside as she remembered how she'd thought he was coming to hit her again. She didn't think she could take much more of it – only where could she go to escape him? Not to her sister's, that was sure. Jethro was a friend of her husband's. He'd just bring her straight back to Tappersley.

Two days later her husband gave her permission to visit Backenshaw and Harriet set out in their luxurious carriage. The coachman had strict orders not to stop at the Packhorse on the tops. She'd overheard Andrew telling him that though she had no idea why. When they came to the place the horses slowed down after the steep pull up the hill and she looked out, wondering why her husband hated this inn. It looked very ordinary to her, though a trifle run down in appearance.

And then *he* came out, the man she and her sister had seen in Halifax, the one who'd said he was a distant connection of Jethro's. He was giving orders to someone, but not as Andrew did it. No, this man was smiling, a truly charming smile that lit up his whole face. The fellow he was speaking to was nodding and smiling back at him, then hurried off to do his bidding. It hadn't taken nastiness to get whatever it was done, she thought, craning her head to look out of the window as the carriage pulled slowly past. What made her husband think you had to deal so viciously with everyone?

Tears came into Harriet's eyes. How was she to stand a lifetime of this? No wonder she hadn't fallen for a baby. She didn't *want* his baby. She loved children and knew she would be devastated if a child of her body were treated as Andrew treated his daughters for he slapped them quite often, though they were the meekest, quietest pair of girls she'd ever met, hardly daring to open their mouths, even when he was out of the house.

She was beginning to suspect that the governess, who'd apparently been there for years, protected them as much as she could. If so, Andrew didn't suspect. Harriet didn't dare try to interfere with what Miss Swainton was doing in case she spoiled things for them. It was a pity. She'd have liked to be a real mother to Kate and Marianne.

When she got to her sister's Harriet was still feeling emotional but tried to hide that. Out of pride she had never told her sister how Andrew treated her, though she knew Sophia suspected something was wrong. Well, suspecting wasn't knowing, was it?

They went inside, Sophia with one hand on her slightly swollen belly, gesticulating with the other as she talked. How lively she was! How happy she seemed!

Harriet sat down, not saying much but enjoying being here nonetheless. It was such a relief to know *he* wasn't within reach of her. Sophia had asked a question twice before she realised how her thoughts had strayed. 'Sorry, I was wool-gathering. What did you say?'

'I asked what was wrong.' Sophia's voice was very gentle as she added, 'And don't tell me nothing's wrong, Harriet dear, because I know you too well. Has he been hitting you again?'

'How did you—' Harriet broke off and tried to regain her composure, but for once she couldn't hide her feelings. Instead tears filled her eyes and flowed down her cheeks, betraying her, and words built up in her throat, try as she would to hold them back.

'Tell me, Harriet love.'

Out it all poured. By the time her tale ended she was sobbing against her sister, who began patting her shoulders and making soothing sounds.

After a while Harriet drew herself upright. 'I mustn't – go on weeping. He'll see my reddened eyes and then he'll stop me coming here. And if I can't s-see you and have just an hour or two of –' she had to take a deep breath before she could finish her sentence '– respite from him, I'll go mad or kill myself. I've thought of that, you know, only I don't want to die, just get away from *him*.'

After she'd finished speaking they sat in silence, and when she couldn't bear that any longer Harriet said bitterly, 'If only I could get with child! Maybe then he'd be kinder.'

'I can't see how a child would change him. Look how meek his daughters are. They're clearly afraid of him. A baby should be born to people who love it. No, it's better you don't fall for a child.'

Jethro was walking towards the room, whose door stood open a crack, when he heard his sister-in-law's next words, spoken in a shrill, terrified voice.

'I don't know any more what's better and what's not,' Harriet said. 'But Andrew's planning to kill someone. I overhear things, but not always the full tale. I think he might kill me if he knew how much I've overheard. I don't know for certain who it is – but I suspect it's your husband's half-brother, the one who looks just like him.'

Jethro waited outside the door to see if she knew anything else.

'It seems to me Andrew's getting worse lately. Worse than he was when I first married him, I mean. He shouts at the servants, hits them too, and as for his workpeople . . . they go in terror of him and his overlooker. Jad Mortley is a dreadful man. He beats the children in the mill, everyone knows it. Many of them are parish apprentices who have to live and work there. I feel so sorry for the poor little creatures. They lead a dreadful life.'

She said no more, but he could see through the narrow gap how she was sitting, read the dejection in every line of her drooping body.

When he guessed she wasn't going to say anything else, Jethro walked away. He was furious that Andrew would make her so unhappy. What good did it do anyone? And to take such a step when Jethro had told him he didn't want his half-brother killed – fury boiled up in him at the thought.

Only what was he to do about it? He couldn't go to the law because he had no proof. And he didn't want to act with similar violence to stop the killing, he just didn't. He'd never approved of violence which was a crude instrument and could rebound on the user as much as the victim.

Since his marriage he'd changed, grown softer, was only too aware of that. Sometimes he felt afraid of the man he was becoming, but whenever he determined to control his emotions better the mere sight of his son was enough to make him feel more kindly towards the world, a depth of feeling he had never experienced before. He'd not expected that of fatherhood and continued to worry about it. And Sophia had cast a similar spell over him. She was everything he wanted in a wife – and more.

Could you live in quiet content and still keep your life in order?

However, he still wasn't comfortable with the fact

that Fletcher lived nearby, looking so like him. Toby wasn't as bad as he'd expected and everyone in Calico seemed to like him, but Andrew was right about one thing. That man's continued existence was a threat to Jethro and to those he held so dear.

John Greenhalgh had a lot to answer for, leaving such a mess behind him for others to clear up.

Cully pulled up outside the Packhorse and left the patient donkey standing in the lee of the building, where it was partly sheltered from the wind. He strode inside and demanded a pot of beer from Alice, who was standing behind the counter.

She drew herself up. 'Don't you speak to me like that, Cully Dean!'

'Like what, you silly bitch?'

'Like I'm nothing. If you can't be polite, I shan't serve you.' She folded her arms.

'If you don't get me that beer, I'll shove you out of the road an' get it myself,' he roared, incensed.

A man in the corner stood up. 'Don't you treat my niece like that! You'll not touch her – or Toby's beer. You'll wait to be served like everyone else.'

All the other men were staring at him now.

'Doesn't hurt to be polite,' one of them said mildly, but his expression was disapproving. 'Especially to one of our own.'

Cully swallowed his anger and turned back to Alice. 'A pot of beer, *please*.'

She stood looking at him for a moment then turned and got it.

He paid in silence and went to sit down. When he got closer he saw that the men at the corner table had turned their backs and pulled their stools closer together, leaving no space for him, a sign of their annoyance. What was the world coming to when a man had to be polite to uppity girls who should be at home with their mothers? Everyone knew the sort of females who served in inns, knew they weren't decent or respectable women – except those who were married to innkeepers, of course, and even they had probably got there by lying on their backs. He sat down by himself at a table on the other side of the fire from the group of men and sucked down some beer, enjoying the slurping noise, the silky feel of the foam on top and the taste. Good beer, even if the innkeeper was Toby Fletcher.

After a few minutes he said loudly, 'Got to go outside a minute. Don't clear my pot away, girl. I'm coming back for another.'

No one spoke. Alice only tossed her head at him.

There was no one outside, so he went quickly into the necessary and relieved himself then came out again and made a quick tour of the stable area. There was quite a bit of lumber lying round because Fletcher was doing up the inn. One rickety wooden shed had had most of its front removed and was propped up on pieces of wood as the front wall was being rebuilt. That might just serve his purpose. Memorising where various things were he went back into the public room and ordered another pot, drinking it slowly.

When he went home, his wife wept with joy at the sight of a whole sack of potatoes, then looked at him in puzzlement. However had he found the money for all this? But she didn't ask because she didn't want him thumping her again.

Cully settled down for a nap on the settle in front of the fire while Sal boiled some potatoes, working as quietly as she could. However he'd got them, she was delighted to be able to feed her children properly.

16

Toby woke with a start. What had disturbed him? He could usually identify most sounds and get off to sleep again, but tonight there had been something different . . . After a few minutes, just as he was drifting back to sleep, he heard it again. A door banging in the stable yard. Only there were no doors left open to bang like that. He always made sure everything was closed properly when he went on his rounds last thing at night and, thanks to his careful maintenance, there were no loose catches. From his bedroom at the rear you could see most of the yard so with a sigh of resignation he left the warmth of his bed and went to peer out of the window.

At first he didn't see anything out of the ordinary then a light flickered inside the shed he was in the middle of repairing. It looked like a lantern being moved around. Somebody must be trying to rob him – only what would they find to steal in there? Then he realised. His tools! Well, they weren't going to get them!

He slipped on his trousers, tucked in his night shirt anyhow and shrugged into his old leather jerkin. Thrusting his bare feet into his shoes, he left his bedroom. Although he tried to walk quietly some of the floorboards and stairs creaked. He hoped he hadn't woken Meg and Phoebe, but didn't stop to find out.

No one was going to rob him!

He found his way through the dark house by feel but as he was about to open the side door, he hesitated then decided it'd be more prudent to have some sort of weapon. As he went back he stumbled over Phoebe's small but sturdy footstool and picked it up with a grin. When he'd made it he hadn't expected to use it as a weapon, but he reckoned it would do as well as anything else. The grin faded. He hoped it wouldn't be necessary.

Holding it firmly by one of its short legs, he opened the side door and went outside, standing for a moment in the darkness listening. He couldn't hear any sounds of movement but there was definitely a light flickering in the old shed. Anger welled up in him again. He hated thieves who took what other folk had worked hard for! If he caught this one, he'd give the rascal a beating that he wouldn't forget in a hurry.

At the door of the shed Toby hesitated again, because although there was obviously a flickering candle inside, there was no sound of movement. But if the thief had left the inn completely, he reckoned the rogue would have put out the candle so as not to arouse suspicion. The fellow must still be around somewhere. He'd check quickly inside here then either hide behind the door or look elsewhere. Very slowly he pushed the door until it was fully open.

He'd greased the hinges himself so it swung silently forward.

As he took his second careful step into the shed something crashed down on his head and he staggered, pain stabbing through him. Before he could gather himself together again, another blow landed.

Cully watched in great satisfaction as Toby crumpled to the ground. He set down his cudgel and fumbled for his knife, knowing he had to stab the bugger now, to kill him.

But he hesitated for a moment because it was hard to do that in cold blood to a man you knew. Images of Toby laughing with the other drinkers, teasing Phoebe, sending Sairey home with pieces of bread and butter, stayed his hand. Only the thought of the money and the freedom it would buy made Cully raise his arm and thrust downwards with the knife he'd sharpened earlier.

Meg couldn't settle to sleep that night. If she dozed off, the wind would blow and something would bang or rattle, then she'd wake up with a jerk. She was too new here to know what was making the noises. The moon was shining fitfully because of the racing clouds and she watched its glow shine through the curtains then fade, only to grow brighter again a minute or two later.

When she heard a noise inside the house her heart began to pound with anxiety, so she slid quietly out of bed and went to listen at the door. The stairs creaked as someone went down them, first the top one, then two together in the middle, and last of all, the floorboard you stepped on to at the bottom. It must be Toby because Phoebe wouldn't be wandering around in her condition. What could he be getting up for in the middle of the night? Had he heard something too?

She tiptoed back towards the bed, lifted the edge of the covers to climb back in and stopped. It was none of her business what he did during the night. For all she knew he might be going out to meet someone. Only . . . she dropped the covers again. It was no good! She definitely wouldn't be able to sleep until she found out what had made him get up. Grabbing her skirt, she slipped into it quickly, fastening it over her nightgown, then wrapped her shawl round her shoulders.

The stairs creaked beneath her footsteps, not as loudly as they had under Toby's weight but loudly enough for him to hear her coming down.

Only he wasn't in the house place, which was dark and full of shifting moonlight and shadows. Pressing her back against the wall she looked round and for a short time there was enough light for her to see that the room was empty. She moved sideways to peer through the doorway into the public room, but there was no sign of him there either. Feeling nervous, she listened carefully, but could hear no sounds of movement anywhere nearby.

Had he gone outside? The moon went behind some clouds just then and she hesitated before moving through the darkness towards the side door, feeling her way by touching the edge of the table. She found that the big bolt had been pulled back so opened the door.

Just then the moon came out again and revealed two figures in the doorway of the shed opposite. One was very tall, and must be Toby, and the other much shorter, standing behind him with one arm raised. He hit out and Toby fell.

'Noooo!' Meg started running across the stable yard, not noticing the cold and mud on her bare feet. When the knife blade gleamed in the moonlight as it stabbed downward towards the figure lying on the floor she began screaming at the top of her voice, terrified Toby had been killed. Heedless of the fact that she had nothing to defend him with, she ran towards him.

The attacker turned but she couldn't make out his face, only hear the low rumble of a curse. He shoved her away so roughly she fell sprawling in the mud and by the time she'd rolled to one side in case he tried to stab her, he'd set off running.

She jumped to her feet, not even trying to follow him. Had he killed Toby? *Please no, please no!*

She fumbled at his chest as the moon played games with her, now hiding behind the ragged clouds, now peeping out. When her fingers encountered a stickiness, she guessed it was blood and icy dread filled her.

'Toby! Toby!' She glanced behind her to make sure the attacker hadn't returned, then felt the face of her employer, leaning closer to see if he was breathing.

He gave a low groan and she sobbed in sheer relief before calling out his name again. *'Toby!'*

Another groan then he muttered, 'Hurts.'

'Where does it hurt?' she asked. 'Toby, answer me. Please, *please* answer me!' She cast another glance over her shoulder.

'Head – hurts.'

The moon stopped its games and shone steadily. When Meg looked down again she discovered that the sticky wetness wasn't coming from his chest but from the fleshy part of his arm.

'You've been attacked,' she said, still keeping a wary eye on the yard. 'Can you stand up? We need to get into the house and lock the door in case he comes back again.'

With her help, Toby struggled to his feet, sagging against the wall as he tried to stay upright. 'Lean on me,' she ordered. 'Quickly, now.'

So they staggered across the yard together, with him weaving unsteadily and pulling her from side to side because he was so much heavier. She kept trying to look round, to check that no one was about to attack them, but it was difficult and she knew with a sick certainty that they were very vulnerable. Toby could hardly stay upright and she was struggling under his weight.

When they got to the house she pushed him inside and followed, with her neck prickling uneasily in case the man had crept back to stab her too.

Slamming the bolt shut behind them, she leaned against the door for a minute, panting with the effort

of supporting such a huge man and shuddering with
sheer relief that they were safe. Toby was propped
up against the wall beside her and didn't seem fully
aware of what was happening.

'Got to sit down,' he muttered, still in that thick
voice.

She helped him across to Phoebe's rocking chair
and as he collapsed into it, she left him for a minute,
pulling the damper out and getting the fire burning
up. It was the work of a minute to stick a spill into the
red glow and use the flame to light all the candles she
could find. She didn't want darkness anywhere if she
could help it because with a big building like this
someone might get inside through another door or
window and attack them again.

There was no doubt in her mind that the man had
been trying to kill Toby, else why would he have
stabbed him when he was lying unconscious and no
longer a threat?

When she looked up from lighting the last of the
candles she saw Toby staring across at her, looking
as if he was starting to think more clearly. He stared
down at his arm and the bloody, slashed sleeve of his
nightshirt, then across at her again.

He spoke slowly but in a clearer voice. 'That fellow
set a trap and I walked right into it, fool that I am. But
why? Why would anyone want to kill me?' He closed
his eyes for a moment then looked at her. 'I reckon
you saved my life tonight, Meg. I heard you screaming and moved, so he missed my heart. Thanks, lass.'

She tried to speak lightly, but her voice wobbled

and betrayed her. 'What would I do if anything happened to you?'

He was frowning in thought as he studied his wound. 'The stool must have deflected the blow. Eh, I never thought when I made it that it'd help save my life one day.'

His expression was very serious, unlike his normal one, and there was no twinkle in his eyes tonight. Suddenly Meg felt so dizzy with relief she had to sit down with a thump on the nearest stool. 'I'm glad.' The words didn't begin to describe how she felt. And what she really wanted to do was cling to him and weep tears of joy all over him because he was alive and she just couldn't have borne him to be dead.

'You're a brave lass.'

'Anyone would have done the same.'

'No, Meg, they wouldn't. But *you* risked your life for me and I won't forget that.' He looked down at his arm and tried to move it, wincing. 'It stings.'

'We'd better have a look at the wound.' She tried to sound brisk but knew she hadn't succeeded. She pushed herself to her feet. 'I'll get some water boiling and we'll wash the cut clean.'

He nodded and sagged back in the chair. 'I feel a bit unsteady and my head's thumping like a drum.'

'I'm not surprised. He must have hit you hard.'

'What's happened?'

Meg swung round to see Phoebe standing at the bottom of the stairs, her grey hair tumbled on her shoulders, her nightcap askew. 'Someone attacked Toby.'

'Eh, dear, no! Whatever is the world coming to?'

The older woman was holding on to the door frame so Meg hurried across to help her to a seat, scolding gently. 'What are you doing out of bed?'

'I heard you screaming, heard the side door slam, and couldn't stay in bed wondering if someone was coming up to kill me.'

Meg eased her down onto a stool.

'I'm all right, Phoebe love,' Toby said gently. 'There was a fellow in the shed and he attacked me, but it's just a bang on the head and a bit of a cut in the arm. Meg's going to wash it for me.'

But Phoebe couldn't sit quietly until she'd checked for herself that the injury wasn't serious. 'It's a long cut, that one. It'll need stitching together if it's to heal without puckering. I'll do that for you. I've done it a few times afore.'

He looked at her in surprise. 'When did you learn to do things like that?'

'When I had to.' She wouldn't let him talk any more but supervised Meg and then showed her how to stitch a cut.

When the two women had finished Toby lay back in the rocking chair, his eyes closed, his face drawn.

'You're not to use that arm till it's healed, mind!' Phoebe warned.

He opened his eyes and managed a smile. 'No, ma'am.'

'I'll make sure he doesn't,' Meg said firmly.

He smiled at her in turn, then moved incautiously

and winced, wriggling as if he didn't know how to sit comfortably.

'I think we should all get back to bed now,' Phoebe said.

'I don't think I can sleep,' Meg said with a shiver. 'What if that villain comes back?'

'I doubt he will,' said Toby, 'but you can get in with Phoebe and I'll use your bed, if you don't mind. That way we'll all be close enough to hear one another.'

When they'd helped him into Meg's bed, he lay there wondering who had attacked him and why. Surely his half-brother wouldn't go to these lengths to get rid of him? Apart from anything else, he didn't seem the type to commit murder. And anyway, surely Jethro would have attacked him or paid others to attack him before now if he'd wanted him dead? After all, Toby had had the inn for over three years.

So who was it?

Eh, thank goodness Meg had come to his aid tonight! He smiled at the thought of her. So thin she looked as if a puff of wind would blow her away and yet she'd saved his life.

As he'd saved hers the other day.

It seemed as if fate had had a purpose in bringing them together.

He snuggled down, liking the idea that she had lain here before him.

In the next room Meg was also awake, staring into the darkness, listening in case the intruder came back. She'd intended to stay awake all night, but woke next morning to find the grey light of a winter dawn filling the room and Phoebe lying next to her still asleep.

She just had to check that Toby was all right, so eased herself out of the bed and crept next door. Yes, he was fast asleep. She stood looking down at him, at his huge frame nearly filling her bed, at his untidy brown hair and rosy skin, and smiled in sheer relief. He was showing no signs of fever, not tossing or turning.

Even in sleep he had a kindly expression on his face. Eh, he was a lovely man and she couldn't have borne it if he'd been killed! She'd lost so many people, father, husband, child! Not her new friend as well.

She blinked in surprise. Friend! Had he become a friend so quickly? She smiled. Yes, indeed, and a good one too.

Late that afternoon Cully nerved himself up to go to the inn as usual for a pot of beer, surprised that no one had come to tell him Toby Fletcher had been killed by an intruder. He found the place abuzz.

No sooner was he through the door than someone called, 'Hey, Cully, have you heard?'

'Heard what?' He listened, trying to look shocked as someone explained what had happened the previous night. 'What's it coming to when folk can't sleep peacefully in their own beds? Eh, to think of Toby being killed like that!'

'He hasn't been killed, just injured.'

'But I thought you said—'

They forgot him as they continued to debate the matter and Cully looked down, trying to hide his disappointment. How had he missed? It must have been that damned female's fault. How *could* he have missed at such close quarters? Well, he wouldn't miss again. Oh, no! He'd been planning how to get away once he received his payment. It wasn't *fair* that after all his efforts that sod was still alive. Voices were raised around him, but he didn't join in.

'Who could it have been?'

'Not one of us.'

'Why would *anyone* attack a decent fellow like Toby Fletcher?'

When the female who seemed to be working here now appeared, Cully went across to buy a pot of beer from her. She must be the one who'd disturbed him. He'd pay her back for that if he ever got the chance, by heck he would!

Scowling, he carried his pot across to the table round which all the regular late-afternoon drinkers were crammed and continued to listen to their wild guesses. He didn't join in. Even the beer tasted sour in his mouth today because the job was all to do again. This time the bugger was forewarned and would be on his guard, so it'd be harder.

When everyone fell silent and turned round, he did too. Toby was standing in the doorway of the house place, his arm in a sling, his face a little pale, but otherwise looking much as usual.

'Tell us exactly what happened,' Ross demanded, going across to escort him to their table.

Knowing it was the best way to stop wild gossip Toby complied, refusing to let them buy him a pot of beer because Phoebe had made him promise not to drink any for a day or two.

He looked round the group as he told his tale, wondering if it was one of them. He didn't think it was, though who else could it be but someone from the village? His eyes settled on Cully then moved on. If he had to guess, he'd guess Cully Dean had done it, simply because he was a nasty type who didn't even provide enough food for his own children.

Only there was no reason on earth why the man should attack him, no benefit to be gained by Cully from his death. The attack just didn't make sense, rack his brain as he might. Toby saw Meg watching him anxiously so smiled across at her to show he was all right.

He stayed with the group for a few minutes then pleaded exhaustion and returned to the house place, where Phoebe was sitting in her rocking chair, well enough to come downstairs, but not well enough to do much.

'She's a nice lass,' Phoebe said suddenly.

'Who?'

'Meg. Who do you think? Has she agreed to go on working for us?'

'Yes.'

'Good. You could do worse for yourself, you know.'

He nearly choked when she said that. She smiled and went on with her mending, not explaining her statement, not needing to. His mother had been just the same, reading his mind.

'I'll do my own choosing,' he growled.

'I sometimes think it's fate as does the choosing for us,' she said, and sighed.

To Toby's relief she didn't say anything else.

But when Meg peeped in to check that they were all right he looked at her with new eyes. She *was* a nice lass, not pretty exactly but with lovely eyes and an alert, happy look to her now as she bustled around. He admired folk who weren't afraid of hard work. He admired her.

But it was a bit soon for anyone to talk of him courting Meg – wasn't it?

Trouble was, he kept thinking about her, seeing her face as she lit those candles last night, feeling her arm round his waist as she staggered under his weight. He shook his head, annoyed with himself and got a book to read. Only he couldn't concentrate.

It was the blow to the head.

No, it was the thought of Meg with her arm round him.

It was a couple of days before Jethro heard about the attack on the landlord of the Packhorse. He listened grimly as his overlooker passed on the gossip and afterwards couldn't get it out of his mind.

Was this the attack Harriet had heard her husband arranging? He considered going over to Tappersley and asking Andrew directly, but decided in the end to do nothing.

He was, he found to his surprise, glad the attack had failed. And whatever the danger to himself and his family, he doubted he was capable of killing anyone in cold blood, or even arranging to have them killed.

His father would say he was too soft for his own good. Perhaps he was. All he knew was that without the old man's dour presence and harsh ways, life was more pleasant. All he wanted was to enjoy his wife and growing family.

There was only one thing stopping that, and Fletcher was involved, whether the fellow knew about it or not. Jethro didn't think he knew for he had never given a hint of it in their dealings and surely he would have tried to take advantage if he had known? Most folk would.

Only Fletcher wasn't like other folk.

Harriet trod carefully for the whole of that week because her husband was in a murderous rage. It was all the more terrifying because he didn't hit her this time, though the anger was there in his face, in his every movement, simmering, lethal.

One day, she thought in surprise, he'll kill someone. I pray it isn't me.

That evening over dinner he was all forced amiability, which made her feel even more threatened for some reason.

That night he was indefatigable in bed, taking her twice.

'I'll get you with child if it's the last thing I do,' he muttered as he rolled off her the second time. 'And if I don't, we'll know whose fault it is. I've already fathered two children, even if they are only girls.'

That remark made her shiver.

But even though she knew it would make him treat her more kindly, she still didn't want to bear that man's child. She hated him too much.

Toby found time passing more slowly because he couldn't do much of his normal work without opening the cut and if he tried to pick up a tool, Meg seemed to appear out of nowhere and take it from him.

He tried reading, but even that palled after an hour or two. So he took to prowling the house, planning what he'd like to do with it if he had the money. Only he didn't have it.

Inevitably he ended up in the back place, sitting on his bench and letting thoughts drift idly through his mind. One day he decided to have another look at the stuff in the secret chamber and went back to the house place for a candle.

'What are you doing with it?' Meg asked at once, arms akimbo.

'Just looking round the corners up at the back place. I can't do owt about things just now, but there are a few places which need work up there. It's a bit dark in those little rooms. Well, it's a dim sort of day, isn't it?'

She glanced out of the window. Dark grey clouds,

flurries of rain. It was lovely to be here in the warmth with so many things to do. When she looked back Toby was staring at her, his expression solemn and yet kindly, as if checking that she was all right.

'I love it here,' she said softly. 'I didn't think I'd like working in an inn, but I do.'

'I'm glad.' He took the candle, lit it and wandered off, carrying the memory of Meg's happy expression with him like a warm gift.

The secret room didn't seem as threatening today. He propped open the door just in case it shut on him, hung the candle holder on the wall hook and began to sort through the papers, studying the sketch of the young woman again. She was a bonny lass. He hoped she'd had a happy life.

There were no surprises for him in the papers, but as he started to put them back on the chest of drawers, he was so captivated by its workmanship that he set them aside again and gave himself the pleasure of admiring a master craftsman's work. Beautiful inlay work. He'd never seen finer. He pulled out a drawer to examine the dovetailing, the joints as tight-fitting as was possible.

It was when he pulled out another drawer that he found the secret compartment at the back. There were papers in it, old and yellowing. He spread them out on the top of the chest and began to read.

He was so shocked by the contents of the first page that he couldn't move for a minute or two, then he heard footsteps and shoved back the papers with the rest unread before slotting the drawer into place.

By the time Meg poked her head through the doorway, he was piling the other things on top of the drawers again – and hoped his expression didn't betray the turmoil inside him.

'You look tired, Toby Fletcher,' she said, folding her arms. 'You should go and lie down for an hour.'

'Aye. Happen you're right, love.' He shepherded her out and closed the secret door. He wished he could shut off what he had learned as easily.

Hell, what was he to do about this?

PART 5
1832

17

January

Toby went to sit down in the house place for a few minutes' rest while Phoebe cleaned behind the counter in the public room. He could hear her humming, hear too the patter of Meg's footsteps overhead as she cleaned the bedrooms. On the stove a large pan was bubbling and the smell wafting from it made his mouth water.

All was right with his little world and he didn't want anything to change it.

The Christmas season had been busier than usual, what with those folk from Calico who could afford to celebrate doing so and also an increase in passing trade as people took advantage of a mild spell of weather to visit relatives. He knew Meg preferred to keep herself busy, but he liked to have a bit of free time to read, something he hadn't been able to do much lately.

He also had something worrying him. A man had taken to stopping regularly at the inn for refreshments. Toby hadn't liked the looks of him from the first though he'd been civil enough, wanting a hot meal and a pot of beer to wash it down, and expressing his appreciation of the service offered afterwards. So of course an innkeeper had to be civil and linger for a chat when the customer clearly wished this.

But Toby had seen the cursory way the stranger tended to his horse's needs and that had annoyed him. He'd taken it upon himself to offer the poor creature a carrot, for it looked jaded, as if it'd been ridden too hard. It had leaned against him with a sigh, chomping the carrot and clearly welcoming a friendly human touch.

After the man had gone the first time Phoebe had come out to help Toby clear up the private room. 'Did you know who that was?'

'Eh?'

'That man. He's Jad Mortley, the overlooker at Tappersley.'

'No, I didn't know.'

'I caught a glimpse of him as he was leaving. What did he want? He's never stopped here before.'

'He wanted a meal and a drink. I hope he doesn't come again. I can't refuse to serve him, though I'd like to.'

On his third visit Mortley complimented Toby once again on his cook. 'Simple food, but properly prepared. You can't beat it.'

'She's a good cook,' Toby admitted, 'and a hard worker.'

'More than a cook perhaps?' asked the man with a wink.

'No.' Toby suddenly realised that he was smiling fondly at the thought of Meg and grew annoyed with himself. This was the last man he wanted to share his personal feelings with.

After he'd served the unwelcome customer he stood near the beer barrel, wiping down the little counter and thinking about Meg. Perhaps one day they could become closer, but not just now because she still had days when she was sad and her eyes sometimes looked red in the mornings. Both he and Phoebe reckoned she was still grieving for her little daughter, but Phoebe said she wasn't grieving for her husband any longer. Well, he'd died a couple of years before the child.

Toby had seen the way Meg still avoided children and babies, whether in the village or at market down the hill. It was as if she couldn't bear to go near them. Perhaps they brought back too many memories.

But she'd shown no more signs of that half-crazed grief he'd seen the day he first met her and had seemed a lot better altogether since she'd wept it all out against his chest, sitting in the back place.

He realised Mortley was ringing the little handbell for service and went with a sigh into the private parlour. 'Would you like a piece of apple pie to finish off with, sir?'

'I would indeed.'

It was only after the man had left that the pedlar, Bram Craven, who'd been sitting very quietly in a corner of the public room, came across to the counter. 'I didn't think to see you speaking so friendly to that sod.'

'I can't refuse to serve him, can I?'

Bram scowled. 'I would. I've never seen the bugger dressed up so fine afore, but I'd recognise him anywhere. I'm surprised no one else in Calico has done.'

Toby frowned in thought. Now he came to think of it, Mortley usually arrived in the late morning, at a time when the men from the village were still at their day's work. He always went straight into the private parlour and stayed there. In fact, he'd done that the very first time, as if he already knew the layout of the inn.

'I wonder what Mortley's doing travelling to and fro so much? He doesn't often leave Tappersley unless he's on his master's business.' Bram took another mouthful of beer, then set his pot down and snapped his fingers. 'I remember seeing him in Todmorden last month. He was talking to someone from Calico then, come to think of it.'

'Who?' Toby's voice came out more sharply than he'd intended.

Bram shook his head. 'Don't know the fellow's name, only that I've seen him round here.' He looked at Toby, eyes shrewd in his weatherbeaten face. 'Maybe he's doing a job for Mortley or his master? Moor folk have trouble putting bread on the table now that the handloom weaving's nearly gone an' folk'll do owt to turn an extra penny. Eh, there was a time when I were young that handloom weavers lived like princes. Meat every day, new clothes every year. Now all the spinning an' most of the weaving's done inside those damned mills an' folk have to jump when they're told or they're thrown out of work and home.'

'What was the village like in those times?' Toby asked.

'Busy. Full o' happy folk. There were bundles of cotton wool coming up Calico Road an' packets of calico as had been woven from it going back down to the putters-out. Why dost think the place is called Calico?'

Toby knew that already, but humoured the old pedlar. 'I like to hear tales of the old days. I like to read about them too. But I wouldn't like to work in one of those damned mills. I was always grateful my mother put me to learn the carpentering trade instead, though it was a struggle for her.'

'Ah, well, the mills are here to stay now, aren't they? And if they were all as well run as Greenhalgh's, they wouldn't be too bad. By, that place has changed for the better since the son took over.'

'It has? How?'

Bram shot him a sly glance and grinned. 'Curious about your brother, are you?'

Toby could feel his expression growing stiff. 'He doesn't feel like a brother. Let's just call him a relative, eh?'

'Anyone who's seen the two of you together would know you at once for brothers.'

'Never mind that. Tell me about his mill. Why is it better now?

'Well, it were never as bad as Beardsworth's. Few place are. And Greenhalgh is still strict with his operatives. Don't get me wrong, he expects them to work damned hard. But they aren't treated as harshly as when his father were alive and it stands to reason that must be because of young Jethro. There aren't as many fines as there used to be an' the children aren't beaten to make them work harder. Even the rent collector behaves different. I heard last time I was in Northby that folk aren't thrown out of their houses if they're sick and some have even been let off paying the back rent when they got better.'

Toby blinked in surprise. He'd never even considered that Jethro Greenhalgh might have a better side to him because the air fairly seemed to crackle with tension on the rare occasions when the two of them met. 'I'm glad to hear that, though I still don't consider him a brother. Now, are you hungry?'

'I am and I've heard tell your new cook is good.'

Toby smiled. 'She is that!'

Bram chuckled openly. 'That smile says she's more to you than a cook.'

'Not yet.' He went to the house place to get Bram's food, a bit worried now. Did he betray his feelings about Meg so easily? Had he done so with Mortley? What *was* the fellow doing calling here, lingering, chatting?

He took out Bram's food. 'How about a free night's lodging and supper in return for pointing out the fellow you saw in Todmorden?'

'All reet, lad. Suits me. I've some stuff to deliver to Mrs Pickerling an' I've no doubt I'll sell a few odds and ends more once folk realise I'm here.'

*

The following day, after Bram had left, Toby went up to the back place to think about what the pedlar had said. The identity of the man Mortley had been talking to was no surprise. Cully Dean was a bad lot if Toby had ever met one and didn't seem to have any real friends in a village where folk stuck together and half of them were related.

Toby had heard one or two of the other men asking Dean where he was getting his money from lately. Not that they'd received an answer except for, 'Mind thy own business an' I'll mind mine.'

Bram's revelation suggested that Beardsworth was paying Dean, dealing through his overlooker, but why should he do that? Toby couldn't remember ever meeting Beardsworth, let alone upsetting him enough to have him hire someone to kill him.

He was wondering whether to get out the secret papers and read the rest of them when he heard footsteps. He turned to see Meg bringing some washing to hang on the indoor lines they'd strung back here for rainy days.

She stopped at the sight of him and set down her basket of wet clothes. 'Oh. Am I disturbing you?'

'No, lass. It's my own thoughts that are doing that. I'm still worried about who'd want to kill me, to tell you the truth – aye, and how best to protect you and Phoebe in case they try again.'

She smiled at him. 'We'll all try to look after one another, eh? That's what my brother always used to say.'

'He sounds a nice fellow, your brother.'

She nodded, her eyes suddenly bright with unshed tears.

'Don't you want to write to him, let him know you're all right? You *are* all right now, aren't you? Settled here, I mean?'

'I'm happier than I've any right to be, Toby, but I'm not writing to my family because I don't want anything to do with my mother – and besides, Jack has enough on his plate without worrying about me.'

'Don't you think he's already worrying?'

She sighed. 'Yes, I suppose so. But there's nothing he needs to do for me. I want him to enjoy his own life – as much as *she* will let him.'

'Well, I've got paper if you ever want to write and in the meantime you've us two looking out for you.'

A smile transformed her face as she said softly, 'Yes, I have, haven't I?'

She didn't smile like that very often and he was always amazed at how much difference it made, how attractive she looked. But he didn't know whether to tell her so and risk losing their friendship, risk her leaving.

She began pegging the washing on the lines. 'It's very useful to have this place, isn't it? And I like coming here. It makes me feel safe – and peaceful.'

'Me, too.' Strange that she felt the same, because it made Phoebe nervous to come here. Was that because of the goods her husband had left here or for some other reason? No, he was too fanciful about this place, should have more sense.

But Toby couldn't quite convince himself that

there was nothing here or that it was only his imagination when he heard faint chanting sounds or distant footsteps.

Once Meg had finished he patted the bench beside him and they sat there for a while, not speaking, enjoying a short rest together in this special place. After a while he reached out and took hold of her hand. He didn't say anything, afraid to break the spell of the moment, but after a while he gave hers a quick squeeze.

She looked down at their joined hands, stole a quick glance sideways at him, then bowed her head again. But she didn't pull away.

He was sorry when she let go and stood up.

'I'd better get on. Phoebe will be wondering what's happened to me.'

He smiled a farewell then looked down at his hand, pleased that she'd let him hold hers.

Maybe it would soon be time to be more open about his feelings? It was strange how sure he was of his fondness for her.

Was she getting fond of him?

Meg walked back to the house place, worrying. Why had Toby taken hold of her hand? She hadn't pulled hers away, had liked the feel of his fingers twined around hers. Had he *wanted* to hold her hand like a fellow did with a woman he fancied or was he just being kind to her?

She didn't know. She wished she did.

She could feel a blush creeping up her neck. *Meg*

Pearson, what's got into you? she scolded herself and began to bustle about in the kitchen, keeping busy, trying not to think about what had happened.

Unfortunately she couldn't prevent the memory of how right his hand had felt in hers from creeping back into her mind. Couldn't help remembering the slow warmth of his smile.

Could a man as lovely as Toby be interested in her?

It had been three years since Ben died and although she'd briefly walked out with Liam Kelly, she'd never felt like this about him, nice fellow though he was. In fact, she'd never felt like this about anyone, not even Ben. It frightened her. And gave her hope. And sent heat creeping into her cheeks again.

Andrew Beardsworth scowled at his overlooker. 'It's taking too damned long to get rid of Fletcher. That fellow you hired hasn't even tried to kill him again.'

'He says he needs to wait until our dear innkeeper feels safe and isn't on his guard.'

'A pitiful excuse! I think we'll have to do it ourselves.'

Jad grinned. 'I don't know why we didn't take care of it ourselves the first time. It's only an hour's ride up the valley, if that. While everyone else is sleeping we could be there and back in three hours at most, with the deed done. Why, there's only the two women up there with him. *They* wouldn't be able to help him. You and I could manage it on our own.'

'They might see us, though, and then we'd have to kill them as well. I didn't want to do it myself because it'd increase the risk at both ends. One of my servants might hear me going out or my wife – though *she* doesn't matter. She does as I tell her. It's not like the old days though, Jad, as I keep reminding you. We have to *seem* to obey the law.'

When Andrew crossed his arms in front of his body and began to slap his right palm against his left arm, Jad kept quiet. If his master got that expression on his face, started doing that arm tapping, it meant he was thinking about something and you left him in peace – if you wanted to go on living in peace yourself.

After a few minutes Andrew cleared his throat. 'Look, Jad, we'll give Dean a week or so and see what he manages. We'll have to get rid of him afterwards, though. Can't risk leaving a witness who could lead the constables straight to us.'

'Dean doesn't know who I am.'

'Of course he knows who you are, or at least guesses. Those folk up in Calico have relatives down here and they've no love for us. You were taking a risk even going to the Packhorse, though Fletcher is less likely to recognise you than the others in the village. They're a damned surly, masterless lot up there! My mill helped put them out of business and they've never forgiven me for it. They tried to smash my machines in the early days, but we got the militia in to deal with 'em. Killed a couple, too.' Andrew smiled, a wolfish expression that was as much a snarl as anything else, and began pacing up and down.

'I thought they'd nearly all move down the hill to work for me. Some did, but most didn't, so I had to bring in others from further away, folk who knew nowt about cotton, and then I had to teach them. That cost me good money. And the moor folk *still* don't mind their own business, even now. I'm damned sure it's they who're helping my operatives run away. The law may take a dim view of anyone leaving employment without giving due notice and may even be on my side, but if you can't find the folk who're missing, you can't prosecute them. As for the apprentices,' he threw Jad a distinctly unfriendly look, 'do you *have* to beat them so hard? You make them useless to me.'

His companion shrugged. 'It happens when I get angry, and those stupid children are enough to try the patience of a saint sometimes.' He risked adding, 'And we're neither of us saints.'

'Maybe not, but I keep what I do private. You're getting known for your beatings.'

Jad didn't say it was also common knowledge that Andrew beat this wife and had beaten the previous one, too. He didn't dare. His employer was the only person in the world of whom he was afraid.

That night Andrew found out that Harriet's courses had come again, regular as clockwork, damn her. So for all his extra efforts this month, she wasn't carrying a child yet. His anger and frustration over-flowed and he was unable to restrain himself from thumping her.

For once she answered back. 'What child deserves a father like you?' she demanded, her cheeks flying spots of hectic colour. 'I'm *glad* I'm not having one. The way you treat your daughters sickens me. They daren't call their souls their own. I don't want children who'll be so unhappy.'

He thumped her again and this time she lashed back at him, managing to land a resounding slap across his cheek.

He stilled and gave her a long, level look, watched her wait for retaliation but said only, 'Be very careful what you do and say from now on, Harriet. If you anger me as well as continuing to disappoint me, I might decide I'd be better off without a wife like you.'

She gasped and took an involuntary step backwards, her face paling.

'Exactly. You've taken my meaning. Don't forget it. Now get down on your knees and apologise for this.' He pointed to his cheek.

And heaven help her, she dared do nothing but obey.

He nodded and as she knelt there, kicked out and sent her flying across the room. 'From now on I think you should make up a bed for yourself in one of the other rooms at these times of the month, for I find the sight and smell of you quite repulsive. In fact, go away this minute and don't come back to my bed until you've something to offer a man.'

She struggled to her feet and left without a word, half-expecting him to hit her again as she passed. But he didn't. She had never felt so humiliated in her life.

She hated him even more for what he'd done this night.

He smiled as he watched her go. There was always a way to bring them to heel. He rubbed his cheek, which was still stinging. Why the hell had he married the bitch? She was nothing like her fecund sister. And, truth to tell, he preferred his women plumper and more stupid.

A week later Andrew allowed his wife to accept an invitation to visit her sister. He didn't want to upset Jethro, after all, needed to make sure he kept the man as an ally. The young fool was acting like an idiot lately, though, treating his operatives far too softly, a practice which made difficulties for other cotton masters. Old John must be turning in his grave at the changes his son had made in the mill.

Andrew made a point of handing Harriet into the carriage himself. 'I trust you'll say nothing disloyal about me?'

'Of course not.'

She sat bolt upright until the carriage left Tappersley, then leaned back and let out a long, low groan of relief. For a few precious hours she'd be free of him. She'd been terrified ever since he'd made that veiled threat to kill her, had hardly dared open her mouth – and hated herself for this cowardly subservience. She was sure now that he'd do her real harm if she stayed with him – and kill her if she remained barren. But how was she to escape – and stay free?

She sat lost in thought, not noticing the scenery. The only way Andrew allowed her to go away from home was in their own carriage with the coachman and another man riding with her. Even when she went to Halifax she was escorted round the shops by one of them.

Her only chance, she decided, was to get away by night and on foot. That might be possible at the time when she was sleeping alone. Only where could you get to on foot from Tappersley? Halifax? She knew no one there and was doubtful she could reach it during the hours of darkness. The only person she knew would help her was her sister, but Backenshaw was also too far away for a night's walking. Andrew would catch her before she got there, she was quite certain. And then he would kill her.

As they drew near the tops she looked out at the Packhorse. Suddenly she pressed closer to the carriage window, struck by an idea. She could make it this far on foot, surely? And if the landlord could be persuaded to hide her then maybe he'd also agree to let Sophia know that she needed her sister's help in getting away. She'd heard the servants talking about the inn, just snatches of conversation here and there which she'd pieced together afterwards. If he'd helped some of the people whom Andrew's horrible overseer had ill-treated to escape, why not her?

It had taken her a few months to realise how brutal her husband was to the children he employed because he refused to let her go inside the mill, saying it was no fit place for a lady. But once again the servants' idle gossip and what she'd seen from the upstairs window had revealed what he was hiding from her. She'd also caught snatches of conversation at the various social events they'd attended. People might behave politely towards her and her husband but she'd soon realised he wasn't liked and that people, even other cotton masters, considered his mill a disgrace.

From what she'd seen things seemed to be getting worse in the mill, the workers there looking more downtrodden and weary, though she wasn't sure whether this was Andrew's fault or that of Jad Mortley. There had been two funerals in Tappersley in the past month – if you could call those hurried burials in paupers' graves funerals. Young children from the mill, they'd been, because the splintered wooden coffins were too small to hold an adult body. She'd gone up to the rear bedroom to watch the pitiful little boxes carried out and taken to the church-yard with no ceremony, not even the church bell tolling, and certainly no mourners attending. It was as if the dead child apprentices were so much rubbish being carted away. That thought upset her greatly.

And yet workhouses from all over the North continued to send children here as 'apprentices'. Andrew gloated whenever another group arrived, saying they were the cheapest of all his workers. They weren't apprentices, in Harriet's opinion, but slaves. The poor things looked hungry and gaunt whenever she saw them in church on Sundays, more like shrunken old men and women than children.

When she'd mentioned to Sophia how much she pitied the children their husbands both employed, her sister had been surprised. Jethro treated his much more kindly, apparently, and had made a lot of changes for the better in the mill when he took over from his father. None of their apprentices had died during the time she'd been married, Sophia was certain. They weren't rosy-cheeked, she agreed, because they rarely saw the sunlight, but they were decently clad and properly fed. She knew that for a fact because she saw them in church every Sunday. What's more Jethro had discussed their diet with Tettie and the nursemaid had told her what they'd arranged. Better food than most of them would have got at home, the nurse said, and she was no fool.

Harriet sighed. Andrew was a monster in so many ways.

She was surprised to find the carriage drawing up in front of Parkside already. She'd been so lost in her thoughts she hadn't noticed anything since the inn on the tops.

She was shown up to her sister's bedroom, where Sophia had been resting. The child was showing quite clearly now and she was moving a little more slowly than usual, laughing at how sleepy she felt sometimes. But she looked to be in blooming health.

Tettie was there with her and studied Harriet shrewdly. 'I hope you don't mind me speaking out, but you don't look well, Mrs Beardsworth.'

Harriet tried to smile at her, but didn't succeed.

'I know you're wanting a child and I have a herbal potion that may help you.'

Harriet would have liked to refuse this kindly offer, but realised suddenly that it might soften Andrew's attitude towards her, so nodded. 'I'd appreciate that.'

'I'll find you a bottle before you leave, Mrs Beardsworth.'

When she'd gone Harriet looked at Sophia, tried to speak normally and couldn't. Her sister looked so plump and happy, while Harriet's own reflection in the mirror told quite another story. 'You're lucky in your husband, so very lucky.' Unable to hold back the tears, she covered her face with her hands and started sobbing.

'Is he still beating you?'

For answer Harriet took off her frock.

Sophia gasped at the sight of the yellowing bruises which covered large areas of her sister's body. 'Oh, Harriet, no! The man's a monster!'

'He often hits me, but now—'

Sophia moved across to gather her into her arms and hold her while she wept.

But Harriet knew better than to continue crying, which would make her eyes reddened and swollen, so forced herself to stop. 'I'm terrified of him. Last week he threatened to kill me if I angered him in any way, because I'm already disappointing him by not giving him a son and am therefore worth nothing as a wife.'

Sophia gasped and put one hand up to her throat. 'Harriet, no!'

'I'm quite sure that if I don't get away from him, you'll be attending my funeral.'

'Stay here. Don't go back today.'

'I can't. He's my husband, has rights over me, can demand my return by law. And anyway, what would your husband say? The Greenhalghs have been on friendly terms with Andrew for many years.'

They sat in silence for a minute or two, then Harriet went on, 'I think I can get away, though. If I do and send you word, could you send someone to fetch me from my hiding place? Not your carriage but someone in a cart perhaps, so that I could hide in the back. You see, he makes me sleep on my own now when my courses come and I think next time will be my chance, my only chance, to leave. I'm very carefully watched the rest of the time, because he doesn't trust anyone. I've been thinking about it on the way here, planning how to do it. I'd have to leave the house at night then go somewhere on foot and send you word. The only place I could think of was the inn, the one on the moors, the Packhorse.'

'Jethro's half-brother owns that inn! I'm not supposed to go there.' Sophia paused, then smiled. 'Mind you, he's softening towards him. I've heard Jethro say a couple of times that the inn is at least better run than before and Toby Fletcher has earned a reputation as an honest man. I think what Jethro dislikes most is that his bastard brother resembles him so closely.'

Harriet looked at her in dismay. 'But there's nowhere else I can go.'

Sophia looked at the bruises where her sister hadn't pulled up the neck of her gown properly. 'If you do escape, even if it's to the Packhorse, I'll find a way to fetch you, I promise, whether it angers Jethro or not. I have plenty of money because he's very generous with me. I can give you some now and send more later.'

'That would help. Andrew doesn't give me any money. His men pay for what I need.'

After a pause, Sophia asked, 'Where shall you go afterwards?'

'I don't know. Anywhere. London, perhaps. The further away from *him* the better.'

Jethro didn't join them for the midday meal this time because he was busy and would eat in his office. Harriet was glad of it, didn't feel she could have chatted cheerfully today.

After they'd eaten Sophia went across to her pretty little desk and pulled out a drawer. 'Here. Take as much as you want.'

But Harriet hesitated. 'Andrew might find it. How could I ever explain where I got it from?'

'He wouldn't find it if we sewed it into the lining of your muff.' Sophia took out her sewing box and they sat together as they had so many times before, setting stitches and speaking quietly.

But the time passed too quickly and Harriet looked at the clock with a sigh. 'I'll have to leave now, I'm afraid. Can you send for my carriage, please?'

It was getting dark as they reached Tappersley.

She found her heart thudding in apprehension as she climbed the steps to the front door.

She joined her husband for the evening meal, feeling sick with worry about the night to come. When he took her tonight, would he use her roughly, beat her? She tried not to show her fear of going to bed, but knew he sensed and enjoyed it.

For something to talk about she told him about the herbal potion Tettie had given her.

'I'm glad to see you behaving more sensibly,' he said. 'Go and fetch it.'

She left the table and went upstairs for the brown glass bottle.

He took off the stopper, sniffed it and pulled a wry face. 'Let's hope it works.'

'She said – Tettie, I mean – that it might take two or three months to work and she'll send me some more bottles when she's brewed another batch.'

'Good.'

The trouble was, Harriet was even more certain now that she didn't want to bear him a child. She hoped desperately that the potion wouldn't work. But she'd take it ostentatiously and perhaps this would allay his anger, buy her some time without beatings, because she felt that if he didn't stop ill-treating her she'd go mad.

18

One fine day in January Jethro rode up Calico Road with his groom Peter, on his way to visit the Packhorse and claim his free pot of beer. He didn't know why he bothered to do this when it was so much trouble, but he liked to keep an eye on his bastard brother and derived a certain secret amusement from the man's stiffness with him. It was a relief to him that Fletcher wasn't as bad as he'd first thought, that the fellow had made no attempt to benefit from their relationship and had kept his promise to stay away from Backenshaw.

What Jethro couldn't understand was why he kept coming here.

When he got close to the inn he saw a carriage getting ready to leave, the coachman fussing with the reins, the attendant groom shutting the door on the occupants. He reined in his horse till it had creaked away down the hill, the horses' hoofbeats seeming to echo for a long time in the frosty air.

He looked at Peter, waiting patiently behind him. 'I don't want the people in that carriage comparing my face to *his*.'

His groom pulled a wry face. 'You can't change his face, sir, whatever you do.'

Only Peter dared speak to him like that. Only from Peter would Jethro ever accept criticism. But that damned resemblance between him and Toby continued to irk him. It was unreasonable, he knew, but there it was.

'See to the horses and then get yourself a pot of beer at my expense,' he told the groom as they stopped in front of the inn. 'And keep your ears and eyes open while you're here, see if you can find out what they think of Fletcher.'

Jethro stopped in the doorway of the public room, letting the warmth generated by its fire wash around him. There were a couple of locals enjoying a drink in one corner and a young woman he didn't recognise was carrying a tray of empty dishes out from the private parlour. She stopped dead at the sight of him and the tray shook in her hands, so that the platters on it rattled and seemed in danger of falling off. He hurried forward to steady it.

'I'm sorry, sir. I thought for a minute – but you're not him.'

'No. I'm a relative. Is Fletcher around? I need to speak to him.'

'I'll go and find him for you. He's probably out in the stables.'

Meg whisked into the house place and told Phoebe about the new arrival in a whisper, keeping a watch over her shoulder in case the gentleman followed her. 'He wants to see Toby.'

'Well, you'd better go and fetch him.' Phoebe hesitated then said, 'He's Toby's half-brother. Comes every January for a pot of beer. It was a condition of Toby's getting the inn. Jethro Greenhalgh is a rich millowner so I don't know why he bothers to claim the beer, but he does.'

Meg shook her head in bafflement as she went outside. She found Toby showing the newcomer's groom where to leave the horses and waited for them to finish speaking before calling his name.

He turned and saw her. She was not quite so thin now, her cheeks delicately pink and her eyes shining with life. Involuntarily he smiled across at her and her lips curved in response. He wished he could make her smile more often. 'I gather my half-brother's here again.'

'Yes. Only he told me he was a distant relative.'

'I wish that's all he was! Maybe then we wouldn't have to wear each other's faces.'

'He wants to see you.'

'Well, I don't want to see him!'

She looked at him in surprise. It was so unlike Toby to speak sharply about anyone, but now that his smile had faded he looked tense. 'Do you dislike him?'

He nodded, then paused and shook his head. 'I don't know how I feel about him, actually. Sometimes I dislike him, sometimes I think – eh, I don't know what I think. But I reckon we both dislike seeing our face on someone else. That feeling is probably the main thing we have in common. But this,' he pointed to his face, 'doesn't stop him looking down his nose at me every time he sees me!'

Without thinking she reached out to catch hold of his arm, threading her own through it. 'Well, he just looked down his nose at me too. So I stared right back at him.'

That brought a reluctant smile to Toby's face. He loved the way Meg was gaining confidence in herself. 'Let's go inside, love. I'd best get this over with.' He was sorry when she took her arm away.

On the way through the public room he poured a pot of beer. In the private parlour he found Jethro pacing to and fro. 'Come for your free drink, have you?' he mocked, holding it out.

The other took it and sipped. 'You keep good beer.'

'A compliment!'

'Why not, when it's deserved? Aren't you going to join me in a drink? You did last year.'

The two stared at one another, eyes at almost the same height, the main difference between them the way they dressed.

Jethro took another sip, then burst out, 'Hell, it's like looking in the mirror. I hate that.'

'You're not the only one. But there's nowt we can do about it.'

'No, there isn't. Look, I'd like a meal as well, if that's all right. Something smells good and the ride's given me an appetite. My groom would probably appreciate one too.'

'I'll go and tell our new cook.'

'Are you talking about that young woman? She's too young to be a cook, surely?'

'She's a good cook and needs to earn her daily bread like the rest of us. What does it matter how old she is?'

'You seem to make a habit of helping waifs and strays.'

'What does that mean?'

Jethro shrugged. 'I've been hearing things.'

'I'd help any folk who were afraid for their children's lives.' He didn't see any reason to hold back the anger that boiled up in him every time he thought of that place down the hill. 'Do you know how badly your friend Beardsworth allows his overlooker to treat his operatives?'

Jethro surprised himself by saying, 'I've been hearing things too, rumours.'

'They're more than rumours.'

'You're sure?'

'Yes. He's a harsh master. I pity anyone in his power.'

'He's the master in his own mill so what can I or anyone else do about it? I only have power over my mill and operatives.'

'Well, you've made things easier for them, I hear. Can't you at least have a word with him?'

Jethro looked at him in surprise, then shook his head. 'Believe me, it'd only make matters worse.'

It was the nearest they'd got to having a proper conversation. Each looked at the other surreptitiously, crossed glances and then Toby grinned.

'Well, at least you have a good reputation as an employer, so I won't be too ashamed of our relationship.'

Jethro was betrayed into a crack of laughter at this turning of the tables on him. Strange how much more often he had laughed since his marriage and the birth of his son. 'If you've not eaten, will you join me for a meal?'

Toby gaped at him. 'Join you!'

'Unless you're too busy.'

'Why?'

'I don't know. Call it a whim.'

'Very well.'

Jethro hesitated, then asked, 'While we're waiting for the food, would you show me the rear part of your inn? The Curate of our church is very excited about it and is coming out to see it when the weather gets warmer. Apparently your Curate corresponds with him and told him it was probably built by monks hundreds of years ago. I'd like to see it for myself.'

It'll be interesting to see how he reacts to the place, Toby thought. 'Why not?' He led the way, startling Meg and Phoebe by taking Greenhalgh through the house place. 'We'll both want a meal when we get back, Meg love, served in the private parlour. The groom will need feeding too.'

'All right, Toby.'

Jethro looked round with interest as he passed through. The place was spotlessly clean and the young woman who'd carried his message had just taken a big platter of pies out of the oven. She was staring at him openly, challengingly almost, but Dixon's widow was avoiding his eyes and continuing to knead some dough. 'The food smells good.'

'It *is* good,' Meg said. 'We wouldn't have so many folk wanting to buy it if it wasn't.'

He was surprised to be addressed so pertly by a servant but he might have guessed that Fletcher wouldn't run a normal household. His half-brother was standing smiling at the young woman, who was probably his mistress. She looked clean and neat, but you couldn't call her pretty. Jethro would rather have Sophia's lush curves any day.

'This way.' Toby was holding a door open on the other side of the room.

When they got to the rear part of the inn Jethro walked slowly up and down the big room, staring around in amazement. He put out a hand to touch the huge wooden uprights, ran a fingertip over the rough old bricks, then bent his head back to stare up at the ceiling. 'They made a good job of this place, didn't they?' He didn't seem to expect an answer, just stood quietly as if letting the feel of the huge room wash over him. Even the expression on his face looked different: less arrogant somehow.

Toby didn't know whether to be irritated or pleased by Jethro's reaction. He'd expected his damned half-brother to feel uncomfortable here, had felt it would be a judgement on the Greenhalghs, but the fellow was clearly enjoying the place, appreciating it as only a few people did.

'It's peaceful here.'

'We could sit down for a minute or two.'

By unspoken consent they sat at either end of the bench, not even trying to speak, each busy with his own thoughts.

Damned if I know what to think of him, Toby decided. He's not looking down his nose at me today. Why has he changed? What does it mean?

After a while he stood up. 'Well, do you want some food now? I'm hungry if you aren't.'

'Yes, please. I'm famished.'

'I shan't accept any payment from you for the meal, so don't try.'

'You're a stubborn fellow, Toby Fletcher.'

'Aye, I am. So are you, Jethro Greenhalgh.'

Their eyes met in another challenge, which neither seemed to win, then Toby grinned. The grin widened, turned into a laugh, and to his surprise, Jethro joined in.

The encounter gave Toby a great deal to think about. He was surprised by the new mood in which they'd met and guessed that Jethro was too. Eh, there was nowt so strange as folk!

As he and his groom rode away, Jethro asked, 'Well, did you find out anything else about him?'

'No more than last time. He's well liked, though they think he's a fool to spend so much money on books and waste good working time reading them.' He paused, then asked, 'Did *you* find anything out, lad?'

Jethro shook his head. 'No. It's always been a

puzzle to me why my father gave him the inn and wanted me to come here every year.'

'You're brothers. Maybe that's why.'

Jethro blew out a scornful puff of air. 'You knew my father. Do you really think he cared about that? He never had anything to do with Fletcher.'

'I think he cared for your brother's mother, though. Just once or twice he said kind things about her: that she was a hard worker, an honest lass, a caring mother for the lad.'

Peter's answer had surprised Jethro. 'Did you ever meet her?'

'I saw her in the street, nothing more. I came to Backenshaw with *your* mother so my loyalty was to her. And since I wasn't brought up in these parts, I didn't know anything about what had gone before until I'd been here a while.'

Jethro shook his head, no wiser for his visit.

Peter let him ride along in silence. He was fond of his master, very fond, as if he were the son Peter had never had. But sometimes it was best just to let Jethro be. He called him 'sir' when other folk were around, 'lad' sometimes when they were on their own.

But this business about the brother – well, Peter was damned if he could work it all out, either. Jethro knew more than he would tell, but when he wanted to keep a secret, you couldn't pry it out of him. He was too close-mouthed for his own good, but how else could you grow up with a father like that?

It had been a bad day when Peter's mistress married John Greenhalgh, a very bad day, but what choice had she had? He had money and her father was desperate for some of it.

Sold her, her father had, and she'd paid a heavy price for saving her family because John had never really cared for her. That was more than obvious. Had he cared more for Fletcher's mother? Who could tell? He hadn't been the sort to show his feelings. Father and son were alike in that, at least.

Cully was a frightened man. He knew Mortley was waiting for him to act and didn't dare let down a fellow with that one's reputation. Besides, there was the money he might earn. He wanted that quite desperately – only, he didn't know how to kill a fellow as big and frightening as Toby bloody Fletcher, and the more he tried to work out a way to do it, the harder it seemed.

In desperation he went across to the inn to have another look round. He chose a night when there was only a thin crescent of moon in the sky because he didn't want anyone seeing him. He forced himself to lie still and pretend to be asleep till his wife and children were deep in slumber and he reckoned the folk at the inn would be too. It wasn't difficult to stay awake because he was so worried.

His wife woke up as he rolled out of bed and asked what he was doing so he told her he was going out for a piss and she turned over in the bed with a sleepy little murmur.

Cully knew the path down to the inn by heart, he'd staggered home along it so many times, and he knew the inn buildings pretty well, too. Hadn't he looked down at them from his field often enough and wished he was sitting drinking in the warmth there instead of digging or planting or feeding his pig? Or worse still, stared along the road at them while doing menial farm chores for others in the village, who were richer than him, the sods, and treated him like dirt while paying him a pittance.

At the inn he tried all the outside doors which used to be left unlocked. This time Fletcher had locked them all. The door that led from the outside into the middle part was a new one, too, solid and fitted with a proper lock. Cully kicked it in a fit of anger and stood for a moment thinking, hands shoved deep into his pockets to keep them warm. There was only the back part left to try and he hated going in there. The whole time he'd been putting the owl inside it, he'd felt as if someone was looking over his shoulder, whispering at him. It was definitely haunted. They should pull down places like that! Or burn them down. It'd make a fine blaze with those big wooden beams.

Maybe he should set a fire? No, that wouldn't kill Fletcher.

As he moved towards the back of the inn he slowed down and squinted up at the old building. Why had he been given such poor eyesight when his damned wife could spot a baby rabbit from clear across the field? There was something moving, he was sure of it. Then he saw that the movement was in the air vent over the outer door. It looked like – it was! There was a face staring down at him!

No, he was imagining it, he told himself firmly, squinting across at it again. It couldn't possibly be a face. That was the air vent, not a window. But if you stood on a bench or you had a ladder, you could peer out through it if you wanted to see what was going on at that side. Maybe someone had heard him moving round the buildings? Maybe someone was watching him, waiting to pounce?

Or it could be a ghost!

Fear skittered across his skin at that thought and he gulped. He took a quick couple of steps to one side and the head moved as if following him. It was light-coloured, round, with big staring eyes, definitely a man's head, a bald man. Who the hell was it? Not Fletcher.

The thought came unbidden: one of the old monks come back to haunt the place. He didn't know which he'd fear most, Fletcher or a ghost.

Then it left the air vent and came swooping down towards him, silent and terrifying. A ghost! With a hoarse cry of terror, he turned and set off running towards the wall of his field, his only thought to get away from that damned place.

Something swooped noiselessly past his shoulder and he cried out again in panic, missing his step and tripping to fall flat on his face. But he was up again in seconds, cursing the mud that slowed him down as he stumbled on. He kept looking back over his shoulder as he lurched up the slope that led from the inn.

The ghost hadn't swooped on him again, but suddenly he heard footsteps behind him and sobbed aloud in panic, trying to run faster, desperate to get away from whatever was chasing him. By now he was gibbering in sheer terror. His father had seen boggarts in the clough, had used to terrify them when they were children with tales of those fearsome creatures. Let other folk scoff! Tonight Cully realised his father had been telling the absolute truth.

When he reached his own wall he slowed down, his heart still pounding, and forced himself to look behind. Sweat was chilling on his face now as a light wind began to whine softly round him. There was definitely something moving in the shadows, so he scrambled over the wall and ran for the house, moaning under his breath.

Beardsworth could keep his sodding money! Cully wasn't going near the back part of the inn again, not even in daytime.

As the running footsteps faded the owl returned to its perch where it made a hearty meal of a plump field mouse it'd plucked from the rough grass on the sloping upper edge of the clough. The sheep, which had been disturbed by the man's yelling, settled down again to sleep.

But Cully slept hardly at all, jerking awake, listening, worrying that something or somebody was hunting him. And what would Mortley and Beardsworth do to him for failing? Those buggers down the hill were vicious brutes, as everyone knew.

When dawn began to lighten the sky he got up, decision taken. As he was creeping out of the bedroom he shared with his wife and children, Sairey asked in a sleepy voice if it was time to get up. He told her in a savage whisper to shut up and go back to bloody sleep. In the kitchen he got the embers burning up and gathered together a few possessions by the light of the fire, all the time listening in case his wife woke up.

As he opened the outer door he suddenly remembered the donkey. How could he have forgotten that? Why, he could drive down to one of the nearby towns, sell the animal and the cart, and that would give him some money to add to his savings for a new start. Not as much as if he'd killed Fletcher, but enough. What was there to keep him up here? Nothing. Only a wife who nagged him, children who ate him out of house and home, and boggarts that chased after him.

He'd never made a decent living since those damned mills started weaving cloth, taking away honest men's livelihoods. He should have left Calico years ago.

He put the pouch of money in his pocket, then as he was leading the donkey out of the lean-to stable, his wife appeared in front of him.

'What are you doing, Cully?'

'Going to market.'

'It isn't Market Day.'

'Going to do a little business over in Tod, then. What's it to you?'

'You took your spare clothes from the box and a few other things too.'

In the grey dawnlight she had such a stubborn look

on her face that he yelled, 'Shut up and get out of my way!' He gave her a shove, but although she staggered sideways, she came back to stand in his way.

'You're leaving us, aren't you?'

'Yes, I am, you stupid bitch.'

'But you can't. How shall the children and I manage?'

'I don't care how you manage. I've had enough of you and those squalling brats.'

'Then you shouldn't have put another in my belly, should you?'

'What!' Fury swelled within him. 'You're lying! You can't be having another already.'

'I am. You never let me alone. The children are more your fault than mine. You don't think I enjoy you doing that to me, do you? But I won't let you go and leave us to be put in the poorhouse. I won't!' She ran round him to the back of the cart and started throwing his things off it.

Fury turned into a red rage and the only thing he knew was that he wasn't going to let her or anyone else stop him. When the red haze faded, Cully stepped back, took a few deep shuddering breaths and stared down at her still body on the ground. Cursing, he reloaded his things and yelled, 'It's no use pretending to be knocked out! You tried that trick on me afore an' I fell for it. This time you're *not* going to stop me leaving!'

He finished harnessing the donkey and looked across at Sal, surprised that she was still lying there in the rain. She couldn't be . . . no, of course not.

He'd only given her a tap or two. No, she'd played this trick afore, and what a good actress she had proved to be then, frightening him into doing as she wished. He clicked his tongue to the animal to start walking, looked back once and saw she still hadn't moved. *Oh, no!* he thought. *You're not catching me like that again, missus!*

As he went past the Packhorse Cully made a rude hand gesture in its direction. Once it had disappeared behind him he began to cheer up. Sal would be back in the cottage by now, weeping. He was sick of her weeping. Sick of skriking kids, too.

Even the rain which started mid-morning didn't dampen his good spirits, for he was free at last, could go where he wanted, wasn't letting any woman trap him again.

From the window of the back bedroom she used every month Harriet watched the trio of new child apprentices walk wearily into the mill yard behind a stern-looking man. Her heart went out to them, for they'd find no comfort here. The oldest still had a hint of spirit showing in the way she stood and stared back at those who'd brought her here.

When Mortley strode out to inspect them he soon found an excuse to slap that girl about the head and Harriet clamped one hand to her mouth to hold back a moan of sympathy. If she tried to intervene, she'd make things worse for the poor child. Oh, the man was a brute!

She heard her husband come in for his mid-day

meal and with a sigh went down to join him, feeling her pulse quicken with fear as Andrew gave her one of his scornful looks.

'Well?' he asked.

She had to tell him. 'I've started my courses.'

'You're taking the potion?'

'Yes. Every day.'

'We'll give it three months,' he decided.

She bowed her head and tried to eat, but couldn't force much down, feeling quite sick with relief that she was not to be beaten again.

'You've moved into the back bedroom?' he asked.

'Yes, Andrew.'

'Good, because I've a new maid starting this afternoon and she'll have other duties beside the cleaning. *Special duties.*'

His leer told her what these duties would be and Harriet had to dig her fingernails into the palms of her hands to prevent a protest escaping her. She was horrified that he would insult her in this way, shamed to the core because everyone in the district would soon know about it.

When the new maid arrived she proved to be a plump young creature who said she was fifteen and hadn't worked as a maid before. Nor, Harriet soon found out, did the girl understand the ways of respectable households like this one. She could guess where Andrew had found Prissy. Even the cook shared one glance of dismay with her mistress before she took a deep breath and said woodenly that she'd better start Prissy's training.

That night the sounds coming from Andrew's bedroom were loud enough to keep Harriet awake until the small hours. She smiled, happy not to be the object of his attentions. If this happened the following night, she'd have no trouble getting away.

And she'd kill herself if they caught her and tried to bring her back, would take a sharp knife with her 'specially for that purpose.

A person could only take so much pain and humiliation.

Meg heard a sound at the door and opened it to find Sairey standing there, her face dirty, her hair a tangled mess. 'Do you want something to eat, love?'

But the child said nothing, just began to weep.

'Shhh now, what is it?'

The weeping continued. Meg hadn't willingly touched a child since Nelly died, and hesitated even now. But Sairey's distress was so overwhelming that she had to take her in her arms, filthy though the girl was. She carried her into the house place and sat down at the table with Sairey on her lap.

The child burrowed against her and gradually stopped weeping. 'Mammy's lying out in the rain and she won't talk to me. She won't move.' She knuckled her eyes and volunteered a further piece of information. 'She's all wet.'

Meg exchanged startled glances with Phoebe, who had stood quietly at the other side of the room watching them.

'An' the baby won't stop crying, neither. We're all hungry.'

Meg stood up, setting the child gently on her feet and smoothing the tangled hair from her eyes. 'I'd better go home with her, Phoebe, and find out what's wrong. Sal may have had an accident and be hurt.' Or Cully might have knocked her unconscious. She wouldn't put anything past him.

Phoebe nodded, moved across the room to thrust a piece of bread into Sairey's hand then went back to work, shaking her head. What next? That Cully had a lot to answer for.

As they walked along the road, Sairey gobbled down the bread, not looking where she was going. When she fell over she didn't cry, just stuffed the last of the crust into her mouth, muddied though it was, and got up again, brushing some dirt off her face with the back of one hand.

'Is your mammy groaning?' Meg asked.

'No. She's looking up at the sky. She won't say nothing.'

Startled by this, Meg began to walk faster. Surely the woman wasn't dead? When Sairey lagged behind, she took the child's hand and fairly dragged her along.

The cottage seemed to be sagging against the rain-soaked ground. The smell from the pig sty was disgusting and the door of the lean-to shed was banging to and fro in the wind.

'Where's your mammy?'

Sairey pulled Meg round to the other side of the

shed and she gasped as she saw Sal lying there. There was no doubting that the woman was dead and had been for an hour or two, because not only were her clothes soaked and her hair plastered to her skull, but her pale face was bloody and bruised on one side from a massive blow. Remembering Ben and how he'd died, Meg couldn't move or speak for a moment.

Sairey knelt down to shake her mother's shoulder and call, 'Mammy! Wake up, Mammy.'

Somehow Meg found the strength to pull the girl away. There was no helping the woman but there were children to be cared for. 'Where's your dad, love?'

'Gone away. In the cart.'

'Where are the other children?'

'In the house.'

There were three others, all younger than Sairey. The baby was crawling around in the filth of the kitchen floor, howling dolefully and getting perilously close to the open fire.

'Dear heaven!' Meg whispered. 'What's to be done with them all?'

'They're hungry,' Sairey said with that hopeful look on her face.

'Don't let the baby burn itself.'

Sairey hauled the baby towards her by the stained and tattered shirt which was all it was wearing and sat down on a stool, picking it up and shushing it.

All the children were thin and filthy, their clothes little more than rags. It was no use leaving them here so Meg searched the two-roomed cottage, found a few clothes and pulled them on to the scrawny little bodies. Then she took the matted grey blankets from the beds and wrapped them round the chidren's shoulders against the chill rain still teeming down outside.

'Give me the baby and hold your sister's hand. We'll all go back to the inn and have something to eat, eh?'

Her face brightening, Sairey took a firm hold of her next sister and Meg held the baby in one arm so that it could look over her shoulder while taking the hand of the child who could just totter along.

Toby was coming out of the stables when he saw them approaching. He was amazed to see Meg, who'd avoided children ever since she arrived here, surrounded by them. Cully Dean's children, too. Poor dirty little brats! He took a step forward, then ran towards her because from the expression on her face something was very wrong.

'What is it, Meg?'

'I'll tell you in a minute, Toby. Can you pick the little one up? She's not a very good walker yet.'

He scooped up the child, gestured to Sairey and her next sister to start moving, then fell into place beside Meg.

With his help they made better progress, entering the house place by the side door and startling Phoebe into an exclamation.

The three little girls clustered together, looking from one adult to the other as if they expected someone to thump them. Meg joggled the baby boy up and down, shushing it, but it kept grizzling. 'Can you keep an eye on these four for a minute, Phoebe? I have to tell Toby something.'

She handed the baby to Phoebe, took him aside and quickly explained what she'd found.

'Sal's dead?' He was so stunned by this he couldn't for a moment think what else to say or do. Then he shook his head and said, 'I'd better go and fetch help. Can you see to the children?'

'Yes.' Meg went to whisper the news to Phoebe who looked at her in horror, then beckoned the three little girls nearer the fire.

'We'll feed them while Toby fetches the Curate,' Phoebe decided. 'The babby will probably be able to eat some pobbies and I dare say the others will enjoy them too. I'll get some milk heating at once and you cut bread into small squares, Meg love. We'll put in some honey. It's comforting, honey is. Eh, the poor motherless lambs! To think of such a thing happening in our village.'

The two women sat the children down at the table and watched them gobble down the contents of the bowls, picking them up to drain the last of the warm milk, impatient of the spoon. Neither woman had the heart to scold them for this.

Meanwhile Toby ran up the clough, clambered over the stone wall and found the dead woman. He didn't stay long. There was nothing he could do for poor Sal and he'd better leave her where she was.

He went on to see the Curate.

Mr Pickerling gaped at the news, then reached for his overcoat. 'I'll come with you.'

At the inn there was a shout from the public room and Meg looked in to find Ross standing there smiling.

'I'm going down the hill, love. Do you need owt from the shop?'

She moved closer to him, looking over her shoulder to make sure none of the children was within hearing distance. 'I found Sal Dean lying dead outside their shed a short time ago. Cully's disappeared. Phoebe and I are looking after the children. Toby's gone to fetch the Curate.'

'Sal's dead?'

Meg nodded. 'It looks like someone hit her.'

Ross closed his eyes for a minute then looked at Meg sadly. 'Sal was the same age as my eldest lass and pretty with it. They used to play together. Why she wanted to marry a ne'er-do-well like Cully I never did understand.'

'Can you help us?'

'Aye. I'll go down the hill another day.'

Within two hours, he had organised relatives of the dead woman to look after the children and was on his way down the hill to fetch the nearest Constable, at Cornelius Pickerling's suggestion.

Only when Sairey and the others had been led away by a plump woman who hadn't stopped crying the whole time she'd been in the inn did Meg find reaction setting in. She sat down suddenly in a chair and looked at Phoebe. 'I feel a bit – dizzy like.'

The older woman was round the table in a trice and pushed her head down. 'Sit like that for a few minutes. It helps.'

Toby came in and looked from one to the other. 'What's the matter?'

'It's just hit her what's happened.'

Meg looked up at him. 'She was lying there – like my husband. There was so much blood. I can still see – his blood.'

He wanted to take her in his arms, comfort her, love her. But she had a closed look to her face and Phoebe was hovering over her like a mother hen.

'Do you want to go and lie down?'

Meg stared at him as if she didn't understand the words. 'What? Oh, no. No. I'll just – carry on working.'

He and Phoebe exchanged glances, but left her to it. He'd rather she'd turned to him for comfort. Much rather.

19

Jethro came home from his trip to Calico in a strange mood. Sophia had been wondering whether to tell him about her sister's dilemma but as he sat and frowned into the fire after their evening meal, she hesitated to interrupt his reverie.

'That damned brother of mine!' he exclaimed abruptly.

Sophia had deliberately avoided asking him how his visit to the inn had gone because he usually snapped at her if she did and she'd found it best to leave him alone at these times. But since he'd started the discussion, she asked, 'Did he upset you?'

'No. Yes. Of course he did!'

'Then why do you keep going there?'

'I don't know. Yes, I do. Because I promised my father I would. He wanted me to keep an eye on Fletcher.'

'You could have gone on and visited Andrew afterwards. You were quite close to Tappersley.'

'Ha! If it weren't for your sister, I'd cut the connection with Beardsworth. He's always had a reputation as a harsh master, but now there are rumours of actual deaths among the children working at his mill, not accidents but deaths from beating – rumours one can't help but believe.'

She was shocked. 'Surely not? Why hasn't the local magistrate done anything about it?'

Jethro shrugged. 'You need to have proof to do something. But apparently whole families are fleeing from his mill – and my brother's involved, helping them escape. Damn Andrew! What does he think he's doing?'

'He's not a very comfortable husband, either,' she began.

'I suppose you're going to blame me for introducing him to your sister! Well, I didn't know how bad he was, and at least he's wealthy enough to keep her in comfort.'

'That's no consolation when—'

There was a knock on the door and the maid opened it. 'Please, sir, you're wanted in the mill. Urgent, the engineer says.'

He rolled his eyes in frustration but stood up immediately. 'I'm coming.'

Sophia watched him go, biting her lower lip and wishing she'd just told him straight out about Harriet when he returned from Calico. Now she'd have to wait till he came up to bed.

But as she was sitting in front of the mirror brushing out her hair, the maid brought a message that there was something wrong with the steam engine and Mr Greenhalgh would not be back till much later.

In the morning Jethro's side of the bed wasn't slept

in and when Sophia went downstairs the maid informed her that the master had snatched a couple of hours' sleep on the sofa and gone back to the mill again without even changing his clothes.

Sophia knew she'd not have his full attention while something was wrong with his beloved steam engine, and indeed the mill couldn't function without it. She tried to wait patiently for an opportunity to speak to him but it was hard when she was so worried about Harriet.

An hour later Jethro came into the house like a whirlwind, saying he had to ride over to Rochdale where there was an engineering works. They needed new parts in a hurry, perhaps a whole new steam engine.

He had enough on his mind, Sophia decided. She'd wait till he returned. One day couldn't make much difference.

The day after the so-called maid had shared her master's bedchamber, Harriet went into it and found the girl peacocking up and down the room in one of her better gowns.

'Get that off this minute!'

The girl smirked at her. 'Master said I could have one of your gowns an' this is the one I like.'

Outraged, Harriet slapped her across the face. 'Get it off at once and don't you dare touch my things again!'

'I'll tell him, I will. He said—'

Harriet dragged the gown from the girl's plump

body, disgusted by the odours that emanated from it. 'Get dressed in your own clothes and go downstairs to the kitchen. Cook will see that you're kept busy.'

Pouting, the girl did as she was told, moving as slowly as possible and letting out an occasional sob or mutter of ''Tisn't fair!'

When Andrew came into the dining room for his midday meal he was angry. 'What's this I hear about you countermanding my orders to Prissy?'

'How did you know about that?'

'She stopped me on the way in, told me what you'd done.' He glared at her. 'I told her she could have that gown and, by God, she'll keep it.'

Harriet stared at him in amazement. 'I can't believe what I'm hearing. You'd make your *wife* a laughing stock because of a common trollop like her?'

He leaned back, balancing his chair on two legs and clearly enjoying her outrage. 'I don't give a damn what people think about you, and they won't know about the dress unless *you* tell them. Besides,' his mood changed rapidly, 'it's me who's the laughing stock for having found myself a barren wife.'

Harriet stood up and left the room, too angry to worry about whether he'd come after her and thump her. But he didn't this time.

When he'd gone back to the mill, she tiptoed into the bedroom, opened the bottom drawer and took out her jewellery box. There was a brooch missing already, one of the pieces she'd brought with her, inherited from her grandmother. Anger filled her and she tipped the rest of the pieces into a scarf, putting the box back again. After locking it and removing the key, she carried the small bundle of jewellery into the back bedroom. Taking the muff out of the cupboard, she unpicked the stitches, removed the money and sewed it up carefully again.

Just as she was finishing that, there was screaming and shouting from the mill yard and she hurried to look out of the window. Jad Mortley was belabouring the new girl apprentice about the shoulders with a strap and she was squealing and wriggling in his grasp. She was no match for the burly man, however, and gradually her struggles became feebler until she sank to the ground, curling up and trying to cover her head with her arms as he continued to hit her.

There were red lines on the thin arms and legs where the strap had cut in, blood trickling from them. Harriet could bear it no longer and rushed down, pushing Cook aside and flinging open the outside door. She ran across the mill yard, shouting, 'Let her go, you brute!'

He didn't even seem to hear her, so she seized his arm and hung on to prevent him from hitting the girl again.

Jad swung round, fist raised to thump her, then realised in time who she was and merely shook her hands from his arm. 'This lazy brat needs a lesson, Mrs Beardsworth,' he panted. 'Kindly leave me to do my job.'

Andrew came striding out to join them. He glowered at his wife and slapped her hard so that she staggered backwards, nearly falling. '*Don't* interfere in my business again!' Then he turned to his over-looker. 'I think the girl has been beaten enough now, Jad. We'll lock her up in the coal shed without food tonight, eh, just to make sure she learns her lesson?'

For a moment fury turned Jad's ugly face into a gargoyle's, then with a visible effort he nodded. 'Right, sir. I'll take her there.'

'No, we'll let my dear wife do that.' He gave Harriet a look that threatened more trouble later. 'Go and tell Cook to make sure the coal scuttles are full, then lock this girl up. She's to have nothing to eat or drink till morning, mind.'

Harriet drew herself up, gave him one icy look and took the child's hand, helping her to her feet. He watched her go then turned to Jad. 'I warned you not to go too far. I don't want any more of 'em killing.'

'And I don't want your wife interfering in my job!'

'You saw my little reminder to her of that. Let it suffice. Anyway, she wouldn't need to interfere if you didn't make a public spectacle of your rages. I'll remind you just once more that I'm in charge here, not you. *No – more – killings.*'

Jad watched him go, furious at being taken to task so publicly, then went back into the mill to make the operatives' lives a misery. But nothing would stem the anger that roiled inside him. That uppity bitch! Couldn't even give her husband a child. Worthless as a woman, she was. He'd get his own back on her one day. Oh, yes. He always did.

Harriet led the unresisting child into the kitchen. The girl wasn't sobbing, just drooping and wincing at the pain of the beating. Cook turned to face them, not seeming at all surprised so she must have been watching through the kitchen window. 'My husband wants this girl locked in the coalhouse overnight, so could you please see that all the scuttles are full before I do it?'

When Cook had sent the maid scurrying to check this, Harriet asked, 'Where's the new maid?'

'Asleep. I sent her to bed because she was too tired to do anything properly – not that she knows how to do an honest day's work anyway.'

'You were right. She's a whore.' The word would once have shocked Harriet. Now, it was simply the correct term for the creature her husband had introduced into the household. She touched her cheek, which was still sore from the vicious slap she'd received, and saw Cook looking at her with sympathy.

'I'm sorry about everything, ma'am.'

'Yes. So am I.' She turned to the child, who was standing beside her waiting in dumb resignation for more unkindnesses. 'What's your name?'

'Jane.'

'And what did you do to anger Mr Mortley today?'

For a moment anger sparked in the child's eyes. 'I don't know, missus, honest I don't. He hit me yester' 'fore I even spoke, an' he's been hitting me ever since.'

Harriet saw Cook shake her head and press her lips together, so took a risk. 'I'm feeling hungry, Cook. Do you have any bread and cheese?'

Cook looked at her sharply. 'You're not going to—'

Harriet raised one eyebrow. 'Well, do you?'

The woman got out a loaf and cut off a thick slice of bread then some pieces of cheese, before setting everything on a plate. 'I'll just get some more butter out.'

'Never mind. There isn't time.' Sitting down at the table, Harriet took the bread and passed it to the child. 'Eat it quickly before Mr Beardsworth comes in.'

The girl stared at her as if she didn't understand the words.

'You're hungry, aren't you? Hurry up and eat it!'

Jane grabbed the bread and began gobbling it down. When Harriet passed her the cheese, she ate that with the same rapidity.

Cook set a glass of milk down in front of Harriet. 'You'll be thirsty too, ma'am.'

'Indeed I am. Thank you.' She pushed the glass towards the child. 'Quickly.'

The minute the girl had finished, Cook cleared the plate and glass away, rinsing them in the scullery bucket and drying them before putting them back on the shelf, a job usually left to her underlings. She let out an audible sigh of relief as she returned to the kitchen.

When the maid came back to report that all the scuttles were full of coal, Harriet took Jane out to the coalhouse, which lay beyond the scullery at the very rear of the house. 'I can't give you any blankets,

I'm afraid, but there are some sacks over there.'

Jane smiled. 'Thank you, missus. For everything.'

'I wish I could do more.' Harriet locked the coal-house door and went back into the kitchen. 'I'm extremely grateful to you, Cook.'

'For what? I did nothing.'

Harriet saw the anxiety in the woman's eyes and said no more, going up to her bedroom to plan what to take with her that night. She tried not to think of how Andrew had humiliated her in front of everyone, but shame still welled in her every time she remembered the scene.

By the time the siren sounded for the end of the day she was sitting in the parlour sewing. She knew that her cheek was still red, but held her head high and ignored it.

Andrew's eyes rested on her face for a moment, then he gave her a gloating smile. He remained in a good mood throughout the meal and as soon as they'd finished, said, 'You look tired, my dear. Better go to bed early tonight.'

She nodded and began to gather up her sewing things, watching him pour himself another glass of port from the decanter, then fill a second glass, which he set ready.

He saw her gaze going to the second glass. 'Prissy does enjoy a glass of port,' he murmured as he pulled the bell.

Harriet pressed her lips together and left the room. It was the last time, she told herself. He'd not taunt her again because either she'd escape or she'd kill herself. Even death would be preferable to staying with a brute like him.

It wasn't until she was in the bedroom that she began to wonder what he'd say and do when he found she was missing. He'd be furious and come searching for her, she was sure. And he'd take out his anger on anyone near.

What about the child? What would he do to Jane?

Harriet would have liked to pace up and down the room, because she'd always found it aided thinking but didn't dare betray the fact that she wasn't asleep. After taking off her outer garments and putting her nightgown on over her underclothes, she blew out her candle and lay down on the bed.

But though she forced her body to be still, her mind wouldn't stop dwelling upon the events of the day and she couldn't get that poor child out of her mind. The girl was in for a miserable life here and Harriet had made it worse.

In the end she could only come to one conclusion: she couldn't leave Jane to Jad Mortley's vicious attacks and her husband's possible reprisals, so would have to take the child with her.

What felt like hours later she heard footsteps mount the stairs, one pair of feet heavy, the other light. The girl was giggling and sounded drunk. As soon as the disgusting noises began issuing from the front bedroom Harriet got up and dressed herself in her warmest gown. She tied up the money and jewellery in a handkerchief and put it into her bag under the clothes. Could a wife be accused of theft if she took her own jewellery? She suspected that she could, from Andrew's taunts, but didn't care.

As she was walking along the landing there was a loud bump from the front bedroom and a squeal of pain from the girl, followed by pleas not to hurt her. Dear God, what was he doing in there?

As the pleas were cut off abruptly and the bed began to creak Harriet hurried down the stairs, putting her carpet bag by the kitchen door and going through the scullery to the coal house. The key was hanging nearby on the wall. She heard a sound inside as she turned it and called in a low voice, 'It's me, Jane. I'm running away. Do you want to come with me?'

The child stepped forward from the darkness into a patch of moonlight, staring at Harriet. 'Won't *he* come after you? Isn't he your mester?'

'Yes, he's my husband, and yes, he may come after me, but I have a – a friend and if I can get to her she'll help me.'

'He'll kill me if he catches me.' Jane stared up at Harriet, head on one side, then her teeth gleamed in a brief smile. 'But I reckon that Mr Mortley will kill me if I stay. All right, missus, I'll come with you.'

'Don't speak from now on, just follow me. And wrap this round you.' She gave the child an old shawl she'd brought 'specially for her then turned to lead the way to the back door.

'I'm sure I heard a sound from down here, Cook,' a voice said.

Harriet pressed back against the wall. Jane didn't need any warning to keep quiet.

Cook's voice came to them. 'As you can see, there's no one here. It'll have been a rat. I'll get the rat catcher in tomorrow. You go back to bed now. I'm a bit peckish so I'll just have a piece of cake before I come up. And go quietly. Don't disturb the master.'

'All right, Cook.'

The kitchen door shut quietly and footsteps came towards the scullery and coalhouse. As the door swung open, the light of a candle shone in, clearly illuminating Harriet.

For a minute the two women looked at one another, then Cook said quietly, 'As I thought, no one here!' and turned away.

Harriet felt so sick with relief she couldn't move for a minute, then took Jane's hand and led her into the kitchen.

Cook was sitting at the table eating a very small piece of cake. She didn't look up as they passed through the room, but the cake shook in her fingers and crumbs fell from it.

Harriet opened the back door with the spare key, leaving the usual key on its hook as she had planned. She wanted to leave no signs of how she'd escaped from the house.

She looked back at the other woman and for a minute their eyes met, then Harriet picked up her bag and took the child's hand.

When they'd left Cook took a cloth and wiped up the coal dust the girl's feet had carried in then forced herself to eat the rest of the cake, washing the plate carefully and putting it away.

★

The moon was shining brightly, showing the road ahead quite clearly, but the child slowed Harriet down more than she had expected because Jane was weak and unused to walking, especially uphill. She had to take rests, panted and wheezed at the steeper gradients, and more than once she tripped and fell. She didn't complain, did her very best, with a look of dumb suffering on her face that made Harriet quite unable to leave her behind.

Several times she fingered the knife in her pocket wondering whether to kill herself first if Andrew caught them, or try to kill him and thus save the lives of many others. No, she'd have to kill herself. She couldn't face death by hanging, just couldn't.

At four o'clock in the morning Andrew decided that the night's romping had made him hungry. He sat up and kicked the girl out of bed. As she lay where she'd fallen, still sound asleep, he decided she'd be useless at getting him some food. Then he grinned. His lady wife could do the honours.

He erupted into the back bedroom, holding a candle in one hand. Harriet was sleeping as primly as she did everything else. With a roar, he kicked the bed and shoved her body hard. Only it wasn't a body but a rolled quilt, its softness mocking him. He looked round. Where was the bitch? What was she doing out of bed at this hour?

He ran down the stairs but there were no lights burning in any of the rooms and his candle showed him that Harriet wasn't sitting in the darkness anywhere. He went back to the foot of the stairs and yelled, 'Get up! Everyone get up and come down here!'

Within minutes Cook, the two housemaids, the governess and his daughters had gathered in the kitchen. Prissy was still asleep, but he didn't send for her, because he knew she wasn't involved.

'Where is she?' he shouted, thumping the table.

His daughters clung to one another, Marianne starting to sob. He grabbed her arm and shook her hard. 'Shut up, you stupid little fool!'

It was the governess who spoke. 'Excuse me, sir, but who exactly are you looking for?'

'My damned wife!'

There was silence. Everyone stared at one another in shock then back at him.

'Well? Someone must know where she is.'

They shook their heads.

'You!' He pointed to Cook. 'Go and search all the attics.'

Praying that the maid wouldn't betray their visit to the kitchen during the night, she left.

Andrew stabbed a finger in the direction of the governess. 'You go and search all the bedrooms. The rest of you, stay here.'

He searched the ground floor himself, properly this time, looking in every cupboard, behind curtains, anywhere she could have hidden. Harriet wasn't there.

He rattled the door of the coalhouse as he passed

to make sure it was still locked, but didn't think to look inside.

When everyone, including a yawning Prissy, had gathered again to report that they'd not found a sign of his wife, he stared at them in bafflement then ordered, 'Stay here!'

He went upstairs to his bedroom, grimacing at the untidiness and smell. Prissy was a hot little wench, but she'd have to learn to wash more often. He'd used others like her over the years, because a virile man could never be satisfied by a *lady*. They didn't even enjoy it, ladies didn't.

Harriet had run away, of course. He should have locked her in her room. With a muffled exclamation of exasperation, as much with himself as with her, he began to dress. He'd gone too far. But hell, it was frustrating to be tied to a barren woman when you knew you were capable of siring children.

He stopped on that thought. She'd run away. Who was to say she wouldn't fall in the darkness, even kill herself? He had been going to call out a search party, but now he changed his mind. He'd take Jad with him and they'd easily overtake her because there was only one place she could go – to her sister's. Not that Jethro would harbour her. He knew the law as well as anyone.

Andrew went pounding down the stairs again and yelled, 'Get the fire burning in the kitchen and make me something to eat, quickly!' He ran across the mill yard and went to hammer on the door of his over-looker's house, cursing the fellow for being slow to answer. When the door opened at last, he explained what had happened, sent Jad to saddle the horses and went back home.

In the kitchen, he found one of the maids weeping and Cook comforting her. 'What's the matter now?'

'The girl you locked in the coalhouse isn't there, sir,' Cook said calmly.

'What? How the hell could she get out?' Then a smile slowly spread across his face. 'My stupid wife must have released her.' Excellent, he thought as he grabbed a piece of bread and butter from the plate Cook held out to him. Harriet had made a big mistake. The child would slow her down and they'd easily catch up with her. The bitch was stupid as well as barren. But she'd signed her own death warrant now.

20

Meg couldn't sleep that night. Holding Sal's baby in her arms had stirred up so many memories of cuddling her own Nelly at that age. Helping the older children had brought back more: small arms clinging to her, a head drooping against her, a sticky mouth opening to be fed. She lay staring up at the ceiling, fists clenched by her sides, wondering if she was going mad again. After a while, when her thoughts didn't swirl away into darkness and she remained fully conscious of the bedroom and the faint night noises around her, she decided this grief wasn't like before. Then she'd nearly gone mad from the pain of her loss and had hardly noticed what was happening around her as she tramped the moors. This time it hurt, yes, but so much had happened since Nelly's death that the grief was more distant, somehow – part of her, always part of her, but not skewering into her life until it made no sense.

And she didn't want to run away, but to stay and make a new life here.

She couldn't get back to sleep so eventually got up and wrapped a shawl round her shoulders, unable to lie there a second longer. She crept down to the kitchen through the darkness of the stairwell, trying to avoid the creaky stairs and nearly falling in the process. With a muffled yelp, she caught hold of the banister and clung to it, bringing herself to a halt halfway down with her heart pounding from shock. After a minute or so she continued slowly and carefully down the rest of the stairs, avoiding the creaky patch at the bottom.

In the house place it was cold, the flagstones chill beneath her feet. Most folk wouldn't want to be up at this hour without a light, but she'd never felt afraid here.

She poked a splinter of wood into the faint red glow at the centre of the stove and lit a candle, then pulled out the damper to get the fire burning up. There were all sorts of things she could have been doing, but she just sat there at the table. Eh, it was strange. It was as if she was waiting for something to happen, though what she couldn't imagine.

Worried sick by their slow progress up the hill, Harriet had to wonder if she should leave the girl behind, trying to hide her somewhere away from the road.

As if Jane had read her mind, she tottered to a rock to one side and plumped down on it with a groan. 'Sorry, missus, but I can't walk no more. I hurt all over where he hit me.'

'I know.' Harriet looked at the scrawny figure in the faint remains of the moonlight and put down her valise, decision taken. She removed the bundle of jewellery from it and tied that to her waist with a ribbon belt, then hid the bag behind a rock about twenty paces from the road, taking careful note of the place. 'Stand on that rock, child, and I'll give you a piggy-back. You're too tired to walk any further and I'm not leaving you behind for them to catch.'

When Jane was settled Harriet looked back, exclaiming in dismay as she saw lights bobbing about further down the hill. It was her husband coming after her, she was certain of that! Who else could it be?

She didn't say anything, wasn't sure if Jane had noticed, but set off again, grimly determined to make it to the inn before daylight.

Surely an innkeeper who had helped others escape would agree to hide her?

Jad ran across the village to warn his deputy to take his place at the mill come starting time at six o'clock, then knocked at a few doors to each end of the main street to see if he could find any clue as to which way Mrs Beardsworth had gone. One woman, holding a wailing infant in her arms, thought she'd heard someone pass by heading towards the tops as she was trying to settle her sick baby, but wasn't sure and couldn't give a time.

He went back to report this to his master. 'It's not certain, but I think she went up the hill, sir.'

Andrew nodded. 'It makes sense. She'll be trying to get to her sister's, though how she thinks she can get so far on foot without us overtaking her, I don't

know. We'll go up that way and see what we find.'
He looked at Jad meaningfully as he added, 'I only
hope she hasn't gone over the edge in the darkness.'

'It'd be a great pity if she had, wouldn't it?'

'Yes. I'd pay anyone who tried to save her, pay
them well too – even if they failed.'

Jad smiled, knowing perfectly well what his master
wanted. He'd expected to get his revenge on the
bitch, but not this soon. Well, he was always ready to
earn extra money and didn't care how. 'What about
the girl?'

'She might fall over the edge as well, poor thing.
The two of them were together after all and trying to
help one another. Very sad.' After a minute's
contemplation of the pleasure of seeing his wife lying
in her coffin, Andrew said briskly, 'Well, let's not
waste any more time. Have you got some lanterns?
It's still pretty dark.'

Jad squinted at the sky. 'Horses can see better than
we can in the dark and the lanterns will show her
where we are.'

'I'm not going anywhere without lanterns. I'm not
a horse and I definitely can't see in the dark!'

Jad bit off a sharp reply. His master was causing
delay after delay. It would be fully light in an hour or
two and he'd have trusted the horses to find their way
safely on such a well-used road. It wasn't as if they'd
be galloping or riding across open country, after all.
But there was never any use arguing with Mr
Beardsworth.

'Hurry up, man!'

As they left the village, each carrying a lantern on a pole, Andrew gave a nasty chuckle. 'I'd like to catch up with them before there are too many folk up and about – if things are to happen as I wish. We don't want anyone mistaking what's happening, do we?'

If there was so much hurry, why the hell had his master caused so many delays? Jad wondered. But Andrew Beardsworth always went his own way, and so far it'd paid off. Ah, what was he worrying about? They were on horseback and would catch the silly bitch easily enough.

Curtains, or the sacks many folk used for curtains, twitched at windows as they passed by, but only Jad noticed that. Let them peep out, he thought contemptuously. They'd not see what happened up Calico Road. And they would still be toiling in the mill while he was living a comfortable life, with power over others and money put by for his old age. What more could a man want?

Breath rasped in Harriet's throat as she struggled on. Each slope seemed steeper than the previous one and Jane heavier. She had to stop every now and then for a rest, and sometimes Jane hobbled along for a while in her ill-fitting shoes, but could not keep going for long. The inn showed up in the distance now, a black outline against the grey of the pre-dawn sky, but behind her the bobbing lanterns were halfway up the hill and moving far more quickly than she could.

She and Jane would never get to the inn in time at this rate!

When a man strode down the road towards them she was so exhausted all she could do was stand there panting, waiting to find out who he was and what he wanted. She let Jane slip down and sag against her, then reached inside her pocket for the knife. She wasn't going back to Andrew, not under any circumstances.

The stranger stopped a couple of paces away from them. 'Who are you?'

'None of your business.'

'I can see someone's coming after you,' he said curtly. 'If it's who I think it is, I might be able to help.'

Harriet was so surprised by this she couldn't speak for a minute or two, then quickly explained their plight.

He looked at the little girl, waif-thin and even in this dim light showing the marks of a severe beating. 'It's wickedness, that's what it is, beating young childer like that. I'd not send mine to work in that mill, not for anything.' He cast another glance down the hill and stepped forward. 'Come on. I'll carry the little lass. Can you manage on your own?'

'Yes.'

He set Jane down on top of a drystone wall. 'Jump down, love. Good thing the ground's too hard to show your footprints, eh? We'll go across the field here. It's quicker. It was lucky my dog heard you coming and growled to warn me.' He looked sideways at Harriet and his voice grew gentler. 'Not far now.'

'Why – are you – doing this?'

'Because I hate folk being ill-treated, an' as for that cruel sod down the hill . . . I'd like to see him under the ground where he can't harm folk any more.'

She walked on in silence then managed to say, 'I'm – grateful.'

'Better save your breath for walking, love. We mun move as quickly as we can so that we're out of sight afore they get here.'

Ross led her towards a small house, square and whitewashed, showing up like a ghostly presence in the grey half-light. Glancing back over his shoulder at the road which lay slightly below them, he grinned. 'They'll not catch up with you now, eh?'

Opening the door he ushered them inside to reveal a room where firelight glowed a welcome. 'Essie love, can you hide these two in the attic?'

A woman who'd been swinging a kettle over the fire turned and looked at them. 'More runaways?'

'Aye. They'll tell you their story. I've got to go out again, keep an eye on them sods. They'll not find it so easy to bully an' beat folk here in Calico.'

Meg heard the sound of horses' hooves just as grey light was starting to reveal the world. She went into the public room to peep down the road and saw two men riding towards the inn. What were they doing out at this early hour? She ran upstairs, feeling suddenly anxious, hesitated outside Toby's room then rapped on the door.

He came and opened it so quickly he must already

have been awake. 'Is something wrong, love? I was woken by the sound of horses.'

'Two men are coming up the hill. They'll be here in a minute. It's not light enough to see who they are, but it's a strange time to ride out, isn't it?'

'Aye. I'll just get dressed, be with you in a minute.'

But before he joined her, he went into her bedroom and looked out of the window. It was getting lighter by the minute, that false light of pre-dawn still, not the true dawn, but if your eyes weren't dazzled by candlelight, it was enough to see by.

It wasn't hard to recognise Beardsworth and his overlooker. There was only one reason Toby could think of for them to be out on the tops at this hour: chasing more fugitives. Unfortunately the fugitives hadn't reached the inn this time. He wondered where they were, how they'd managed to hide from their pursuers, and spared a few seconds to wish them luck.

He slipped down the stairs. 'Put out that candle, Meg. We'll go back up to our bedrooms and pretend they've woken us up. I'm in no hurry to let *them* in.'

'Who are they?'

'Beardsworth and his overlooker, the one as beats young children.'

Andrew and Jad rode up to the front door of the inn, pausing to study the place.

'No lights showing,' Jad commented.

'Well, there wouldn't be, would there? They'd know better than to let us know they're awake. Knock on the door! We're not leaving till we've found my wife.'

Jad grinned as he dismounted. This was going to be very enjoyable. He'd taken a dislike to Fletcher on sight and his various visits had only reinforced that. Soft, that's what the fellow was, and Jad hated soft folk, especially ones who'd fallen lucky and not had to work hard for what they owned. He hammered on the door. When nothing happened he thumped his clenched fist on the wood again. 'Hoy there! Open up!'

A window opened above their heads and a man's voice asked, 'Who is it?'

'Mr Beardsworth. Get that door open, you!'

Toby said in a slow, stupid voice, 'Eh, I never expected anyone to turn up at this hour. There's no food ready. We haven't even got the fire going.'

Impatient with this, Andrew yelled, 'Open this door or we'll break it down. It's not food we want.'

Toby put his arm round Meg. 'I'll have to open up. I don't like the sound of this, though.'

When he unlocked the front door, Jad thrust it open so roughly that Toby stumbled backwards.

'Bring her out.' Jad held up his lantern so that its horn pane was directing the light at the innkeeper.

'Bring who out?' Toby blinked as the light shone into his eyes, casting everything else into a blur of shadows. Anger rose in him at this rudeness. He was just about to push the lantern aside, and the fellow holding it as well if he resisted, when the other man walked past them both into the public room.

Another lantern was shone in Toby's direction. 'Bring out my wife.' Andrew's voice was rough with anger. 'It's no use pretending you haven't got her here because there's nowhere else she could have gone.'

'There've been no carriages here since—'

'She's not in a carriage. She's run mad and is wandering round the moors. We're trying to find the poor creature before she does herself harm.'

Toby said nothing, wondering how best to deal with two men, both of whom had the look of fighters.

'Answer my master, you dolt!' Jad poked a finger towards his chest.

Toby saw surprise on the man's face as he side-stepped to avoid it. Did the fool think he'd stand still and let them treat him like that?

A woman's voice interrupted them. 'Who is it, Toby?'

He saw Meg standing in the doorway, candlelight shining behind her in the house place now. 'A man looking for his wife. You get on with your work, Meg.' He didn't want her putting herself in danger.

But she didn't like the way the two men were standing as if threatening Toby. 'I thought you might need me.'

Jad laughed scornfully at the idea she could help her master. He moved across the room before she'd realised what he was doing and caught hold of her arm, swinging her round to shine his lantern in her face.

Furious at this, she slapped him before he could stop her and stamped on his foot for good measure as she wrenched herself away. 'Get off me!' She stepped quickly backwards out of his reach, her eyes wary now. This was like the times she'd faced angry customers in the pawn shop, only worse. This man exuded confidence and something else, something evil. She wished she'd brought the poker with her.

'Shut up and keep out of our way, you stupid bitch!'

'Leave her alone.' Toby moved across to Meg's side. He wasn't having them ill-treating her.

Andrew said, 'Go and search the place, Jad. Harriet's got to be hiding somewhere.'

Toby tried to use words to protect them, always his favourite tactic, but his patience was almost at an end. Anger such as he hadn't felt for years was welling up in him. 'I keep telling you, we've seen no one. *You* woke us up hammering on the door.' As Jad turned towards the house place, he blocked the entrance. 'And no one is searching my inn.'

'I'll have you up before the magistrate for this,' Andrew yelled. 'Get out of my man's way.'

A voice from the outer doorway startled them all. 'I were up with a sick sheep and saw the horses, wondered who was out at this hour. You can't be too careful, can you? What's going on, Toby lad?' Ross Bellvers stepped forward from the shadows, his expression grim.

'Mind your own business, fellow!'

Toby answered. 'Mr Beardsworth is looking for his wife. Seems she's run away.' He turned back to the millowner. 'I've heard of your operatives running away, but what did you do to make your own wife flee from you?'

Andrew gave him a look that said he'd regret that remark, but Toby merely smiled at him and waited to see what they'd do.

'As I've already informed you, landlord, my wife is in a disturbed state of mind and doesn't know what she's doing. For her own safety I need to find her.'

'Well, she's not been here.'

'I'm not taking your word for that. I intend to search the place myself. She may be hiding in one of the outhouses.'

'I'll come and search the outhouses with you, but the inn has been locked up all night and the only door that's unlocked is the one you came in by, so I know for certain she's not in here.' And, he thought, even if she was, I'd not give her up to you.

'I'd prefer to search the inn as well. People whose wits are troubled can be very cunning.' Suddenly there was a pistol in Andrew's hand. 'In fact, I insist.'

Toby thrust Meg behind him. 'Go into the house place, lass. Leave this to me.'

She did as he asked but was shocked by how sharp her anxiety was for him. If that man killed him . . . if *anyone* harmed her Toby . . . She stopped just inside the house place as she admitted to herself what she'd been trying to deny: she loved him, loved him so dearly it hurt even to think he might get hurt.

So much for her saying she'd never let anyone get close to her again. She stood listening to the men talking, every sense alert and watchful.

'It seems I've no choice but to let you search the inn, but you'll find I'm speaking the truth,' Toby said.

'And I'll come round with you,' Ross added, 'just to see fair play done.'

Toby gave him a nod of thanks. He wouldn't have put anything past these two after what he'd seen of the fugitives he'd helped.

For a moment Beardsworth stared at Ross, the issue clearly in doubt, then gave a curt nod. 'Make sure you stay out of our way.'

The two men searched every room, every cupboard in the inn, beginning with the house place, where Meg stared at them resentfully and Phoebe sat clutching a shawl round herself looking terrified.

'Make sure you two don't leave this room!' Jad warned the women as they left. 'Mr Beardsworth would be very angry with you if you did.'

Meg opened her mouth to protest, caught Toby's warning glance and shrugged. They could take her silence for acceptance or not, but she was going to keep an eye on them.

As they went round the various rooms, Ross and Toby leaned against the nearest wall and watched them, and always either Jad or Beardsworth would position himself to see that no one slipped past while the other searched.

When they got to the rear building, Beardsworth looked round scornfully. 'Places like this should have been pulled down years ago. It's clearly unsafe.' He still had the pistol in his hand.

'We only use it for drying the wet washing so who's going to get hurt?' Toby asked, managing with an effort to sound his normal genial self, though he was itching to kick these two out of his inn. If Mrs Beardsworth had run away, he was sure it wasn't because she had lost her wits, but because she'd regained them. Who in their right minds would marry someone like this? Eh, she must have been desperate, poor woman.

He remembered seeing her in Halifax. For all her fine clothes, she'd seemed downtrodden and nervous, faded-looking compared to her sister, Jethro's wife, who'd been in vibrant blooming health.

Jad went into every room of the rear place while his master kept the pistol trained on Toby and Ross. He studied the cupboard and thumped the back of it, but the old timbers sounded solid and he came out of it shaking his head to signify he'd found nothing there.

It felt to Toby as if they were dirtying his inn with their presence and he didn't trust them an inch. He noticed Ross hadn't stood or walked next to him if he could help it and knew that for a wise precaution in case Beardsworth tried to use his pistol.

Jad hardly spoke the whole time they were searching the inn, but the looks he gave Toby and Ross said he didn't believe they didn't know where Mrs Beardsworth was.

When they got back to the public room Andrew said to Ross, 'You can stay here. We'll get mine host to show us round the outhouses.'

'I'd rather come with you.' Ross moved forward and Andrew raised the pistol to aim it towards him. 'Do as I say or suffer the consequences.'

Meg and Phoebe had been listening to them speaking and as soon as they'd gone outside, she rushed into the public room. 'I don't like this.'

'Me neither,' Ross said grimly. 'Yon bugger's up to no good, Meg lass. If he hurts Toby I'll bring out the whole village against him and he'll not get away, believe me.' He went to glance out of the window. 'I'm going to slip out while they're in the stable yard and make my way up the clough. I know one or two men nearby who'll come back with me to make sure he doesn't hurt Toby. You and Phoebe had better stay inside, out of harm's way, but if you can watch what they're doing through the window, it wouldn't hurt.' He went out of the front door and moved quietly round the far side of the inn from the stables.

Meg went back into the house place and found Phoebe sitting at the table looking terrified.

'They'll kill him, I know they will,' the old woman said. 'They've killed enough men already that one more won't make any difference.'

'How do you know that?'

'My husband worked for them years ago and they'd have killed him too once he was no use to them, only he had some papers they wanted to destroy. He told them he'd left the papers with a lawyer and that if anything happened to him, the lawyer would deliver them to the nearest magistrate.'

'What papers?'

Phoebe was sobbing incoherently, so Meg shook her shoulder gently. 'What papers? Tell me.'

So distraught was the older woman that she blurted out the whole story, leaving Meg standing dumbstruck.

'And Toby doesn't know about this?'

'No. And think on, it's safer for him if he doesn't.'

'Where are the papers? Still with the lawyer?'

'No, they never were. They're in the back place in the secret room, hidden behind a drawer in a bureau there.' She got up to look out of the window. 'What are they *doing?* If they hurt him, I'll . . .'

Meg took a deep breath. 'They're not going to hurt Toby. I won't *let* them.' She picked up the poker and went to the side door. 'You stay here, Phoebe.'

'But what can you do?'

'I don't know. Something. I only need to delay them till Ross gets back.'

Under Andrew's watchful eye Jad searched every outhouse and shed. 'There's nothing, sir, no sign of them.'

Andrew turned to Toby. 'Where have you hidden them?'

'Them? I thought it was your wife you were looking for.'

'She has a girl with her. She's fooled the silly child into helping her. And I don't believe you know nothing.'

Toby moved to lean against a wall so that Mortley couldn't take him by surprise from behind.

The two men stared at him and Andrew slowly brought the pistol up to aim it at Toby.

Peeping round the corner, Meg forgot everything in her terror that they would shoot him, that she would see his precious blood spilling on to the cobbles as Ben's had. 'Don't you dare touch him!' she shrieked, and ran across the yard brandishing the poker.

Toby moved swiftly sideways to prevent Mortley from attacking her and as the two men began to struggle with one another, Beardsworth tried to get a bead on Toby. But they were moving to and fro, and he couldn't. As he took a couple of steps nearer, still trying to get a clear shot at Toby, he forgot about Meg. Seizing her moment, she knocked the pistol from his hand with the poker.

He swung round quickly and thumped her hard enough to knock her to the ground before she could use the poker again. She was struggling to breathe properly and could only watch in horror as he picked up the pistol and raised it again.

But at that moment Bram drove his cart round the side into the stable yard, reining in his poor donkey hard with a cry of, 'What's this?'

'Mind your own business and get out of here if you want to trade in Tappersley again,' Andrew snarled.

'I'd be glad never to go there again, and this *is* my business since Toby's my friend.' Bram watched warily as the pistol wavered from him to Toby and back again. Behind Beardsworth, Meg was inching along the ground, trying to reach the poker.

But rage at seeing her ill-treated had made Toby forget his usual rule not to let anger rule him when fighting, and it fuelled his strength. Jad yelled in shock as he suddenly found himself picked up like a toy and smashed into the nearest wall. As he slid to the ground and lay there, groaning and dizzy, Toby marched across to Beardsworth, heedless of the fact that the man was still holding a pistol trained on him.

He smacked the weapon from his hand and shook Beardsworth like a rat. 'Touch her again and you'll be in no fit state to beat anyone.'

'You can bear witness that he's threatening me!' Andrew said to Bram.

'I heard no threats, only a man defending his lass,' the pedlar said at once.

'Nor we didn't hear any threats, either,' another voice said from the rear of the yard. Ross's voice. This time he was accompanied by two neighbours, men who glowered at the millowner and his over-looker in a way that said they knew who they were and didn't like them.

'I think it's time you left Calico, Beardsworth,' Ross said.

'And if you ever so much as step over the threshold of my inn again,' Toby said, 'I'll be the one laying a complaint about today before the magistrate. I've enough witnesses.' He took the pistol, discharged its two barrels into the air and handed it back to its owner.

Jad hauled himself to his feet, swaying and holding on to the wall. Blood was dripping from his cut, swollen lip and he said thickly, 'You'll be sorry for this, Fletcher.'

'I can bear witness that he's threatening you,' Ross said, mimicking Beardsworth's earlier words and tone.

Andrew also looked at Toby. Though he said nothing, his expression spoke more clearly than words.

Everyone could see that Toby had made a dangerous enemy. Beneath the gentleman's clothes was a killer, those eyes said, as their chill gaze moved from one man to the next as if memorising their faces.

But the men of Calico were not to be intimidated. Ross and his two companions accompanied the unwelcome visitors out to their horses, which were cropping the grass by the side of the road. The three men stood in front of the inn while the others mounted and began making their way down the hill.

'Didn't think Toby knew how to fight,' Ross said thoughtfully. 'He's allus so calm and cheerful.'

'He looked like he could take on anyone today,' one man said appreciatively. 'I'd like to see him in a fight. I'd put money on him.'

'Never mind that. We're *all* in trouble now,' the other said. 'That bugger won't rest till he gets his own back at us. Where's his wife got to, do you think?'

Ross shrugged. 'Don't know. But I pity the poor woman, I do that, an' I hope she gets away.'

'Has Toby got her hid somewhere, do you think?'

'Who knows? If he has, he's not telling – an' I'm not askin'.'

When the others had left the stable yard Bram watched Toby go across to Meg and put his arm round her. With a grin he went into the house and left the two of them alone.

'Are you all right, love?' Toby asked gently.

'A bit bruised.'

'Eh, was there ever such a brave lass? That's the second time you've come to my aid out here.'

She buried her face in his chest. 'I couldn't bear it if they hurt you, Toby.'

He held her close and murmured in her ear, 'Nor I when that vicious devil thumped you, Meg love. Are you sure you're all right?' When she didn't answer, just continued to cling to him, he lifted her chin so that she had to look him in the eyes. 'It's time we talked about how we feel, don't you think, my little love?'

She looked at him, shy now, almost as afraid of what was happening between them as she had been when Beardsworth pointed his pistol at Toby.

Just then Ross came back into the stable yard, laughing at something one of his companions had said, and although he stopped and held out one arm to stop his friends from moving forward, the moment was lost.

'Later,' Toby whispered, giving Meg a gentle push towards the house. 'Go and get your breakfast now, lass.' Then he turned to the men. 'Is it too early to offer you a pot of beer?'

'Never too early for me,' one said, and clapped him on the shoulder.

21

O nly after the two men who'd come to Toby's aid had drunk their beer and left did Ross reveal that he had Harriet Beardsworth and a little lass called Jane hiding in his house. 'I reckon it's better they stay there, too, because yon buggers will be keeping an eye on this place from now on. Beardsworth won't let up, you know. His wife running away will make him a laughing stock.'

He looked at Toby, drained his pot and added, 'I haven't told anyone else in the village. My wife and kids know how to keep their mouth shut an' so does Bram here, but other folk's childer sometimes let things slip.'

'Where was Mrs Beardsworth heading?' Toby asked.

'Here, I reckon, but if I'd not taken her in she'd never have made it. She was carrying the little lass piggy-back, because the child had been so badly beaten by Mortley she could hardly walk.'

'They're an evil pair, those two.' Toby could remember another little girl with strap marks gouged deeply into her tender flesh. The mere sight of them had made him feel physically sick.

'I reckon you'd better hire Bardy Thomas to work in your stables for a few days. He's a big lad and he dearly loves a fight.'

'Well, I don't love a fight and I don't want anyone here who'll stir up trouble,' Toby said irritably.

'Bardy won't stir it up, just help out if necessary.' Ross looked at him, saw the stubborn expression on his face and grinned. 'You've got no choice, lad. One man can't defend a place this size. Oh, and I'll send my Pippa across to help with the cooking. You needn't pay her, just feed her. There's no one as nimble as that lass. She could slip through a line of men in broad daylight and no one would even notice her. If there's trouble she'll run home for help without being told – an' she'll get there, too. Good as a lad, she is.'

Before he left he went into the kitchen to speak to Phoebe, who seemed to have aged five years in the past few hours. 'Cheer up, old lass. Us moor folk know how to look after our own.'

But she shook her head. 'My Hal used to work for Beardsworth and Greenhalgh years ago. I know what they're capable of – murder and worse.'

Ross and Toby exchanged quick glances then turned back to Phoebe, who didn't need urging to continue speaking.

'They're wicked to the core. You're a fine pair of men, but you won't be able to stop them.'

'They've turned respectable now, though,' Ross reminded her. 'They'll have to be a bit more careful-like.'

'That's only the coats they're wearing. They'll never turn decent inside,' she threw back at him. 'I keep telling you, they'll stop at nothing. Why won't you listen to me? We should leave here, all of us. It's the only way we'll stay alive. It doesn't matter for me, my life is nearly over, but you and Meg have so much to look forward to, Toby love.'

'I'm not giving up my inn,' he said firmly. 'Nor am I running away.' He patted Phoebe on the shoulder then went to the door with Ross, saying quietly once they were standing outside it, 'She knows something else, but she won't tell me what, says it's too dangerous.'

'Aye, well, I'll find out from Mrs Beardsworth how she was planning to get away from here. You send Bram round in an hour or so pretending to sell goods and I'll tell him what I find out. And don't forget, lad: you've friends all around you.' Ross shook his hand and went striding off to his farm.

Toby stood there for a moment, feeling a warm glow at his neighbours' support and remembering how suspicious everyone had been of him when he first arrived – especially with a Greenhalgh face. He took a deep breath of the chill air, but even the memory of today's trouble didn't dispel the warmth and determination inside him. This was his home, something worth fighting for, and he was damned if he was going to be driven away.

And Meg loved him. His grin broadened. Eh, what a brave lass she was! His mother would have loved her, he was sure – but not as much as he did.

*

Meg waited until everything was quiet in the public room except for a couple of men on horseback who were on their way back from Halifax and seemed to want to chat. She'd persuaded Phoebe to go upstairs and rest, because the older woman still wasn't well. Now, after checking that Toby was still chatting, Meg left Pippa in charge of the house place with instructions to stir the pan every few minutes.

This might be her only chance to check what Phoebe had told her.

She took a lit candle with her, shielding its flame as she walked along the draughty corridors and hoping the travellers would keep Toby occupied for a while. In the ancient room at the back of the inn she sighed and stood quietly for a moment or two, finding some of the peace of mind she needed simply by being in this place.

Things were going to get worse before they got better, she was sure of that, and she wanted to be able to open the hidden room in case Mrs Beardsworth needed to hide there. She'd never met the woman but felt deeply sorry for her, especially after Ross telling them how she had been carrying the little girl on her back, putting her own hopes of escape at risk to save the child. When she'd heard that Meg had determined to help her if she could.

Just like the other people up here on the Calico Road were doing, she thought dreamily, still standing with her eyes closed. They were banding together to defy an evil man and she wanted to be part of it, wanted to stay with Toby and make this inn her life from now on.

Shaking her head at her own fancies, she went across to the cupboard and found the key. The back panel seemed so solid that if she hadn't seen Toby open it, she'd not have believed it possible for it to be a door. Using the candle, she located the knots in the wood which concealed the locks. Turning the key in each, she then pushed at the side panel as instructed and was surprised by how easily the heavy old door swung backwards.

Holding up the candle, she looked round the long narrow room, then hung the candleholder on a wall hook and went to the chest of drawers Phoebe had mentioned. Such a pretty piece of furniture! She pulled a pile of old papers off the top and saw the pattern of leaves and flowers inlaid into the wood. She ran her fingers over it because she'd never seen anything as lovely, not even in Peggy's front room.

Then something seemed to chide her for wasting time, so she pulled out the drawers one by one, finding that the next-to-bottom drawer was slightly shorter than the others and had a slot behind it on its rear panel. It contained some yellowing old papers. Meg had no hesitation in pulling them out and reading them. Slowly and carefully she traced out what the words said. Some of them were long and meaningless, but she understood enough to know that Phoebe had told her the truth. It was all written down in fading ink and dated nearly thirty years ago.

From somewhere far away she heard a bell chiming faintly and it seemed like a warning that it was time to leave. She put the secret documents back, slid the drawer into place and placed the pile of papers on top again. One slid out as she moved them, a sketch, and she stared at the young woman in it, seeing at once the resemblance to the man she loved, the man whose features she knew by heart.

Who was this woman? If Phoebe didn't tell her, she'd ask Toby. But not till they'd got over the present trouble.

Her final impulse was to blow out the candle and leave it in the room.

When she got back Toby was looking for her. 'These two gentlemen want a meal, love. They set off at dawn and they're famished. It's a bit early, I know, but can you find them something?'

'Yes, of course.'

Danger and dinners, she thought wryly. Life has to go on. She realised he was still standing in the doorway, looking at her and smiling. She smiled back, her heart warmed by his loving expression.

But as she worked her face set in lines of grim determination. They were not going to harm her Toby while there was breath left in her body. Nor were they going to deprive him of what should be rightfully his. He might not fight for it but she would.

Bram came back after about an hour, driving his cart into the stable yard and knocking on the side door of the inn. 'I need to speak to Toby quickly, love.'

Meg let him in and went to find Toby. She took his place serving beer in the public room, wishing she could stay to find out what Bram had discovered. But there were a few men from the village in for pots of mulled ale to warm them on this frosty day as well as the two travellers finishing their meal.

Raised voices from the house place made everyone fall silent. Toby and Bram were quarrelling, though the cause of their disagreement wasn't clear. Meg was so surprised she stood like the others, gaping in shock, because she'd never heard Toby quarrel with anyone before. And come to think of it, Bram wasn't the quarrelsome type, either.

Then she saw the strangers exchanging glances and suddenly wondered whether they'd been sent here by Beardsworth to keep an eye on the place. She looked away from them quickly, not wanting to betray herself, but saw one or two of the men from Calico giving them suspicious sideways glances as well.

'Damned if I'm coming back this way again,' Bram yelled. 'Fighting and guns one day, and who knows what the next? I'll stay in Lancashire from now on. I can make my living anywhere and I'm not giving yon mad bugger down the hill another chance to kill me. What's more, if you had half an ounce of sense in that big, thick skull of yours, you'd leave too.'

'Ah, you're a coward.'

'Better a live coward than a dead hero!'

When she heard the side door slam, Meg went into the house place. 'Toby love, what's the matter with Bram?'

'Don't mention that name again to me!' he roared, but at the same time gave her a wink.

Pippa was grinning in one corner, Phoebe muttering to herself. Clearly they knew more than Meg did about the so-called quarrel. She went across to stir her stew, throwing Toby a dirty glance. 'You'd better get back to your customers and please try not to quarrel with *them*,' she said loudly.

There was a guffaw from the public room, and when Toby went in there was a buzz of conversation from the locals, but the strangers had finished their meal and were ready to pay and leave, it seemed.

Bram drove as fast as he could down into the valley. The donkey, unused to such speed, kept trying to slow down to her usual amble, but for once he wouldn't let her. He kept a wary eye behind him, hoping that no one was following. But he caught a glimpse of the two men on horseback further up the road behind him. They were trying not to be seen but could only be following him.

When he got to a crossroads down the hill he turned in the opposite direction to Backenshaw, which was his eventual destination, to fool his pursuers. He drove for nearly an hour to a village where he had friends he could rely on, aware all the time that he was being followed.

By the time the two riders reached the village,

Bram was selling goods on the green. He watched them go into the small alehouse and come out again a few minutes later. They stood watching him then mounted their horses.

Only when they'd ridden away did he close his eyes for a moment in relief and pray that his intuition would continue to keep him safe. What it said now was that they weren't going to leave him alone. He left his donkey and cart in a friend's care and paid that same friend to drive a cart of hay to Backenshaw, with him hiding underneath the dry scratchy stuff.

He kept still as they rumbled along and wasn't surprised when his friend exclaimed, 'Bugger me, you were right! It's them two as followed you, Bram. They're waiting by the side of the road.'

'Pray they let you through without looking under the hay.'

The cart continued to jolt along and just as Bram thought his nerves could stand it no longer, his friend said, 'They didn't stop me and they're not following me, but I'm going to turn off the road now and ask my cousin to take you further in his closed cart. What's more, I'm coming with you. I didn't believe you when you said you were in danger, but I do now.'

It took longer to get to Backenshaw like this, but at least he'd got there, Bram thought later as they drove into the small town. It would soon be dusk. A good time to leave the place again quietly.

They left the cart at an inn where his cousin was known, then made their way out to Parkside.

★

Sophia hadn't been able to settle all day. Jethro had come back from Rochdale but gone straight to the mill to oversee the installation of the new engine parts. He sent a message that he'd be working with the engineer until late at night.

She paced up and down in frustration, wondering whether to go to the mill and insist on seeing him. But she hadn't heard anything from Harriet, so perhaps it wasn't urgent.

It felt urgent though, she couldn't think why.

When the maid came to say that there were two men at the back door insisting on speaking to her, she didn't hesitate. 'Show them in.'

'But, ma'am, they're dirty and covered in bits of straw.'

'Do as I ask.'

They stood just inside the door of the parlour, one of medium height and sturdy, one smaller, with a weatherbeaten complexion and eyes bright with intelligence. It was he who spoke.

'I'm Bram Craven, Mrs Greenhalgh, and I've brought a message from your sister.'

Sophia put one hand up to her throat. Trouble. She knew it. 'Tell me.'

He looked over his shoulder and moved closer. 'Don't want anyone to overhear, do we?' He explained quickly what had happened and she could only stare at him in shock.

'She's worried your husband won't agree to help her escape, begs you not to tell him.'

And heaven help me, Sophia thought, but I haven't

been able to find out how he feels. Well, it was time to act and since he wasn't here, she must do something. 'I'll go up there in my carriage and bring her back.'

'Beg pardon, missus, but Beardsworth might try to stop you.'

Sophia stared at him in shock. 'He wouldn't dare!'

'He'd dare anything, that one would.' Bram told how he'd had to conceal himself to get through to her. 'We don't want you getting hurt, do we?' He looked at her belly meaningfully.

Sophia began to pace to and fro. She didn't want to risk her baby, either, but she wasn't leaving Harriet to face that man's violence any longer. 'I'll write a note to my husband and have it taken to the mill just as we're setting off so that he has to follow.' She looked at him. 'You *will* come with me, won't you?' Somehow she trusted him. He had such an open, friendly face.

'We'll both come with you, missus.'

She set the bell pealing, gave orders for Bram and his friend to be fed, then sat down to write a note to Jethro, scattering sand everywhere as she tried to dry the ink quickly. Worried about the reliability of her young maids, she decided to send Tettie with the note because she trusted the older woman implicitly.

The nurse was very disapproving. 'In your condition, ma'am, this isn't wise.'

'Wise or not, I'm going to help my sister and I'm not letting you or Jethro stop me. Now will you take the note to the mill or not?'

'Of course I will.'

Within minutes Sophia was sitting in the carriage, praying she'd get to her sister before Andrew did.

A man stepped out in front of her as she was making her way into town and Tettie let out a squeak of fear just as another man put his hand over her mouth from behind and dragged her into an alley.

'Where are you going?' one asked.

'None of your business.'

'That's for me to decide.' He held a sharp knife to her throat. 'I'll ask you again: where are you going?'

Terrified, she said, 'I'm taking a note to my master at the mill.'

'What's in it?'

'I don't know.'

'Show it me.'

She fumbled in the pocket of her cloak and brought it out. He snatched it from her and took it to the street to read it beneath a watch lantern.

When he got back he stared down at her and she thought he was going to murder her there and then. Instead, he said, 'Tie her up and gag her mouth. She'll not recognise us again. It's too dark here.'

Trussed up like a fowl for roasting, she was left lying in the alley, unable to move, unable to call for help, terrified now for her mistress and the unborn child.

As time passed and the carriage went higher and higher with no sign of Jethro following them, Sophia began to worry.

'I'd expected my husband to have caught up with us by now,' she said to the pedlar.

'I was thinking the same thing, missus.' He hesitated then said, 'Perhaps we ought to turn back. We don't want you getting hurt.'

'We can't very well turn the carriage round on this road. And anyway, I'm worried sick about my sister. No, we'll press on.'

Behind them the two riders held back, not wanting the driver of the carriage to know he was being followed.

The men in the public room of the Packhorse drank less that night than usual and there were people sitting there who didn't usually come out for a drink. Meg alternated between standing with Toby behind the counter and sitting with Phoebe.

Pippa sat quietly in a corner of the house place. Her dad said she was to be ready to run for help, but if something happened in the front of the inn, she couldn't go through there, and the side door was just as easy for people to enter by. 'Can I take a candle and go and look round?' she asked when Meg came in for a moment.

Meg looked at her in surprise. 'Why?'

'For another way out. Just in case.'

Meg liked the girl, who was willing and cheerful. 'I'll show you round, if you like.' She took a candle and led the way along the corridor to the middle part of the inn, then to the rear, shadows fluttering and weaving along the walls as they walked.

'They say this part is haunted,' Pippa said.

Meg looked at her, but all she could see in the young face was excitement, not fear. 'If it is, it's good spirits who haunt it, not evil ones. I like this back part.'

Pippa went across the big room to the outer door at the side. 'Is there a key?'

Meg fumbled above the lintel. 'It's here.'

The girl opened the door and peered outside. 'I'll know where to come, then, if I have to get away quickly. This would be the best way to get up the clough.' She closed the door, locked it and stood on tiptoe to replace the key.

Her young friend's cheerful assumption that she would need to fetch help didn't make Meg feel any better.

Peter, alerted by his mistress to the need to have horses saddled ready for himself and his master, waited for Jethro to come home from the mill in response to the note she'd sent. When he didn't, the groom was puzzled. He was well aware of how fond his master was of Mrs Greenhalgh so he'd expected him to come rushing home.

And Tettie hadn't returned, either, though she'd been gone long enough to get to the mill and back twice over.

What could have happened?

After pacing up and down for a little longer, he decided to go to the mill himself. The streets were quite empty because it was cold and getting late. He walked quietly, carrying a stout knobbed stick, alert for anyone following him or trying to attack him.

As he was passing an alley he stopped. Had he heard something? He listened, but all was quiet. No, he must have been mistaken. But just as he was about to move on, he heard it again. A muffled groan.

This could be a trick to get him into the alley, so he walked past it, found a couple of men lounging outside an alehouse and offered them sixpence each to come with him and make sure no one attacked him while he checked the alley.

In the light streaming from the alehouse he could see them straighten up and nod happily at the prospect of earning money so easily. 'Follow me, then. And keep your eyes open. You'll not get paid if you let anyone attack me.'

In Tappersley a group of men began assembling as dusk started to fall. They were carrying cudgels and other weapons. Most of them had been brought in from Halifax by Jad that afternoon.

In the mill house Andrew paced up and down impatiently, glancing at the sky and then at the clock. He'd told his daughters to stay in the schoolroom with their governess. If they knew their step-mother was missing they hadn't said anything about it and he knew Miss Swainton wouldn't let them. She knew her place, always did what he wanted.

When the siren went at the mill for the end of the working day, he looked out and saw the operatives going home as quickly as they could. Jad had been absent from the mill most of the day, but his deputy had been chosen for the same personal qualities and would, Andrew was sure, have spent the day enjoying the exercise of full power.

One moment the streets were full of people and the noise of clog irons clattering on the hard ground, the next the streets were empty and everything was quiet. Too quiet. There was really only one main street and Andrew could see down it from his vantage point. No one was walking towards the alehouse or standing on the doorstep having a word with a neighbour.

He smiled. Everyone knew something unpleasant was going to happen – it always did when Jad was absent from his post and strangers came into the village – and no one wanted to get in their way or attract attention to themselves. Which was just as he wanted it.

He took a pull of brandy, put his silver flask into his pocket and went to find his overlooker. 'Time to go. Is everything ready?'

22

Tettie clung to Peter for a minute after he cut her bonds, shaking and muttering, 'Thank goodness you found me. Oh, thank goodness!' Then she took a few deep breaths and pulled away. 'We have to tell the master.'

'I'll take you to him as soon as you're able to walk.'

'I can walk well enough now.'

At the end of the alley, she gasped and drew back as she saw the two men waiting there.

'It's all right. They're with me.' Peter felt in his pocket and tossed them the promised payment. 'Thanks, lads.'

Except for the engine room, the mill was mostly in darkness by the time they arrived, but the gatekeeper recognised his master's groom and let them through at once.

Jethro was helping the engineer to put the machinery together again and the two men were exchanging low-voiced comments.

Peter had to call, 'Sir!' twice before his master turned round. 'Sir, there's trouble. It's Mrs Greenhalgh . . .'

Jethro was instantly alert. 'I'll leave you to it, Don.'

Wiping his hands on a piece of cotton waste he came forward, shooting a worried glance at Tettie. 'Well?'

When they had explained what had happened, he threw the cotton waste on to the ground. 'Why the hell did you let her go off on her own, Peter?'

'She said you'd follow straight away, seemed very sure of herself.'

'Damnation!' He set off at a cracking pace, so that poor Tettie was left behind and could only pant along painfully and pray she wouldn't be attacked again. By the time she got to the house, the two men had already left and she could only stagger into the kitchen where for once she gave in to weakness and let the other servants bathe her wounds and fuss over her.

Jethro and Peter didn't bother with lanterns because there was enough moonlight to see by. Fretting, but not letting that make him do anything foolish, Jethro said curtly that it'd be best to let the animals set their own pace.

Halfway up the hill, however, his horse suddenly stumbled in a pot hole, and when it started moving again, it was limping.

'You take mine, sir,' Peter said. 'I'll find some-where to tie Beauty up and follow on foot. Keep your pistol handy. You never know who you'll meet on such lonely roads.'

Once it was fully dark Ross told his wife he'd go and warn the neighbours to be ready to act, but would come back and take Mrs Beardsworth to the inn as soon as her sister arrived. An hour passed and he didn't return, just sent a lad to say he'd been delayed.

'Delayed by what?' Essie asked the boy sharply.

The lad wriggled uncomfortably. 'He an' Dad went for a pot of beer, said they were thirsty.'

Harriet turned to Essie. 'I think I'll go across to the inn now and wait for my sister there.'

'Ross said to keep you here till he came back.'

'He hasn't come back, though, has he? And if he's at the inn, I shall be all right. I do want to be there when Sophia arrives, to explain and –' her voice faltered '– I need to see her so badly.'

'I'll send our Tony across to ask his dad if it's all right for you to go there.'

'I'll go with him. No, I insist.'

Essie stared at her, read determination on her face and hesitated. She couldn't very well tie their visitor down. 'What about the little girl?'

'She can come with me.'

'She needs to rest.'

Jane came down the stairs, proving she'd been listening. 'I want to come with you, missus. I'm all right now.'

The child wasn't all right, Harriet knew, but it was only a short walk to the inn. The important thing was for them to be ready to leave as soon as Sophia showed up, which they could do if they were already there. She had to get as far away from her husband as possible before he came searching for her again.

'I'm going,' she repeated.

Essie gave in. 'Show the lady the way, son.'

*

When there was a knock on the side door Meg went to fetch Toby. She wasn't opening any doors at night when she couldn't see outside.

Ross's son was standing there with a woman, or rather a lady from her clothes. Her face was haggard and she had her arm round the shoulders of a thin little girl with a bruised face. Both Meg and Toby guessed immediately who she was.

'You'd have been better staying where you were, Mrs Beardsworth, till we came for you,' he said bluntly.

'I was going mad sitting doing nothing. I just couldn't bear it a minute longer. Besides, I want to leave as soon as Sophia arrives.'

'You seem very sure she will.'

'I know my sister.'

Toby gestured to the lad. 'You get off home then and I'll look after the lady.' And he'd tell Ross what he thought of him, too, for leaving her alone like that.

Meg drew Harriet and Jane across to warm themselves by the fire. 'You sit down and I'll get you something hot to drink.'

Toby interrupted. 'They can't stay in here, love. Someone only has to poke his head round the curtain to see them. Take them up to one of the bedrooms, but don't light any candles or fires up there.'

A voice from the public room calling for more beer had him turning away, muttering under his breath.

When he'd gone Meg looked at the stairs. The two fugitives would be trapped up there with no way to escape except by coming back down them. 'I think it'd be better if I took you to the back part of the inn.'

Phoebe looked at her in dismay. 'You'll not put them in the storeroom. There's things there.'

'I'll just leave them in the big room,' Meg said soothingly, knowing Phoebe meant the secret chamber. 'I'll fetch them some blankets, though. It's a cold night.'

She nipped upstairs and was back almost immediately with the blankets from her bed. She handed one to each fugitive and led the way through the dark inn, holding a candle up to show where they were going.

'I'm sorry to be so much trouble,' Harriet said. 'I'm sure my sister will soon be here, though, then we can leave.'

'I'm happy to help you, Mrs Beardsworth.' Meg's eyes went to the child, who had a gaunt famine face and skinny limbs. This was another one who reminded her of Nelly, though it had been ill health that painted such a look on her daughter's face, not brutal treatment.

She settled them on the bench with blankets wrapped round them. 'It's nice and peaceful in here. I daren't leave the candle, though, because it'd show that someone was inside.'

As she went back she had a sudden urge to put the two fugitives in the hidden room. But that place was Toby's and contained secrets. She didn't like to betray its existence when there was no need for it.

★

Sophia arrived at the inn and tumbled out of the carriage without waiting for anyone to open the door. She hurried inside but stopped dead on the threshold at the sight of a room full of working men, who had all stopped speaking and were staring at her.

Flushing, she looked round for the landlord, or better still, the landlady, but could see no one who appeared to be in authority.

Then the man who looked like her husband walked through a doorway at the back of the room.

She hurried across to him. 'I believe you know where my sister is, Mr Fletcher?'

Even as she was speaking four rough-looking men pushed into the public room from outside, followed by her brother-in-law. She gasped in dismay and clutched Toby's arm.

Meg, who'd been watching from behind the curtain, snatched up a candlestick. She had to get to the back place before anyone else did. She should have trusted her instincts and hidden those two in the secret room from the start.

When she set off through the corridors, Pippa pattered along behind her. The girl was sharp enough not to need telling what to do.

In the back place Harriet jumped to her feet when Meg ran in. 'What's wrong?'

'Your husband has turned up with some men.'

'I'll kill myself before I go back to him!' She fumbled for the knife in her pocket.

Meg pulled her across the room and thrust the

candlestick at her. 'Better to hide than die. There's a secret room here. He won't find you. It's well hidden.' She fumbled for the key, muttering in agitation as she had to feel around in the dark for it. She could hear voices yelling, footsteps coming nearer.

Pippa had disappeared through the outer door and Meg could only hope the men wouldn't catch the girl.

Opening the secret door, she pushed the woman and girl inside and followed them because there was no time to get away and it'd look strange, her walking out of an empty cupboard. She didn't want to be thumped – or worse! – by Beardsworth or his men. As she was pulling the door closed, the key slipped out of her hand again and she couldn't see where it was in the dark. When she heard the sound of someone in the corridor just outside the back place, she closed the heavy door as quietly as she could and fumbled for the key kept inside the room, locking the top lock, relieved to hear it snick into place.

Hearing voices close by now on the other side of the door, she hesitated to put the key in the second lock, afraid that the noise it made would be heard by whoever it was on the other side. Surely the top lock would hold it fast? She slipped the slender piece of metal into her pocket instead.

Only as she tried to move did she realise that her skirt had caught in the door. She pulled, but couldn't release it except by tugging until it tore. She looked at the other woman then down at her skirt.

'They may not notice,' Harriet said.

'If they're searching carefully, they'll see it and guess that this place is here! I'm angry at mysen for being so careless! Shhh!'

They all fell silent and listened.

In the public room Beardsworth pointed his pistol at the group of men, as did Jad. 'Stand still or we'll shoot!' he yelled. 'I've another loaded pistol in my belt as have the others. We'll account for quite a few of you before we're through if you try to resist.'

The men from Calico froze, anger on their faces as their eyes went from one man to the other, assessing the risk.

Andrew looked across the room at Toby, smiling at the thought that he had the fellow in his power now. Then he realised who was standing next to the innkeeper and fury coursed through him. His men had been told to make sure Jethro's wife didn't get up here because he didn't want to hurt her and her unborn child. This was one wife who was doing her duty by her husband, providing him with heirs.

Somehow he'd have to keep her in ignorance of what he intended to do to her sister – and to Fletcher. Killing him and maybe a few other 'rioters' from the village would stop it from being a hotbed of rebellion against him and other millowners, stop his operatives from having anywhere to flee to, give him absolute power over them, as was only right.

'You shouldn't have come here in your condition, Sophia,' he said gently. 'These men are dangerous.' He turned to Jad. 'Take her upstairs and lock her in one of the bedrooms where she'll be safe. We definitely don't want Jethro's wife getting hurt by accident, do we?'

Jad put his pistol in his belt and grabbed Sophia's arm.

'I'm here to see my sister,' she said, shaking his hand off her arm, 'and I'm going nowhere until I do.'

'Take her forcibly but don't hurt her!' Andrew ordered.

As Jad pulled her out of the room, Sophia struggled in vain against him, almost weeping in frustration at being so close to her sister and yet unable to help her.

Another man pulled a pistol from his belt and brandished it.

Toby saw no opportunity to intervene and indeed would be glad to have a woman in her condition out of the way of harm, so let Jad drag her into the house place. He listened carefully, because if Meg were still there and that villain tried to hurt her, he'd not hold back any longer. He kept a careful eye on the millowner, seeing the relish with which Beardsworth held the pistol and the bulge at his waist where the other one was tucked away. If it was at all possible, Toby hoped to prevent those pistols going off in his inn, because he didn't want men from the village being killed or maimed, let alone the woman to whom he'd given shelter.

'There's no one else back here,' Jad called. 'But there's a maid and an old woman somewhere. They aren't in the public room, sir.'

'Be careful how you go, then. If you see them, lock them up too.'

In the house place Jad shook Sophia's arm and said in a low voice, 'You'll hurt yourself if you keep struggling, Mrs Greenhalgh. And your baby might get hurt too. Your choice.' He clenched one fist and tapped her lightly on the belly with it.

Furious and terrified, but not daring to risk his carrying out his unspoken threat to punch her belly, she let him grab a candle and light it at the fire, then went with him up the stairs. He peered into every room, keeping tight hold of her arm.

In one of them they found a candle burning and the covers rumpled. Jad flung Sophia down on the bed and yelled, 'Stay there!' He bent to peer under it and laughed. 'Come out, you!'

Phoebe crawled from under the bed, staying as far away from him as she could.

He smiled as he recognised her. 'Not got a husband to protect you now, you old hag, have you? Should have left here while you could.'

He backed towards the door, taking the key and locking it from the outside, then pocketing it.

Inside the room Phoebe sat down abruptly on the bed, pressing one hand to her chest and moaning slightly.

'Are you all right?'

'It's just – a dizzy turn.'

Sophia went across to the window and saw that it looked down on the front of the inn. If she could open it, she'd perhaps be able to shout down to

Jethro when he arrived. It was a struggle, but she managed, leaning out and looking down the road. There was no sign of any men riding up from the Backenshaw direction.

When she turned round she saw that the old woman was still looking unwell and went across to her. 'I think you'd better lie down for a while. Yes, that's right. Let me pull the covers up. He's locked us in so there's nothing to do but wait.' She prayed that Jethro would come soon and rescue her, but most of all, that he'd be able to stop Andrew from hurting Harriet. He was the only one who could do that, she was sure, because although Jethro's half-brother was also a big man, he had no weapons. 'Who are you?'

'Phoebe. I help in the inn. Who are you? Why have they locked you in here?'

'I'm Sophia Greenhalgh and—' She was astounded to see terror in the old woman's eyes. 'Why do you look at me like that?'

'You're a Greenhalgh.' She began to sob. 'Please don't let your husband kill my Toby! There's been enough killing.'

'I'm quite sure my husband doesn't intend to kill anyone.'

'He's a Greenhalgh, isn't he?'

There it was again, this expectation that Jethro would behave cruelly. 'He's not like his father, I promise you.' But Sophia could see that the old woman didn't believe her.

There was silence for a few moments, then Phoebe said, 'This is the best place to be if they're on the rampage again. I used to hide under the bed in the old days.'

'What do you mean by "on the rampage again"? What old days are you talking about and who used to be on the rampage?'

Phoebe stared blindly at the ceiling as she murmured, 'Thirty year ago John Greenhalgh and Andrew Beardsworth were the leaders of a gang of men who'd do anything, kill anyone, for money. That fellow who brought you up here was one of them, and heaven help him, so was my husband. Hal didn't hold with so much killing, but he didn't dare leave the gang because he knew they'd kill him if he tried. When they turned respectable and used their money to set themselves up in business, they put him here to run the inn. It was here they used to hide things, in the big room at the back. And from here you can see all the comings and goings across the tops.'

Wanting to hear anything the old woman had to tell her, Sophia made encouraging noises and then listened in horror to her tale of murder and thieving and mayhem. And to what was going on in Andrew Beardsworth's mill. Surely Jethro wasn't like that? Surely he hadn't been involved in his father's crimes, wasn't treating his operatives in Backenshaw so cruelly? She couldn't bear it if he was.

Then she remembered his tenderness towards her and their son, and knew deep within her that he wasn't involved, couldn't commit murder.

*

Pippa crept quietly up the clough, knowing her little world well enough to be sure she wasn't being followed and that no one was keeping watch here. But when she got to the outskirts of the village it was a different matter. There was a burly man stationed there, constantly looking from side to side.

She backed away carefully and chose another route, but there was a second man further along the road and it took her a while to get to the rear of the first house where she knew she'd find help for her father.

She hoped Meg was all right. She'd seen her making for the cupboard, which was a strange place to hide and wouldn't keep them safe for long. Pippa had wondered whether to suggest they come outside with her, but they'd have slowed her down and she knew she had to get help quickly because her dad was in danger. She could have sobbed in frustration at having to be so careful and slow as she checked that no one was watching her and then tapped on the window.

'Where is my wife?' Andrew asked Toby. 'I know you've got her hidden here.'

The two men measured one another up and Toby knew it was no use to pretend he hadn't seen her. 'She *was* here. She's moved on.'

'We've had the place watched day and night. We know she hasn't left.' He raised the pistol and stepped forward to hold it at the nearest villager's head. 'Tell us the truth or your friend here will die.'

There was no question of letting a man die, Toby thought bitterly. At worst Beardsworth would beat his wife, but she'd be alive and they could try to help her escape later. Seeing the wild, almost lustful look in Beardsworth's eyes told him more than anything else that the man wouldn't hesitate to kill. 'She was in the room next to this. I can only guess that she's hiding somewhere else in the inn.' He looked directly at the other man. 'I promise you that's the truth. I *don't* know where she is now.'

'Then you and I will take a walk round the place once Jad comes back and if we don't find her, I *will* carry out my threat, believe me.'

Jad came back, grinning. 'I found the old woman and locked her in a bedroom with Mrs Greenhalgh. Silly old bitch was hiding under the bed. There's still the young 'un to find, though.'

'She doesn't matter. You keep an eye on this lot and I'll take one of the men with me to guard Fletcher while we search the rest of the inn. We'll no doubt find the cook-maid hiding somewhere and we'd better find my wife or there'll be trouble.'

Jethro reined his horse back as he approached the inn. He could see that something was happening there from the lights inside, but his carriage was standing outside so his wife must be there. When a man stepped out from the shadows just before the inn and suggested he ride on to the next inn as there was 'a bit of trouble' at the Packhorse, Jethro glared at him and dismounted.

The man moved forward, saw his face by the light of the lantern hanging outside the inn door, and gasped in shock. 'How the hell did you get away from my master?' He bunched up his fists as if about to attack.

Jethro took a quick step backwards. The fellow must be referring to Fletcher, but what did he mean by 'get away'?

'Who is your master?' Jethro asked.

'Mr Beardsworth, and he'll pay me well for stopping you from getting away.'

'You're mistaking me for my half-brother. I'm Jethro Greenhalgh, not the innkeeper, and that's *my* carriage so my wife must be waiting for me inside. Go and tell your master that I've arrived.'

At that moment, Sophia poked her head out of the bedroom where she and Phoebe were locked up and yelled to attract her husband's attention.

He looked up briefly, which was enough for the man he was confronting to rush at him and knock him over. Suddenly, out of the shadows, other men appeared and hauled the guard off, knocking him unconscious then helping Jethro to his feet.

The minute he thanked them, one of them said, 'Hell, it's not Toby. It's bloody Greenhalgh!'

'What's going on here?' Jethro demanded. He looked up. 'Sophia, come down and let me take you away from this madhouse.'

'I can't. They've locked me in this bedroom. Oh, Jethro, go and see if you can find Andrew and stop him! I'm safe enough here but I'm sure he means to hurt Harriet. She's run away from him because he's been beating her black and blue. If he goes on like this, he'll kill her.'

He hesitated, looking sideways at the roughly dressed men who had saved him thinking he was his brother. They were now keeping watch on him as if they didn't trust him. 'Do you know what's happening here?' he asked them.

'Ross sent his little lass to fetch us, said there was trouble,' one said. 'When we looked through the window we saw that devil of an overlooker from Tappersley and another fellow pointing pistols at folk. Beardsworth isn't there that we could see, nor is Toby.'

Another said, 'We didn't like to rush in while they've got pistols.'

Jethro looked at them. Moor men by the look of it, probably Toby's neighbours. 'I can go in and disarm Jad Mortley,' he said. 'I don't want anyone threatening people with pistols while my wife's in there. Will you trust me?'

They looked at him, then at each other. Jethro waited. He'd learned since he took over the mill to respect men like these, yes, and their womenfolk too – something his father never had done.

'Aw reet,' one said. 'But don't try to trick us. There'll be more fellows coming in from the village to help. We're not having *them* shooting honest folk here in Calico, whatever they do down the hill.'

Jethro looked up to the bedroom. 'You heard, love?'

Sophia nodded, 'Yes. Find my sister before you release me, *please*, Jethro.'

So he went inside.

As Sophia watched him, she realised he'd called her 'love' openly and joy ran through her.

Jad swung round as the door opened behind him, but relaxed when he saw his master's friend, Mr Greenhalgh. 'Thank goodness you've got here, sir. There's been rioting and mayhem.'

Jethro nodded as if he agreed and walked forward. 'Have you seen my wife?'

Before the man could answer, he wrenched the pistol from him, and the men who'd been drinking took this as a signal to knock the other man's weapon out of his hand and attack the bullies. The men behind Jethro rushed in enthusiastically to help tackle the intruders.

Ross managed to avoid being caught up in the fighting and edged his way round the room to join Jethro. 'We need to find Beardsworth. He's taken Toby away at gun point to search for his wife.'

'Damn the man!'

'Beg pardon, but damn who, sir?'

'Damn Beardsworth, of course. My wife says he's been beating her sister – and badly. She's terrified he'll kill Harriet.'

'He's killed a few in his time. What difference will one or two more make?'

'*Killed a few?* What do you mean by that?'

'Ask Phoebe. Her husband was involved in it, so

she knows more than anyone about what happened in the past. I don't know how Hal Dixon managed to stay alive so long, given the threat he offered to Beardsworth if he'd told what he knew.'

A man rolled across the floor, grappling with another, and they both had to jump backwards to avoid being knocked over.

'Best if we go round the outside, I think,' Ross said. 'This way. We'll leave the lads to enjoy themselves. They'll give these buggers a lesson they won't forget.'

23

Toby was only too aware of the pistol Beardsworth was carrying and of the other brute of a man breathing down his neck. As they passed through the house place he wondered where Meg and Mrs Beardsworth had got to and hoped they'd left the inn and were hiding somewhere in the village.

'Get a candle and light it,' Beardsworth snarled, emphasising his point by poking Toby in the side with his pistol.

Thankful for his years of training at not reacting to insults, Toby did as he was told, keeping his face expressionless as he chose the heaviest of the spare candle holders which they kept sitting on the mantelshelf for convenience. Given half a chance he'd smash this down on Beardsworth's head.

'You can carry a candle too,' Beardsworth told the man with him, watching as he lit one. 'Now, we'll search the rest of the inn and we'd better find my wife, Fletcher, or you'll be in trouble. Oh, and from here onwards, you speak only when spoken to. All right?'

'Yes.'

'Yes, *sir!*'

Toby repeated the words in a mild tone of voice but it was an effort because he had never felt such strong hatred for anyone in his whole life before. He led his two captors to the middle part of the inn, where the rooms were mostly unfurnished, and then stood where he was ordered as each room was searched again, as Beardsworth had searched the day before.

It didn't take very long but the way the doors were banged open would, he hoped, give Meg warning to get away.

As they drew closer to the narrow corridor that led to the rear part he found himself listening carefully, hardly daring to draw a deep breath in case he missed something that would give him a clue to Meg's whereabouts. But he heard nothing ahead of them, no sounds at all apart from the wind and their own footsteps.

When they entered the rear part, Beardsworth ordered curtly, 'Hold the candles higher! Let me look round.'

The taciturn man carrying the other candle shivered suddenly and exclaimed, 'Eeh, it's cold in here, sir.' Then he pointed. 'Look, there's an open door.'

Even as he pointed the door swung wider, its hinge creaking, and then slammed shut. But the catch was faulty and it opened and closed a few times before blowing open and shut again.

'They must have left that way,' Toby said.

'Shut up. And you, watch him carefully.' Beardsworth took his man's candle and marched across to fling the door fully open and peer outside. When he looked down he saw footprints in the soft earth and lowered the candle to check them, shielding its flame carefully. But a few seconds' study showed him that they were too small to belong to a grown woman, certainly not his wife because Harriet had long, narrow feet. He laughed and turned back to Toby. 'She didn't leave by this door, so she must still be inside the inn somewhere. Now, are you going to tell us where you've got her hidden or do I have to start killing your friends one by one to persuade you to speak?'

'She may be in one of the rooms over there.' Toby indicated the side wall.

Beardsworth thrust the candle back at his henchman and gave his prisoner a shove. 'You go in first.'

So Toby opened each door in turn and stood inside with the candle held high while his captor checked that no one was hiding there.

Last of all he opened the cupboard door and stepped back out of the way, but not before he'd noticed the scrap of material caught in the bottom of the hidden door and recognised it as the colour of Meg's skirt. He looked away immediately, holding his breath, hoping desperately that Beardsworth wouldn't notice it.

But he did, damn him!

'What's this?' After glancing round the empty

cupboard, he bent down to retrieve the piece of cloth wedged in the almost invisible crack. He had to tug hard to get it out, leaving a few threads still caught. Smiling broadly, he stood up, holding the shred of material in his fingers. 'From a woman's dress, I should say. Not Harriet's, a poor woman's dress. The child or your cook, probably. But what I don't understand is how it got caught there.'

He thumped the wall at the back of the cupboard. 'How can a scrap of material possibly get caught in a solid wooden wall? Well, it can't, can it?' Bending down he followed the crack with his fingers, tracing it up, then across, then down again.

Toby watched, sick at heart to see the secret place revealed.

Andrew turned round, smiling. 'So this isn't a solid wall. What lies on the other side? A secret tunnel or a room?'

'A room.' Toby regarded him stolidly, hoping he wasn't betraying his anxiety and knowing he couldn't easily get out of this.

'And how do we open it?' He took the candlestick out of Toby's hand and used it to inspect every inch of the door. He found the upper keyhole quite quickly but continued to examine the surface. As he felt along the bottom, he said, 'Ah!' in a satisfied tone and stood up. 'Two keyholes. Very ingenious. Now, where's the key?'

Toby stared at him, trying desperately to work out what to do.

'The longer you keep me waiting, the angrier I'm

going to become – and then who knows what I may do to your little cookmaid? Is she good in bed? I do like a little romp every now and then.'

Anger strained inside Toby, but by a superhuman effort he still held it back. 'We usually keep the key on the lintel of the outer cupboard door.'

Beardsworth felt along the top. 'It isn't there.'

Toby took a step forward. 'But it's always there.'

'Careful! Keep your distance.'

The other man jabbed his pistol into Toby's back and he stilled, looking from one man to the other, bitterness filling him at the thought of what this evil creature might do to his own poor wife – or to Meg – if he found the key.

Beardsworth searched again, shuffling slowly side-ways, and they all heard something scrape under his foot. 'Ah.' He bent down to pick up the object. 'The key!' Smiling triumphantly, he inserted it into the top lock.

Meg pressed her ear against the door. She could hear men speaking, Toby's deep tones and Mr Beardsworth's harsher voice barking out orders. She looked at Harriet and whispered, 'It's Toby and I think – your husband.'

Harriet came forward to squeeze in beside her and listen, then said in a low voice, 'Yes. That's him.'

'He won't be able to get to us without the key.'

'Then let's pray he doesn't find it.' Harriet's shudder was very eloquent.

Meg looked round, put one finger to her lips and

tiptoed along the narrow chamber, taking the candle and holding it high.

The girl watched them in silence, but after a minute or two, Harriet asked in a whisper, 'What are you looking for?'

'Something to defend us with in case they open that door and try to hurt us.'

Harriet looked at her wonderingly. 'You're very brave.'

'I won't let folk hurt me without fighting back, whoever they are. You go and listen at the door.'

Shortly afterwards Harriet gasped and, when Meg turned round, beckoned.

'What's wrong?'

'He's found the key.'

Jethro followed Ross round the outside of the building, through the stable yard and then up the slope to the rear part. He touched Ross on the shoulder and when the other man stopped, whispered, 'There are lights there.'

'Aye. I've noticed 'em. But we'll find out who it is afore we go rushing inside, eh? You still got that pistol?'

'Yes. And I'll use it if I have to. Beardsworth's not hurting anyone while I'm around, especially Harriet.'

Ross studied him in the moonlight, his eyes searching Jethro's face, then gave a little nod as if he had decided to trust him, before moving on again.

*

Andrew turned the key in the upper lock and bent to insert it into the bottom aperture but found it unlocked.

Toby let his shoulders slump as if he had lost the spirit to stand up for himself, but held himself tensed to attack the other man, pistol or not, if he tried to hurt Meg.

'This village has been a thorn in my side for a long time now,' Andrew said in an almost conversational tone. 'No wonder we couldn't find any fugitives. You had them hidden in here. Well, before we leave the inn, this door will be destroyed. I *will* be master of those I employ.'

Watching Toby and keeping the pistol aimed at him, he pushed the door open, stepping back quickly and shouting, 'Come out, you stupid bitch! *Come – out – at once!*'

As the door swung inwards, Meg quickly blew the candle out and stepped as far back as she could, muttering, 'I don't see why we should make it easier for them to attack us.'

Harriet stayed where she was, frozen by terror of her husband. A candle was thrust forward to shine in her eyes, half-blinding her, and she heard a familiar, mirthless laugh. Her worst nightmare came suddenly true as the candle was moved back and she saw Andrew standing there aiming a pistol at her.

'Well, my dear wife, it seems I've found you again. How could you ever think you'd get away from *me*?'

He waved Toby back. 'Keep your distance, Fletcher.' Then he gestured to Harriet with the pistol. 'Come out now, but move very slowly.' He set the candle down on the floor, all the time watching her carefully.

She stepped forward, waited for him to step further back into the main room, then followed him out of the cupboard.

'You too, cookmaid!' he called into the darkness of the secret room.

Meg followed Harriet but she didn't move slowly. She took everyone by surprise, hurling a heavy book at him, then following that with a little brass ornament which hit him on the cheek, gashing his cheekbone.

He cursed and started to move towards her. 'You'll regret th—'

Toby used the distraction to leap forward and grab their captor by the collar, jerking him backwards between him and the other man.

Beardsworth resisted for long enough to take aim at his wife and indeed the pistol went off, but by then his hand had been pulled upwards so that the ball flew wide. Toby chopped at his hand and sent the pistol clattering across the room.

'Get that!' Meg shouted to Harriet, who rushed across to pick it up. She turned towards the other man in time to see an ornament hurled by Jane hit him on the temple. He dropped to his knees, half-stunned, grunting, the candle going out as he dropped it.

As Andrew fell, he rolled sideways so that Toby's second punch only grazed his shoulder. While his back was turned towards Toby he fumbled in his belt for the other pistol.

But although he was usually very quick, something seemed to be slowing him down. In fact everything around him seemed to slow down. He heard voices chanting in the distance and hesitated a moment, wondering who was coming towards them. He knew he should fire the pistol but his fingers seemed very stiff and he couldn't even get it out properly.

The other man had a similar dazed expression on his face.

There was a sound of distant chanting and a bell tolling faintly a long way away. For a moment or two no one moved.

Meg picked up the candle Beardsworth had set down and held it up. When she saw the butt of the pistol in his hand as he was pulling it out of his belt, she shouted, 'He's got another pistol, Toby!'

That brought Andrew out of his momentary paralysis but by this time Toby was near enough to kick out. He sent the millowner rolling across the floor.

His eyes mad with rage, Andrew used every last ounce of his strength to finish pulling out the other pistol to fire at Toby. But the damned chanting had started up again and there was a buzzing sound in his head. And somewhere in the distance a bell was tolling.

By now Harriet had picked up the first pistol and moved forward, aiming it at her husband. She was so close she couldn't miss, but like the others she saw him pause, shake his head as if something was annoying him and then shout, 'Stop it! Stop making that damned noise.' So she held back, not understanding why he wasn't firing at them.

Meg's hand was shaking so much that the candle she was holding sent shadows jerking to and fro. *Toby,* she prayed, *Toby, stay safe!*

Before anyone could take further action Andrew finally succeeded in jerking the pistol out of his belt but there was a loud explosion and it discharged into his face. He jerked just once and fell slowly back to the ground, to lie still, his eyes staring at the ceiling.

There was dead silence in the room, then they all heard a bell tolling in the distance, as it would to mark someone's death. It seemed louder this time.

Harriet dropped her unfired pistol and took an involuntary step backwards, covering her face with her hands.

Jane ran to her side and now it was the girl who was supporting the woman, for Harriet was trembling uncontrollably.

The other man scrambled to his feet, staring at the body of the man who had hired him, then from Toby to Harriet. The ghostly bell tolled again and he yelled in terror and ran for the door.

Toby let him go. Taking a long, deep breath to steady himself, he went to tug a piece of washing off the line at the far end and cover Beardsworth's shattered head with it. Then he turned to Meg, holding out his arms. 'Are you all right, lass?'

She nodded and moved towards him, needing to touch him, to feel his warmth. For a moment only they pressed close together, then he drew away. 'See to Harriet, love.'

Meg walked across to put her arm round the other woman.

'He is dead . . . he really is, isn't he?' Harriet asked.

'Yes. He can't hurt you any more.'

Toby picked up the candle dropped by the fleeing man and lit it from his own.

'Where is that bell?' Harriet whispered. But even as she spoke it stopped tolling and time seemed to move at its normal pace again, instead of slowly.

'There is no bell,' Toby said, 'but I reckon there used to be once. This place was built by some monks, the Curate says.'

He and the two women stared at one another.

'It isn't possible,' Harriet whispered. 'What happened just isn't – possible.'

'Well, it happened anyway,' said Meg, 'and good riddance to him.' She scowled down at the dead man.

'If we told anyone else about the bell and the way Beardsworth suddenly began behaving strangely,' Toby said, 'they'd think we'd run mad.'

Harriet stared round. 'Are you saying you both believe this place is haunted?'

He nodded. 'Oh, yes. I'm quite sure it is. I've never *seen* any ghosts, though I've heard noises many a time. Only nothing has ever hurt me and, actually, I always feel peaceful in here.'

Meg went to thread her arm through his. 'I do too.

I love sitting here. And whatever helped stop *him*, I'm grateful. I thought he was going to kill you and oh, Toby love, I couldn't have borne that!'

He put an arm round her shoulders and for a moment gazed down at her with love blazing in his eyes.

It was so different from the expression on her husband's face, Harriet thought, so very different. She turned to Jane and gave the girl a quick hug. 'I'll make sure no one hurts you any more, child.'

'That overlooker is just as bad. Please, missus, I still don't want to go back to the mill.'

The child's fear helped Harriet pull herself together, though she still tried to avoid looking at her husband's body. Suddenly she realised something. 'I'm Andrew's widow now and I know what was in his will because Jethro insisted on it. I own most of the mill, with smaller shares left to his daughters. Things are going to change there, Jane, I promise you. There'll be no more beatings. And Jad Mortley won't be staying on at the mill, even if he escapes the law.'

'He won't,' Toby said grimly.

The outer door burst open and he swung quickly round, but it was his brother and Ross, not more of Beardsworth's thugs, so he relaxed again.

'Are you all right, Harriet?' Jethro asked. As he moved round Toby he caught sight of the corpse. 'What the hell's happened here?'

Harriet's voice wobbled as she explained. She shuddered. 'See for yourself. No one's touched him since it happened.'

He knelt by the side of her husband and uncovered him briefly. 'He's dead.'

Harriet looked across at him. 'I'm glad! Not sorry, glad!' Then she burst into wild sobbing, so that Jethro had to take her in his arms and comfort her as best he could.

A few men had gathered in the corridor outside the old place, men from Calico, watchful, waiting to see what was going to happen. Ross walked across to them. 'Well, have you lot fettled them buggers at the front?'

'Aye. We've got 'em trussed up nicely. What do you want doing with them? If it were up to me, I'd roll 'em ovver t'nearest cliff.'

Jethro said sharply, 'There'll be no more violence. We'll deliver them to the nearest magistrate and explain what happened here tonight.'

Then a woman pushed past the men and ran across the room. 'Oh, Jethro, Harriet, you're both safe! I was so afraid for you. Andrew was insane, I'm sure of it. His eyes were wild tonight.' As she was speaking, Sophia hugged her husband, then her sister, then hugged her husband again for good measure. 'Harriet, I'm so sorry I let you d—' Her voice trailed away as she saw the still body on the floor. 'That's Andrew. Is he—?'

'He's dead,' Jethro told her. 'Killed himself.'

'And I'm glad,' Harriet said fiercely. 'You didn't let me down, Sophia. We both knew it'd be hard for me to escape from him.' She looked across at the body of her husband and repeated, 'I'm glad he's dead and

I won't pretend otherwise.' Suddenly she began to weep.

Sophia put her arms round her tearful sister. 'Shh, love. You've escaped him for ever now.'

Jethro looked at the group of men. 'Will you get the prisoners ready and make sure they don't escape?'

There were grins and rough assurances. One man said, 'Jad Mortley's hurt bad, though. Got kicked about a bit in the scuffles.'

Jethro didn't comment on that. 'Someone in the village must have a cart to put them in. I'll ride down behind you in my carriage and make a deposition before the nearest magistrate about what happened. Harriet, can we get Sophia to your house? I want her to lie down and rest.'

'I don't need to rest,' she said mutinously.

'I want you and the baby safe, love,' he said, smiling at her.

Harriet felt envy spear through her. They were so close, so loving. 'Yes, of course we can go to my house. And, Jethro, I'd be grateful for your help with the mill tomorrow. I don't know what to do there, but I do know I won't have any more cruelty – to children or anyone else.'

'There's no need for it. If a mill is run efficiently it makes more than enough money for its owner.'

Ross grinned at Toby. 'If he means that, there'll be a lot of happy folk in Tappersley.'

But Jethro heard him and swung round. 'I'm not in the habit of saying things I don't mean.'

For a moment the resemblance between the brothers was stronger than ever before, then Toby's face relaxed into a grin and Jethro's expression grew tighter and they looked less alike.

Now that the tension had abated, Meg began to feel angry. She and Toby had been in the thick of it, had risked their lives tonight, and this rich man had just taken over and started telling everyone what to do, as the rich always did. Yet he was ignoring Toby, his eyes sliding sideways rather than rest on his brother's face. Determination rose in her to do something about that because it wasn't *fair* for anyone to look down on Toby, any more than it had been fair for him to be treated as a bastard all these years.

'Let's go and sit in the house place,' she said. 'It'll be warmer and brighter there.'

As they walked through the inn two men passed them carrying a gate, going to collect the body.

'Sit down a minute, Sophia,' Jethro said, his eyes on his wife. 'I'll go and make sure the carriage is ready for you.'

With a wry grimace she did so while Harriet joined Phoebe who was warming her hands by the fire.

Meg glanced round. There were only the two ladies, herself and Toby, Phoebe, Ross and the girl present. Now was the time to say it. She stepped forward and called, 'Just a minute, Mr Greenhalgh. There's something else needs sorting out before you leave. About your brother—'

Phoebe gasped. 'No, Meg, no! Don't do it.'

'Why not? He doesn't deserve all that money and I can't *bear* to see him looking down his nose at my Toby.' She pushed the old woman gently away, looked at Jethro and then turned to the man she loved, saying very loudly, 'You're not bastard born, Toby Fletcher. You're the oldest son of John Greenhalgh and Alice Dixon. He married your mother before he ever married *his*.' She looked at Jethro scornfully. 'Alice was dead by the time he married *your* mother, so you're not bastard born either, but you're *not* the oldest son and you shouldn't have inherited all that money.'

The silence that followed this announcement was louder than any shouting.

Jethro scowled at her, saying nothing but looking angry.

It was left to Toby to step forward and take charge. 'We can discuss that later, Meg lass.' He looked at his brother. 'You have things to see to tonight that can't wait. Come back tomorrow and we'll sort this out.'

'It can't be true!' Sophia exclaimed.

'It is!' Meg said, not willing to give an inch. 'And I'll prove it tomorrow.'

Jethro looked across at Toby. 'You knew,' he said flatly.

'Aye, I've known for a while.'

'You didn't say anything.'

He shrugged.

Meg wasn't having them ignore it. 'But Toby—'

'Shhh, love.' He pulled her closer and set his arm

possessively round her shoulders. 'It doesn't matter to me, not any more, whether I'm bastard born or not.'

'Well, it should.'

With a grin he kissed her and stopped further protests.

24

T he following morning Toby took Meg and
Phoebe up to the back place, leaving Pippa in
charge in case any customers arrived.

'Now, tell me everything before anyone else
arrives,' he ordered.

Phoebe sat staring down at the ground looking
anxious. Meg opened the secret room and retrieved
the hidden papers, passing them to him. 'Read
these.'

'I've already seen some of them.' But he read again
the marriage lines of his mother and John
Greenhalgh, then looked at Phoebe. 'You've known
about this for a long time, love, haven't you?'

She nodded.

'Why didn't you tell me when I first arrived.'

'I thought it'd put you in danger with *them*. I *care*
about you, Toby. You're like the son I never had.
Please don't be angry with me.'

'I'm not, love. But there's something I don't understand. Meg said my mother was dead when John
Greenhalgh married Jethro's mother . . . but I lived
with a woman I called mother until I was eighteen.'

'Marjorie wasn't your mother. She was your aunt

and – she was my Hal's sister as was your mother.'

He stared at her in shock.

'She loved you like a mother, I know. You were all she had left of her twin sister Alice. Me and Hal didn't dare go and see her or Greenhalgh said we'd regret it, but she sent word sometimes and we talked to folk from Backenshaw. Hal was frightened of upsetting *him*, so we never did get to see her again and I'm sorry for that. After Hal died, Jethro Greenhalgh told me to leave Calico and asked if Hal had said why he got the inn. I pretended I didn't know anything, but he still said I had to leave.'

Toby was trying to understand how all this had come about. 'Why did John Greenhalgh marry my mother in the first place when he was so ambitious? If she was anything like my m—, my aunt Marjorie,' he corrected, 'then she was just an ordinary lass.'

'They made him, your mother's brothers did, because she was expecting you. They said they'd kill him if he didn't marry her and kept him locked up till he agreed.'

When neither of them drew the obvious conclusion, Meg said it for them. 'It's you who should own the mill, Toby. You're the eldest son.'

He couldn't help laughing at that. 'Not me! I've no desire to be a millowner. All I want is here.' He took her hand, and Phoebe's too. 'If you'll marry me, lass, and you'll stay on to help with our children, Aunt Phoebe, then I'll be a happy man.'

But Meg jerked her hand away. 'But you're the eldest son! It's yours by right.'

'I definitely don't want it. And do *you* really want to be a millowner's wife, Meg love, and live in a fancy house tripping over servants every time you turn round?'

She was the one staring down now, avoiding his eyes. 'You deserve someone better than me, Toby.' She loved him so much, she wanted the very best for him.

He let go of Phoebe and lifted Meg's chin with one finger. 'You *are* the best, love. And I never thought you'd turn me down.' He pretended to sob.

'Stop making a joke of it. They've cheated you out of your inheritance.'

'If you'll wed me, I'll be a happy man. What more can anyone want than that?'

She could only look at him, tears welling in her eyes. 'I don't deserve to.'

He reached out and brushed one teardrop away. 'No crying, my lovely lass. We're going to be happy from now on, you and me.' He looked across at their companion. 'Don't go, Phoebe! There are other things I want to know about, and Meg should know too. The stuff in the secret room, the painting and the sketch . . .'

She sat back down on the bench. 'The furniture was your mother's. After they were wed John Greenhalgh gave it to her, because he wanted her to be comfortable. It was probably stolen. I reckon he loved her in his own way, even though he didn't want to marry her. She died a few months after you were born, just faded away and died, so your aunt took you to raise and John let her have a cottage in Backenshaw and work in his new mill. Marjorie wouldn't take anything else from him unless she really needed it, though.'

Toby went to get the sketch out of the secret room and brought it back, staring at his mother's face. But somehow all he could see was the woman who'd brought him up. 'Marjorie was my mother, really,' he said softly.

'Aye. And she did a good job with you.'

'So did Meg. She's changed me too.'

She gaped at him. 'What did *I* do?'

'Taught me to love. I never did want a woman to wife till I met you, lass.'

More tears brimmed in her eyes, this time tears of joy. 'That's the nicest thing anyone's ever said to me.'

'So you'll wed me and stay here?'

'Of course I will.'

It was so beautiful to see their love that Phoebe burst into noisy sobs.

Toby threw back his head and roared with laughter. 'She always cries like that when she's happy.'

As both women hugged one another, alternately crying and laughing, he rolled his eyes. 'I can see I've got a right pair here.'

Meg pretended to hit him but he caught her hand and raised it to his lips.

Which made Phoebe give another loud sob for joy at their love for one another.

*

That afternoon Jethro came riding up the hill, looking very stiff and solemn. When he entered the inn, Toby looked up and patted Meg's shoulder. 'I need to talk to Jethro on my own.' He turned to his brother. 'We'll go to the back place, if that's all right with you?'

'Yes. Yes, of course.'

When they were seated on the bench, Jethro said, 'What do you want to do about it? You *are* the eldest son, after all.'

'I don't want to do owt.' Toby grinned. 'Stop scowling at me, little brother. I really don't want what you've got. I'm happy here.'

'But your maid is quite right in what she says. You *are* entitled to more than this.' He looked round him scornfully.

'Eh, what would I know about running a mill? Or care either? I hate the damned places. And Meg isn't my maid. She'll be my wife as soon as we can arrange it.'

'Oh, I see. Well, she's very loyal to you.'

'Aye, she is. A right fierce woman, my Meg. She's saved my life twice, and had a hand in saving it a third time, too, last night.'

Jethro looked at him in bewilderment. 'I doubt I'll ever understand you.'

'Well, I don't really understand you, either, but that needn't stop us both getting on with our lives. How's your wife? She seems a nice lass. And Mrs Beardsworth? Is she feeling better now?'

'They're both well, thank you.'

'Good, then you go back to them and sort out that mess in Tappersley.'

'I will, but not until we've come to an agreement.'

There was an edge to Toby's voice now. 'I've said, I don't want your bloody mill!'

'And I believe you. But I shan't feel right unless you have something.' Jethro looked round. 'I'm a rich man and I'll not notice it if I give you the money to brighten up this place, make it an inn to be proud of.'

'I'd rather do it under my own steam.'

A voice from the doorway interrupted them. 'He'll take it, Mr Greenhalgh. I'll make sure he does.'

'Do you hanker after money, love?' Toby asked, disappointment ringing in his voice.

'No.' Meg went across and took his hand, looking at him very seriously. 'But I do hanker after security. For me and – and for our children one day. If anything happens to you, I want to be sure there's enough put by that they won't be sent to the poor-house.' She shuddered. 'That's where they nearly put me and Nelly after Ben died.'

Toby sat down again and pulled her to sit beside him, smiling at Jethro. 'Eh, she'll nag the life out of me, this one will.'

Jethro laughed suddenly, surprising himself as much as them. 'I think you'll be very happy with her, as I am with my wife.'

Toby waved one hand. 'Well, then, get your lawyer to sort something out, whatever you think right.'

'You don't even want to discuss details?'

'Not me. If I've a bit of money to spare, I'll be too busy reading the books I can buy with it.' He stood up, pulled Meg to her feet and gave her a hug, then pushed her towards the door. 'Leave us a minute now, lass, and no more eavesdropping.'

'It was only because I care so much about you, because you *deserve* so much.'

When she'd gone, he held out his hand.

Jethro took it and they shook solemnly.

Then Toby chuckled and clasped his brother to him, feeling how the stiffness of the other man's back relaxed gradually, then holding Jethro at arm's length. 'Get off back to your lady wife now. Make her happy. But don't drive past again. Stop and say hello. I haven't got any other brothers.'

Jethro was speechless for a minute, then said huskily, 'Nor have I.'

'Can you find your own way out? I'd like to have a bit of time here, in the peace.'

When his brother had gone Toby wandered round the room. Eh, Meg was a cheeky devil, but maybe she was right. He wanted lots of children and it would be good to know they were safe in case anything happened to him.

There were no bells and chanting today, only winter sunlight slanting through the windows and the moors he loved so much were spread out around him outside like a living cloak.

After a while Meg peeped through the doorway again. 'You're not angry with me, are you, Toby?'

For answer he opened his arms wide and, when she

ran into them, pulled her close and kissed her until she was dizzy. 'I doubt I'll ever be able to stay angry with you, love.'

She rested her head against his chest and they stayed like that for a few minutes, then went back to the front part of the inn to get on with their work.

Both of them smiled a lot that day.

Three weeks later there was a wedding in the tiny church in Calico.

Toby refused point-blank to let the Parson wed them, though now it was known that he was a Greenhalgh the man was treating him differently and had even called in at the inn to introduce himself. But Toby insisted on being wed by the Curate and invited all the Pickerlings to be there too, and come to the feast he was providing at the inn afterwards.

Sophia sent a dress for the bride to wear, a simple silk in a pretty pink that lent colour to Meg's cheeks. When she unpacked the box and read the accompanying message it took her breath away, and she could only hold out the piece of paper to Toby and give him a tearful smile.

On the wedding day Phoebe helped her put it on and cried over how pretty she looked, but although that helped make Meg a bit more confident, she was still feeling very nervous as they waited for their most important guests to arrive. When two carriages came into sight from the Lancashire side, pulling up the last of the hill towards the Packhorse, she looked uncertainly at Toby.

'Why two carriages?' She didn't wait for an answer. 'Whatever will I say to Jack? I haven't seen him for over a year.'

'He's still your big brother, love. He won't have changed that much.'

'Come and greet him with me. *Please*, Toby.'

So he stayed beside her, resplendent in his own new clothes, one arm around her shoulders.

And when the first carriage door opened and Jack got out, giving a hand to his wife Emmy, the girl he had always loved, Meg lost the last of her nervousness, squealed in joy and rushed across to hug them. 'I was so *glad* when I heard you two were wed.'

Shad, Ginny and Joe got out after them and were also hugged and kissed, but to Meg's enormous relief her mother wasn't there.

'I wouldn't have brought *her*,' Jack whispered. 'It's a day for celebrations, not sour-faced old harridans. She's living in lodgings now, on her own.' He smiled ruefully. 'And still complaining all the time.'

When the second carriage door opened, Jethro and Sophia got out of it, followed by Harriet and her two step-daughters, all very finely dressed, and Meg stared at them in shock.

Toby walked across to greet them. 'I didn't tell her you were coming,' he said with one of his wide smiles. 'She was nervous enough as it was.'

And Jethro found himself laughing again, as he always seemed to now when he was with his brother.

Her arm linked in Jack's, Meg introduced her

family to Toby, hardly pausing for breath as she tried to tell Jack all her news at the same time. She included the Greenhalghs and Harriet in her torrent of words because she was too excited to be nervous now.

Jack looked at Toby, liked what he saw and said quietly, 'You've made her happy. I'm so glad.'

'I am too. She's made me happy as well.'

Meg, who had led the ladies inside, stuck her head out of the inn door. 'What are you men doing, standing there chatting when there's so much to do? Come inside at once or we'll never be ready in time!'

Grinning, Toby clapped Jack on the back, winked at Jethro and led them off to do her bidding.

But after the wedding and the feasting were over, Toby took his bride up to their bedroom and locked the door on the rest of the world. When he turned round, she was staring at him solemnly, looking nervous, hands clasped at her breast.

'You're not afraid of me, are you, my little love?'

She took a hesitant step towards him, then let him take her in his arms.

'You've been wed before, you know what to expect,' he continued, puzzled. But she didn't brighten as he'd expected. 'What's wrong, lass? I'm not moving another finger till you've told me.'

'I – don't like it very much, the bed play, I mean,' she said gruffly. 'With Ben I pretended, but with you, Toby, I can't pretend.'

'Eh, I don't want you to, love. Let's just get into that bed and see what happens, shall we?' When he blew out the candle and took her in his arms again, he could feel her heart pounding against his chest.

Tenderly, trying to show the great love he felt for her, he began to kiss her and caress her. As he felt her relax he held himself back and put all his efforts into making his bride happy . . . .

When they'd finished, he chuckled.

Her voice was husky. 'What are you laughing at now, Toby Fletcher?'

'You. For someone who doesn't like making love, you certainly enjoyed that.' Then he felt the dampness trickling on to his bare chest. 'Meg darling, I didn't mean to make you cry. Did I hurt you? What's wrong?'

She gave a watery chuckle. 'I'm crying because I'm happy, you great fool.'

He rolled over on to his back, laughing. 'Oh, no! Between you and Phoebe, I'm going to drown. Why do women cry when they're *happy*, for goodness' sake?'

She fell asleep shortly afterwards, exhausted by the long day. But her hand remained fast in his – which was just the way he liked it.